FREE FLOATER

PAUL R. BRIERLEY

Also available from this author

Loving Those You've Lost, Loving Those You're Losing

"The bloom of a twelve year old boy is desirable, but at thirteen he is much more delightful. Sweeter still is the flower of love that blossoms at fourteen and its charm increases at fifteen. Sixteen is the divine age."

(Straton: Anthologia Palatinus)

"Love is a lie. Poet's write of it, our great art represents it, it inspires our musicians, but it does not really exist. Only lust."

(Anonymous)

Chapter One

The stench of death had filled the room. Having previously fought the unmistakable musky aroma of damp for dominance, against which, there could only have been one winner, death. The body had lay on the bed for three days, undisturbed as *rigor mortise* settled in and then passed it by, stiffening the joints and making the skin waxy, an almost translucent greenish-red colour. A pungent odour now generated from the bed, similar to the fetor of rancid meat, making those unfortunate to be in the airless room feel nauseous and light-headed. Entrance to the room was being prohibited by a uniformed police officer who was weighed down by his thick and heavy stab-proof vest, a sign of modern policing, and not relishing in his current location. The officer, barely out of training and his early twenties, was attending his first dead body and found that he was resisting his body's natural desire to vomit up the previous days meals and flee his post in pursuit of some fresh air.

He had though allowed two men past him and into the room of death, one a doctor, the other a detective. The doctor, balding and pot-bellied, looking older than his sixty years, was the closest to the deceased. Wearing latex surgical gloves and a facial mask he examined the body. It was a morbid task, but also a necessary one. He was searching for any clues and evidence which would reveal the possible cause of death.

The detective, twenty odd years younger than the doctor, tall and with a head of shortly cropped dark brown hair, greying in places, offering a total contrast to the physician, had not expected the sight before him. The barely audible message which had crackled through his radio, had

told him to attend the scene of a death, a possible suicide. He had then been given an address, which was still written on the back of his left hand. Attending the scene of a death was unfortunately an almost routine part of police work these days, one that the detective had carried out before and almost certainly would do so again in the future. Each one had filled him full of woe and that most natural of emotions, depression, that followed the investigation plunging him to new depths of despair as he discovered the abyss of misery felt by somebody who thought that their only form of escape was suicide.

What brings somebody to take their own life was a question often pondered by Detective Chief Inspector McKenzie Hollister, but one that he has never understood. Maybe it was a broken relationship, the death of a loved one or even any number of reasons. Maybe these were just excuses used instead of searching for a solution to whatever their problems were? Nothing though, thought Hollister, should have reduced a person to this. However the sight of this particular body told him one was going to be far from routine. Almost subconsciously he was already treating the room as a crime scene, being careful not to disturb anything that may reap clues at a later time.

While the doctor went about his grim duties, the detective looked around the room, both aware of the macabre eeriness of the silent room. A hand-written piece of paper caught the eye of the police officer, positioned on a piece of furniture where it would clearly be seen. After donning a pair of blue surgical latex gloves that he produced from his jacket pocket, he picked it up and read it; *"If life is a game, then I must be its natural loser. I have striven to find peace, happiness and above all, love. All my life I have silently cried out for love, but nobody has*

ever loved me. I was just another face, a nameless entity amongst others. I cannot continue this terrible existence. Maybe in death I might achieve something."

It appeared to be a suicide note. Discovering it in such a place only added to its credence, but something did not seem right to Hollister. He was a career police officer who had joined the police when he was aged seventeen and spent the next twenty five years going from a cadet to his current rank, Chief Inspector. The carefully written and worded note troubled him. Whether it was the notorious 'coppers instinct', used so often to explain the gut feeling of police officers, or not did not matter. His own personal experience was enough to cast doubt on the poetically phrased contents, let alone the near perfect grammar.

The doctor's cold and clinical almost rasping voice snapped him out of his thoughts. "He's been dead a couple days. I'd say three or four based on the *livor mortis*. Judging by the smell and the blistering and swelling of the body confirms this. No signs of violence or of a struggle. No obvious indications of any physical assault. In my opinion, I'd probably say it was a suicide. We'll know better after the *post mortem*."

Hollister sighed and nodded. "I've got what appears to be a suicide note saying, I think, that he's going to kill himself."

"That'll confirm my initial findings," the doctor replied almost smugly. "I'll notify the Coroner's Office and they can handle things from here."

Carefully and methodically he packed away the tools of his trade, removed his mask and gloves and left the room. Hollister had met the medical man several times before. Not every occasion had involved a

body, sometimes they were still alive, but, whenever their paths crossed, the doctor had succeeded in annoying him. There was something in the doctor's mannerism and attitude that riled the detective, never caring about the person before him, only seeing the body, be it alive or dead. Maybe it was due to the differences in their careers, with the police officer seeing, the sometimes innocent, victim and the individual behind the death or crime, while the doctor only saw the body and/or the wounds and occasionally this was only for a few minutes, before he handed over to somebody else.

Hollister shuddered as he realised that he was left alone with the body and he continued to look around the room. The once brightly coloured flowers on the wallpaper had faded with age, as had the gaudy floral print curtains, which were still closed, adding to the melancholy of the plateau. Bulky wooden furniture, which must have been as old as him, helped fill the room, typical for a bedsit, thought the detective. The largest object in the room was a two-door wardrobe and Hollister pulled open the doors, cringing at the grinding of the ancient hinges. The contents took him by surprise.

Nothing. Not a single item of clothing hung on the rail or rested on the inner shelves. He then crosses to the chest of drawers, pulls open these drawers one by one and was again taken aback when he discovered that all, bar one, was empty. The only drawer that did contain something was the top one and this only held three white sheets, all neatly folded and placed in there with care. Apart from those that were neatly folded on the chair over in a corner, the deceased did not appear to have any other clothes in the room. Not even a change in underwear, which troubled the detective. No matter whom you were or

where you lived, even if you slept rough on the streets, you had at least one change of clothing but the person who lived in the bedsit did not appear to have any other clothes.

Another thought then dawned on the detective. There was no pen or any paper in the room. How could the person who was lay on the bed write a farewell note if there was nothing either to write it on or write it with, wondered the detective? Hollister now finally looked at the body on the bed.

Standing alone, the silence filled the room as the police officer stared at the motionless figure before him. It was that of a male youth, in his late teens or early twenties. He was naked, having previously been covered by a white sheet, which was now around his ankles, having been pulled back by the doctor. The slim youth had a finely toned and muscular body. His skin was, despite the greying of death, still a golden brown, not overly tanned but a healthy hue. His fine blond hair was precisely cut, perfectly framing his young handsome face, which showed no sign of pain and looked perfectly at ease with himself, almost peaceful. Whoever he was, he had obviously taken care of himself. The youth, if nothing else certainly had his looks going for him and yet, here he was alone, dead, in an almost seedy looking bedsit and this was the thought that troubled the detective.

It was only now that Hollister heard his own heart beating, pounding away inside his chest, making his ribcage strain under the constant pressure, thinking that his heart was going to explode at any moment. He had never known a potential suicide victim to have this effect on him, making his adrenaline flow through his body and this was something else that troubled the detective. Most suicides he attended

were adults and only rarely it was youngsters who had taken their own lives, but never in a place or way like this. They usually jumped off buildings or drowned in remote ponds or deliberately crashed cars into walls, but never usually like this. This was different.

The nameless youth had come here, undressed and neatly folded his clothes, went to bed and died. That was it. Another thought suddenly struck the detective. If he had just killed himself, then how did he do it? His cursory search of the bedsit had not revealed any tablets or anything else with which he could have used to kill himself.

Then he started to ask himself questions. Why would a good looking and apparently fit young man decide to end his life in such a grubby looking bedsit? Where were his family? Then again, did he have any family and friends here in Manchester? But more to the point, who was he? Was this his home? If so, where were all his personal belongings, such as his clothes and the implements for personal hygiene? The youngster had obviously taken care of his appearance while he was alive, judging by his neatly trimmed hair, suntanned body and his well-defined physique and so, to Hollister, it just did not ring true to him that the clothes on the chair were all that he had. So many questions and yet somehow the detective knew that the answers were going to be hard to come by.

From all the juveniles that he had come into contact with and from his own personal experience of the education system, the wording of the 'suicide' troubled him too. The grammar appeared to be all wrong for a person of his age. Over the years, Hollister had seen several final messages, scrawled by a soon to be suicide statistic in the hope that their final words and act would be understood by somebody but this

particular one sounded more like prose, rather than a cry for help, as most suicide notes and indeed suicides were. It had an educated sound to it. Almost that of a teacher, but clearly the youngster was not old enough to have been one. He was barely old enough to be working and yet, if this was indeed his final testament to the world, it was a very articulate one. Had he wrote it himself or had the words been dictated to him by some unknown person? It was yet another mystery for the seasoned detective to figure out, possibly another question that may go unanswered over the passage of time and his investigation.

McKenzie Hollister found himself sitting opposite the distraught landlady of the bedsits. She was a stocky woman in her sixties, her silver-grey hair tied tightly in a bun. Her face, wrinkled from the experience of age, showing her grief. Hollister took a few seconds and viewed his surroundings while the woman prepared herself for the questions soon to be posed by the detective. He could have almost been in an adjoining room to the one occupied by the recently deceased young man, he thought to himself as he waited. The same type of wallpaper hung on the walls, the furniture was similar and even the smell reminded him of the other room.

When the woman was finally settled, he began. "I know all this has been an ordeal for you Mrs Longman, but I do need to ask you a few questions."

"It's all right dear," she replied in a deep voice, gravelled by age, constantly wavering as she fought back the tears. "I know you're only doing your job."

"Thanks," Hollister feigned a smile. "I'll try to be as quick as I can. First, can you tell me the young man's name?"

"Martin, Martin Foxford" came the reply.

This may not have been his real name but an alias, thought Hollister, once again based on his experience and his inclination that the dead youth only used this address as a place to sleep. "And how long has he lived at this address?"

"Oh, quite a while really dear, I think he moved in about a year ago. I'd have to check his rent book for an exact date. My tenants don't usually stay that long. They're mostly students who stay a term or two and then move on somewhere else once they've got used to Manchester."

"I don't think that I'll need the rent book yet, but somebody from the Coroner's Office will be along and they will need it. Now…" he paused briefly, "…how often did you see Mr Foxford?"

The woman began to weep again and a well-used handkerchief was produced from a sleeve to wipe away her tears. "It was not very often dear. I think that he worked nights." She paused briefly, "No, I'm certain that he worked nights. He used to go out about eight o'clock and he returned around breakfast time."

"Have you any idea where he worked or what he did for a living?" From experience, Hollister knew that this woman was not going to be able to tell him anything of great importance, but he still had to go through the motions and ask her these questions. For some unknown reason Hollister already had a good idea what the youth actually did for a living.

"Not a clue dear. He paid his rent on time, always with cash and was never late. He kept himself to himself, minded his own business and had very few visitors. You could say, from my point of view, that he was an ideal tenant."

Hollister was beginning to get irritated at constantly being addressed as 'dear'. "Did he have any girlfriends?"

"That always surprised me did that," she replied almost excitedly, as if she held the answers to all the riddles about him. "He is...I mean...he was such a good looking and polite boy and yet I never saw him with any girls. I thought that was strange."

The detective however, did not. "Who exactly did you see him with Mrs Longman?" already knowing the answer he had just asked the sobbing landlady.

"Over the period he lived here dear, just two or three men. I guessed that they were men that he worked with. They'd pick him up at night and drop him off in the morning."

"Could you describe them for me Mrs Longman?" Once again, Hollister already knew the answer to this before he had even asked the question.

"Not really dear." She thought for a moment and then continued, "I'd say they were about thirty to forty years old. They looked like businessmen or something professional. I didn't really pay that much attention. I'm not one of those nosy landlady's you hear about you know." The tears started again.

"I didn't mean to imply that you were and if I've upset you then I'm sorry," Hollister explained. Ignoring the plight of the woman he pressed on. "Did he ever speak about his family or where he came

from? Even you, Mrs Longman, must have been a little curious when one so young turned up on your doorstep looking for a room."

The landlady thought for a moment, wiped away another tear, "Not that I can recall dear. I just thought that he was just another student. I don't think that we ever had a proper conversation after he moved in. Like I said earlier, he just kept himself to himself."

"Did he ever have any friends nearer to his own age call on him or was he friendly with any of your other tenants?"

The landlady once again paused while she thought and eventually she shook her head and answered. "Not that I ever saw dear."

"I can see that you're upset Mrs Longman, we might as well leave it there for now." Deep down Hollister was pleased that he was bringing the interview to a halt and let out a long silent sigh. The landlady had inadvertently posed more questions than she had answered. Reaching into his inner jacket pocket Hollister pulled out a printed business card which he handed to the sobbing woman. "If you do remember anything that you think might be useful, then please don't hesitate to 'phone me at Heller Street police station. Somebody else will call and see you later and take a full statement. Just purely routine, you've got nothing to worry about. Thank you for your time."

"I'm so sorry to keep blubbering like an old woman. He seemed such a nice boy. I've got a grandson about the same age. His mother will be heartbroken when she finds out."

Hollister stood up from the lumpy and uncomfortable chair and let himself out of the woman's flat and then went out onto the street. Once outside he passed a small group of woman, curious neighbours no doubt, standing behind a single strand of blue and white tape sealing off

the building and he gulped the fresh air, secretly relieved to be away from the woman. Whilst leaning against a waist-high wall which divided the small gardens, Hollister lit up a cigarette and puffed heavily on it. Talking to her had only fuelled the suspicion already implanted in his mind, almost confirming that, for some unknown reason, the dead youth was a 'rent boy', the slang expression for a young male homosexual prostitute.

To Hollister, all the obvious signs were there, 'working nights', only being seen in the company of men, a ready supply of cash. But searching the bedsit had raised another question, where were his clothes and personal possessions? This was clearly not his 'working' address. He obviously had somewhere else where he took his clients but where was it? From what Hollister could figure out, he only used this bedsit as a place to sleep, possibly as a means of escaping the demands of his clients and his lifestyle. Would finding this other home offer any clues as to who he was or why he had taken his own life? Would it offer the detective an explanation as to why this youth had even chosen such a sordid lifestyle?

Throughout his time in the police, Hollister had occasionally come into contact with both 'rent boys' and those that used them, but this was the first time that he had to investigate the death of one. Even at this early stage he was troubled at the prospect of this. He had a great deal of difficulty in understanding what makes a boy choose, if this was the right word, this particular way of life and then suddenly ending it all by taking their life in such an anonymous location and manner. No sooner had he been told it, Hollister realised that the name given by the

landlady was probably a false one and that he may never even find out his real name or who he really was.

Hollister considered himself fairly liberal in his outlook to life and liked to think that he was tolerant towards the gay community of Manchester, but he did not like to openly associate with the few homosexuals that he knew. He acknowledged their right to live their lives the way that those chose, but the very thought of them actually committing any form of sexual act with each other abhorred the detective. The thought that a grown man having sex with a boy, like the recently deceased youngster he had just seen, no matter how willing he may have been to enter into the tryst, repulsed him and brought out his natural homophobia. He could not understand how anybody could find themselves so attracted to young boys that he would actually pay them to have sex with him. Hollister simply could not grasp the very thought of it.

Hollister also did not like the thought of leaving such a youngster anonymous in death. For a reason that he did not know, nor understand, he thought that he owed it to him and his family to try and discover the truth about his life and death.

Now sitting in the ample seat of his car, the air conditioning turned full on, filling the vehicle with cold air as he tried to rid his nostrils of the smell of death, Hollister thought how much he disliked cases like this. Too many questions and too few answers always left him with a feeling of despair and hopelessness. Silently he cursed himself. Even though he was the senior detective on duty this day, he was actually on his way somewhere else and now regretted taking the call. Part of him wished that he could pass this case onto another officer and yet there

was something nagging deep in the brain of the detective. He knew that this was going to be *his* case and no matter how much he disliked what the boy did or those that abused him, he *was* going to come up with at least some answers to the multitude of questions milling around deep inside his brain.

Forty-eight hours later, a tired looking McKenzie Hollister sat in the canteen of Heller Street police station. The red-bricked building, originally constructed in the 1950s, had become too small for the area that it served and rather than relocate to other premises it had been extended. Now, two decades later, it was again far too small. Prefabricated huts had been brought in and one of these now served as a restroom for the officers of Heller Street. Hollister was sipping his second cup of coffee of the morning, oblivious to the cacophony of noise around him, the clatter of plates and cutlery, the constant crackle of radios, the mumbling chatter of colleagues recounting the exploits of the previous days shift or their personal stories. Breakfast had consisted of his first cup of coffee and a cigarette and now he wished that he had not opted for a second coffee. The smell of bacon, sausages, eggs, amongst other things, being cooked was making him feel hungry.

He was just about to succumb to temptation when a colleague brought him the results of the post mortem on the dead youth. Detective Sergeant Phoebe Boston, a twenty-six year old brunette that was tall, standing around six feet tall, with a shapely figure. She was rapidly building a reputation for herself as a hard-working and dedicated officer, but originally being from the Scottish city of Glasgow she also had a feisty temper and was not afraid of speaking her mind or standing

her ground with fellow officers, of all ranks, in what was still a male dominated environment.

After attending the morgue and witnessing the post mortem, at Hollister's request, she had carried out some further research before reporting back to Hollister. She was already addressing Hollister before she sat opposite him at the table, her voice still heavily accented despite leaving Scotland over a decade earlier. "The Doc's confirmed that the youth died of a drugs overdose. He had a cocktail of Librium, Thorazine and Lorezepam, all prescription drugs for anxiety and mood swings, mixed with the painkiller Lithium and these had been washed down with vodka. There was no sign of a struggle. In fact, he found nothing suspicious whatsoever. It was as if he just took an overdose and then went to bed and died. Suicide was his conclusion."

"If you consider the fact that he had at least four different prescribed drugs in his body, plus vodka and yet a search of the room didn't come up with any medication or booze as 'nothing suspicious', then you're not as bright as some people say you are," replied Hollister, his voice tainted with sarcasm.

The female detective could feel her cheeks burning as they filled with blood, a combination of humiliation and rage. "Maybe he took them somewhere else?"

Hollister ignored the remark and without even looking up from his coffee, "Anything else, Sherlock?"

"Yeah, he was definitely gay. There was evidence of recent sexual intercourse, anal penetration. However, there was no semen in him, nor any bleeding, so we can rule out rape. I doubt it was his first time either. There was some kind of water-based lubricant though. He

appeared to practice safe sex. I didn't think the name given was his own so I took a look at the computer, you know the missing persons file and then contacted the Child Protection Unit and got a definite ID on him..."

Not being known for his calm temperament, especially early on in the day, Hollister snapped and finally looked up at Detective Boston. "For Christ's sake, get on with it."

Once again she felt flushed, only this time she knew it was with rage. "His real name was Cameron David Ian Robinson and...he was only sixteen years old."

Hollister looked straight at her and was now giving her the attention that she deserved, "You sure about this?" Why he had not thought to check the computer himself escaped him.

A smug grin now appeared on her face with a feeling of deep satisfaction "Oh, you're interested now are you Mac?"

"Cut the crap Phoebe. I'm tired. I've been up all night."

And that gives you the right to be an arsehole, thought the woman but she let it go, knowing that she had got one over on Hollister had given her a great deal of personal pride and satisfaction. "Yeah, I'm sure. After finding him on the J.P.U. computer, I dug out his file. He'd been missing from home for two years. Apparently he just upped and vanished shortly after his fourteenth birthday. At the time there was a big search, but to no avail. He just vanished of the face of the earth. His file was still open, but the last comments recorded that he was either in another city or even dead. Mundy was in charge of the search for him. He wasn't on the 'At Risk Register' with Social Services, wasn't even known to them. Vice didn't know him either. If he was a 'rent boy', he

was either new to the game or just very careful not to get caught. Maybe he was just a private plaything of some 'paedo', kept off the streets, used just by them?"

"What makes you think he was on 'the game'?" asked Hollister.

"Come off it Mac," Boston had been taken a little by surprise by Hollister's question. "Everything just points to it. Didn't you suspect it when you first saw him?"

"The thought did cross my mind," replied Hollister with a shrug of his shoulders as he finished off his coffee. "Tell me Sherlock, how does a fourteen year old just vanish of the face of the earth and then survive on his own, get a flat and everything else and nobody even know or suspect anything?"

It was the turn of Boston to shrug her shoulders, but as she did, she held out her hands, palms up as she did. "Search me Mac. He did look older for his age and had the build for it as well. I don't think that it would've been that hard for him to pull it off."

Silently Hollister agreed with her. When he had first seen him, the detective had thought that he may have been in his early twenties and so he found the speculation of his Sergeant feasible. "Got a final address for him?"

It was the turn of the female detective to be abrupt. "Of course I have. I've checked it out and his parents still live there."

Hollister rose from the table, "Let's go and see the family. We'll keep it quiet about him being a 'rent' for now. It's going to be hard enough for his family when we tell them that he's dead."

Sergeant Boston nodded in agreement and followed Hollister out of the police canteen and restroom, having to almost run to keep up with

him. At last, Hollister thought to himself, he finally had something to go on, a real name to the dead youth and sadly a soon to be grieving family which might explain some of the mysteries that troubled him and had kept him awake since the discovery of the body. It was at that moment, despite its morbidity, the best news in the world for him.

Chapter Two

Around ten miles to the south of Manchester city centre and close to the airport is Wythenshawe. This vast, sprawling estate, said to be one of the largest housing estates in Europe, spanning an area of just over ten square miles and offering homes to over seventy thousand residents, was once the pride of Manchester but in recent years it had become a bleak place. Built during the 1920s as an over-spill garden estate, parts of it until recently, had been neglected and the unsavoury elements of suburban life had taken over the streets. Crime, including violent crimes, drug abuse and vandalism was rife in some areas and many people felt that they had become prisoners in their own homes, too scared to venture outside when the sun set and nightfall descended over the city.

It was not all like this though. Part of it, known as Moss Nook, was made up mostly of three bedroom terraced and semi-detached houses and it straddled the Cheshire border. This was the acceptable face of Wythenshawe. This was where the Robinson family lived and where Detectives Hollister and Boston found themselves.

Immediately on entering the lounge of the terraced house the police officers could tell that it was a family home and pride was taken with its appearance. Almost the entire wall over the fireplace was devoted to framed photographs of three children, two boys and a girl. They covered the years from birth to their early teens, each looking resplendent in their school uniforms, their smiles beaming at you from various angles. Both detectives recognised the dead boy immediately,

dispelling any lingering doubts that Hollister may have had. He let out a deep, almost silent sigh, his heart heavy with remorse at having to break such dreadful news to an unquestionably loving and devoted mother and family.

Like her closest neighbours, being neighbourly, but not nosey, with their curtains peeled back a fraction to see who the strangers were, Mrs Robinson had seen them walking up her path and met them at the door before they had a chance to knock. After seeing their warrant cards, she showed them into the privacy of the lounge. A knot tightened in the pit of her stomach and she knew, as if by a mother's instinct, that they had brought bad news.

Hollister cleared his throat, his mouth dry and really wanting the drink that had been offered, which they both declined, not wanting to impose on the woman, if only it had been to delay his task. "I'm afraid that we have some bad news for you Mrs Robinson. Is there anybody, a neighbour perhaps that can come in and be with you?"

Defiantly she shook her head. "The least they know the better. You've come about my Cameron, haven't you?", her voice still heavily underlined with a strong Scottish accent despite it now being many years since she moved down to England.

Hollister nodded his head slowly and once again cleared his throat. "There is no easy way to say this Mrs Robinson, but a youth, we believe to be your son Cameron, was found a couple of days ago. He had apparently taken an overdose..."

The response was immediate, an emphatic denial. "My Cameron would never take his own life."

Hollister was a little surprised by the lack of grief shown by the mother, "I'm very sorry, Mrs Robinson, but we could find no suspicious circumstances and no evidence to assume any other conclusion."

A cold glare came from the normally warm blue eyes, sending a shiver down the spine of Hollister. "Believe me, Chief Inspector, I know my son better than you. He would never do such a thing. It would be against his faith. My Cameron has been brought up a good Catholic boy, he sang in the choir at St. Anthony of Padua church not far from here and his priest thought the world of him. No, I'm sorry, if this boy you've found had killed himself, then it won't be my Cameron."

It was the turn of the female officer to try and convince the mother. "I'm very sorry, but it was me that positively identified the deceased as your son. I've double checked everything. I'm very sorry Mrs Robinson, but there isn't a mistake."

Slowly realising that the female detective was right and that the police would have done everything possible to confirm the identity of the dead youth before setting off and coming to see her, the mother slowly began to accept the inevitable, no matter how painful it was to her. "Where did you find him?"

"He was found in a bedsit over in Longsight. It appears that for the last year or so he had been…" A harsh glare and a jolt into the ribcage from Hollister silenced his colleague.

"How could he be living somewhere like that? He would've only been fifteen," asked the mother.

It was Hollister that replied this time, "That is something we are still investigating. We know that this is a very traumatic time for you, Mrs

Robinson, but we need to make arrangements for somebody to positively identify your son…"

Seeing the distress now on the face of Mrs Robinson, Sergeant Boston interrupted her superior officer for the second time. "Let's go and make that cup of tea."

The two women left the rather surprised McKenzie Hollister sat on his own in the lounge, while they disappeared into the kitchen and made some tea. All he could do was sit and look at the photographs on the wall in front of him and also dotted around the room on various pieces of furniture. His trained eyes searching for anything that appeared out of the ordinary, but he could not find anything. The lounge, the adjoining dining room and probably the rest of the house was clean and spotless of dust. It was a nicely furnished room, with all trappings of modern life, a large television set, DVD player, satellite TV box, computer and games machine, which would have kept the children, not to mention their friends, happy and contented for hours. It was indeed a nice family room, one to be proud off.

The images of the children stuck in the mind though. They were all good looking. The two boys, with Cameron being the eldest, were extremely handsome in their school uniforms, whilst their sister, the second of the three children, could be described as having the beauty of a fashion model. Was it any wonder that their mother was having difficulty in accepting that her first born child was dead mused the solitary detective whilst sitting on the sofa, lost deep in his own private thoughts and contemplated what he was going to do next.

Hollister had been sitting alone in his car around fifteen minutes after letting himself out of the Robinson's home, leaving the two women talking in the kitchen, hearing the occasional sob from the mother, when he was joined by Sergeant Boston. "Well?" he asked curtly, annoyed that he had not been privy to the conversation.

"She still won't accept that he committed suicide, but she has at least come to terms with the fact that one of her son's is dead." A deep sigh followed as she joined Hollister in smoking a cigarette. Sergeant Boston had been deeply moved by the courage of the mother.

"Why won't she admit that he took his own life?" asked Hollister.

"They are a religious family, devoted Catholic and the notion of suicide just doesn't figure with them. It's easier for her to accept his death. Did you know that ever since he left home, she's known that she'll never see him again and for the past two years she's already grieved for her son, she told me this over the tea. Every time that the body of a young male had been found, she's hoped it would be her Cameron, only to have her misery continue when his identity was revealed. We've finally put her mind at rest. She can finally rest at night knowing what happened to her son. In a way, I'm glad he's turned up, even if he's dead."

Hollister was a little surprised by his colleague's bluntness, "That's a bit heartless, isn't it?"

"No it's not," snapped back Sergeant Boston. "I've just been talking to a woman who has lived a lie for the last two years, dreaming of seeing her first born child again and yet, all along, knowing that she wouldn't. But she still hoped to with all her heart. Did you know that for the past two years she's been keeping a fresh set of clothes ready

for him and a bed made up, just in case he did come home but knowing all along that he wouldn't? Her faith in God and hope were the only things that kept her going all this time. As soon as she saw us at the door, she knew that he was dead and that we were there to tell her. Have you any idea of just what she's gone through the last couple of years? My heart really goes out to her. She's one of the strongest people that I've ever met in my life."

A somewhat surprised Hollister set the car in motion and the journey back to the police station was conducted in complete silence, only interrupted by the crackled messages coming through their radios. Boston's outburst was never mentioned again by either of them, but Hollister never forgot it. He too could not understand why the youth had taken his own life, despite being in the privileged position of knowing about the seedier lifestyle of the dead youngster. Driving back in silence he resolved to himself that he would do everything in his power to protect the mother from any further heartbreak and to find at least some answers too many of the questions troubling him.

McKenzie Hollister had to get out of bed early the following morning, which was something that he always disliked doing. For the third consecutive night he had been unable to sleep, tossing and turning until the early hours, before drifting off into a restless slumber, settling for whatever sleep he could get. Every time that he closed his eyes, he saw the young face of Cameron Robinson staring back at him. The youngster had looked so peaceful and tranquil in death, and yet, he must have been so tormented by his lifestyle that he ended up taking his own life, if that was indeed what he had actually happened.

Three days after the body had been found Hollister still doubted that it was an open-and-shut case of suicide. Something just did not seem right about it to the experienced detective and yet there was nothing he had discovered that indicated otherwise. It had all the classic hallmarks of a suicide, so why did he doubt it? This was, above all the others, the main question that Hollister kept asking himself.

The previous day, after leaving Sergeant Boston at Heller Street police station, he had returned to the house that Mrs Longman had converted into bedsits and interviewed all the other tenants. They had all told such similar accounts that Hollister could have sworn that they had all connived together. Nobody really knew him, or saw or heard anything suspicious but, then again, nobody ever did these days. Only a couple of the tenants even saw the youngster while he was at the flat and those that did could not offer any clues as to his behaviour. They did, however, confirm what the landlady had told him and that he had been seen in the presence of a couple of men, all very similar in their description. Finally he went to the now empty bedsit.

The Coroner's Office had completed their routine tasks and after removing the body, had cleared away the clothes and the suicide note, to be used later at his inquest. A window had been prised open, possibly for the first time in a long time and allowed some fresh air into the room but Hollister could still smell the body. The sweet odour of decaying flesh still hung in the air and all the time Hollister was in the room, he found himself retching. If he had actually eaten anything he would have no doubt vomited it up. The room had, however, offered the seasoned detective no new clues and so, resigned to defeat, he left it, went home and the futile effort of sleep.

Now, several hours later, after taking a shower, Hollister dressed and made his way downstairs. After making himself a cup of coffee, his first of many throughout his day, he sat in an armchair in his lounge, still thinking about Cameron Robinson. One of the things that really troubled him was why had he become a prostitute? From his previously limited experience of them, he thought that most 'rent boys' were the victims of some form of abuse, both sexual and physical, usually at home, and they had run away from their homes as a means of escaping it and then found themselves drawn ever deeper into life of sleaze in order to survive. But, having seen his home and spoken to his loving and devoted mother, this was not even a consideration in this case. So, why had he left home in the first place and how and why had he become a 'rent boy'?

Why did the detective find this so troubling? If it was indeed a suicide and three days after he had been discovered there was still nothing to suggest otherwise, then it did not even matter to the police. It was now in the hands of the Coroner's Court. To them, he was just another teenage runaway that had killed themselves rather than go home. Officially, to the police, he was just another statistic, an incident number logged on a series of pieces of paper, first as a runaway and now as a suicide. To the police bureaucrats, he was not even a person, just a number. So why was this particular detective losing sleep over the death of a 'rent boy'?

Mrs Robinson had also once again returned to sleepless nights. After her son had first disappeared, she spent the first few weeks barely sleeping. Most of her waking hours had been spent roaming the streets

of Manchester desperately searching for her son or staring out of the windows of her home, looking and waiting for him to once again walk up the path and come through the front door. From sunrise to sunset, she sat watching out for her beloved son and when nightfall came and darkness descended, she listened out for his key to go into the lock and for the front door to open and her eldest child, still only fourteen years old, to walk in.

As the days turned to weeks and the weeks dragged on into months and the police, with nothing new to go on, scaled down their search for him, she slowly began to accept the fact that he had either run away from home or that the unspeakable had happened and Cameron had been abducted and murdered. As her torment continued and the months rolled by, the prospect that her son was dead seemed ever more likely, despite all her hopes and prayers.

It is every parent's worst nightmare that their offspring may have run away from home, but to comprehend that they may have been taken against their will and murdered is incredibly difficult to come to terms with. Whenever there is a report in the media that a child has gone missing, every parent's heart goes out to the family of the missing child, saying that it could never happen to them. But, when the unthinkable does happen, no matter how much that they think they can handle it, the strain eventually becomes unbearable.

For months after her son, her baby, had disappeared Mrs Robinson had somehow managed to convince herself that she had actually done something wrong in order to make her son leave home in the first place. The devoted mother had searched for answers to questions that had no answers, constantly asking herself what she had done wrong to make

him leave home in the first place. Like every mother, she had protected him as best as any mother could. She had taken him to church every Sunday ever since he was old enough to understand what was being said. She had sat wiping away silent tears of pride when he took his First Communion. Beamed with the same pride when he took his first place in the church's choir and once again when he became the senior choirboy, singing solos with his sweet, angelic voice. She had seen him off on his first day of secondary school, the Catholic school with the same name as the church that it was attached to, looking so grown up in his brand new uniform and then she radiated with pride at him doing well academically and athletically, especially with his talent for gymnastics.

Had she over protected him? Had she pushed him too far? She could not accept the fact that he had been abducted. In her eyes this only happened to small, defenceless children, not to teenagers. So for her son to have run away from home must have been her fault, something to do with the way in which she had brought him up. If he was that unhappy, why had he not tried to talk to either her or his father about what was upsetting him? Had he actually tried to reveal to them that he was indeed unhappy and they had missed the hints? All these questions and many more, had swam around inside her head for the past two years and never finding the answers to them had taken its toll on her. She had been placed on antidepressants by her physician and, on several occasions, had come close to having a mental breakdown.

It was only when the rest of her family were safely in their beds that she allowed herself to shed tears and grieve for her missing son. During the darkness and silence of the night, while the rest of the household

slept, she would sit alone in the kitchen, endlessly sipping cups of warm milk and wept silent tears. She would never allow anybody to see her weep for her son, putting on a charade for all to see, a vision of strength for the remaining members of her family. But deep down her heart was broken.

A mother never expects that she will have to bury those of her loins. It should always be the other way around. But having finally been told that her son was dead, she had to find the inner strength to see her 'baby' laid to rest. She would have to dress him one last time. Give him one final kiss and be able to hold him in her loving arms one more time. The prospect of having to do this was harder for her to contemplate than to face up to all the months of doubt and the ever growing realisation that he was never coming home. Now she needed all the strength she could muster from all the years of praying to her God. She needed all her inner strength to comfort the remaining members of her now heartbroken family, to offer them support and love in this, their darkest times. While he was 'only' missing there was hope, now there was none and as a loving wife and devoted mother, she would have to console the others in the grief.

But who will be there for her? Dark times lay ahead for her, but at least she finally had the peace of mind to know where her beloved son was and what had happened to him.

Chapter Three

Three weeks had passed since the funeral of Cameron Robinson and McKenzie Hollister had moved onto another case. With the Coroner, as expected, recording a verdict of accidental death on the youth, the police case had been concluded and the missing person file on him had been closed. The new case for Hollister could not have been any more diverse, a series of armed robberies had led the police to suspecting a particular gang, robbing banks and post offices in order to finance their future involvement in the lucrative drugs trade. Hollister was heading the team of a dozen detectives that were in the early stages of this investigation.

As a final official involvement into the death of Cameron Robinson, he and Sergeant Phoebe Boston had attended the funeral of the youth, offering the grieving family the moral support of the Greater Manchester Police force and letting the heartbroken parents know that, even though the files regarding Cameron had been closed, they had not been forgotten. As he watched the hearse pull up, bedecked with multi-coloured garlands of flowers, Hollister found himself with mixed emotions. His heart went out to the family, each of them wrapped up in their own sorrow, openly sobbing and seeking comfort in each other, but he was also filled with guilt at having lied to the family as to the real reason why the teenager had taken his own life.

When the priest, looking very solemn in his black vestment, decorated with a purple stole over his shoulders, adding a touch of colour to the solemnity of his dress, began his eulogy about the brief

life of the youth before him in an ornate oak casket, his voice was punctuated by the sobs and wails of the grieving congregation, Hollister wondered whether he would be giving him such a glowing testament if the darker side of Robinson's lifestyle was known? With his private knowledge about the life, and death, of Cameron Robinson, the highly trained eyes of the detective scanned closely the gathered congregation, made up of family members, friends of the family and school friends of the youngster, together with a token representation from the teaching staff, each of them with their own memories of him and their tribulations. Hollister found himself wondering whether any of the assembled male adults fitted the vague descriptions given by the fellow lodgers at the bedsits of Mrs Longman.

Starting at the front, the priest did not. He was much too young and had blond hair. There were two candidates from Robinson's former school, one later turning out to be the head teacher and the other, the physical education and gymnastics coach. There was a couple of uncles that also fitted the description, but then again, it was such a vague description that it could have applied to about half the male population of Manchester, including Hollister himself.

When the discovery of the body had been made public, the local press had taken another interest and they had also attended the funeral, much to the annoyance of the Robinson family. They had tried to be discreet, but their very presence was seen as an intrusion into the private mourning of a grieving family. Although the family did not blame anybody, other than themselves, for the death of Cameron, they did however think that if they, the media, had taken this much interest and concern after the police had finally called off their search for him, then

they might not actually be burying him today. This was the unanimous view of every member of his family. Only his devastated parents had been told that he had taken his own life. With the surprising collusion of Hollister's senior officer, a cover story had been concocted telling of that he had contracted pneumonia whilst sleeping rough, to protect the family from any unwelcome attention from journalists.

The police had also decided, again at the recommendation of Chief Superintendent Mundy, Hollister's boss and the man that led the initial search for Cameron Robinson, to spare the family from the anguish of knowing about his secret life as a 'rent boy'. How long they would be able to keep this from the family was anybody's guess but, everybody had agreed, that disclosing it would have served no purpose, only adding to the pain and suffering of his family and friends. Whilst Hollister was happy to go along with this charade, he was however a little surprised by the almost unprecedented decision.

This particular death had deeply affected Hollister in ways that he had never known before. Something had struck a raw nerve in the mind and conscious of the street-hardened detective. Even now, whenever he thought about the youth, he still had difficulty in understanding why a boy from a 'normal' and loving family had just suddenly run away from home and become a prostitute in order to survive? The bedsit in which his body was found was less than ten miles from his family home but the difference in lifestyles meant it could have been in another city. The difference in his life could not be more diverse either, from living in what appeared to be a strong, close loving family home to spending his last days all alone in the bedsit. His body was found so close to his family's home, less than ten miles, and yet for whatever

reason, the truth known only to the boy, when he was at his lowest ebb, he still had not returned there and died alone. Why? At first, in the first couple of weeks following the discovery of his body, Hollister spent a great deal of time thinking about the dead youth and trying to come up with at least some answers to all these question but since his funeral, slowly he had put the plight of the youngster out of his mind and continued with his own life and other cases.

The one day, completely unexpectedly, all this changed. Hollister was on duty and answered his ringing telephone to hear a male voice, obviously a youth, his speech heavily accented. "Are you the copper who saw Martin Foxford?"

Hearing the alias used by Cameron Robinson sent a shiver down his spine and Hollister into a moment of blind panic, but very quickly regained his composure and gathered up his thought. "Yes…yes it is. Who's this though?"

"It don't matter who I am," replied the mystery voice. "Except that I knew Martin. I used to work with him, if you know what I mean." The youth appeared to be trying to reveal something about Robinson, without giving too much away.

"What exactly do you mean when you say you worked together?" asked Hollister, without pushing further for a name to his mystery caller just yet.

There was a brief, awkward silence as the youngster hesitated before he answered the question. "You know what he was, don't you?"

Hollister, sensing they could keep playing this game for a while, each trying to figure out what the other knew, without revealing too much themselves, decided to take a gamble with the male caller and called his

bluff. "Yes, I do. But you've got to tell me yourself, in your own words."

This was followed by another brief pause, "He was on 'the game'. You know, a 'rent boy'. Well, I don't think he killed himself."

Hearing the mystery voice reveal the closely guarded secret about Robinson sent another chill down the detective's spine and he felt the hairs on the back of his neck stand on end. "He didn't, he died of pneumonia," replied Hollister, maintaining the lie.

"Well, we both know different," teased the voice. "Don't we?"

Having been caught off his guard momentarily, Hollister had now composed himself. "I think we need to meet, you know, face-to-face and talk some more."

"Yeah, but no tricks though," the owner of the anonymous voice came back with. "No tricks though or I'm off. You try picking me up and I'll disappear and tell you nothing."

"You sound like that you might be a minor. I can't talk to you without another adult being present, you know, like a social worker or another appropriate adult..."

"That's only if you arrest me," countered the voice.

Realising that he had been out manoeuvred, Hollister tried another ploy to get the person into the station. "You obviously know who I am, I can't just drop everything and go off and meet a perfect stranger, especially someone who sounds like they may still be a juvenile. I need to know that I'm not walking into a trap or something or that I'm not wasting my time."

After a brief pause the boy answered. It had been his turn to be outsmarted. "Martin was being blackmailed by a punter. Somebody

recognised him, knew who he really was and then blackmailed him into free sex."

Hollister felt a rush of excitement flow through his body. He had always doubted that he had committed suicide and now, here was somebody possibly offering him proof of his suspicions. "You're right. We do need to meet up."

"Like I've said no tricks though or I'm off. You won't see or hear from me ever again."

"You've got my word on that. Where and when?" Hollister knew that he was taking a huge gamble but thought it might be worth it, if only to put his own mind at ease.

After another brief pause, the voice replied. "Piccadilly Gardens, in the middle, in an hour. You know, near the water fountain thing."

"How will I know you?"

"You won't but I'll know you. Saw you at his funeral. Nice touch that was. That's why I'm coming to you and nobody else. I told you, he was a friend."

The line went dead and Hollister hung up the phone, scribbling a few notes recounting the call on a piece of paper on his desk. It was only now that he realised how much his hands were sweating and he dried them by wiping them on his trousers legs. He was both intrigued and excited. How had the mystery caller managed to get hold of his name and direct telephone number? How did he know that Robinson had been a 'rent boy'? And what, if anything, did he know about the life and death of Cameron Robinson, or Martin Foxford? Once again, the plight of the dead teenager was foremost in his thoughts.

An hour later, McKenzie Hollister found himself leaning on a metal railing in Piccadilly Gardens, chain smoking cigarettes and his eyes darting in every direction, waiting to be approached by the male youth he had just spoken too, looking out for a familiar face that he had seen at Cameron Robinson's funeral. If ever two people wanted an anonymous meeting place in the centre of Manchester, then this must be the perfect location, he thought to himself. Tens of thousands of people must past through one of the few green areas left in the city every day, a lot of them rushing to catch buses or the 'Metro' trams that criss-crossed the city, many others making their way to the shops to be coaxed out of spending their hard-earned money. The most recent of variations of Piccadilly Gardens was about the size of a football pitch, with a sunken area and a water feature of fountains, an ideal place for those wishing to meet somebody or to grab a hasty lunch throughout their working day. A huge concrete wall did an excellent job of sheltering the noise of the constant stream of buses and the wind could be heard rustling through the leaves of a few trees, creating a sanctuary for the throngs of ever cooing starlings.

Hollister had kept his word to the youth and, despite a nagging doubt in his judgement, he had gone alone to meet the mystery caller. As a senior ranking police officer, protocol dictated that he had to report his every movement whilst on duty, but Hollister had only told the control room at Heller Street police station that he was meeting an informant. He had also informed them that he had with him a two-way radio and his mobile phone, just in case of any unforeseen emergency, but he seemed to know by instinct that on this occasion, they would not be needed. The person he was due to meet sounded like he was only

young, possibly around the same age as Robinson and so Hollister deemed him as no risk or threat to himself and had attended alone.

He had been waiting around ten minutes past the stipulated meeting time and was just about to give up, cursing to himself as he thought what a waste of time it had been, when he was approached by a male youth. "You Hollister?" he asked in a softly spoken, heavily accented voice.

The detective recognised the boy's voice immediately and nodded. Quickly looking the youth over that took a place next to him revealed a smartly dressed teenager with a slightly tanned complexion, green eyes and looking Eastern-European, his dark hair cropped short at the back and sides and longer on top. He was wearing black jeans, a white sweatshirt and a black quilted jacket. Hollister got straight to the point, with an embittered tone in his voice, slightly annoyed at having been kept waiting. "I hope you're not pissing me about?"

The youngster, completely unfazed by Hollister abrupt attitude was very relaxed and composed. "Chill out man, and no I'm not. Let's go and sit over there," motioning to seats on a platform served by the trams. "We'll be able to talk better."

As man and boy crossed the Gardens, Hollister found himself relieved to be away from the stench of alcohol and urine soaked grass and they made their way to the platform. Hollister knew what the youth was up to but had decided to go along with him. The youngster, if he thought threatened by the detective would have been able to either jump onto a tram or leap off the platform and run, leaving the older man unable to keep up with his youthfulness.

After taking a seat on the platform, Hollister spoke first, still convinced that he was doing the right thing. "Right, what can you tell me about Cameron Robinson or Martin Foxford, as you knew him and his death?"

"All I know is that Martin pulled a trick one night that knew him. This punter then made him do it for free whenever they met?" replied the boy.

"How do you know this?" asked Hollister, lighting up another cigarette.

The youth motioned for one of Hollister's cigarettes and was given one. With his other hand he ran his fingers through his hair, playing with the gold stud earring in his left lobe, delaying his reply as long as possible. "Martin told me about it one day."

"Have you any idea who this guy was or even how he knew Martin, Cameron, in the first place?"

The teenager shook his head. "Nah, he never told me that bit." He then paused briefly and gave a little impish smile. "I met him once though, about your age, going grey."

Hollister became a little excited by this disclosure and felt his heart beat quicken at being given the same description as others had given. "Would you be able to recognise him again?"

The youngster once again shook his head. "Nah, doubt it."

Somewhat perplexed, Hollister pushed the point. "If you met him though, then surely you should be able to give me a slightly better description?"

With another shake of his head, accompanied by a shrug of his shoulders, "We don't usually see their faces for long. We're either on our knees, giving them a blow or they're giving us one from behind."

The frankness of the teenager's reply shocked the detective and he realised just how naïve he was about this sort of thing. Although he should have been repulsed by the candour of the youth, talking about his homosexual activities, instead he found that he was hanging onto every word the boy said. "Okay, okay...I get the picture. How did you meet this guy?"

"Martin told me that he had this thing about watching boys do it to each other. He wanted to watch Martin in action, you know, with another lad and he asked me. We went back to his place and did the business..."

Hollister interrupted the youth, "That's where I've caught you out..."

It was now the turn of the teenager to interrupt the detective. "Not that dump where you found him but the place where he lived, you know, where he met his regular punters."

The detective had already come to the conclusion that Robinson had another place, where he had taken his clients but the thought that this was actually his home simply had not occurred to him. It would though explain the absence of any other clothes or personal possessions, he thought to himself. "Do you know where this place is?"

"Yeah," came the reply and then the youth paused briefly. "But, it'll cost you."

Hollister found that he was not exactly surprised by the youngster's mercenary attitude. "I thought it might" he said with a slight smile. "I'll do you a deal. You take me there, you know...his other place and tell

me everything that you know about him and this particular day, plus anything else that might be useful to me and we'll see how much it's all worth, how's that?"

"Sounds fair enough," he replied with a smile, showing his pearl white teeth. One way or another he was onto an earner, he thought to himself. Either he was going to 'pull a trick', a term used by prostitutes for picking up clients, or he was going to get paid for his knowledge. Either way, he was going to earn money.

After a short journey, Hollister pulled his silver grey Vauxhall Vectra car up outside a modern three-storey block of flats, one of an identical pair situated on Alexandra Park Road and directly opposite the large park that gave the road its name. The leaves on the trees in the park had just began to fall as autumn drew in and those still on the branches were a multitude of colours, green, brown, orange and gold contrasting against the almost black branches and Hollister could not help but look in awe at the view before him, thinking how pleasant it must be waking up to the vista of the park as the sun rose on an autumn morning. The detective and the youth both got out of the car and the few people out on the street did not even give them a second glance, no doubt thinking that they were father and son returning home from a shopping expedition.

Their ten minute drive out of the city and to the Whalley Range district of Manchester had been conducted in almost total silence. Hollister had not even put on the cars radio. The youngster had given the detective directions as to where the flat was situated giving away to the experienced detective that he had been to the location on more than

one occasion. Whilst driving, almost out of habit, Hollister had scrutinised the teenager sat next to him. He appeared to be a little under six feet tall with a slim build, light brown hair and a clean, fresh and slightly tanned complexion, which reinforced Hollister initial thoughts on hearing his voice that he was originally from somewhere in Europe. The lack of any facial hair and the odd acne spot on his near-olive skinned face indicated that he must only be in his late teens, a similar age and appearance to that of the dead youth that had brought them together. Hollister had maintained his silence throughout the journey because he knew that if he had started asking any questions whilst driving, the boy would have either kept quiet, or even worse for him, he would have leapt from the car no sooner it was stationary at a set of traffic lights, never to be seen again.

It was the boy that spoke first, "Martin's place is on the second floor, flat twenty eight."

"How are we going to get in?" asked the detective.

"I know where he hides the key. He has…or I should say…had a cleaner come in for him once a week," replied the teenager.

Hollister shook his head in disbelief. "I don't believe what I'm hearing. You've waited nearly a month to come forward and tell me about this place. The cleaner must've been in at least three times by now. Any possible evidence or fingerprints that we could've got are now well gone. I just don't believe you've done this to me."

The teenager was annoyed at Hollister. "I didn't have to come and see you in the first place. You obviously had no idea he even had this place. Not only that these punters that use us are all legit. They don't have no police records, they're all part of the system, part of the

establishment. They pick us up, fuck us and then go home to their nice little homes and their wives and their kids. It's them that get away with it and the likes of me that get the shit."

What the boy said had made sense though, thought Hollister, as he followed him up the flight of stairs and stop outside a door. From under a nearby fire extinguisher a set of keys were then produced and the teenager let them into the flat.

If he was honest with himself, Hollister had no idea of what to expect inside the apartment as the boy opened the door but on seeing the decor of the flat he was more than a little surprised. It was not a flat that fitted the stereotyped image of a young man and was in complete contrast to the ghastly bedsit where Robinson had been found. Considering that he was now entering into the realm of homosexuality and the seedier domain of 'rent boys', the flat was decorated with style. Both the hallway and lounge were painted a very pale grey and you walked on black laminated flooring. Three large multi-coloured prints, which Hollister recognised as by being by Mark Rothko, hung on the wall that was dominated by a large black leather sofa, a second, but smaller sofa was against a wall under a window and a large TV sitting on a white cabinet, which matched the tables in the room. A brief tour of the rest of the flat revealed a kitchen, pair of bedrooms and a bathroom that were all decorated and furnished with equal style.

"Nice place," the detective said as he joined the youth now sitting on one of the sofas. "He must've worked hard for it," choking on his words when he remembered that he was talking about a teenaged prostitute and what he must have had to do in order to have such a nice home.

"Yeah," replied the youth. He had lost all his earlier arrogance and now seemed quieter, more solemn.

Hollister detected this change in mood. "What's up?"

The boy shrugged his shoulders before replying. "Just don't feel right being here...you know...with this Martin or whatever his name was being dead and all that."

The detective was having no such problems with guilt, but realising that he needed the teenager on his side, offered the street hardened youngster some sympathy. "I can understand that. Tell you what I'll do, I'll see if I can make us a drink and then we'll have a chat. The cleaners obviously been in, I can still smell the polish and she would've wiped away any fingerprints, so I don't think it'll matter. You okay with that?"

The thought of being waited on by a detective amused the youth and he gave another quick mischievous grin. "Yeah, that'll be all right. I'll have a coffee, two sugars, if you can."

A couple of minutes later Hollister reappeared with two mugs of coffee and sat on the larger sofa. "Now," began the detective, "You don't have to tell me anything that you don't want to. We both know that we can't hold a formal interview because you're obviously still a juvenile and I can't prove or use anything that you do tell me. I need to call you something though, what's your name?"

"It's Spencer, Spencer Drury," replied the youngster. The alias now coming more natural than his actual name, but then again, it had been a while since he had used his real name.

Hollister guessed that this was probably not his real name, but chose to go along with him for now. "How old are you Spencer?"

After briefly hesitating, Spencer answered the question, "I'll be eighteen in a couple of months and before you ask, I'm not going to tell you where I come from."

Hollister again shook his head, this time it was in despair. "How long have you been on 'the game'?"

"A couple of years," Spencer said in a softly spoken, barely audible voice.

A despondent Hollister was taken aback by his answer. He knew that asking the next question would probably shock him, but it was something that he needed to ask. "The next question is fairly obvious, why?"

Spencer paused briefly, took a sip of his coffee and then plucked up the courage to answer the embarrassing question. "Have you any idea what it's like being the worst dressed boy in your class? I'm the youngest of three boys and I've got two older sisters as well. I've only either had second-hand clothes or their cast-offs. All me mates knew that I was wearing me brother's old clothes and they took the piss out of me..." he paused briefly, almost too embarrassed to continue. "I've even had to wear me sister's knickers 'cause me mum couldn't afford proper pants for me. You any idea of the shit that I got of me mates when they found out? All me mates had top clothes, all the right labels and makes, know what I mean? I had nothing, fuck all. I just wanted to be part of their gang, be one of them, to look the same as them. But I couldn't. They just took the piss out of me daily. I used to go home and cry myself to sleep at night. So I just stopped going to school. Used to hang around train stations and shopping centres and did a bit of

begging and thieving for me dinner. Know what? I enjoyed being on me own and so one day I just didn't go home when I was supposed to." Hollister found that he was genuinely touched by his story. He was now feeling sympathetic towards the boy, but Hollister was also a realist. Had he been taken in by a story, a collection of lies? The way that he had rattled this account off had led Hollister to believe that he was actually telling the truth. "Where are you originally from?"

The reply was immediate, "I've already told you, not telling you that." After a brief pause, during which he took another drink of his coffee, he continued. "I didn't come straight here though. Went to London first, hung out around the theatre area. You know, streets paved with gold and all that bullshit. Didn't like it though, too many paedo's after your arse. I came to Manchester 'bout a year ago and I've been here ever since. I like it here, won't never go home now."

"I know this might be difficult for you, embarrassing too, but how did you end up working as a prostitute?" asked Hollister, not really expecting an answer.

"Don't matter to me talking 'bout it…" he paused. The youth had lied and Hollister had seen through it. He was embarrassed about his way of life and, without letting on to the detective it was Hollister who became the first person that he had ever spoken to about it. Spencer finished his coffee, cleared his throat and continued. "I met this bloke one night in town. Alright bloke he was too. I was outside *Burgerworld* on Market Street, 'bout ten at night. It was raining and I was cold and soaked to the skin. I'd been here 'bout two weeks by this time, doing a bit of begging, bit of robbing to get by. Nothing much, just stuff I could eat and then this night though I was starving and freezing. I was so cold

that I was shivering and I actually started to cry. Just couldn't help myself and it was the only time that I've ever wanted to go home. Then this bloke starts talking to me and offering to buy me something to eat. I hadn't eaten anything for a couple of days and needed something, so I said okay and he took me inside. He said I could choose anything that I wanted and so I had two full meals. I had no idea of when I'd get a chance to eat like this again and so I made the most of it."

Hearing that once again *Burgerworld* was being used as a meeting place for men and 'rent boys' brought back some very unpleasant memories from many years ago, when Hollister was stationed in London, soon after becoming a Detective Sergeant. The area around Piccadilly Circus, including the burger bar, had been given the nickname of 'The Meat Rack' and its reputation as a pick up place had acquired near legendary status.

"Did you know what he was really after, you know, because these days nobody offers to help anybody these days, without wanting something in return?" asked Hollister as he lit up yet another cigarette, offering one to Spencer, who accepted it.

"Had an idea. We talked while I ate and then he said 'bout going back to his place. I was a bit reluctant at first, but I thought 'bout it and said 'fuck it, why not'. Anything had to be better than yet another night on the streets."

"Then what happened?"

Spencer gave one of his cheeky impish grins, "You getting off on this?"

The mere thought that this was going through the mind of the teenager mortified Hollister and he was deeply offended. "No, of

course not," he snapped back. "I just can't understand why people…lads…like you go on 'the game'. Call me naïve if you want."

Spencer realised that he had over stepped the mark and offered the detective an apology. "All right man, chill out. I'm sorry, right." He paused briefly and continued recounting his experience, "Any way, we went back to his flat, over in Manchester, one of those new ones. He then ran me a bath and stuck me clothes in the washer. Just lay there for ages. It was me first bath for ages, I must've stunk. I thought 'bout what was expected from me while I lay there. Knew he'd want something in return. Barry, that was his name, came in and gave me a brandy. There was no lock on the door. He said it'll warm me up on the inside. We talked for a bit and then he told me to get out of the bath and after he dried me off, we went to bed. I got the impression that he did this sort of thing a lot. After spending weeks sleeping rough, you know on park benches and in doorways, you've no idea just how good it feels to be in a nice warm and clean bed again…"

"Oh, I can. I've spent days on end in a car doings 'obs' on a place. I know how welcoming a bed is…" Hollister cut himself short, realising he was entering into dialogue with a teenaged prostitute. "When did anything sexual happen, assuming that it did?"

"The next morning. Didn't touch me all night long. Just cuddled up next to me. After this Barry had made me breakfast, he asked if he could give me a 'blow job'. Then he told me to do it to him." The youth spoke about what must have been a humiliating and degrading experience in an almost casual, matter-of-fact way, as if it was the most natural thing in the world.

"Did he force you to do it?"

"Nah, not really. It wasn't the first time that I'd done something like this, but it had been a while. I wasn't used to doing it and I knew all along that he would want something in return for the bed and something to eat. So I reckoned that I owed him something. It was a small price to pay. He'd been okay with me and so I thought 'why not be nice to him back.'"

"But surely you didn't have to resort to that?" Hollister could hardly hide his moral indignation towards this man that had taken advantage of a vulnerable youngster.

"Shit man," snapped back Spencer. "You just don't get it do you? What the fuck else could I do? How else could I have paid him back? Didn't have no money. If I did, do you think that I would've been there in the first place?"

Realising that the patience of the youth was wearing thin and that he was in danger of walking out on him, Hollister finally got around to the point. "Okay Spencer, calm down. I didn't mean to upset you. I want you to tell me about the night that you told me about on the phone, the one where you came here with Cameron."

"Like I said," began Spencer, now a lot calmer. "Martin...or Cameron...or whatever his name was had this punter that knew him and got his fun from watching boys together. He offered me two hundred quid for an all-nighter. Don't mind admitting that I jumped at it. After all, if it wasn't going to be me, would've been somebody else and so I might as well have the money. Then when I got here, there were four blokes, including Martin's punter. Don't mind admitting that I was a bit scared, but Martin said it'll be okay. Said he knew them all. We all went into the bedroom and one bloke gets a video camera out

and started filming us. He was telling us what to do. Seemed to know what he was doing, probably done it before. First me and Martin had to kiss each other, then strip each off…" Spencer hesitated and then continued, "…I then had to give him a 'blow-job', letting him cum on me face. Then I had to give him one up the arse, while Martin sucked them off. Then me and Martin had to do them all night. They fucked us over and over again and we had to suck them off over and over again. Don't mind admitting that I was glad when it was over."

Hollister sat in a stunned silence for a moment, shocked by the boys account. Eventually he found the inner strength to reply, "Do you think that you'd be able to recognise any of them again, especially the one with the video camera?"

Spencer shook his head and shrugged his shoulders, "Doubt it. Seen lots of punters since, you know, being a 'free floater'. After a while, they're all the same…"

"Sorry, but what's a 'free floater'?" asked the detective.

"It's somebody like me who goes from punter to punter. Not one with a 'sugar daddy' that looks after them and is his alone. Anyway, might recognise the punter with the camera. You don't forget a bastard like him."

Hollister could hardly believe what he was hearing. The police had long suspected things like this were happening, but up until now, had never had any proof. Now here was a youngster that had actually taken part in a gay orgy, with the intent of turning it into a pornographic movie, and he could not use the youth as a witness or reveal to anybody what he now knew. "How long ago was this?"

The teenager thought for a moment, "Must've been 'bout a year ago, maybe eighteen months, max."

"That would put you very close to sixteen and under the legal age."

Another shrug of the shoulders followed, this time with a nod of his head. "Right, told you all I know, where's me money?"

As Hollister reached for his wallet, "If I need to speak to you again, you know, like this, where can I find you?"

"In 'The Village'. Just give me fifty quid. After all, he was a mate."

Some friend you are, thought Hollister as he handed over the money and watched the youth walk out of the flat, leaving the detective alone and in a state of shock. He knew, that his duty as a police officer, should have been to try and prevent the youngster from leaving and take him into custody, for his own safety and protection if nothing else, but the reality of this course of action would have created too many questions. So instead, he just sat there, paid the youth and watched him disappear.

Nightfall had long descended on Manchester and, once again, McKenzie Hollister was having difficulty in sleeping. He had tossed and turned for what seemed like hours before he finally gave up on the notion of any sleep and, in an effort not to disturb his sleeping wife beside him, he got up and went downstairs. After fixing himself a large shot of whisky, which he sipped neat, Hollister eased himself onto the sofa. He had not turned on any lights, opting to open the curtains and allowing the room to be illuminated by the streetlight that shone through the window, bathing the room in an orange glow.

The detective, despite being hardened by years of experience, had found himself deeply affected by his encounter with the young boy and this had unsettled him for the remainder of the day. Having returned to the police station, locking the flat behind him and taking the keys with him, he found it almost impossible to concentrate on any other matters and his fellow officers had seen a marked deterioration in his mood and temperament. Hollister could not stop thinking about the teenage prostitute and the calmness, almost matter-of-fact way that he had recounted his terrible experiences and by the way that he had quickly accepted this as a way of life.

Hollister had learnt a long time ago never to get too personally involved in his cases, although at times it had been very difficult to avoid forming some form of attachment to either the victim or those that had committed the act, and relying on his training and experience to remain impartial, but this time he did actually feel a great deal of sympathy for both boys. Whether it was because he had met Spencer so soon after the death of Cameron Robinson, with the detective drawing parallels between the two youths, or, in the case of Spencer, whether it was due to his own upbringing, was uncertain to the detective. He too had come from a large family and while he was growing up in the Springburn area of Glasgow, recollected Hollister, as he sipped his whisky, the family had to endure periods of financial hardships and hard times, but he had never resorted to even thinking about doing anything like the two boys now troubling him.

When he was their age, the subject of teenage prostitution, especially amongst boys, was almost unheard off. On reflection though, Hollister

thought that it must have happened, but it did not happen as often or as casually as it does today.

As he felt his body sinking deeper into the comfort of his armchair, the warm, soothing whisky helping him to relax, Hollister thought about his current predicament. Robinson was, unfortunately, dead and there was nothing that he could do about that. But Spencer was very much alive and kicking and in his thoughts. But what should he do about him? Despite what Spencer had told him, the detective very much doubted that he was nearly eighteen years old. He was probably nearer to sixteen and Hollister knew that he should bring his plight to the attention of Social Services and arrange for him to be picked up and placed into care. He should also notify officers of the Child Protection Unit, the arm of the police that offered help to those under the age of seventeen and in need of protection, and let them pick him up and investigate his claims. But reporting Spencer to either created another dilemma, they would want to know how Hollister had got to know the youth in the first place and why he was having a drink with him, a self-confessed under-aged male prostitute, in the secret home of another, recently deceased, 'rent boy'. Now that alone, thought the detective, would take some explaining away.

Hollister considered another option available to him. Should he report this latest development to his superior officer and then let him decide on the next course of action? But he too would want to have the answers to the same questions, except, being a long-time friend, he would be more insistent in getting answers. He would also want to know why Hollister was still 'investigating' the death of a youth that had already been declared as a tragic suicide and his case closed. It was

the answer to this question that was the hardest for Hollister to come up with or even justify to himself. What exactly was his macabre fascination with the death, and indeed, the life of Cameron Robinson?

An hour later, as Hollister was draining the last remnants from the bottle of whisky, he found himself thinking more and more about Spencer. The detective glanced at a clock, twenty past two in the morning, and he wondered where the boy was tonight? Was he alone on the sometimes violent streets of Manchester, running the gauntlet of those that preyed on vulnerable boys, and girls, like him? Had there been anything that he could have said in order to get the youth off the streets and to do something positive with his life? But the youngster had spoken so openly and casually about having sex with men for money. He did not seem that embarrassed about it, just a means of earning money. Maybe he even liked it? But how could he like it? Having some pervert breathing down on him, probably under the influence of drink, his breath stale with alcohol, while he was having sex with him.

The deeply unsettled detective found that, for the second time during that day, he had an involuntary erection. The first time had been when Spencer was recollecting the occasion with Robinson and the nameless, faceless men. This time it was because he was thinking about Spencer being with a man tonight. Having gotten himself into a state of drunken stupor, Hollister dropped the glass onto the carpet, spilling the last few drops of his precious whisky, and reached inside his dressing gown, his hand almost involuntarily snaking its way inside his underwear. His nicotine stained fingers gripped his hard manhood.

It had been many years since Hollister had masturbated. Like many boys, he had done so frequently during the painful years of puberty and adolescence until he was in his late teens and 'discovered' girls, never having to resort to it since. But now he did through a subconscious choice. He closed his tormented eyes and the image of Cameron Robinson was once again fresh in his mind, lying naked on the bed, his finely tuned, suntanned body almost inviting him to join him. As he tugged on his penis that image was replaced by Spencer. The face of the boy was still fresh in his memory, as if he was there with him now and Hollister's imagination begun to run wild.

Spencer's cheeky, impish grin beamed from his face as he slowly and seductively undressed, revealing his young body until he was naked and by his side. Hollister thought he could feel the breath of the teenage boy on his stomach as he leant over him and grasped the hard penis. They were now not his own fingers that were wrapped around the pulsating manhood imagined Hollister, but those of the mysterious Spencer. Faster and faster the hand worked on the phallus until he could stand it no more and let nature take its course, with semen bursting from it and onto the blue robe of the detective. It was only now that he realised that his body was trembling and rigid and that his heart was pounding away in his chest, his breathing fast and heavy. It was as if he had just had sex with his sleeping wife upstairs.

Then guilt took over. He had just masturbated while having a fantasy about having sex with a young boy. Why? Almost immediately the detective seemed to sober up as he was overwhelmed with contrition and he cleaned himself up before returning to his bed. Not that his conscious would allow him any respite from his recent activity.

Chapter Four

Over the following three days McKenzie Hollister submerged himself deep into his work, desperately trying to erase the haunting memory of *that* night, trying to block it completely from his consciousness. The following day, after *it* had happened, he had reported for duty late and then because he was consumed with guilt, his mood and temperament had succeeded, without having to try too hard, in annoying almost every other police officer that had the unfortunate luck of coming into contact with him. Even members of his own squad of detectives, fairly used to his mood swings, were reluctant in approaching him unless they had no other option. Each of them had decided to leave him sitting alone in his office, staring at him through the large windows and wondering what had caused this seismic mood swing. It got to such a stage that a delegation of them went as far as complaining to their Chief Superintendent about Hollister's obnoxious attitude and then he was told, officially, to calm down. Hollister never offered anybody any explanations or apologies to his colleagues, but most of them, having worked together for several years, had seen this type of behaviour before.

Eventually though, Hollister heeded the well-meant advice and did try to relax and calm down a little but no sooner had he returned to the sanctity of his home, shame and self-reproach once again consumed him as he found himself at the scene of his misery. This set the pattern for the next few days until eventually the detective could stand it no more. For nearly a week now he had been wallowing in self-pity and

going through the motions both at home and at work, never really taking anything in that was being said to him nor offering anything of great importance himself, but no sooner had he come off duty, then he headed straight for the nearest bar and over an indeterminate number of hours, sitting alone on a stool at the bar, sinking deeper into a depressive drunken stupor.

What really troubled the detective were his deep, innermost feelings and his failure to understand why he had done what he had and why he felt like he did. Was it pity and sympathy for those like Cameron Robinson and Spencer? Was it the sense of hopelessness for a generation of boys, and girls, who thought nothing of selling their bodies for sex with strangers, turning their childhood into a commodity to be exploited just for a few pounds, or in Spencer's case, for the price of a meal and a bed for the night? Still further questions kept returning to the mind of Hollister, adding to his depressive mood and maintaining the near constant headache brought on through the lack of sleep.

After he had contacted him and knowing that he was a teenage 'rent boy' he knew that he should have secretly contacted Social Services and agreed to meet them, secretly, in Piccadilly Gardens and arranged for them to pick up the teenager when they had first met? He should have him placed into care for his own protection or even reunited him with his no doubt worried family. They were probably feeling the same despair and hopelessness that the Robinson family had when Cameron had first disappeared from his home.

Over a period of time, Hollister began to think more and more about Spencer. He was a fairly good looking young man, with a cheeky smile and an air of bravura about him, instantly likable and Hollister

wondered to himself that in the couple of years he had away from his family, had he ever contacted them to let them know that he was still alive and safe or, at the very least, sent them a letter or postcard? The detective knew, from the experience of previous cases of runaways, just how much a simple gesture like this would have meant to his family. Thinking about this, Hollister recalled an occasion from when he himself was a youngster, barely into his teens, and had failed to come home on time. His mother had worked herself up into a state of near hysteria as the hours passed by, worrying about her son. What had happened was that Hollister had met up with some school friends and lost all sense of timing while playing football with them on a hot summer's night. All perfectly innocent and when he did eventually realise the time, as the sun cast an orange glow to the sky and darkness descended, he set off for home. He never gave it a thought to find a way of letting his anguished parents know that he was safe and was playing football with friends. Teenaged boys simply do not think about doing such things.

What turmoil Spencer's parents must be going through, wondered the detective? He had been missing from home for a couple of years and his parents, wherever they were, would be desperate to know that at the very least he was still alive, being able to discard any fears that would have built up over the passage of time that he was lying dead in an unmarked grave. Then the detective remembered the strength shown by Cameron Robinson's mother and her refusal to give up hope for her son, even when Hollister had informed her that he was dead. As it turned out, her son was living less than ten miles away from his family but Spencer, by his own admission, was in another city and who knows

what his family had gone through since his disappearance, not to mention what he may have had to endure or put himself through in order to survive on his own.

For the first time in his long and distinguished career, and as he found himself drinking more and more, desperate to try and find a solution to his current turmoil, Hollister found himself questioning being a police officer. For as long as he could remember, it had been all he had ever wanted to be. He had lost many so-called friends when he first joined up, but he did not really care. Feeling the pride of wearing the dark blue uniform far outweighed any personal loss and, over the years, he had made many more friends. Even his wife, Kate, was a former police officer, having been forced to retire a few years ago after suffering a back injury whilst investigating a burglary and now living on her generous pension. Now Hollister found all this pale and insignificant when compared to the plight of Cameron Robinson and Spencer and who knew how many more like them.

Something had snapped deep within the brain of the detective. Hollister decided that he simply had to do something to help them. He simply could not just ignore them and their plight. He slowly began to sober up and focus his mind on helping Spencer, not really knowing exactly what he was going to do. He just knew that he simply could not sit back and do nothing. Hollister eased himself from the stool at the bar of a public house close to Heller Street police station and, once he had steadied himself using the glass-topped bar, his balance impaired due to sheer volume of alcohol that he had just drunk, he headed for the door. Once through the doors, the cold chill of an autumn night and the light rain helping to sober him up some more, he crossed the gravel car

park to his car, the small stones grinding themselves together under his feet. It never occurred to Hollister that he was well over the legal limit for driving. But, even if he was stopped by an eager uniformed traffic officer, he would rely on the camaraderie of the police and encourage the officer not to report him and to see him safely home.

Setting off, but not really knowing what he was doing or where he was going, Hollister tried to focus his mind and found that, once again, all he could focus on was Spencer. The youth had managed to embed himself into the psyche of the detective. He was all he thought about. He was determined to find him and do something to help him. What exactly, he did not know. This time, when he found him, he was not going to ignore the youth and turn a blind eye to his plight and life on the streets and his depressing circumstances. As he set out on his personal crusade, Hollister wondered what he would actually do if he actually found Spencer? At that precise moment in time, Hollister did not have an answer. All he knew, that as a police officer, he had to do something to help the boy, even if this meant taking him to the correct authorities and letting them decide what to do with him. He just knew that he would be failing in his duty not to try and find him and do something about getting him safe.

As he drove, Hollister found that everything was a brightly coloured blur. The reds, yellows and greens of the neon lights of the city seemed like smears of paint on an artist's palette as they passed him by until he somehow found himself driving slowly around the square mile of bars and clubs that formed 'The Village'. The homosexual community had become a great deal more respectable over the past two decades and now they openly advertised *their* bars and clubs by flying the

distinctive rainbow flag outside their premises. The flag symbolised 'pride' and it was these flags that Hollister searched for, being surprised at just how many there actually were flying and the sheer throng of revellers within the area.

It was only as he snaked his way around the dimly-lit side streets leading off the two main brightly lit streets that he realised just how many people appeared to be prostitutes. Almost every corner, darkened alleyway and drinking establishment had, what seemed like, prostitutes loitering around outside. Some were obvious ones, others not so. They ranged from their late teens to their later years and were both male and female. Their ages it did not seem a barrier and many had the unmistakable appearance of prostitutes. As he searched for one in particular, not even sure if he was even out on the streets hustling for a client, Hollister became filled with despair at the sheer number of youngsters that were out on the streets.

Not all of them were possible prostitutes and many were out enjoying themselves with their partners but a significant number appeared to be just that. How could there be that many lost souls out on the streets Of Manchester and he not even known about it before? But then again, why should he know? Until the advent of this particular case, he had very rarely ventured into 'The Village' before, let alone get involved in anything to do with child prostitution. This was always the domain of the Vice Squad.

After about an hour of fruitless searching and before he could fully sober up the detective decided to give up for the night. The elusive Spencer was nowhere to be found. It was only now that Hollister realised just how futile his efforts were in the first place, no matter how

well intentioned they had been and, after letting out a heavy sigh, he headed off for home. The sixty minutes that he had spent looking for the youngster had only succeeded in adding to his feeling of despondency and hopelessness. He would have to wait even longer before he could once again see the youth that he had become besotted with.

Kate Hollister had, over the years, got used to her husband's long and unsociable hours, but as he almost fell through the doors on his eventual return home, she realised that he had been drinking and not working. Any sympathy that she originally felt for him quickly disappeared. After giving him the cold harsh glare of disapproval, she passed him in the hallway, their shoulders almost brushing, and headed up the stairs, the banister of which that her drunken husband clung to tightly, desperately trying to prevent him crashing onto the floor. Eventually though, he somehow managed to make it to the lounge and collapsed into a chair, falling asleep almost immediately.

He awoke a couple of hours later. The room had been plunged into darkness and his heavy eyes searched for a clock and when the numbers had stopped being a blur and became readable, Hollister realised that it was a little after four in the morning. He sat upright in the chair, his lower back aching due to the uncomfortable position that he had just slept in and using both his hands, the detective rubbed his eyes, finally shaking his head. He found that his head ached more than his body and he had a gritty, dryness in his mouth which he had not experienced for a long time. Slowly he stood up, clinging to the chair in order to prevent himself falling over, painfully, onto the carpeted floor.

The entire room seemed to be spinning and eventually his balance allowed him to stand unaided. He ached from his head down to his toes and he longed for his bed.

Climbing the stairs he found every step an effort. Each step sent a jolting pain from his right temple to the middle of his forehead, but almost like a baby taking its first tentative steps, he made it up the stairs. Eventually, after what seemed like an eternity, he stood in the bedroom. Despite the darkness, he could make out the motionless outline of his wife as she slept in their bed and he began undressing, dropping his clothes onto the floor, with them forming an untidy heap, before moving over to the bed and easing himself under the covers, inching closer to his wife. His hand slid over her shoulder and along the silky gown until it cupped on of her breasts. She stirred, but did not wake up. Gently at first he kneaded the soft bosom, his breathing getting heavier as he increased the pressure on it, before he moved his hand lower, searching for her pubic mound. Finding it, Hollister rubbed the area, inching up the gown until he could touch both the naked flesh and the matted hair. Kate stirred a little more, realised what her drunken husband was trying to do and pushed his hand away. Hollister though was not giving up that easily.

Both his hands this time went straight back to his wife's vagina and forced her legs apart so that he could manhandle her better. She was now fully awake and aware of what Hollister was trying to do and attempted to fend off his unwelcome groping, but he used all his strength against her. He forced her over onto her chest, pushing her face into a pillow to stiffen her cries and climbed on top of her, forcing him body between her now outstretched legs. Kate Hollister, writhing

and struggling to free herself, was already having difficulty in breathing due to her head being forced into a pillow and now, due to the sheer weight of her husband lay on her back, she found it even harder.

Driven by his own carnal desires, the muscular naked body of Cameron Robinson and the roguish smile of Spencer in his mind, imagining that he was with either of them, the detective gripped his wife and pulled her hips upwards to meet his erect penis. Stabbing blindly at her nether regions with his hard member, Hollister eventually found an orifice. Kate let out a muffled scream as the penis was forced up his wife's anus, and, having found the hole that he wanted, Hollister took great pleasure in having his wife. Ignoring her struggling and her pleas and sobbing, Hollister roughly had sex with his wife, never once showing any tenderness or loving until he could stand it no more and let his juices flow inter her.

Spent, he rolled off his wife and flopped onto the bed. His breathing was heavy, his heart pounding in his chest and he soon fell asleep, ignoring his near hysterical wife next to him. In all her years of knowing him, she had never known him to act like this before. He was not her loving husband of two decades but a savage. He was like a wild animal. She had witnessed his violent mood swings before, never once assaulting her though, but she had never witnessed anything like this. He had not made love to her as a husband should, showing her gentleness and signs of loving her. He had just raped her, anally raped her. She was not even sure how long the assault had lasted and was so relieved when it was all over.

Over their years of marriage she had got used to her husband's mood swings and occasional bouts of depression, but this was something

completely different. Having been a former detective herself, Kate Hollister knew full well the trials and tribulations of being a police officer's wife. On many occasions she had spent hours some evenings waiting for him to return home, sometimes in vain, because he was so absorbed in a case and simply could not come home. All the time though she had worried about him. Other nights she had cried herself to sleep having waited for that dreaded knock on the door that would have brought the heart-breaking news of his untimely death and now he was treating her like this. What made it all the harder for her to understand was that she did not know why he was behaving like this, no longer the loving husband but somebody cold.

Had he stopped loving her or found somebody else? This thought had already crossed her mind and now this. Her husband had changed over the past few weeks. His sullen and silent moods coming ever more frequently and his increased drinking had made him cantankerous, but after this latest episode the once loyal and loving wife had reached breaking point. As she lay in her bed, curled up in the foetal position, offering herself some comfort and protection, crying rivers of tears, her entire body aching from her husband's brutal and vicious assault, she knew that their marriage was now over. He had treated her nothing better than an object for deviant sex and she wished him dead.

The morning following his vicious assault on his wife, not knowing exactly what had happened but judging by his wife's coldness towards him that something horrible had happened, McKenzie Hollister did not bother reporting for work until mid-afternoon and, as a result of this, he had missed an important briefing. There had been a breakthrough in the

armed robbery case that he had been heading. His action, or inaction, had only succeeded in alienating him further from his colleagues to such an extent that when he did finally show up, he was instructed to report to his own immediate superior, Chief Superintendent Mundy. Mundy was not the highest ranking officer at Heller Street police station, but he was a long-time friend of Hollister's and had been 'volunteered' to speak to him.

From meeting each other in their teens, they had grown up together, joined the police force at the same time and had risen through the ranks together. They had attended each other's weddings, each taking a turn a being best man at the others wedding and Hollister was Godfather to Mundy's eldest son. Even Mundy had noticed, from a discrete distance, that his friend was troubled by something and had gone off the rails recently and he was only too willing to try and help him.

Hollister knocked on the door and was beckoned into the office. "Mac, come in and take a seat."

The weary detective could tell that, despite their friendship that this was going to be more than a friendly conversation. Once Hollister was seated, Mundy continued and, in his usual way, came straight to the point. "What's the matter with you these days? You're late for duty, you're missing briefings. Your team are complaining about your attitude and, just look at you, you look like shit. You look like you've been on the piss all night. Mac, what's up?"

Hollister cleared his throat, the dryness making it hard for him to speak and played with his tie before taking a deep breath, "I can't stop thinking about anything except..." His voice trailed away. He knew that at last he had the opportunity to talk to somebody about how he

felt, safe in the knowledge that not only would his friend listen to him sympathetically, but would not judge him either.

"About what exactly Mac," Mundy asked calmly, sensing the distress in his friend's voice and encouraged him to talk about whatever his problem was.

Once again Hollister cleared his throat before talking, "You remember a few weeks ago, when I attended the death of that young lad in Longsight, you know, the runaway from Wythenshawe? Well, I just can't seem to get him out of my head."

"Yeah, I remember him. I know that lad and his family. I led the search for him when he first went missing a couple of years ago when I was a D.I. Even back then it was a troubling case. From what I remember, the boy just upped and vanished of the face of the earth a couple of weeks after his fourteenth birthday. It's always heart-breaking when a child goes missing. No matter how much you try, you can't help but get involved and a feeling of hopelessness comes over you as the weeks drag on. We looked everywhere for him, pulled out all the stops, but nothing. He just disappeared one day. His death was put down to suicide wasn't it, so what's the problem?"

"That's just it, I don't think it was suicide," stated Hollister.

"What makes you think that Mac?" asked Mundy. There was now an unmistakable edgy tone in his voice and his forehead was briefly marked with worry lines. If Hollister had not been so hung-over and more in tune with himself, he might have noticed these slight changes. "Because I was involved with the original search for him a couple of years ago, I took an interest when he turned up dead and checked the

pathologist report myself. There was no sign of a struggle or anything to suggest anything else. Even the Coroner agreed with this."

Hollister continued regardless of the dismissal from Mundy. "It just doesn't fit with me, you know, that he took his own life. It's hard to describe in words. It's just a gut feeling that I've got. Normally these runaways come from broken homes, escaping from some form of abuse but not this one. He came from a good and loving family. He just turned his back on them and left home. Why? Then he turns up, two years later, in a bedsit in Longsight and even this doesn't seem right. You had to be there. It was all too neat and tidy and I don't just mean the room. The so-called suicide note just didn't seem right. It was as if it had been dictated to him. Then there was the lack of any other clothes and anything personal..." Hollister cut himself short, realising that any further disclosure might only incriminate himself and his secret investigation into Robinson.

Mundy was a little surprised by his friend's feelings with this particular case. "Mac, I can understand you being emotional about this, after all, he was only a child. Fourteen when he left home, sixteen when he died. Believe me, there's nothing to investigate. I know, because I've checked it for myself."

As Hollister watched his friend push his gold-rimmed glasses up from the bridge of his nose and into his grey hair, the words of Spencer flashed back to him, 'about forty, greying hair'. Now he was even beginning to suspect his friends involvement in the case. Mundy's voice brought him back to his senses, "Believe me Mac, there's nothing to investigate further with this case. He was just another runaway that took his own life rather than go back home and face the music. It's all

very tragic, but that's it. Now snap out of this depressive mood and concentrate on something that does need investigating, before I have no option but to put you on sick leave."

That was it. The meeting was over and Hollister left the office. The thought was still in his mind though as he made his way back to his own office, forty year old man with greying hair. They were everywhere, Mundy, fellow detectives within his team, the desk sergeant, everywhere. Even outside, on the streets of Manchester, they were on every street, in every doorway, shop and vehicle. Hollister could feel a sharp jabbing pain in his head and he rubbed his temples and sought some fresh air.

Once outside Hollister lit up a cigarette. Perhaps, he thought to himself as he smoked it, desperately in need of the nicotine it provided that Mundy was correct, maybe there was nothing suspicious and he was searching for something that simply was not there.

After stubbing out the remainder of his cigarette Hollister turned on his heels and once again entered the police station, determined to put Cameron Robinson, and his death, to the back of his brain and resolved to continue other investigations. However, the plight of Spencer, or whatever his real name, was proving harder to forget.

Chapter Five

After spending the following weekend digesting what he had been told, or had been ordered, by his superior officer, Chief Superintendent Mundy, Hollister thought long and hard about what he should do next. The notion of actually dropping the 'case' and his private investigation was never a serious option to him because each night, when he closed his eyes and attempted to get some sleep, the memories came back to him. First it was of Cameron Robinson, his naked body lying on the bed, cold and motionless and looking so peaceful. How Hollister wished that he could now find such peace. Even in death the detective could tell that the youngster had been very handsome, with a well-defined and toned body and it was this image of his nakedness the stuck in the mind of the detective. Seeing him naked, Hollister could understand why he had people wanting to have sex with him and what disturbed Hollister was that nearly every time that he thought about the teenager, lying there on the bed, naked, he now developed an involuntary erection.

After Robinson came thoughts about Spencer. There was something about this particular youngster that intrigued Hollister. He very much doubted that 'Spencer' was actually his real name and that he was nearly eighteen years old. From his experience, most teenaged boys never gave their original name at first, trying to bluff their way out of whatever predicament that the found themselves in, and Hollister suspected that he was probably nearer to Robinson's age of sixteen rather than eighteen, as he had claimed. Hollister had also realised that

Spencer had been very careful with his words and had not revealed too much about his background when recounting his earlier life, before leaving home and ending up on the streets, leaving Hollister with nothing significant to go on in trying to discover his real identity. Then there was the candidness in which he spoke about being a prostitute. Hollister recalled being of a similar age to the boy and was very shy and reticent about any matters regarding girlfriends and sex and yet the youth had spoken to casually about having sex with men for money. He had even performed oral sex with a man just for a meal, a bath and a bed for the night. What else was the teenager prepared to do for money Hollister wondered and this thought led to all manner of vivid images flashing through the mind of the detective, resulting in yet another embarrassing and unwanted erection, desperately attempting to hide it and unsure as to why he was getting aroused by teenaged boys.

Finally though was his own living nightmare and the need to face up to the consequences of his own actions. Through a series of flashbacks, he had slowly pieced together the events of the incident with his wife and felt deeply embarrassed. He had forced his wife to have anal sex against her will, which was he knew was rape, no matter how much he dressed it up and tried to justify his actions as being under intoxication, she simply did not deserve it. No woman deserved to be raped, especially by their spouse, thought Hollister. If it had been a criminal case that he was investigating he would have despised the assailant and would have found it incredibly difficult not to administer some form of physical retribution against him and yet here he was, *he* was the perpetrator of the heinous and barbarous ac and the victim had been his own wife, the wife that had always loved him and stood by him.

Having forced himself to recall the details of his heinous assault and what was troubling Hollister the most was that while he was raping his wife, he was imagining that he was having sex with the 'rent boy' Spencer. It was not his wife Kate that was in bed with him but the teenage boy. The youth had somehow crawled so much into the psyche of the detective that he was all that he thought about and he had no idea as to why? He was not that particularly special, he was not what somebody could describe as a vision of beauty, like *Michelangelo's David,* and until very recently Hollister had never even known him and yet now he was all that the detective currently thought about. Why? This, above all the other questions swimming around inside his head, was the one question that he needed an answer for and the one that was proving to be the most elusive. What exactly was it about the boy that fascinated the detective so much? Why was he so obsessed with him? He was not exactly the first teenager that he had met in the course of his police work, he had met many over the years, but there was something fascinating about him, something that Hollister found captivating, an unknown magnetism that drew Hollister towards the youngster, something that could not put his finger on or explain why and this deeply troubled Hollister.

Realistically he knew that there was no way he could ever let this 'case' go until he had succeeded in coming up with at least some of the answers to the multitude of questions that haunted him and discovered whether Robinson's suicide was indeed that, which he now doubted. Not just because of what Spencer had told him but his own gut instinct had told him the day that he attended his apparent suicide that there was more to it than suicide. He knew that he had to find Spencer once again

to try and get some more information regarding Robinson and also to try and get him off the streets and to stop working as a prostitute. Hollister tried, in vain, to remember any previous case that had affected him in such a way, but no matter how hard he thought, or how far back he went, he simply could not recall any such case.

McKenzie Hollister once again visited the secret former home of Cameron Robinson. On this occasion he went alone. Having kept hold of the key the detective let himself in and the first thing that he noticed was the freshness of the air and, on closer inspection, that there was not a speck of dust anywhere. It had been over two weeks since his first visit and yet the place was spotless, which meant that the cleaner was still coming in. This posed yet another question to Hollister, if Robinson had been dead for over a month, then how was the cleaner still getting paid? When he had first seen Robinson over in the bedsit in Longsight he knew that there was going to questions without answers, but this latest one defied all logic. Hollister set about searching the flat and, hopefully, finding at least some answers.

Standing in the lounge he looked around. How could a sixteen year old boy be able to afford such luxuries? It then became obvious to the detective that either the youngster earnt a lot of money or he was being kept by somebody. If the latter was the case, then who was he and where was he now? Could this be the mysterious professional looking businessman that everybody he talked to mentioned? Hollister continued to survey his surroundings as he thought about this matter. Then another thought struck the detective, how could the young Robinson have got this place in the first place? When he died, he was

still only sixteen years old but it clearly looks like that he had been here for a while and so, around the age of fifteen, guessed Hollister, he would have moved into this apartment. How? How could such a young boy be able to rent such an apartment? Somebody must have helped him, but whom? Two more puzzles for Hollister to try and figure out. Apart from the furniture and the television, surveyed the detective, the room was bereft of any other objects. There were no ornaments doted around on the furniture, as he saw in most homes he visited, but noticeably there was not a single photograph of the dead youth or his family. There was nothing.

It was as if he had completely exorcised them from his life. There was not a single thing in the room that could have given it any warmth and character. It was in fact a very cold and impersonal room. It soon became clear to the detective that this room was not going to yield any clues and so Hollister moved to the bedroom, his footsteps on the wooden floor creating the only sound in the flat.

A large white metal framed bed, decorated with brass finials, dominated the room. On each side of the bed were matching bedside tables, each adorned by a brass lamp and an entire wall was covered in four mirrored doors that housed a wardrobe. Over the bed was a print of a work of art that the detective recognised but did not know its name, a smiling young girl dressed in gold and blue, dominated by its black background. Once again, the room was decorated and furnished with style and finesse and, like the lounge it looked almost like a display in a furniture store, with nothing personal to offer any clues as to the identity of the occupier. Hollister crossed the room to the full room height mirrors, glancing briefly at his reflection, then slid one open and

for the second time he looked inside a wardrobe belonging to Cameron Robinson and as with the first time, he was taken aback by what he saw. Row upon row of expensive designer label clothes, all either hanging on rails or neatly folded on the shelves within the robes. Sliding each of the doors open revealed the extent of Robinson's clothing collection and its value must have ran to several thousands of pounds.

A black leather case, one normally for laptop computers, that rested on one of the top shelves finally offered Hollister some clues. It contained the boy's passport and three bank cards. There was a wad of bank notes and when Hollister counted them, they amounted to nearly five hundred pounds. However, the most important find was a burgundy covered *'Filofax'*. Finally, the detective thought to himself, he was getting somewhere and that he would soon be able to answer at least some of the questions mulling around inside his head.

He went back into the lounge and settled onto the larger sofa, this time realising how comfortable it was, whilst he looked at the diary section of the *'Filofax'*. Recorded in neat handwriting, almost daily, were initials and numbers. To the trained eye, this was obviously a coded record of who he had met and how much they had paid him. The amounts were staggering. One hundred and one hundred and fifty pounds were the most common, sometimes two or three in a single day. Occasionally there was an entry of two hundred and fifty pounds and there was even one for five hundred pounds. Could this be an entry for the night that Spencer had told him about, mused the detective?

A bit of mental arithmetic revealed that Robinson was earning over two thousand pounds a week, more than three times what the detective

himself earnt and yet this was being earnt by a teenaged boy for sex. No wonder he could afford such a nice apartment, thought Hollister. The notion of a single rich 'sugar-daddy' sponsor now receded in the mind of the detective. The address and telephone section did not have anything in it, over twenty pages and not a single name or telephone number. Surely he must have had some friends and contacts, thought Hollister. However, he was not going to find them in this book of startling surprises.

Hollister went back into the bedroom for another look around. The drawers in the bedside chests contained evidence of his sordid career. They contained several types of lubricants and condoms and several rubber penis' and plastic vibrators in a multitude of sizes. Hollister declined to touch these objects, simply shaking each box to see if there was anything concealed at the bottom. He was very relieved not to find anything and returned each box to its drawer.

He then crossed the bedroom and looked, a lot more closely this time, on the high, eye level shelves that ran the full length of the wardrobes. Here he found, pushed right at the back and in a corner, another case and when he opened it he discovered that it contained around a dozen video cassettes. Eureka! He thought as he took the box into the lounge, with the intent on watching them.

Using the remote controls Hollister turned on the television and video player and after inserting a tape, settled back on the sofa. He discovered that it was a homosexual pornographic film. It showed men having sex with each other and in every position imaginable and not just two men. Sometimes there was anything up to five men on the screen at a time. At first the detective found the scenes portrayed disgusting, his stomach

churning over and over, adding to his moral indignation. He had wanted to stop the video recorder and destroy all the tapes, but he thought that maybe at least one of them could yield some clues as to who Robinson's clients had been or even why he had killed himself, if indeed he actually did and so he continued watching them.

There was another reason why Hollister did not stop the tape machine, one that he found much more disturbing. After spending over an hour watching the explicit images he realised that he was actually beginning to enjoy them. Only a few months ago the very thought of sitting down and watching a homosexual porn film would have repulsed him, making him feel nauseous and outrage him and yet, here he was, getting aroused by one, in the home of a former 'rent boy' who had probably done many of the things being depicted on the television screen. This only added further to the maelstrom of emotions that the detective now felt.

Two hours and five tapes later, four of which were watched at twice the normal speed, Hollister eventually found the one that he had secretly and eagerly anticipating, a home-made tape that contained Cameron Robinson. After over a month of mental images of the youth lying dead on a bed, Hollister finally found himself face-to-face with a living Cameron Robinson. He was wearing a school uniform, which the detective immediately recognised as the one which he had been wearing on the photograph that hung proudly on the wall of his former home. If his mother could see her son now, thought the detective, then he doubted whether it would still hang so proudly in the room. Strong back-lighting shone through his fine blond hair, immaculately cut and combed, again as in the photograph and also on the first time that

Hollister had seen him, as a death tableau in a bedsit. The powerful lighting gave the effect of giving the boy a halo, giving the youth an almost angelic appearance.

Robinson was dancing to music, slowly removing his clothing as he gyrated and twisted to the rhythm until he was completely naked. The striptease had been done slowly and seductively, expertly performed by Robinson, clearly not the first time that he had done it and once naked, Hollister could not help but stare in awe at the superb athletic physique of the youngster. Hollister also noted that the camera technique was not that of an amateur either. Each change of direction was perfectly framed and the focusing was sharp and precise, not like some of the cheap porn movies he had come across, where the camera operator only used one hand-held camera, doing who knew what with his other hand. This one was a professionally filmed video.

Intuitively, Hollister found himself sexually aroused as he sat captivated by the beguiling dancing of Robinson and subconsciously he began to copy the hand movements of the boy, running his own hand over his chest and then caressing his erect penis. He was no longer surprised to have an erection and caressed it until he could stand it no more and unfastened his own trousers. After pulling his trousers and underwear down to his knees, Hollister gripped his penis and began masturbating it, just as Robinson was doing on the television screen before him. An object was passed to the boy by the camera operator.

Robinson licked and then sucked on the large black sexual aid, known as a dildo. He let the hard rubber object fill his mouth, pushing as much in as he could without choking on it. The unknown camera operator zoomed in close and the screen was filled with the near saintly

image of the youth as he performed fellatio on the grotesquely large object. There was a brief pause in the music and the only sounds that Hollister could hear were the whirling of the video player and his own heart, pounding away inside his chest and his own heavy breathing. The thought of being sexually aroused by teenaged boys should have repulsed the detective and yet he found that he could not take his eyes of the screen, watching Robinson with ever increasing fascination. Long repressed and previously forgotten memories of his own childhood came back to Hollister.

He had, as a teenager, enjoyed masturbation and once, while at school and at a very similar age to Cameron Robinson, had taken part in and enjoyed mutual masturbation and fellatio with another boy. But the innocence of youth and the tribulations of puberty profoundly affected both boys. They were caught naked and heavily involved with the sexual act by a teacher, who, after he had secretly watched them for a couple of minutes, interrupted them and made both boys stand up before he allowed them to get dressed. The teacher, thought Hollister with hindsight, revelled at the sight of two naked schoolboys and the feeling of humiliation taught Hollister and the other boy a valuable lesson in life.

Yet here he was, many years later, fully aroused and masturbating, whilst watching the antics of a naked Cameron Robinson. The film continued to show Robinson and his exploits with the dildo. He was now lying face down on a white sheeted bed, his knees tucked up to his chest, raising his backside high of the bed, as he stroked the crease between his buttocks with the shiny imitation phallus. With a twist of the wrist the dildo began to be pushed into his rectum and very soon he

worked the dildo in and out of his anus, the black object standing out boldly against his sun-tanned flesh. When it first entered his rectum Hollister let out a gasp of amazement and then continued watching in fascination. This scenario was filmed for several minutes before the naked torso of a man came alongside the bed.

Without any hesitation Robinson took the man's erect penis into his mouth and sucked on it, as the man took over the thrusting of the dildo up the boy's anus. It was no longer being done with any sensuality or passion. The man was forcing as much of it up Robinson as he could, making the boy's body jerk with every upward push and making him gag on the penis that now filled his throat. After several minutes, the mysterious faceless man eventually could stand it no more and, judging by the shuddering of his body, apparently ejaculated into the mouth of the schoolboy.

Hollister's head was buzzing with mixed emotions at what he had just watched. He was disgusted at the sordid and degrading manner with which the unknown man had abused the youth. But then again, thought Hollister, had he just abused him? Robinson seemed perfectly compliant with the situation and what was being done to him and never once objected or asked for it to be stopped. It was clearly not the first time that he had participated in something along these lines, even Hollister could tell that the boy had done this before, and at certain times Robinson seemed to be in complete control of the scenario.

Having just watched the appalling video and knowing a little about his past, Hollister kept wondering why Robinson had left his obviously loving and devoted family to take up a living of a prostitute and doing such licentious acts? What terrible, unknown secret had made him

leave his clearly loving family and allow himself to get drawn him into this sordid lifestyle?

The emotion that troubled the detective most though at this precise moment in time was that of his own sexual arousal as he watched Robinson performing sexual acts on the television screen before him. Why did he suddenly find himself enthralled by teenaged boys? While he was watching the video Hollister had felt like a voyeur, a 'peeping Tom' and this disgusted the detective. He thought that his life had hit new lows.

Turning off the video Hollister tried to figure out what it was that had actually aroused him. Was it actually Robinson himself or had it been the sexual act or was it because he had been reduced to watching it as a third party, unable, but not unwilling, to participate? Sitting in silence he realised that he was no longer rubbing himself and moved his trembling hand. Sweat trickled down his forehead. Was it caused by sexual arousal, embarrassment or paranoia? What if somebody, the cleaner for example, had come in and caught him, pants down and masturbating whilst he watched the explicit and obscene videos, especially the one featuring Robinson? How would he ever live down the shame and humiliation if he had been discovered?

But then again, who could come in and interrupted his watching of the videos? As far as he knew, only two other people knew of the existence of the flat, one of them was the cleaner, the other being Spencer, which thought Hollister would not have been such a bad thing. It would have saved him the time and effort of searching for him on the streets of Manchester, not that he really knew where to look for him. Neither of them could have actually got into the flat because Hollister

had subconsciously locked the door behind him, leaving the key in the lock to prevent another kept being used.

As he packed away the video tapes, making a mental note to return and watch the remainder of them in the faint hope that they may reveal the identities of those adults abusing Robinson. He also secretly hoped that he wanted to find a copy of the film that Spencer had spoken off, where he and Robinson had sex together, before having sex with the men. The thought of finding this tape excited the detective and he allowed himself a brief smile.

Making sure that nobody saw him, Hollister slipped out of the flat and continued his private and now very personal quest into the life and death of Cameron Robinson and his search for the elusive Spencer.

Sitting alone in the now darkened and deserted office that was the base for Hollister's Serious Crimes Squad, he pondered his next move. He had already decided that, despite the 'advice' from Mundy, he was still going to investigate the life of Cameron Robinson. He was under no illusion that it would be one of the hardest 'cases' that he had ever investigated because he was going to be on his own. He would not be able to tell anybody about his investigation, owing to the fact that officially there was no case to probe. The *post mortem* had recorded Robinson's death as suicide and Chief Superintendent Mundy had agreed, formally closed the missing person's case on him, satisfied that the youth had taken his own life.

If it was all that simple, then why did Hollister have difficulty in accepting it? What was it that stood out in the back of his mind telling him that there really was more to this case than what lay on the

surface? Another question that he did not have the answer to was the suggestion made by Spencer that the teenager had been recognised by somebody and was being blackmailed into giving them free sex. Could there be any truth in it or was the youth only saying as a means of enticing Hollister into a meeting and then duping out of some money? The sincerity of Spencer seemed genuine enough, thought Hollister and he was very adamant about his claim. Hollister now knew that he really did need to find him and talk to him again, this time though he might even have to make it official.

There certainly was a possibility that Robinson could have been blackmailed by somebody, thought Hollister. It was not that unusual for prostitutes to be blackmailed by the clients, and vice versa. History was awash with such incidents. Whether there was any truth in this particular claim was still open to speculation. Due to the nature of any sexual relationship between a man and a boy, which was still very much a taboo subject, though in reality widely practised, they both would understand the need for secrecy and if Robinson's mystery client knew that his life, career and future as a user 'rent boy' was to be exposed by his public naming and shaming, no matter what the personal damage might be, then that presented an ideal opportunity to a less scrupulous prostitute to exploit the situation and if Robinson's client was a respected member of the community and his naming as a user of teenage boy prostitutes would become public knowledge, complete with the shame attached to his 'outing', it would sway the balance in favour to Robinson. However if Robinson's actual age and identity was to become known it would end whatever ambitions the boy had and this could very easily be manipulated and Robinson could find

himself willing to do anything to protect what he had and it could easily be him that was being blackmailed, just as Spencer had told him.

The more that he thought about it, the more certain he was that he had to somehow find Spencer. He was his only direct link to Robinson's life of prostitution. But how would he go about finding the elusive boy again? Hollister now knew that there must be dozens of teenaged prostitutes out there on the streets of Manchester, both male and female, so how would he go about finding one in particular? As with almost every other aspect of this 'case' there was another far deeper and darker reason for the detective to find the youth, he wanted too. Hollister had become obsessed with Spencer. From the first moment that he saw him in Piccadilly Gardens and then later listened, in awe, as he recounted the scant details of his life and then his sexual exploits, Hollister had become fixated with the boy and now, on the rare occasion that he slept, Hollister found that he was dreaming about him. Hollister had developed an unhealthy obsession with Spencer.

Hollister found himself wracking his brain, recalling their brief conversation held in Robinson's flat. Had there been anything that the boy had said that might reveal where he could find him? The detective recalled that Spencer had said that he had met a man outside *Burgerworld* on Market Street. Could this be the place to start looking for him? Many fast food establishments, together with amusement arcades, were notorious as being 'pick-up' places for hungry runaways. They had allowed themselves, sometimes through no fault of their own, to become easy targets for those that preyed on them and been taken advantage of because of their situation, in many ways identical to the scenario that Spencer had recounted.

Maybe Spencer was still seeing his mystery benefactor over in Salford? This would explain the boy's reluctance to go into any details as to who he was. Surely, the detective thought to himself, he could not be that hard to find and maybe he could lead him to Spencer. How many single men named Peter, who also happened to frequent both Manchester gay 'Village' and cruised burger bars looking for young boys and also lived over in some newly developed flats? Surely there could not be many and no doubt, if Hollister could interview some 'rent boys' or runaways on the street that somebody would know him. This prospect offered Hollister with a better option than just looking around the streets and alleyways of 'The Village'.

Pen and paper at hand, Hollister scribbled some notes. First and foremost in his mind was trying to discover why Cameron Robinson had left home in the first place? Was he already 'working' as a 'rent boy' at this time or did it come later? Whatever the outcome of the two previous questions the next one was fairly obvious to the detective, why become a 'rent boy' in the first place?

Hollister knew that, somehow without drawing attention to his secret investigation, that he would have to interview all those that knew Robinson, from his family, to his school friends and teachers alike. His mother had told him that he had been a choirboy and so the local priest might know something that could help Hollister. The detective wrote all this down and wondered just how he was going to be able to talk to so many people and for it to still remain secret from Mundy?

Hollister also knew that he would have to speak to members of the gay community and try and seek out those that used 'rent boys', but this presented the detective with another dilemma. How could he go

about finding these people and nobody get the wrong impression as to why he was looking for them? Such was the moral paranoia about underage sex that it would be easy to assume that he was trying to infiltrate this no doubt secret and closely-knit group in order to expose them or prosecute them or that he wanted to have sex with these young boys. If he, a high ranking police officer, was ever discovered out there on the streets of Manchester, secretly searching for teenaged male prostitutes, being unable to prove that he was working covertly on a secret investigation, he knew that he would be on his own. He would find himself out on a limb, isolated from everybody and with nobody to turn too. He would become a pariah, an outcast to everybody that knew him but he judged it a risk worth taking. Even if it only helped him once again sleep at night, it would be worth the risk.

There was an even more pressing reason, thought Hollister to continue his investigations. If Robinson was indeed being blackmailed by somebody and this had led directly to his death, which was then disguised to look like a suicide then there was a very dangerous and resourceful murderer out there. He might be searching for or even grooming his next victim, which might even be Spencer.

Chapter Six

"Thank you for seeing me again, Mrs Robinson," began Hollister. The detective had spent the weekend not only thinking about what exactly to say to Cameron Robinson's mother but deliberating just whether or not to visit her in the first place. He knew that he really did need to speak to the still no doubt grieving mother but the last thing that he wanted to do was to cause her any further anguish. She had been through enough, first with her son leaving home and, more recently, being found dead, and Hollister had no desire to add to her grief. Eventually he had made his decision, chosen his words carefully, with each one having been selected so as not to reveal too much or to offer her any false hopes.

Mrs Robinson, despite it being several weeks since her son's funeral, still wore black clothing as a mark of continual mourning and the grieving mother, black rings circling her eyes, showed Hollister into the lounge and, once seated, the detective continued. "I know things have been very difficult for you recently, but how are you and how do you feel?"

Mrs Robinson was a little surprised by the concern shown by the detective, a virtual to her and her plight. "I'm very well, thank you. You're right, it has been a very trying time for all of us, but Joe and I have to be strong for the other children. Would you like a cup of tea or coffee, Mr Hollister?"

"Coffee would be nice. I have milk but no sugar," replied Hollister.

Mrs Robinson left him alone for a couple of minutes and he found himself staring into the smiling faces of her children on the wall in front of him, with particular emphasis being paid to Cameron, desperately trying to read any tell-tale signs of sadness in his eyes. There was nothing. The largest photograph of the boy now had a black silk ribbon running diagonally across each corner, a mark of respect and mourning. The innocence of the schoolboy in the photograph contrasted sharply with images of his debauched behaviour in the film which Hollister had watched and he had difficulty in reconciling the two completely contrasting personalities of the dead boy.

Eventually, after what seemed like an eternity, Mrs Robinson returned carrying two mugs of coffee and sat opposite Hollister, her eyes now reddened where she had wept silent tears whilst in the kitchen. "Now, then, what can I do for you?"

"I've got to be honest with you Mrs Robinson…"

"Please call me Eileen," she interrupted.

Hollister acknowledged her request with a nod of his head. "I've got to tell you that I'm not here in any official capacity. I'm her on my own accord. In fact, my superiors don't even know that I've come to see you." The nodding head of the woman offered him some comfort, as he hoped his words would to her. "I know that this might be difficult for you and I've got absolutely no intention of upsetting you or adding to your suffering but…I'd like to talk to you about Cameron."

"I'm really pleased that you've come around and I appreciate that, for some reason, you want to keep it quiet." Mrs Robinson gave him the slightest of smiles that radiated genuine warmth. "You seem to be a

caring man. I can tell that from your eyes. I knew that from when you attended...my Cameron's...funeral. How can I help you?"

Feeling rather embarrassed at her platitudes and making reference to his notes from his previous visit, which he had read over and over again until he had memorised them. "I recall that the first time that I came over and saw you, just after...well...when we found Cameron that you were adamant that he would not take his own life."

"He didn't" came the immediate reply. "Oh, I know that on the surface that you've got no reason to doubt it, but, believe me, as his mother I know that my son did not kill himself."

"How can you be so sure?"

"Call it a mother's intuition if you like, a bit like your copper's instinct. A mother just knows these things. I also knew that while he was away from me, my Cameron suffered. I know, because I felt it."

Hollister was taken aback by her candour. "What I'm going to tell you is by no means official, in fact it is only my opinion, but I too personally doubt that Cameron took his own life."

There, he had finally said it to somebody. A heavy burden seemed to have lifted of his conscious from the moment he finally uttered the words. He let out a brief sigh and continued, "Let me explain why. I was the police officer that was called to the bedsit that Cameron had and, with the exception of the police doctor, I was the first person to see him. Without going into any great detail that would no doubt upset you, the bedsit where we found Cameron did not give the appearance of a place of suicide. There was a carefully written note that was supposed to be seen as a suicide note, but to me, the wording and the grammar just didn't fit with somebody of his age. Don't get me wrong, I'm not

suggesting for one minute that your son was stupid or anything, far from it. But, from my experiences with other suicides and I've attended a few over the years, but it just didn't seem right."

"As long as I've got a breath in my body, I will never accept that my Cameron took his own life. Since the very first day that I was told that my Cameron was dead, I have told those close to me that he did not kill himself. Most people think that I'm only saying it out of a mother's love for her son, but I know my son better than anybody else."

The grief and sadness was now showing through the woman's tough exterior and Hollister thought twice about continuing. It was only the obvious devotion to her son that persuaded him to continue. "This may be hard for you to remember, but how was Cameron the last time that you saw him?"

Lost in a moment of personal thoughts and memories, Mrs Robinson smiled to herself before letting out a long deep sigh and eventually answering the question. "No, Mr Hollister, it's not hard for me. I've carried that moment in my heart for the past two years. Cameron went off to school as he did every morning. He went to the local school attached to the church, St. Anthony of Padua. Cameron came home for his lunch like he always did and secretly packed a few belongings and went back to school. Or so I thought. But I never saw him again. When he was having his lunch, on hindsight, he did appear a little quiet, a bit sullen. I remember that because I caught a glimpse of his eyes and now I know that there was sadness in them. I now know that it was because he was leaving and he knew that it would break my heart. He was right. It has and will continue to do so until my own dying days. I'll never forget that last time that I saw my Cameron Mr Hollister."

Sipping his coffee Hollister sat enthralled, "How could you tell, you know, the sadness in his eyes?"

"A mother can tell these things. Cameron was such a happy boy, full of love and affection. He always had a beautiful smile on his face and that smile could light up a darkened room. He loved life and everything about it and Joe and I had brought him up to love everybody and everything about life. But on this particular day, June the twenty forth, it was, he just seemed different. Nothing that I could put my finger on at the time and I was going to ask him about it…later…you know when he came home." A lump swelled in the throat of the heartbroken and devoted mother as she fought back her tears. "I've had over two years, two long and torturous years to remember that day and think about it and wish that I had asked him, there and then, what was on his mind. How I now regret not asking him. At the time I didn't want to pry, but now I wish that I had. When my Cameron didn't come home from school on time I called the school and it turned out that he hadn't gone in at all that day."

"Did he often play truant?" asked Hollister.

His question was met with another emphatic denial. "No. Never. He was absent sometimes through illness, but he never stayed off without mine or Joe's permission. His attendance was nearly one hundred percent."

"Did you ever find out where he had been on that day?"

Mrs Robinson let out another gut-wrenching sigh as she shook her head. "No. Every day since I have wondered this and I will not rest until I find out where he had been. Something must have been wrong

with him for my Cameron to lie to me, which is something he had never done before."

The detective, feeling that there might be something here, pushed the point. "Could he have been at a friend's house, you know, encouraged to take the day off school by one of his friends?"

"That is what I thought at the time and so I checked, as did the school and the police. All his friends were in school that day. None of them even saw him."

Drawing a blank, Hollister tried another avenue. "What were his friends like? Did he ever get into trouble with them, you know, like most teenagers do these days?"

Once again the woman shook her head. "My Cameron only had a few close friends and they're all good lads, from good Catholic families. They had given him the nickname of 'Pud', you know, after *Robinson's* jam. It wasn't meant in a nasty way. None of them have ever been in trouble with the police. Joe and I had brought Cameron up properly. He knew from an early age the difference between right and wrong. This had also been taught to him through his dealings with the church." The tone of her voice had changed.

"I'm sorry if I've upset you Mrs...Eileen. I certainly wasn't trying to suggest otherwise." Realising that he may have touched a raw nerve with the boy's mother and he was relieved to see her lips part and break into another smile. "I know these are difficult questions for you, but because I wasn't involved in the search for your son and I've only got the notes of my colleagues to go on, all I'm trying to do is build a picture of Cameron and what his frame of mind may have been on the day that he vanished which might help me come up with some answers.

Sometimes a new pair of eyes might turn up some little detail that somebody else may have missed at the time. So, as far as you know, Cameron wasn't having any problems at school?"

The silence from the mother answered the question. Hollister tried another approach. "What about after school? What did he do in the evenings?"

"Three times a week he stayed late at school to do gymnastics training. He was very good you know. His coach, Mr Foxford, thought that he showed great promise." The pride could clearly be detected in her voice. "Then, twice a week, my Cameron went to St. Anthony's for choir practice. Gymnastics and the church were his life. We, that is me and Joe thought that he might even take up the cloth, you know, become a priest. He was a server as well, not just a choirboy." The puzzled look on Hollister's face signalled that he did not know what a 'server' was. "A server assists the priest, you know he holds the salver with the Communion bread on it or waves the incense orb. Another name for it would be altar boy."

"What's the priest like?"

"We have a new priest now, Father Michael, the one that...you know...performed my Cameron's...funeral, wasn't Cameron's priest. That would be Father Martin. He's since moved on. He was a lovely man. He always had the time of day for you and any problems that you had, no matter what time of day or night it was it was. He took a shine to my Cameron from the first time that he ever saw him. I think that he also thought that my Cameron might become a priest himself. I know that Cameron liked him too. He was always talking about Father Martin. They spent a lot of time together."

Could this be my break, thought Hollister or was he just being too cynical? There had been, over the years, many cases that involved child abuse allegations against members of the clergy, of all faiths, and it might explain where Cameron had been on the day he disappeared. If the boy was such a devout Catholic and he was having some problems, then it would be logical for him to seek help and advice from somebody that he was close to outside his family. Another thought struck the detective, without knowing any details about why the priest had changed parishes, his relationship with Robinson may be the reason behind his move ant there being a new priest.

Hollister brought his meeting with the grieving mother to an end shortly after this revelation, on the promise of keeping her updated with any developments that might come up. Mrs Robinson had been a great help to Hollister but he also thought that he may have been a help to her. She may not have been able to talk to anybody else that thought along the same lines as she did and just for her to know that there was actually somebody else out there, thinking about her son's death the way that she did, must have been a great comfort to her.

As he drove back to Heller Street police station Hollister had solved one of the many puzzles troubling him. He now knew where the alias Robinson had used had come from. It was from the two adult males closest to him, his priest and his gymnastics coach. He also remembered the outburst made by Detective Boston on the day that they had broken the news of Cameron's death. She had been right, as usual, all those weeks ago. Mrs Robinson was a remarkably strong woman and a very proud mother. She did not deserve to be suffering the way that she obviously was. She needed to be able to put her mind

at rest and know why her son had left home and that it was off no fault of hers. She needed to know that her beloved son loved her and had not turned his back on her and the rest of his family. But mostly, she needed closure, if only for her own peace of mind and Hollister was now even more determined to get to the truth, if only for her sake.

As it turned out, it was not hard for Hollister to find Father Martin. A telephone call made to the office of the Bishop of Manchester and his secretary had given the detective with the new address and a glowing reference for the absent priest. It did, however, trouble the naturally inquisitive mind of the detective as to why the secretary thought it necessary to give Father Martin such a glowing testimonial, before he even knew what he wanted to talk to him about. Hollister himself had been very careful not to reveal the reason why he wanted to talk to the priest. He had only told the Bishop's secretary that he was investigating the disappearance of a member of his congregation from a few years ago. No names and no other details were given, nothing that could have forewarned the priest.

After an hour long drive Hollister was tired but when he saw the priest dressed in a dark suit and black shirt, the white collar around his neck offering the only break in the sombre outfit, the hairs on the back of his neck stood on end and he was suddenly wide awake and alert. His heart began to beat faster in his chest until it was pounding, filling his ears with a eurhythmic rhythm, his adrenaline pumping around his body. Father Martin was around fifty years of age, standing around six feet tall and had a head of greying dark hair. He matched perfectly the description given by so many people of the type of person that

Robinson had been seen with but then again, thought Hollister, if Cameron was a close to his priest as his mother had suggested, then it would hardly be unusual for the two of them to be seen together and maybe he was just jumping to conclusions and making assumptions about something that did not exist.

Hollister was finding that his imagination was racing far ahead of his existing knowledge as he parked his care. Surely he could not be this lucky, thought Hollister? Or was he just being too cynical? At this precise moment in time, without even speaking to the priest, he had no reason to suspect that Father Martin had been anything other than a caring and sympathetic priest and yet, here he was, judging and suspecting him of not only abusing a teenaged member of his congregation but being somehow responsible for his death, either directly or by virtue, according to Spencer, of blackmail.

Hollister made his way to the priest and when he was close enough, the clergyman offered an outstretched hand. "Chief Inspector Hollister, I presume?" Taken aback that the priest knew who he was, Hollister shook hands with the smiling priest. "The Bishop telephoned me and told me that you would be coming to see me, although I am a little surprised that it is so soon."

"There's no time like the present," replied the detective. Getting straight to the point, as was his style and manner, he continued, "Is there somewhere more private where we can talk?"

When Hollister asked for a private place to speak, the minister's guard was raised. "Yes, of course. Come into the rectory. I'll get Miss Tennant to make us some tea, or maybe you would like something a little stronger or even something to eat? You've had a long journey."

"No, I'm fine. Coffee would be okay" Hollister replied.

Father Martin led Hollister into his home and study. The room had a typical, stereotyped appearance of a priest's inner sanctum. Old bulky chairs surrounded a huge and cluttered desk. More chairs, none of them matching, were opposite the fireplace and it was in these that they sat. Hollister continued glancing around the room as the priest used the telephone to request the drinks. The white walls were dominated by either paintings of Christ or the Virgin Mary or were stacked high with books, some ancient, others more recent additions and they covered a vast range of subjects, but most were theology books covering all the major religions of the world. Despite the efforts of his housekeeper, they gathered dust and the older ones generated mildew, which could have explained the musky aroma in the room.

Once settled, with drinks in hand, brought to them by the priest's elderly housekeeper, Hollister began his questioning. "Thank you for seeing me Father Martin. I'm looking into the recent death of a former parishioner of yours, Cameron Robinson. Recent information has been passed on to the police that may shed some new light into his disappearance and subsequent death and we are honour bound to look into it. We are doing some preliminary investigations as to whether we should reopen the case."

The clergyman nodded his head as the detective explained the reason for his visit and now he looked straight into the dark eyes of the priest, searching for any hidden emotion. He did not think that he would be able to glean much information, the priest would be far too experienced in not revealing his true feelings and Hollister just hoped for the odd snippet or the hidden hint at his deeper meaning. To the trained eyes of

Hollister, the mere suggestion would be all that he needed. "Mrs Robinson has told me that you were particularly fond of her son," continued Hollister. "And that the two of you spent a lot of time together. Did you see anything of Cameron shortly before he disappeared and the days before he went missing, did he reveal anything to you that was out of the ordinary?"

"I was, like most people, deeply saddened by his disappearance and my heart went out to his family at the time and it still does," replied Father Martin, his eyes offering no clues to the detective. "When I was informed that Cameron had gone missing, my first thought was that he had gone off somewhere to clear his head and that he would return home after a couple of days. However, as the days became weeks and the weeks became months, I just knew that he was gone and would not be returning home."

"Picking up on something that you've just said, you thought that he might be away sorting his head out. What made you think this and did Cameron have any problems before he vanished?"

"You must be fully aware Chief Inspector, that I am bound by an oath of confidentiality and that I cannot reveal anything told to me, either in confidence or in the confessional," was the predicted reply from Father Martin.

"Of course Father and I would never expect you to betray such trust. However, we are talking a young boy, a fourteen year old boy, one that left his loving home for no apparent reason and then died two years later. He died in some rather unusual circumstances, that may or may not, even turn out to be suspicious and anything that you do tell me will, of course, be treated and remain in the strictest confidence

between a very small circle of people and nobody would ever know where the information came from originally," came the much rehearsed reply from Hollister.

The priest detected that Hollister was himself trying not to give too much away. "I'm glad that you understand my predicament detective. It is not that I do not wish to help you, but I need to know that anything that we talk about will remain between the two of us and not be misused or passed onto others."

"You have my word on that Father." Hollister now played his well thought out and rehearsed trump card. "I can tell you though, that after speaking to Cameron's mother in depth, all I have are her best interests at heart. I would never do anything that could cause her any further pain or heartache. She is a remarkable woman, one of great strength and faith and if there does in fact turn out to be anything suspicious in the death of her son, then, we all owe it to her to come up with the answers. No matter how painful they might be." Knowing of the fondness that the priest felt towards Robinson, Hollister was in fact resorting to emotional blackmail.

It appeared to have worked, the priest was impressed. "Yes, you are correct, Eileen is a remarkably strong and proud and loving mother. My heart and my prayers go out to her and the rest of her family. Even now I often refer to her incredible strength and conviction in my sermons. Now Chief Inspector, how may I help you?"

The game of cat-and-mouse over, Hollister came straight to the point. "What was your relationship with Cameron Robinson?"

After a brief pause, while Father Martin absorbed the bluntness of the question, he finally replied, "Cameron was a good boy, a devout

Catholic and a child that any parent would have been proud to have as their son. He was always full of joy and happiness, an excellent chorister and he had a very inquisitive mind. Cameron was always asking questions about various aspects of church dogma. He was, and still is, one of my favourite altar boys."

"What sort of questions?" asked Hollister. He made a mental note that the priest had not in fact answered his question.

"They were all the usual ones regarding Catholicism and about life in general. He had barely become a teenager and was just entering into a difficult period in the life of anybody. There was so much happening to him and all at the same time. Such is the nightmare of puberty. He wanted to know more about the doctrines of the Church, including my own opinions on a few subjects. In many ways he reminded me of myself when I was a teenager. He was forever asking questions, searching for answers, to quell his knowledge of the Church."

A nod of the detective's head indicated that he had an idea of what the priest was getting at. "Did Cameron give you any indications of any specific problems that he had in the last couple of months before he disappeared?"

"Nothing springs to mind," replied father Martin shaking his head.

Hollister suspected that the two men were still playing a game, you ask the right questions and only then will I give you the correct answers. They seemed to be still going around in circles. Maybe Hollister needed to be blunter, he thought. "What was Cameron like, I mean really like? All that I've got is this near saintly image of him and this has been painted by his mother."

Father Martin let out a sigh. He was obviously deeply moved at having to talk about the dead boy. "Cameron was an immensely likable young man. The first time that you met him, you could not help but notice him and his smile. He nearly always had a smile on his face, a broad and genuine and loving smile. He had a deeply sardonic sense of humour and a hearty laugh. He had a terrific personality and was always a sheer joy to be around." Father Martin paused briefly and gave another, barely audible sigh. "I must admit that I was deeply saddened when I learnt that he was dead. It was such a terrible waste of a young life."

Hollister found that he was a little surprised at the depth of feeling from the priest. He could only hope that somebody, one day, would give him such a glowing obituary. "You speak very highly of him, but what exactly was your relationship with him?"

After a brief pause, to collect his thoughts and to try and read any hidden meaning behind the question, the priest eventually responded. "Cameron was not like many of the local youths of his age. He showed a great deal of maturity for one so young, at times almost too mature. He took a great deal of interest in the mechanisms of the Church and would, if he had lived, have made a fine priest."

For the second time Hollister noticed that the priest had not answered his question about his relationship with the young boy and now suspected that he was hiding something. "Did Cameron have any problems that he spoke off shortly before he disappeared? Did he seem different in any way that you noticed?"

"Like what?" the question being met with another question.

Hollister was not certain himself. He was stabbing in the dark, certain that the cautious Father Martin knew more than he was ever going to admit and also knowing that a more thorough search into the life of the priest was needed. "You know any problems at school or anything. Maybe he had problems with his friends or he was being bullied? Maybe there was something wrong at home? Anything really, I must admit that I'm clutching at straws."

"If you've met his mother, then you would know that Cameron came from a very loving and caring family and lived in a very loving home. I can assure you detective that he would not have had any problems at home. As regards to his school and his friends, they would have to tell you the answer to that one. I cannot reveal anything about his school life, even if I actually wanted too, because I simply don't know. Cameron never spoke to me about anything at school."

"But, if you and Cameron were as close as you have indicated, then surely he would have spoken about his days at school?" Hollister had picked up, yet again, that the priest was trying not to answer the question and he pressed the point.

The priest responded with a moment's silence. It had become obvious to the detective that Father Martin was not going to answer any particular questions regarding his relationship with Robinson, which only served to add to the suspicions that Hollister had about the priest. Instead, Father Martin asked a question of his ow. "You said earlier, if I remember your exact words correctly, that 'recent information' led you to think that his death may be suspicious. What exactly did you mean Chief Inspector?"

Hollister took a gamble, "This must remain in confidence," it was the turn of the priest to nod his head in agreement to the request made by the detective. "When we found Cameron, it gave all the appearance of him committing suicide. We that is the Greater Manchester Police, concocted the story of pneumonia to protect his family, but officially he took his own life. Only his parents know the truth."

"A very commendable gesture Chief Inspector, but I think that you are wrong" replied Father Martin without any hesitation. "From what I recall about Cameron, based on what I knew about him two years ago and his interest in the Church, there is doubt in my mind that this young man would ever take his own life."

"That is precisely the opinion of his mother. She still refuses to admit that her son committed suicide. I must admit that at first I thought that she was only being protective, but the more that I mull it over and think about it, the more that I think that she might be correct. I personally, and I must reiterate that it is only my own personal opinion and not one held officially by the force, doubt that he did commit suicide."

Father Martin sat upright and took a deep breath, "Cameron was a deeply religious boy. He was one of my senior choir boys and my server, altar boy, and a shining light towards the Church's policy towards the youth. The taking of your own life, to the Catholic Church, is viewed very much as great a taboo as contraception. No serious Catholic, no true believer in the teachings of the Catholic Church, would ever take their own life."

Secretly Hollister knew that not only was Robinson homosexual but he also used contraceptives whilst having sex with his clients, both of which would break with the Catholic Church's philosophy and then

maybe he could have taken his own life after all. He decided to keep this knowledge to himself, for now at least. "Would you regard Cameron as, to use your own words, a 'true' Catholic?"

"Without any doubt or question," Hollister's question had been answered without any hesitation.

"And what about homosexuality?" asked Hollister.

Father Martin gave a brief, dry guffaw. It was an almost nervous laugh. "Now why on earth do you ask such a question as that?"

"I'm just trying to cover every available option," was the much rehearsed reply from Hollister.

The priest saw straight though the lie. "I do not think that you are being totally frank with me Chief Inspector."

Hollister thought for a moment, running the next sentence through his brain before uttering it, "Let me just say, that while trying to protect the memory and reputation of Cameron and that of his family, that I believe that there may be something, in this case, to the subject matter."

"Officially, the Catholic Church is vehemently opposed to any form of sexual liaisons between couples of the same sex. In fact an organisation within the Vatican known as the Congregation for the Doctrine of the Faith have recently issued a Holy See in which it is stated that homosexuality is 'intrinsically evil'. Unofficially though, and this time it is only my personal opinion, we now need to have a more liberal approach to the subject. We know that in this, the twenty first century that homosexuality exists and is widely practised by some members of our faith, despite the fact that we try to teach a more valued and family orientated lifestyle. Surely though, you are not trying to imply that Cameron was killed because of something like this?"

"I'm not trying to insinuate or suggest anything. Father, nor have I said that Cameron's death was anything other than the official cause, suicide. I am though, as a detective, trying to keep an open mind on everything. Tell me Father, what is your personal view on homosexuality?"

"I follow the edicts of the Church and of the Holy Father. I don't have an opinion. I do though resent this line of questioning." The priest was now twitching nervously in his chair.

It seemed that Hollister had touched on a raw nerve, but he decided that, for now at least, he did not pursue it any further. "I'm sorry if I have offended you Father. That was never my intention. However, the kind of lifestyle that I've recently discovered Cameron was living would, and once again I'm only speculating, imply that there may have been some form of homosexual relationship going on shortly before he was recently discovered. Once again, I'm not trying to imply anything improper had occurred between you and Cameron, but just wondered, as the boy's priest, whether or not he may have mentioned anything along these lines and may have been influenced further?"

After a brief pause, Father Martin responded to Hollister's statement. "At first I thought the notion too ridiculous to even consider. However, on reflection, Cameron was a very good looking young man and a pleasant one at that, with a great of charisma. If Cameron was moving in those circles, then I can imagine that he would be greatly sought after by some men. So, as somebody that knew him well, I think that there could actually be some truth in what you're thinking. No matter how much I would wish otherwise. The very thought of such a nice boy like Cameron being preyed upon by such men appals me, but I have to

be realistic and accept that this kind of lifestyle exists and that Cameron may, in the two years of his absence, have been manipulated by somebody older for their own sexual gratification."

"Once again Father, let me reiterate, I'm not suggesting that this was the reason behind his death. At the moment it is just one of many avenue's that I'm considering."

"But one that you are seriously considering?" asked the priest.

Hollister nodded, "Unfortunately Father, yes."

"As you are fully aware Chief Inspector, most boys at a certain stage of their lives development do go through this quest for sexual identity. I know that I did and no doubt that you probably did so too. Most people overcome these unnatural desires of the flesh, whilst others, unfortunately, succumb to them. In the case of Cameron, only God now has the answers to your questions."

Hollister concluded his meeting with Father Martin shortly after this comment. The detective had deliberately not mentioned to the priest that Robinson had adopted the priest's name as part of alias once he had gone missing, deciding to withhold it just in case he needed another reason to come and visit the priest.

As he drove back to Manchester, with the rain lashing down on his car, the windscreen wipers having to work overdrive to keep his view clear, Hollister thought about his two meetings. The mother, with her undying love for her son, painted a very similar picture of Cameron Robinson to that of the priest. But there was something not quite right with his words and the fact, that despite asking him twice, the priest never explained his relationship to the youth. This he considered deeply suspicious. If it was only a priest and parishioner relationship then why

was Father Martin extremely reluctant to discuss it? As he drove Hollister wracked his brain to try and figure out what it was that the priest had said, or did not say that troubled him so?

Hollister was tired and hungry and as a result found it difficult to think straight, but he knew that there was something there. What it was escaped him for now. He did though have a tense nagging doubt in the back of his brain and decided to investigate the priest more thoroughly.

Chapter Seven

McKenzie Hollister could feel the tension in the room from the moment that he entered the office that was 'home' to the Serious Crimes Squad. He knew that by his unauthorised absence over the last few days that he had overstepped his seniority and that he was now in trouble. All the conversations between his fellow officers stopped and every pair of eyes stared at him, burning deep into him, matched by the frowns on their brows. The faces of previously loyal officers were now twisted with the rage of isolation and an even deeper resentment.

Hollister ignored them and shrugged them off. He had felt their wrath before and chose to ignore his colleagues rather than to respond to them. Arrogantly he strode past them all, without even acknowledging their presence and not uttering a single word to any of them, going straight to his office, his eyes fixed firmly in front of him and closing the door behind him, once again shutting his colleagues out of his own private world. Now inside his private office Hollister lets out a deep sigh and sits behind his desk.

Within seconds of sitting behind the heavily cluttered desk, awash with paperwork and internal messages, the silence was broken by the ringing of the telephone. Hollister had expected this and he knew who the caller was going to be before he answered it. He was proven correct. It was the secretary of the most senior detective at Heller Street and Hollister had been summoned up to see Chief Superintendent Mundy. Having anticipated this, Hollister had spent the last twenty four hours rehearsing a fabricated story for Mundy and his colleagues which

explained his absence. He knew that he could not them the truth and that he was secretly investigating Cameron Robinson's death, this would create too many questions that Hollister himself did not know the answers to and so he had concocted a story for their benefit. Whether his long-time friend Mundy was going to believe him though was another question, but Hollister simply could not afford Mundy to know the real reason for his absence and the lack of any form of inclusion from his colleagues.

Hollister did not exactly rush upstairs to the plush office of Mundy. He took his time reading a handful of the messages splayed over his desk, smoking a cigarette, before taking a leisurely stroll up to his senior officer and to receive the inevitable reprimand. Once there, Mundy retaliated by keeping the junior officer waiting outside, sitting in silence with the secretary, who twitched nervously as she almost silently typed a letter. From experience Hollister knew that this was a deliberate ploy used by Mundy to psyche out the waiting officer, making them sweat at being kept waiting, adding gravitas to their disciplinary reprimand and, as a rule, the longer the wait, the more severe their censure. Hollister was kept waiting exactly ten minutes and this usually indicated that serious trouble lay ahead.

Finally, for both of them, the wait was over. The intercom drowned out the ticking clock on the wall and the tapping of a keyboard and the middle-aged woman motioned for Hollister to go into Mundy's office, where he was greeted with the abrupt and sarcastic voice of Mundy. "Now don't tell me…your name…it'll come to me in a moment. That's it…it's McKenzie Hollister. It's been so long since I've seen you that I nearly forgot who you were." The mocking soon stopped and the tone

of Mundy's voice became serious. "Now, where the hell have you been?"

Hollister sat in front of Mundy, unimpressed by the sarcasm, which was hardly new to him. "I've been laid up with a cold. I've been in bed for a couple of days."

Mundy knew his friend was lying to him but decided to go along with Hollister for the moment, "So ill that you couldn't even pick up the phone and let us know?"

"Do you mean that Kate didn't call you? I told her to. Wait until I see her later" Hollister replied.

Mundy snapped and banged his hand on the desk, which even surprised Hollister. "Do you want to go out and come back in again and this time cut the fucking crap and this…comedy routine and start telling me the fucking truth."

"What are you going on about?" Hollister replied, still protesting his innocence.

"Mac," began Mundy, his voice still slightly raised. "Kate phoned me yesterday and asked me where you were because she had barely seen you for a week. She's asked me to pull you off whatever case you're working on because it's getting to you and she thinks you're losing the plot. You've not been working on the robberies, so where the fuck have you been and what the fuck have you been doing?"

Hollister gulped and tried another ploy, still attempting to hood-wink his senior officer. Internally he was livid that his wife had spoken to Mundy. "What does she fucking know? I might not have been in the office, but who's to say that I've not been working on the armed robberies?"

"I'm say so," snapped back Mundy. "Because yesterday we picked up Willy Hulme and his gang and we're beginning to wind the case down and you were nowhere to be fucking seen. So for the second time, and this time I want the truth, where the fuck have you been?"

It was now time for Hollister to commence his much-rehearsed speech, hoping that Mundy would believe him. "All right, all right, calm down. It's Kate. I think she's having an affair. I've been trying to figure out who it's with, and so I've been secretly following her. That's what I've been doing."

Mundy was clearly shocked by Hollister's disclosure and was not sure whether to believe him or not. Hollister had never lied to me before, thought Mundy, and he hoped he was not starting now. He came from behind his desk and began pacing the room, nervous and agitated almost it seemed as if he had just been told that it was his own wife that was cheating on him. "You must be wrong Mac. Kate would never do that to you. What proof have you got?"

Hollister looked long and hard at his friend and wondered whether he had taken the bait. "Nothing definite. It's just some little things that she's been saying and doing. If she's not shagging somebody else, then she's certainly up to something. I've been telling her that I've been coming here and then, using a friend's car, following her and recording her every movement. I just want to be prepared for it if she is."

Mundy shook his head in disbelief and placed a comforting hand on the shoulder of his friend, who was still sitting and inwardly smiling to himself. "I'm absolutely gob-smacked Mac. I never thought for one moment that Kate would do something like this." He paused briefly in order to let his words sink in and this gave him the chance to choose his

next sentence carefully. "I can now fully understand why you've been away from the office Mac. You don't want the other's to see you like this." Mundy had dropped the anger of a disappointed and let down superior officer and had become a friend again, "What I want you to do is take a couple of days off...no. Take a week off. Longer if you need to, I'll sort the troops out and the Commission, don't worry about them. Go and spend some time with Kate, try and save what's left of your marriage."

Hollister felt a great deal of smug satisfaction. He had succeeded in calling his friend's bluff, relying on their friendship to get away with his lies. Hollister needed to continue his charade a little longer and put on his best acting voice. "Thanks Andrew. I just need a few days."

Mundy was having none of it, "Nonsense. You are to take a week off, nothing less. Go away if you have too. But you must, as a friend, keep me updated. I won't say anything to anybody. Now get out Mac. Go, but stay in touch." Resting a hand on his friends shoulder once again, completely unaware that he had been duped, Mundy felt sympathy for his long-time friend.

Trying to sound humble, Hollister replied to his friends demand, "Thanks and I will."

Hollister stood and left Mundy's office. Deep down the detective was delighted with the outcome of his meeting. He now had at least a week to investigate the life of Cameron Robinson and to try and locate the elusive Spencer without having to worry about coming into the station. The downside meant that he would be unable to use the resources that Heller Street police station offered, such as the historical file on Robinson's disappearance and the records of suspects or known

criminals that might have been able to help him. But to Hollister, this was a small price to pay because he now had the freedom to continue his secret investigation and to try and come up with at least some answers to the myriad of questions mulling around in his head, affecting him in everything that he tried to do and keeping him awake at night.

It was only a fifteen minute drive from Heller Street police station to his home but it seemed like an eternity and the longer that he drove, the more annoyed he got with the actions of his wife. How dare she phone Mundy and ask him to take him off a case, he thought to himself over and over again. When Mundy had told him what she had done, Hollister had immediately become full of rage and resentment that he had wanted to storm out of the office and confront her but instead he just had to sit there, lie to his friend and listen to Mundy. Now he was driving home to confront her.

Despite it being a criminal offence, and one that he knew he would have difficulty in getting away with if caught, Hollister took mouthfuls of whisky at every opportunity and as he neared his home the flat, square shaped bottle was nearly empty. If he had been honest with himself, even Hollister was beginning to get a little concerned as to the sheer amount of alcohol that he was consuming these days.

Ever since becoming a detective, he had always been acutely aware of the copious amounts of alcohol that both he and his colleagues drank. They had, over the years, probably figured out and solved more crimes and cases in the local bar than in the police station, but now even Hollister was getting a little concerned as to his own personal

alcoholic consumption. He was becoming reliant on alcohol to get him through the day and could not sleep unless he had drunk himself into a stupor. He needed a drink to help him sleep and then, the following morning, he needed a drink to help him wake up.

Sleeping at night had now virtually eluded the detective. For the past few weeks, every time that he closed his eyes, Hollister saw the ghostly and haunting face of Cameron Robinson staring back at him. Lying there on his deathbed, looking so innocent and peaceful and yet, in reality, he had been so depraved and corrupt. Why had he felt the need to embrace such a vile and abhorrent lifestyle, selling his body for sex rather than finding some other meaningful employment? What was it that had pushed him over the edge and onto the streets as a 'rent boy'? The all-consuming search for an answer to this question was all that was driving him these days, nothing else mattered to him. That is with the exception of Spencer, whose face he also saw whenever he closed his eyes. This time it was a different set of feelings, adding to the whirling maelstrom of emotions currently in the troubled mind of McKenzie Hollister.

There was something about this youth that also equally haunted and captivated the detective and as with Cameron Robinson, the answer why, eluded him. The detective had guessed that the name 'Spencer' was almost certainly not his real name, so who was he really and where was he from? Why had he apparently chosen, like Robinson, to become a prostitute, literally in his case selling his body for a meal and a bed to spend the night? What about the boy himself? He had a certain charm and charisma that had captivated the detective from the moment that he had first seen him. He had elfin-like and boyish good looks with a

cheeky, mischievous smile and Hollister had been enthralled by his every word regarding his life on the streets and what had happened to him. Hollister had become infatuated with the boy, desperately wanting to see him again and had spent the last two nights searching for him. He had spent hours driving endlessly around 'The Village' looking for him, eating endless bits of cheap and disgusting hamburgers in the brightly lit fast food bars in and around Piccadilly, hoping, in vain, just for a glimpse of him. He had even slept in his car, a bottle of whisky forever at hand, in a deserted side street, waiting for dawn to break over the usually rain-drenched streets of Manchester before beginning his forlorn quest all over again.

Hollister's obsession with both Robinson and Spencer now took second place in his thoughts. As he parked his car in a side street close to his home, so as not to alert his unsuspecting wife, Hollister staggered up to his house and silently entered his home. By now he found that he was completely consumed by rage. A red mist had descended over him, blinding him with fury as he called out to his wife, "Kate, where are you?"

"I'm in the kitchen," was the surprised but happy response.

Using the walls and furniture to steady himself, Hollister made his way to the kitchen and found his wife at the sink. After turning to face her husband and before she could say anything, Hollister lashed out with an open-handed blow to the side of her head. The sheer force of the unexpected blow sent Kate and the plates that she was holding crashing to the floor. "How fucking dare you. How fucking dare you phone Mundy and complain about me," yelled Hollister through gritted teeth. He continued to vent his anger at his defenceless wife, cowering

on the floor, completely shocked by her husband's actions. "Don't you ever fucking phone him again, you hear me? Who the fuck do you think you are?"

By now the near hysterical woman had scrambled to her feet, astonished by his totally unexpected assault. "What's wrong with you?" she yelled back.

"Fucking you, that's what" came a snarled rely.

As Hollister lunged for his wife for a second time and feeling that her life was in danger, Kate reached for a knife to protect herself and waved it widely towards Hollister. "Keep away from me you bastard. Look at you, you're pissed and it's only..."

Dodging out of the path of the sweeping blade, Hollister continued towards his sobbing and hysterical wife. "I'm pissed because I can't stand the fucking sight of you when I'm sober."

Another blow, this time a punch, sent Kate flying backwards into a pine cupboard, its door spitting with the impact of her hitting it and then she fell to the floor again. The kitchen knife, her only means of defence, was dropped, falling noisily to the tiled floor and out of her reach. "Get out you bastard," she yelled.

"Oh, don't worry, I'm going," replied Hollister. This time his words were not shouted, but spoken in a menacing and intimidating manner, though gritted teeth as he moved ever closer to her. The terrified wife caught a glimpse at his eyes, which were filled with hatred. "I'm going, but not until I've taught you a fucking lesson."

Blow after blow rained down on the defenceless woman curled up on the floor in the foetal position, desperately trying to protect herself the best that she could, but she was no match for both the strength and

sheer ferocity of her assailant. She screamed out to her once loving husband to stop the savage beating, but her pleas were to no avail. It seemed the more she cried out and pleaded with him to stop, the worse he got. Hollister did not restrict himself to hitting the defenceless woman. He lashed out with kicks and threw anything and everything that was within his reach at her. Then just as abruptly as his assault had started his assault, he stopped.

He had suddenly come to his senses and realised what he was actually doing. Hollister panicked and ran out of the kitchen, already full of remorse and guilt at what he had just done. Not that this would have meant anything to the whimpering woman who now lay, barely conscious, on the cold floor, surrounded by broken crockery, dented saucepans and blood. It was her blood, from a face that had been pounded into a bloodied and swollen pulp by her alcoholic husband. Every inch of her body ached from his kicks and punches he had rained down on her as he sought to take his drunken rage out on his wife.

She had suffered the consequences of her husband's inability to come up with the answer to the multitude of questions mulling around his head and his inability to find the person who he had become infatuated with and who he desperately sought out, Spencer.

It was only after he had returned to his car that Hollister realised just how much he was trembling. It was not just his hands, but it seemed as if his entire body was involuntarily shaking. His breathing was heavy and the sound of his own pounding heart was deafening, so much that it made his temples throb and the rest of his head hurt. Reaching under his seat Hollister found the whisky bottle and finished off its contents

in one huge gulp, before tossing it onto the rear seat. Having run out of alcohol, he now sought solace in a cigarette, with it trembling so much in his nicotine stained fingers that he had difficulty in lighting it, burning the tips of his fingers with his shaking lighter as the enormity of his current situation slowly began to dawn on him, filling him with a deep sense of sorrow.

Once he had inhaled several drags of his cigarette and in the comfort of his cart was only now that he began to realise the gravity of what he had just done. What had come over him? In over ten years of marriage, Hollister had never so much as laid a finger on his wife and now, for some inexplicable reason, he had just beaten her senseless. He had totally lost control of himself and his innocent wife had suffered as a consequence. If he was honest with himself, he was not really that annoyed by her actions. She had only been looking out for her husband. Hollister was, in fact, more frustrated with himself for letting himself get too personally involved in a case. He would not be human if he had not been touched by some of the things that he had seen, but they had not had the kind of impact on him as the dead Cameron Robinson and the missing Spencer.

But what should he do about Kate? Should he phone an ambulance for her? Doing this though could later be used against him if she brought charges of assault against him. Mobile phone tracking and the recording of the emergency call would have proved that he had knowledge of the assault. The sudden screeching sound of an alarm, which he recognised as the panic alarm fitted to his home, pierced the silence of the residential street sending Hollister into a panic. He started the car and drove off, in the opposite direction to his house.

Hollister had been driving around for about fifteen minutes when his mobile phone rang. He recognised the number and hesitated at first, but decided to answer it, "Yeah, Hollister."

He immediately recognised the voice of Mundy, "Mac, it's me, Andrew. Where are you?"

"I'm in the city. Why, what's up?" asked Hollister, trying to sound calm and innocent.

"Don't get alarmed, but Kate's been hurt. Your emergency panic button was activated at your home and we raced there. When we got there, Kate was in the kitchen," Mundy paused briefly before he continued, "Mac, Kate's been attacked, quite badly."

"Where is she? How bad is it?" Hollister asked the two questions in rapid succession, he already knew the answer to the second question though.

"She's been taken to the M.R.I. for treatment. From what I can make out from what she's told the paramedics, there was an intruder in your house, a possibly burglar. Kate disturbed him and he attacked her, only fleeing when she pushed the panic button."

A huge sigh of relief flowed from his body. He could not believe that after what he had just done to her that his wife was actually protecting him. "Cheers Andrew. I'm on my way."

The car surged forward as Hollister accelerated and turned on the two-tone siren and the blue flashing lights hidden in the radiator and the lights of his car, clearing traffic out of his way as he rushed to his wife's side and continued his almost pathetic charade of the loving and caring husband.

Thirty minutes later Hollister stared down at his sedated wife. A lump filled his throat and tears welled in his eyes, real tears, not 'crocodile tears'. Shame and guilt took over every other emotion that he was feeling. He could not believe that it was him that had actually done this to her. But the shock of Kate protecting him and his actions really surprised him. After what he had just done to her, why was she covering up for him? Why on earth would she protect the man, her supposed loving husband that had just beaten her to a pulp and hospitalised her? Was it out of the love that she professed for him on their wedding day? Hollister doubted this. Was it out of sympathy for him and whatever it was that had recently sent him off the rails? This seemed even more remote. Only Kate knew the reason why she was protecting him and this became yet another issue for the tormented mind of McKenzie Hollister.

Arriving at the hospital Hollister was met by a uniformed officer who led him to the ward where Kate Hollister was being treated. She had been placed into a side room and another uniformed police officer, this time a woman, stood guard outside. As a nurse constantly made herself busy in the room, hovering around the bed, checking this and that, Hollister pulled up a chair and sat next to the sedated woman. He took hold of her hand and gently squeezed it, wiping the tears from off his face with the other. Through bleary tear-filled eyes Hollister stared pitifully at the cuts and bruises on her previously beautiful face and how he had ruined her looks, maybe forever. He leant forward and gently kissed her forehead, his lips barely touching the flesh of his wife. Kate Hollister stirred slightly and the detective mouthed the words, "I'm sorry. I'm so, so sorry."

Hollister found that he was at an all-time emotional low. He felt nothing but shame for what he had done to his wife and confusion as to why he had carried out the attack. He alone knew what was troubling him and could not share it with anybody else. His inability to come to terms with the official cause of death of Cameron Robinson and his futile search for the elusive Spencer were all that he thought about had so derailed his rational thoughts, leading to his increased drinking and now the horrific assault on his wife wracked the detective with guilt. His life had been turned upside down and he simply could not understand why. In all his years in the police force, no single case had ever troubled him like this and there had been some terrible incidents that he has had to investigate, but there had been nothing like this before. Why does a boy from a loving home suddenly leave the safety of his family and become a prostitute in order to survive? Not just any boy, but a fourteen year old schoolboy that seemed to have everything going for him and even a possibly future as a priest.

Then there was Spencer, the mysterious teenager that had approached him. What had led him to adopt such a lifestyle, full of danger and uncertainty, never knowing what he was going to eat or where he was going to sleep, leaving himself vulnerable to the prey of sexual deviants that liked to have sex with young boys. This private investigation had so troubled him, with all its unanswerable questions and inner turmoil affecting every aspect of Hollister's life, had now led to him committing the unthinkable and taking it out on his once-loving wife.

McKenzie Hollister now dreaded the thought of going home. Knowing that he needed to go somewhere and clear his head and try and understand what was going on with him was one thing, but actually knowing what to do and where to go was another thing. He had spoken to Mundy from Kate's bedside and reassured him that she was going to be okay, informing the nursing staff to contact him the moment that she woke up, before driving back to the city centre, where he once again found himself sitting on a stool in scarcely occupied a bar, alone, drinking glass after glass of whisky.

His constant and excessive drinking was finally beginning to get the better of him, wreaking havoc with his already tormented and mixed up emotions, which was now making him incredibly volatile. Not that he was trying to justify the beating of his wife. There was, thought Hollister as he finished off one drink, only to order a replacement, and never could be any excuse for his actions. But, what was done could not be undone and he faced an uncertain future of forever being tormented by the guilt of attacking his wife and the knowledge that she probably would never forgive him. Maybe this alone was a worse prospect than being prosecuted, mused the already drunk detective, eventually realising that alcohol was not the answer to his woes.

As he finished off what he had decided was going to be his last drink, Hollister around at his surroundings. Nightfall had come and the once empty bar was beginning to fill with patrons, out spending their hard-earned wages on drinks that they could hardly afford. Mostly they were in couples. Others were in larger groups and getting more and more boisterous as the more that they drank. There were one or two people like him, drinking alone, either out of choice or like him, out of

necessity. Hollister caught a glimpse of himself in the mirror behind the bar and the sight worried him further.

The last couple of days had taken a heavy toll on his appearance. He had not washed or changed his clothing for the past two days. Nor had he shaven, stubble had grown on his face. Even he had to admit that he looked a mess and using his fingers as a make-be comb he had a pathetic attempt at doing something with his greasy hair. Then the obvious dawned on Hollister.

He knew where there was an apartment not being used. It was clean and tidy and, above everything else, if offered the detective a bed for the night away from his marital home and the painful flashbacks of what he had just done in the house. He even had the keys for it in the glovebox of his car. He was aching all over from sleeping in his car and the prospect of curling up in a bed was most appealing to him. He had decided to use the former apartment of Cameron Robinson.

Whether his emotions had been distorted by the alcohol or not, Hollister had no conscious about using the former home of the dead youngster, after all, it was empty and not being used. The flat was well furnished and had all the necessary amenities for a short stay. It also offered, on reflection, an ideal place to stay while he came to terms with the guilt of attacking his wife. Here he would have the peace and solitude to reflect on his current lifestyle of the past few days and, once clear, his mind would be able to focus on his private investigation of the life and death of Cameron Robinson and trying to establish whether he did or did not commit suicide. He would also use Robinson's flat as somewhere to base himself while he attempted to find Spencer and to take him back there if he was ever to find the youngster again..

Hollister knew that he would not be able to do any of this if he was either constantly drunk or hung over from the effects of alcohol. He knew that he would need a clear head in order to think about the reasons why Robinson had first left home. He also knew that he would have to clean and tidy, but above all, sober, when he interviewed people. Any slip-ups on his behalf would bring complaints and these would, in turn, bring the inevitable questions from Mundy and others as to what he was actually doing still investigating Robinson's death after explicitly being told by Mundy that there was nothing to investigate. Hollister knew, from gut-instinct, that there was something not right with the death scene of the teenager and he was determined to get to the bottom of it, whatever the cost.

It was not long before Hollister was once again parking his car in the side street next to the building that housed Robinson's former apartment. After locking the vehicle and turning on its alarm, the detective made his way to his place of refuge, looking around to see if anybody was watching him. Despite the block of flats being situated on a main road, Hollister was surprised at just how few people were out on the streets, man out walking his dog, a small group of teenaged boys in the park opposite playing football and a couple, arm in arm, returning from a local take-away food shop. Nobody that would remember him, thought Hollister but, then again, why would anybody question what he was doing? Nobody knew he was there and, he supposed, knew about the line of business that the previous inhabitant of the apartment had, so why was he being so paranoid about anybody seeing him on the street outside the building?

Hollister let himself into the flat and the first thing that he noticed was that the flat was still being cleaned on a regular occasion and the detective made a mental note to try and find out just who the cleaner was as he made his way to the lounge, his footsteps sending echoes around the hallway as the reverberated from off the wooden floor. Even though this was the third time that he had been here, Hollister glanced around the room after putting on a light. This was an instinctive reaction that he did wherever he went, coming from years of surveying crime scenes, searching for any tell-tale and minute clues. The detective now viewed the small apartment with a different frame of mind and he was impressed. He knew that it could offer him an ideal location to continue his investigation into the life, and death, of its previous occupant. Not only did it offer him privacy, a place to possibly bring people for a more relaxed meeting without giving away his own identity, but most of all, it offered him sanctuary.

Hollister went to the bathroom. This room offered colour, a pleasant change from the white walls of the hallway and lounge. The walls were painted a bright yellow, with broad stripes of two different shades of blue running horizontal and at eye level. The taps for the sink and bath, together the towel rails were chrome and the towels were a dark navy blue. It was a shame that the youngster was dead, thought Hollister, because if he had chosen the décor and the finishing items in the flat himself, then he would have made a terrific interior designer. The weary detective turned on the shower, adjusted the temperature to suit him and removed his creased clothing before climbing over the side of the bath and standing under the torrent of hot water. He lost all sense of timing while under the spray of water and even whose home he was in

as he lathered an expensive liquid soap all over his tired and aching body and, for the first time in around a month, he relaxed.

When he finally turned off the shower and emerged from the behind the steamed up glass screen, he dried himself off, eventually wrapping the wet towel around his waist and set off in search of some clean clothes. Once in the bedroom he looked at the garments that hung in the wardrobe and silently thanked Robinson for liking gymnastics and building a good physique, for he and the dead boy must have been a similar build because the clothes just about fitted him. The trousers were a little too tight for Hollister's liking but the shirt that he chose fitted him perfectly. Hollister remembered the three 'cash-point' cards in the case. Housed in a black leather wallet, each of the three cards had a four digit number written on a piece of paper and taking the first one, Hollister set off again for the city.

A short time later and standing outside a bank, Hollister once again glanced around prior to using the cash machine. Should he really be doing this, he thought to himself? Should he actually be using the bank account of a dead 'rent boy' for additional money? For the first time he felt a slight twinge of conscious, even a hint of guilt, but, at the end of the day, Robinson was dead and he certainly would not be using the money and, as long as he only used the cash machines, nobody would ever know or suspect that it was in fact him and not Robinson withdrawing money from his accounts. His mind made up, the guilt wiped from his mind as greed and necessity took over and Hollister decided to see how much money the dead youth had in his bank account.

Inserting the plastic card into the slot and typing in the four numbers that he read off the small piece of paper. Hollister was a little surprised to discover that he could still access the account but then again, why shouldn't he? Nobody else knew that it existed and so nobody could use or even close the account. Hollister was given a choice of options and pressed the button for an on-screen balance of the account and was shocked to see the figure before his eyes. So much so that his mind went blank and could not concentrate and stopped the transaction.

Robinson had over twenty thousand pounds in this bank. How on earth could a sixteen year old boy amass such a staggering amount of money he thought to himself? Then another thought flashed into the brain of the detective. This was only one of three accounts that he now had access to. Hollister now found himself in an unenviable position. He had a near luxurious apartment at his disposal and access to several thousands of pounds and none of it traceable. For somebody like himself that now, through other circumstances, found the need to lose himself he was in a perfect position. By now the detective had been able to collect his thoughts and for the second time set about withdrawing some money. He took a gamble by using his own cash machine limit and soon had two hundred pounds presented to him.

Hollister bought himself a Chinese take-away meal and some beer on the short journey back to his newly adopted home. He settled down for the evening, tucked into the food and sipped the cold beers as he watched the remainder of the pornographic videos, having first watched the one where Robinson performs with the dildo for the second time. This time Hollister found that he was no longer repulsed by the images on the television screen. In fact, the very opposite happened. He found

that he became sexually aroused by them. Once again it troubled the detective that he got aroused a little too easily as he watched the various scenarios that usually involved teenaged boys of a similar age to Robinson and Spencer, so much so that once he had decided that he had seen enough for the night, he retired to the bedroom and before going to sleep, masturbated himself, recalling what he had just watched in his mind. Tomorrow he was going to continue his investigation into the life and death of Cameron Robinson, but first he needed some sleep.

Chapter Eight

A rested and contented McKenzie Hollister woke shortly before nine the following morning. It had been several weeks since he had slept so well and felt this relaxed and ready for the day ahead of him. The low autumn sun shining through the closed curtains had broken his slumber, a sleep that had not only helped to soothe his aching body, but that now enabled him to focus his mind on what lay ahead for him. He knew, within seconds of sitting up in the strange, but comfortable, bed that it was going to be another very difficult day for him.

He knew that his first task was to continue the charade of the loving and caring husband. Hollister was under no illusion that, judging by his recent erratic behaviour, certain people would be watching his every move very carefully, ready to pounce on anything that that could either use against him at a later date or to enable one of his many enemies to bring him down, giving him the comeuppance that they thought he needed.

Not only his fellow police officers, but the medical staff at the hospital, were in the mind of the detective. They were, according to Hollister, watching out for him to slip up and discover that it was he who had caused the injuries to his wife and not some unknown and mysterious intruder. Despite the fact that his wife Kate had not, up to now, reported that it was actually her husband that had attacked her, some of his colleagues, especially those that had been privy to his previous mood swings, may either figure out or at the very least suspect Hollister had attacked his wife and this was something that he was

desperate for them not to work out. So it was both out of necessity and desperation that he played the role of the loving and devoted husband, being at his wife's bedside and showing suitable concern for her. He did feel genuine remorse and regretted his actions but he also thought that she had no right to go behind his back and speak to Mundy. In his mind, she had overstepped the mark. She had crossed an invisible line and interfered with an investigation.

After taking his second shower at the flat, Hollister dressed himself in the clothes of the dead youth, this time he wore a tangerine coloured shirt, dark denim jeans and a blue jacket. He was still a little surprised that they actually fitted him, although only just and once again he silently thanked Robinson for his interest in gymnastics and developing a good physique. Even Hollister had to admit that he was getting used to unusual surprises and wondered just how many more he would encounter before resolving his personal quest into the life and death of Cameron Robinson. Breakfast consisted of a cup of coffee and then, taking the two remaining cash machine cards, complete with their PIN numbers, he set off for hospital.

Despite the usual restrictions imposed on most visitors, with Hollister being a high ranking police officer, he was allowed immediate access to his wife's private room, still being protected by a uniformed female police officer, who saluted him as he passed her. It was not the sight of his wife that upset him and brought a lump to his throat, but the fact that it was him that had put her in hospital. Hollister stood just outside his wife's room in the clinical preparation area between the ward corridor and Kate's bedroom, his head bowed, while the hustle and bustle of daily hospital life went on all around him, unseen and

unnoticed by the guilt-ridden detective. He just stood there for a moment, watching his wife sleep, but that moment felt like an eternity. He finally plucked up the courage to confront his wife and entered the tiny room that was overflowing with flowers from friends and colleagues.

As soon as she heard a noise, Kate Hollister turned her head slightly to face the person that was disturbing her rest. On seeing it was her husband her first instinctive reaction, as panic set in, was to reach for and press the call button that would have brought a nurse to her assistance, but she could see the remorse and guilt on her husband's face and she knew instinctively that he meant her no further harm. It was McKenzie Hollister that spoke first, "If you want me to leave, I'll understand."

Kate shook her head gently. The sorrow in her husband's eyes told her what she had wanted to know. "No, please stay."

Hollister crossed the room, pulled up a chair and sat next to his wife. They gripped each other's hands, both of them noticing how sweaty and clammy each other's was. Hollister could now clearly see the extent of Kate's injuries. Her left eye was swollen and now almost black, so much so that it was closed, her right eye was also heavily swollen and bruised, she had a cut across the bridge of her nose and her lips had swelled to about twice their normal size. These were the most notable injuries on the puffed and bruised face, however, her entire body still ached, but what hurt her the most was the fact that it was her own husband, the man which she loved, that had done this to her. She viewed his assault on her as a violation of her personal dignity, her

pride but, despite these feelings, her natural anger towards her assailant, she decided to hide her true feelings from her husband.

"Kate, I'm so sorry. I'm so very sorry." The tears had flowed down his face when he saw the true extent of the savage beating that he had inflicted on her. They were genuine tears, tears of remorse.

The sight of her husband weeping, a proud and strong man, not one to show his emotions easily, set Kate off crying. "I know you are Mac."

Once again they were together, holding each other's clammy hands, both crying, but for different reasons, McKenzie Hollister out of regret and sorrow, Kate Hollister for another reason. After a long and uncomfortable silence it was Kate Hollister that broke the lull. "What's happening to you Mac? Why are you like this?"

Hollister wished that he could tell her, anybody, but he just could not pluck up the courage to do so. In time he might be able to do so, but not just yet. First he needed her to forgive him. At this precise moment in time she simply would not understand why he had beaten her. Not even Hollister himself understood why he had done it. He would be far too embarrassed to tell his wife, or anybody, that he was obsessed with two 'rent boys', one dead and the other very much alive and in his thoughts. How would anybody be able to explain this infatuation? Finally, after much deliberation, he answered his wife's question. "I don't know Kate. I wish I did." At least the second part was true.

"You've been like this for weeks," continued the wife, her jaws aching with every word and her voice trembling with both emotion and fear. "You used to be so strong and now look at you. You're falling apart right before my eyes. That's why I phoned Andrew. I know that I

shouldn't have and I'm sorry that I did. I didn't mean to undermine you but I only did it because I love you."

Hollister had only just regained his composure and had wiped away the last of his tears, only to lose control of his emotions again at hearing his wife apologising to him and still proclaiming her love for him. "You've nothing to say sorry for Kate, my love. It's me that should be apologising to you."

"If I hadn't phoned Andrew, then none of this would be happening."

"There's no excuse for me to hit you, ever. I'd been up for days, I was tired. I'd been drinking and I just lost it. You know that I've never once laid a finger on you before and now...look at you. Look at what I've done to you and yet you still stand by me."

"You're my husband and no matter what you do, I'll always be here for you and be by your side." Strong words from the battered and bruised woman and spoken with conviction, but every one of them were lies. There was no way that she could ever forgive him for this. He had gone too far this time.

Kate Hollister had already made her decision to leave her husband about a week ago and this had only acted as a catalyst in speeding it up. But in her current situation, she could do nothing about it and had decided to act as the loyal and loving wife as a pretence. She needed some time to sort out somewhere to live and have money to survive on. She knew that their joint finances would not permit her to leave her husband on a whim She knew that she had to plan it first. The loving words that she had spoken to her husband felt like acid on her tongue as she mouthed them, burning her mouth with hatred and bile as they

came from her swollen lips, but they were necessary if she wanted to pull off her leaving.

Little did she know though that her husband had already decided to leave *her*, however, his breakaway was going to be immediate. Curtesy of Cameron Robinson he had already found somewhere else to live and had ready access to money. Hollister had come to this conclusion whilst driving to the hospital. What he had said to his wife were once his true feelings towards her, spoken from the heart, but these days he had no feelings for her. He had no love left for her. He knew that he should not of hit her, there was no excuse for that and the fact that he could do it, after all their years together, was proof enough to him that their marriage was well and truly over. His words meant nothing to him, but he knew that he had needed to apologise to his wife for his actions in order for her to continue to protect him and not reveal to anybody that it was actually him that had attacked her. Hollister had realised this as he drove to be by her bedside. He knew that he no longer loved her but was, in fact, in love with the mysterious Spencer.

Having done what he regarded as his duty, McKenzie Hollister returned to his matrimonial home and changed into a more appropriate form of dress, a dark suit, complimented with a shirt and tie, and now he looked the part of a detective. He also sorted out another couple suits and other clothing and belongings, placed them into a suitcase, which he then placed into the boot of his car. Hollister thought that they might come in useful in the future as he drove across Manchester to Wythenshawe and to St. Anthony of Padua's, the former school of Cameron Robinson.

The sprawling modern building, originally built in the late sixties, since then hugely expanded with vast amounts of concrete and glass, was around a fifteen minute walk from Robinson's former home and a place of learning for over one thousand pupils between the age of eleven and sixteen. The detective parked his car and despite it being on the schools car park, but knowing the general area, he made sure that he locked the vehicle and set its alarm, before entering the building and going to the reception desk.

Having shown the receptionist his warrant card, he requested a meeting with the head teacher. The woman, in her fifties and looking every bit the part of an old style school mistress, padded off to inform the head of his presence. Hollister took a seat and awaited her return. He glanced around at his surroundings and recollected, spending many occasions standing outside his own head teacher's office as a boy, for any one of many minor indiscretions and faced the prospect of receiving lashes from a leather strap, the chosen mode of corporal punishment at his school, which is now outdated and illegal.

While he waited for the secretary to return, Hollister thought to himself whether the abolition of this punishment was now partly responsible for the delinquency of the generation of near-feral youths that he and his colleagues were arresting on a daily basis? Petty crime, such as theft, had existed during his own time at school, reflected Hollister, but nothing like the extent that it does today. It seemed to the detective that an entire generation has been raised in a climate where robberies, assaults and drug taking was now considered the norm and tolerated as just a part of modern life. What hope was there, he thought, for the scores of pupils that ambled noisily past him on their way to

lessons with many of the older pupils, both boys and girls, seemingly knowing instinctively that he was a police officer snorting like pigs in a derisory manner, showing absolutely no respect for those that maintained law and order. Another stark realisation came over Hollister while he waited, a feeling of despair and hopelessness for the futures of these children in this day when opportunities to better themselves were few and far between. A former pupil of this school, with a similar age to those that walked past him, had chosen a life as a prostitute and porn movie actor before ultimately taking his own life, because he thought that he had no meaning or future and his only option was ending his life at sixteen.

The secretary returned, breaking Hollister out of his private thoughts, and instructed him to follow her. "Dr McIlvenna will see you now. Follow me." It was more like an order than a request.

Minutes later Hollister was shown into the office of the head teacher, a man with a doctorate in philosophy, its certificate hanging proudly on the wall behind him, greeted the detective with a smile and a handshake. "Please come in and take a seat Chief Inspector. Would you like a cup of tea or coffee?"

Hollister accepted the outstretched hand, but declined the offer of a drink. The secretary left and the two men sat either side of the cluttered desk. "What can I do for you, Chief Inspector?"

As with Father Martin, Hollister had rehearsed his opening statement and chosen his words carefully. "I'm here regarding a former pupil of this school, Cameron Robinson, who, as you are aware, was tragically found dead recently. Certain elements within the police force would

like to know more about his reason for running away from home and what happened to him during the two years that he was missing."

McIlvenna let out a sigh, "Ah yes, Cameron Robinson. His death has cast a dark shadow over the school and our thoughts, naturally, go out to his family, like they did when he first disappeared. A great many here at St. Anthony of Padua have been deeply troubled by recent events. As regards to Cameron, I did not know him personally. I never had any cause to. From what I recall, and I have since been told, he was an ideal student, hardworking and never in any trouble."

"That is precisely why we want to know more about him and his time at this school. As you are aware, he was not only a good student, but he was heavily involved with his local church and his priest at the time has already given him a glowing...eulogy." Hollister was still not letting on that it was a personal quest. "He also came from a warm and loving family and he just does not fit the normal stereotyped youngster which would run away from his home. Since he turned up dead, the police are looking into his case to see if there was anything that was overlooked when he first went missing that may have led to him being found...well, before it was too late. Is there a teacher that did know him well enough to give me an idea of what he was like, both academically and personally?"

Dr McIlvenna nodded, "We have a policy within this school where every student has a personal advisor, usually their form teacher, who is there for them if they ever need help or advice on any matter. I'll take you to Cameron's. He is teaching at the moment and so I would like you to make it as brief as possible so we do not interrupt class."

"I could always come back later if you like. At a more convenient time," offered the detective, secretly hoping that his request was turned down.

"Unfortunately, with budget restraints the way that they are, there would never be a totally convenient time, Chief Inspector. We might as well do it now, while you're here," replied the head teacher philosophically.

Dr McIlvenna stood up, a move replicated by the detective, who now felt a little uncomfortable and uneasy about his visit to the school. He was not sure whether it was the correct thing to do, but he also knew that at some stage of his personal quest that he would have to visit the school sooner or later. It was the thought of being discovered that troubled the detective.

At least the head teacher does not fit the given description of men that were seen with Robinson, thought Hollister as he followed McIlvenna through a myriad of brightly coloured corridors, mostly glass, but others solid walling. Many of them contained all the usual school days graffiti pledging allegiances to various football teams, or boys and girls pledging their undying love for one another. Some were just plain obscene comments, all perfectly spelt and phrased correctly, which at least proved to Hollister that it was a school that did care about its standards of education. Two of these less than savoury comments did actually catch the detective's eyes as he walked past them. One said, *"Bummer Barratt fucked a boy in year nine"* and near to this was, *"Barratt is an arse bandit"*. Hollister made a point of remembering these two remarks, probably the figment of juvenile minds and

imagination, but he did not know for definite that they were and so he made a mental note to try and find out who this Barratt was.

Dr McIlvenna and Hollister finally reached their destination, the school's gymnasium. A comment from Mrs Robinson suddenly flashed through the mind of the detective, *"My Cameron was good at gymnastics"*. McIlvenna instructed the detective to wait in the corridor while he went into the noisy hall and while waiting between the two changing rooms, one for boys, the other for girls, the unmistakable stench of sweaty bodies lingered from the rooms and hung in the air of the confined corridor. Once again Hollister flashed back to his own school days. He too enjoyed taking part in his school's athletics program, but had always hated the communal showers that followed. Why he suddenly remembered this particular aspect though mystified him while he awaited the arrival of Robinson's form teacher.

A track-suited man soon emerged from the gym's doors and joined Hollister in the corridor. Now this teacher certainly did fit the description given by the residents of the bedsits and Hollister felt his stomach churn as his heart missed a beat when he spoke. "Hello, Barratt Foxford. How can I help you?"

Once having regained his composure, Hollister responded, "Chief Inspector Hollister," he briefly showed the teacher his warrant card. "I'd like to talk to you about Cameron Robinson. Apparently you were his form teacher and advisor, for lack of a better word."

Foxford's brow furrowed with concern as he led Hollister into the boys changing room, two square rooms that were connected by an opening and a separate tiled area showering that completed the room. All around the walls and on the benches were the clothes of the boys

that were currently in the gym and the smell of sweat was more pungent than outside in the corridor. The two men went into a crapped annex room that was Foxford's private changing area.

"Such a shame, him dying like that," began Foxford. "We were all devastated when we heard about it. Prayers were said for him in assembly. Such a terrible shame."

There was something that Foxford had just said that was not right, but for now the detective could not put his finger on it. Years of interviewing suspects had taught him not just to listen out for the words that answered the questions but also on *how* they were spoken. "What was Cameron like, you know as a pupil?"

"He was a very likable boy. He was always happy and smiling and willing to help out any way that he could. He was good both academically and athletically. He was an excellent gymnast, showing a great of promise and, had he survived, whatever career he chose, he would have been a success in it."

"I remember his mother telling me that he was a good gymnast. Just how good was he?" asked Hollister.

"He was very good. You could say that he was a natural gymnast. He had worked hard in his early years, before I came to this school, and it showed. All his training was just beginning to show fruition when he went missing. He had excellent potential for the future, but then he disappeared and we never saw him again. I think that he could've been a future champion, had he been given the chance."

That would explain his finely toned and muscular physique, thought the detective, recalling the first time that he saw Robinson on the bed at Mrs Longman's bedsits and how it made him look older than the

sixteen years he later turned out to be. Hollister decided to pursue the athletic angle for now. "How often did Cameron train?"

"Three times a week after school and on Saturday afternoons," came the immediate reply.

"So you could say that you saw a lot of him?" The teacher nodded his head and the detective continued, "I know that it is now a couple of years ago but do you remember what Cameron was like, you know, mood like, just before he disappeared?"

"From what I recall, he seemed fairly normal. You're right Chief Inspector it is a long time ago. What I do remember is that it turns out that I was the last teacher to see him at the school. He had a competition coming up and so we spent a couple of hours together, you know, going through his routine. I think that was the night before he vanished. I gave a statement at the time."

Once again there was something in what the teacher had said, but still Hollister could not grasp what it was as his mind raced into overdrive. "Was there anybody else with you?"

Foxford seemed to hesitate before he answered the question. He knew that his response could incriminate him if the police launched a full-scale enquiry. "No. We were on our own in the gym, but not in the school."

It certainly did incriminate him, even if it was only in the imagination of the detective, especially considering the graffiti that he had just seen and the private knowledge of Robinson being a 'rent boy'. "Was that usual, you know… just you and Cameron?"

The teacher now seemed to be very uneasy. He had become nervous and his actions revealed it. He now avoided direct eye contact with

Hollister and his hands found anything nearby to play with. Even the tone of his voice had altered. It now had a dry edge to it. "No, Chief Inspector, it wasn't. I don't know how much you know about all this from a couple of years ago, but being the last teacher to see Cameron alive I was thoroughly investigated at the time of Cameron's disappearance and as part of the search for him. There was nothing that could be found on me and I was fully exonerated."

Hollister had thought about interrupting Foxford, but decided to see if he could dig himself into a hole. He knew from experience that the teacher was hiding something, but was not certain yet what it was. Once he had finished, Hollister knew that it was time for diplomacy. "Let me clarify something to you, Mr Foxford. I'm not trying to insinuate or imply anything about you or any other member of the teaching staff here at St. Anthony's. I know that all the teachers and a lot of pupils here at the school at the time of his disappearance were interviewed back then and if I've offended you in any way, then I apologise unreservedly. All I'm trying to do is build up a mental picture, a sort of character profile on him. I'm trying to find out as much about Cameron and his lifestyle before he disappeared and whether this had any reflection on what he did during the two years that he was missing. I'm just trying to establish if we, that is the police, missed anything back then that could have found him sooner and maybe prevented his death."

Foxford accepted the apology with a nod of his head and seemed to relax a little. "Because of his obvious talent as a gymnast, and maybe my own desire to train a future champion, I must admit that I did develop a very close relationship with Cameron. On reflection, I did

probably spend more time alone with him than I should have. But I could see his talent and nurtured it and his sudden disappearance did upset me. I cannot deny that."

Realising that he had pushed this line of enquiry as far as he could for now, Hollister changed track. "Do you know, as his sort off mentor or advisor or whatever the head calls you, whether he was having any problems, you know…with his school work or other pupils?"

"Not that I was aware of. After Cameron went missing, the school launched its own independent enquiry to see if there was anything that we could have foreseen or picked up on, but there were no indications whatsoever that Cameron was unhappy. Cameron was a boy that everybody seemed to like. You simply couldn't help it. He worked hard academically, trained hard and generally kept himself to himself. From what I remember he didn't have many friends and the ones that he did used to call him 'Pud', a sort of friendly spin on his surname. Some though considered him a bit weird though because all he did was train and go to church. Two good qualities if you asked me, but unfortunately not to others. You see Chief Inspector…" Foxford paused briefly, let out a sigh before continuing. "…many of the students here in this school, and probably every school in the country, really don't care about their academic work. But Cameron was different. He took an interest in most subjects and excelled at a few. Mathematics, for example, was one. To some students, as long as they can divide into eighths and sixteenths, if you catch my drift, then they really wouldn't care if they couldn't even count up to ten."

"Are you telling me that this school has a drugs problem?" asked Hollister.

"I'm not saying that we have, but then again, as you are probably fully aware off, there is an underlying drug subculture amongst the youth of today. That is where Cameron stood out as different. He wasn't interested in anything like that and as a hard-pressed teacher in a system that sometimes fails the very children that we're supposed to help, when you find somebody like Cameron, then you open up every resource available to you in order to help them as best you can."

Despite having misgivings about the sheer amount of time that he spent alone with Robinson, Hollister was very impressed with the dedication and commitment of Foxford, but now it was time to deliver his sucker punch. "One final question, unfortunately it is a personal one. On my way down here I saw some graffiti on a corridor…"

The teacher interrupted the detective and offered a nervous smile, "I know what you saw Chief Inspector and you can rest assure in the knowledge that there is absolutely no truth in that accusation whatsoever. Children will be children and they can be very cruel and nasty at times."

But usually there is some truth in their allegations, thought Hollister as he thanked Foxford for his time and brought their meeting to an end. As soon as he discovered that the subject of the graffiti and Robinson's school councillor were one and the same and that he was in fact the boy's gymnastics coach, Hollister had already decided to run a background check on him at some point in the future. He was going to find a way of running his name through the police computer and see if anything unusual came up. He doubted that it would, otherwise he would not be teaching in the first place, but he wanted to try, if only to quash the suspicions that he had about him.

Dr McIlvenna came out of the gym, looking slightly agitated that he had taken so long with Foxford, but put on a polite smile. "I hope Barry was able to help you?"

When the head teacher referred to the teacher by his first name Hollister felt he had been punched in the stomach. It took all the wind out of him. He had not even considered that this could be the same person that Spencer had met at *Burgerworld* and who had taken him back to his apartment. He could now see how 'Barry' could be shortened from Barratt and the detective wondered to himself how he simply had not seen it. Maybe it was just a coincidence, like so many other aspects of this case, but then again, it was certainly not something that Hollister could overlook, which now made his reference check on the police computer into the gym teacher all the more urgent.

Once he had caught his breath again, Hollister replied to the question, "Yes. He was a great help. Thank you for taking the time to see me and I'm sorry for interrupting both of your busy schedules."

"Think nothing of it Chief Inspector. We are only too pleased to help in such a terribly sad and tragic affair and if the school or I can do in order to be of any further help, then please don't hesitate in contacting me again."

Hollister acknowledged the offer of future assistance with a nod of his head as the two men walked back through the school in silence.

After he had returned to his car, Hollister produced a small cassette recorder and having turned it to 'record', he made some notes, before stopping suddenly in a moment of excitement as he realised just what was wrong with Foxford's comments. When the name of Robinson was

raised for the first time, the teacher immediately commented about him dying and how upsetting it was. He did not mention though, at first, about him running away from home and disappearing. Surely the teacher should have said something along the lines of "*It was upsetting when he disappeared and later turned up dead.*" Then there was the fact that Foxford stated the "*we*" were devastated. Who exactly did he mean in using the plural? He also specifically said that he was the last teacher to see him alive. Why had he volunteered this information without being asked? Did he secretly know that Robinson had been seen with another adult after he vanished? If so, then who was it?

Hollister thought that he finally had a break and something to investigate.

Chapter Nine

McKenzie Hollister sat and reviewed his accumulated information on Cameron Robinson while sipping a cup of coffee in his newly acquired home. He had completed his day's work by once again returning to his marital home and collecting some more clothing and personal items. On his way back to his adopted home, Hollister had stopped off at the other two banks which Robinson had accounts and checked their balances. Each one had over five thousand pounds in, which gave the detective ready access to nearly thirty thousand pounds. Hollister was astonished and could hardly believe that he now had access to such a staggering amount. He could hardly believe his luck either. At a time when he thought that his life was falling apart around him he now had access to a well-decorated and furnished apartment and he could lay his hands on nearly an entire year's salary, in cash, and apart from himself, nobody else knew anything about it.

The detective, had at first, wrestled with his conscious as to whether he should be using both the former home and the ill-gotten gains of the dead youth. He was slowly beginning to understand what the poor boy may have had to endure in order to have accumulated such luxuries. The fact that he had saved up so much money by performing all manner of sick and depraved acts, either willing or being coerced into doing so, clearly meant that his prostitution had been well planned and had been going on for a while. It was, however, becoming very apparent to Hollister that Robinson knew exactly what he was doing and getting himself in to when he left home nearly two years ago.

Spending so much time thinking about Robinson, Hollister had recently begun to reflect on his own childhood. Despite having a relatively good upbringing in the Springburn area of Glasgow and never really having to go without anything, even when times were hard and money was tight, which on reflection it no doubt was while he was growing up. Then afterwards, as an adult and during his time at college, before leaving home and commencing his training as a police officer, Hollister had never really ever received this form of luck. So, after much deliberation, he had allowed his conscious to be governed by his own current needs and circumstances. Having decided to leave his wife, he knew that he would need somewhere to live and the secret flat of Robinson offered him an ideal opportunity. The money was an added bonus.

His own salary would permit him to pay for the apartment but, as long as it was being paid for out of one of Robinson's bank accounts, he was not that bothered about paying for it himself. With the thirty thousand pounds that the youth had saved up, it now allowed him the opportunity to investigate the lifestyle and subsequent death of the 'rent boy' with impunity, being able to offer cash payments for information, as he had with Spencer a few weeks earlier and he would not have to worry about anybody questioning it at a later date. Hollister had thought about drawing all the money out, just in case it mysteriously disappeared, and paying it into his own bank account but he ruled this out as too much of a risk. The sudden arrival of thirty thousand pounds into the bank account of a high ranking detective could at a later date, if he was ever investigated, be construed as a bribe and with Hollister never being able to reveal the source of his sudden wealth, he decided

to leave the money where it was and only sporadically draw it out when he needed it. Realising that his marriage to Kate was now well and truly over and should they divorce in the future, he would have to give her half of it as terms of a divorce and she too would want to know where it had come from. Hollister decided that leaving it in the banks and under Robinson's name was probably the safest option available to him, but even this was not without some risk.

After he had returned to the flat, Hollister took the opportunity to search it thoroughly for the first time, hoping against all hope, that the rooms might still yield some clues as Robinson's way of life, other than him being a prostitute. As expected, the search proved fruitless. The only items that did turn up were a bundle of letters, addressed to Robinson from a person called Abbie Lovatt. Hollister checked the postmark, London, and when he read a couple of them he realised that they were going to offer no new information, other than Robinson had a friend who lived in Camden Town, North London. The letters were of very little use, but Hollister decided on keeping them for possible future use.

Another mystery for the detective was created by Hollister's search of the apartment. He found no medication. Robinson had died of a drugs overdose, prescription issued drugs aimed at relieving the symptoms of depression and yet when he searched the flat, checking every cupboard and drawer, in every room, he found nothing. This only increased his doubts as to how the boy could have taken medication for depression, enough to kill him and yet not have any either in the bedsit of his flat. To Hollister, this meant that somebody else must have been involved in

the death of the youngster and his suspicion that it was not a suicide was looking more and more likely.

Once again it seemed that up until he left home, Robinson was just another normal youth that stood on the threshold of adult life, surrounded by a warm and loving family, with a lot going in his favour and the suddenly and unexpectedly he throws it all away, leaves home and becomes a prostitute. Then, from what the detective knew about him, he just went through the motions of life and had sex with men in order to survive. It appeared, in the light of what little information he had about the boy, that apart from making pornographic movies, all he did was have sex with men for money. It was a tortuous and abhorrent lifestyle for anybody, especially a young boy barely into his teens but it was the life that Robinson had seemed to embrace until that fateful day when he appeared to have enough of it and taken his own life.

From Hollister's limited knowledge of 'rent boys', and even he admitted that it was very limited, most boys that run away from home and later becoming prostitutes do so because they are escaping from some form of abuse problems at home, be they mental, physical or sexual, turning to prostitution as a means of surviving on the streets or they do so in order to pay for a spiralling drug habit, exacerbated by their lives on the streets. Robinson did not fit into either category. There was nothing that Hollister had discovered that would suggest that Robinson was running away from anything specifically bad at either his home or school. In fact, in his case, it was quite the contrary. Robinson was well loved by his family and well liked at school, with nothing at either location that seemed to be troubling the boy. It was as if he just decided one day to pack his bags and leave home. He seemed to have

planned it carefully and knew exactly what he was doing. He also appears to have entered into prostitution willingly, purely as a means to survive. Despite the fact that Hollister had serious reservations about his priest and gymnastics coach, again there was nothing to suggest that Robinson was running away from them either.

Talking to the boy's former priest had not yielded anything specific about their relationship but Hollister was very suspicious about the closeness of the cleric to the youngster. Hollister accepted that this could just be his own furtive and cynical imagination working in overdrive. However, Father Martin, if he had wanted to, certainly did have plenty of opportunities to abuse the boy and by using the power of the Church as a means of keeping the teenagers silence. Robinson was obviously drawn to the teachings of the Church and it would not have been hard for an impressionable young boy to fall under the hypnotic influence of a priest who was intent on abusing his power. If, like his mother had suggested, that Robinson was indeed considering a future life in the Catholic Church, then he would have been prepared to do almost anything that would help him and those around him and able to help him could easily exploit this. Father Martin also fitted the description given by the residents at the bedsits, but then again, so did the boy's gymnastics coach.

If he had chosen to, he too had the means to abuse the boy. They were often alone together, both in the evenings and at weekends and if he wanted to Foxford could have used the threat of withdrawing the added extra-curriculum training as a way to get Robinson into his malignant clutches, using the same threats to maintain the boy's silence. If Robinson had wanted to do well at school and excel at

gymnastics, then he might have found himself in a very vulnerable position and this may have been exploited and manipulated by the teacher in order to exploit the youth. Then there was the salacious graffiti on the wall on the school's corridor. Using some mental arithmetic and depending on how old they were, Hollister worked out that the comments certainly could have applied to Robinson. He would have been in either year nine or ten when he vanished and the detective made a note of finding out which, if only for his own curiosity.

What Hollister needed more than anything else was somebody that knew Robinson during the two year period between him leaving home and turning up dead at the bedsit's. The only person that Hollister knew off that had seen the teenager and hat gotten to know him during this timeframe was Spencer.

The mysterious and elusive 'rent boy' had been constantly in the thoughts of the detective ever since the one and only time that he had met him. Since then Hollister had searched for the boy, worried about him, drank himself into countless stupors over him, but still he had managed to avoid being found by the detective. What worried Hollister the most about the young boy were his own feelings towards him. He had become obsessed with the boy. Nobody else, not even his wife of ten years, mattered anymore to the detective. He had become infatuated with the teenager. Not only that, he had started to have sexual fantasies about him and had also begun to masturbate while imaging that he was with the boy. The once normal lifestyle of the police officer had been thrown into turmoil by both Robinson and Spencer.

Recently Hollister had, for the first time in many years, started having flashbacks to his own childhood, no doubt as a consequence of thinking

about the two lost youths and this had only succeeded in adding to the confused state of mind of the detective. Hollister had an arduous childhood and a lonely one. His father, whom Hollister had adored and looked up to because he was a police officer, had been killed in the line of duty whilst trying to foil a bank robbery and the image of his dead father, lying motionless in his coffin, haunted the dreams of the thirteen year old boy. The dreams later became nightmares as he struggled to come to terms with his father's death and it was only when he too became a police officer, in homage to his father, that he finally managed to exorcise the demons from his sleep. On the surface though he was a bright and cheerful child, but once alone he was sullen and moody and very introverted. That was until he met Ged, which short for Gerard.

At the age of fourteen, and at a time when his self-esteem was at an all-time low, a new boy entered his class and his life. The first time that they met was during a physical education class and during a game of tennis. Hollister and Ged looked directly into each other's eyes, as if they were the only ones on the tennis courts and they both detected something in common with each other and the sadness in their eyes. They immediately became friends, until then something sadly lacking in Hollister's life. Ged had been transferred from another school, nobody seemed to know why and nobody really cared why, except for Hollister. The true impact of their meeting was now being felt by Hollister three decades later.

The two boys were hardly ever apart. They sat together in classes, stood together at break times and dined together, forever in private conversation and never allowing any other pupils into their own private

world. They were forever in each other's homes after school and it was not unusual for each of them to sleep over at the others home and over a twelve month period, an inevitable and extricable bond grew between them. However, during all their conversation, Hollister never once enquired why his one true friend had been moved from his previous school. He did not regard it as any of his business and knew that Ged would, if he wanted to, tell him why in his own time and one night, after they had been friends for nearly a year, he did so.

At first the fourteen year old Ged was a little reluctant to tell his friend, but he thought that he owed it to Hollister to be honest with him and one night, during a sleep over at his house, Ged finally plucked up the courage to tell Hollister. It was the secret fear of losing Hollister as a friend that had delayed him from telling Hollister that he had been caught performing oral sex on a teacher at his former school. Once the ice had been finally been broken and his secret revealed, Ged finally got it all of his chest and relished the opportunity to finally tell somebody all about it and the way that the 'establishment' had closed ranks to protect one of their own and had ruined his life.

Ged and the teacher, he revealed that he was a science teacher but never his name, had been having a secret relationship for around six months. It had started one evening during rehearsals for the annual school play and purely by accident. Ged had been helping the teacher paint some scenery and had spilt some paint onto his trousers. In order for the paint not to stain and ruin his trousers, the teacher took him to a private area and told the boy to remove them so that he could clean them. Without any hesitation the boy innocently took off his trousers, safe in the knowledge that nobody would disturb them, but realised that

the paint had also gone through the trousers and onto his shirt. The teacher told him that he would also wash his shirt and told him to take it off. Once again, Ged did as the teacher asked and before long he was sat next to the teacher in just his underwear. Little did he know at the time just how much the sight of a near naked fourteen year old boy had sexually excited the teacher, but he soon found out.

The teacher and Ged sat and talked while his clothes dried until the adult could stand it no more and placed a hand on the boys thigh. Surprisingly, Ged did not push the hand away in disgust and the teacher massaged the thigh, going higher until he stroked the boys now erect penis, eventually pulling the briefs down. He introduced Ged to the pleasure of oral sex, later teaching him how to perform fellatio as well, before bending the boy over a desk and having full sex with him, thus starting their relationship.

They both knew the risks of their relationship, fully aware that it was a very dangerous thing that they were doing, something that the teacher explained to Ged on numerous occasions. If they were ever found out it would not be tolerated and bring shame and humiliation on both of them, wrecking the outstanding career of the teacher in the process. Maybe it was the risk of getting caught that excited them both. Ged became infatuated with the teacher and this rang alarm bells in the brain of the teacher. To him, Ged was nothing special. Just the latest of a string of boys, both older and younger, that had been prepared to do almost anything in order to gain a higher grade in the difficult subject of science.

The teacher, in a last ditch attempt to get rid of Ged invited him back to his home, where he had arranged for three of his friends to be there

and all four men then abused Ged where he was spared nothing and subjected to all manner of depraved sexual abuse. He was just something to be played with, used, hurt and then discarded when they had grown bored with him, but all the time Ged had let them do whatever that they wanted to him because, in the mind of the teenaged boy, it was his way of showing the teacher just how much he loved him.

Their relationship continued until they were 'caught' by another teacher. It was a contrived act and after both teachers had abused Ged they closed ranks on him and got Ged transferred to another school. Ged complained about his treatment at the time and reported his sexual relationship with the teacher, but his allegations were ignored. Those in authority knew all along what had been going on because it turned out that Ged was not the first boy to allege a sexual relationship with the teacher, but they valued the academic qualities of the corrupt and depraved teacher more than the wellbeing of a young schoolboy and because Ged admitted that he had willingly entered into the relationship with the teacher, he was held to blame and the school authorities transferred the boy, leaving the teacher where he was and no doubt able to continue his sordid conquests of vulnerable young boys.

On hearing of his treatment, Hollister consoled his weeping friend by putting his arms around his shoulders, which later turned out to be a catalyst for them. Somehow the two schoolboys ended up kissing, a meeting of lips that seemed to bind their friendship ever closer and over a period of weeks Hollister experimented by committing sexual acts with his far more experienced friend. Hollister allowed himself to be educated by his more accomplished friend, fully enjoying most of their

activities, but after their first time together he did not allow Ged to perform full anal sex on him, despite the fact that Ged gave himself willingly to Hollister.

After leaving school, the two boys never saw each other again, both going their own separate ways, but Hollister had never forgotten about Ged and now found himself recollecting their time together with great fondness as he realised that this was why he had become so absorbed in this particular case. Over the past month or so Ged had often come into the thoughts of the detective as he wondered what he was doing these days and whether he had out grown his homosexual tendencies, as Hollister had or, until the discovery of Robinson's body and his meeting with Spencer, he thought that he had. Hollister was thinking about one of their nights together when his brain shut itself down and he fell asleep in the chair.

It was approaching nine thirty in the evening when the detective woke up. The sun had set and the blue sky had turned dark blue, almost black, plunging the room into darkness. Hollister turned on a light, both literally and mentally. As the light filled the room, a thought filled his mind as a stark realisation came over him. He had allowed his mind to become so clouded with his quest to find Spencer and had not realised the obvious. Both he and Robinson would have known other 'rent boys' out on the streets of Manchester. One of these other corrupt delinquents may know where he could find Spencer or may even have known Robinson, which could have been more important and relevant to Hollister. Had the young Robinson ever confided in one of his peers, then he might know the answer the one question that had haunted

Hollister since the first time that he had seen Robinson, the answer to which had always eluded him. Why did Robinson leave his loving family and become a prostitute?

The detective, now feeling refreshed after having a shower and a shave, chose his clothes with great care. The last thing that he wanted to do was give the wrong impression. He did not want to give anybody the notion that he was out on a night out trying to pick somebody up or to be picked up himself by some stranger. Nor did he want to advertise the fact that he was a police officer. From previous experience he knew only too well that if anybody realised that he was a police officer, a wall of silence and suspicion would descend around him and he would not be able to gleam any information. He eventually decided on one of Robinson's blue shirts and a pair of his own denim jeans. Smart, but casual, he thought to himself and he thought that he would be able to blend into his future surroundings and yet not stand out. He knew that his clothing was only part of his charade, his general demeanour would also be scrutinised by others in his chosen bar, when he eventually got there. The last thing that he wanted was to be immediately recognised as a police officer.

Having been on many covert operations, Hollister was used to being in strange surroundings and putting on an act in order to blend in, but this particular assignment filled him with trepidation. He had never previously set foot in a gay bar and until recently found the notion of two men being together fairly repugnant. But all that had changed with the discovery of Robinson's body. Now, not only did he find himself thinking the previously unthinkable, that is him having sex with

member of his own gender, but he was frequently having fantasies about having sex with a teenage 'rent boy'. Why he was having these feelings concerned him, but only a little. He had found that during his brief meeting with Spencer that he had been completely captivated by him. Hollister had hung on to his every word, really surprised at the fact that the young boy recounted his sexual experiences with such candour. Hollister, his own latent and dormant sexual feelings stirred, wanted to hear more.

He was also worried about his cover. He knew that he was playing a very dangerous game and that he also had a lot to lose. Firstly, he was investigating the death of Robinson, despite being ordered not to by his superior officer. Hollister knew that he would find it very hard to explain away, if discovered, why he was using the dead boy's flat and spending money from his bank accounts. The police have very strict rules and procedures to prevent officers from taking advantage of victims of crime and Hollister was now breaking just about every single one of them. Driven by his own necessity, not to mention his carnal desires, he needed access to untraceable money and somewhere to rest his weary head at nights and the dead 'rent boy' had given him both.

Hollister also pondered on what his life wife was going to do once she had been discharged from hospital? Would she leave him? Would she ask him to leave? After his recent treatment of her, he would hardly blame her if she opted to end their marriage. Then there was the thought that she may seek her revenge and press charges against her husband and, in doing so, ruin his previously unblemished career. Or would she, as indicated, just forgive him and simply pretend that his assault had not happened?

If the truth was known, this was the option that Hollister hoped for. Kate, like all the wives and partners of senior police officers, knew the immense pressure that they were under, never knowing if they would be returning home at nights in these often dangerous times, when almost every villain was carrying some kind of weapon and were not afraid of using them. Every police officer needed an internal safety valve, a means of releasing the inbuilt stress and the occasional loss of control was inevitable. Not that Hollister was trying to justify to himself what he had done to his wife. Even he knew that there was no excuse for what he had done to her, but he also knew that it was the slow build-up of unanswered questions regarding this case and his heavy drinking out of frustration at not being able to answer these same questions that had driven him to it. If he ever explained all this to his wife, she would more than likely understand why it had happened and he hoped that Kate would not break ranks and prosecute him.

But what worried the detective the most though was the thought of being discovered by somebody that knew him in a gay bar within Manchester's 'Gay Village'. Having had his own sexual proclivity awakened he realised that there must be many more like him in the police force and dreaded running into somebody that would recognise him. News of this chance meeting getting out and making its way back to Heller Street police station and his peers, then having to tolerate all the abuse and ridicule was something that not even Hollister relished the thought of.

Apart from drinking, another form of letting off steam within the police force was the friendly banter about anything that was regarded as a weakness in another officer. Many a life and career had been ruined

by the 'jokes' and obscene graffiti in their locker rooms. The constant sniggering and innuendoes behind the back of their victim could break even the strongest officer and being found frequenting gay bars would prove enough ammunition to be used against them for months of abuse.

All this flashed though Hollister's mind as he sipped a glass of cold lager in the swish bar. He had spent the previous thirty minutes stood in a darkened recess on the opposite canal bank, unseen and silently watching the activity before him, trying to pluck up the courage to mingle with those that he watched. He had observed the variety of people walking up and down Canal Street, the predominantly car-free street that was the centre of Manchester's 'Gay Village' from the sanctuary of a disused building. Some were obviously homosexual, others not so. Hollister had, like many people, a preconceived idea or image of a typical gay person and had expected to see men dressed in bright flamboyant clothing, 'mincing' it up by swaying their hips whilst they walked and generally advertising their sexuality, but the detective was pleasantly surprised to see how many 'normal' looking people were frequenting the bars on Canal Street. They were all dressed conservatively, not overtly open about the sexuality and, above everything else, they were discrete.

The one thing that he did notice whilst watching the people in 'The Village' was the absence of those that he actually sought, the teenage prostitutes, or 'rent boys'. Without knowing really why, Hollister had expected the area to be swarming with them and was surprised, not to mention disappointed, by their absence. Once again, his preconceived idea of homosexual life had let him down as he slowly realised that he would not immediately meet another 'rent boy' that had known

Robinson and who would be able to tell him what he wanted, coming up with answers all his unanswered questions.

From his obscure vantage point, separated by the narrow strip of still, near glass-like water, Hollister could see virtually all the bars and clubs on Canal Street and wondered which one would be his best bet to go in and begin making his enquires? The detective suspected that he might need to go into a few bars, ask about Robinson and show his photograph before he met anybody that had known him, so one of these bars opposite was going to have to be his starting point, but which one? By using his limited knowledge of Robinson and basing his judgement on both the youth's and his own personal tastes, Hollister opted for one of the more refined looking bars, *'The Last Exit'*, probably called so because it was towards one of the ends of Canal Street, away from the throng of main activity and one of the last bars on the street. Having now decided which bar to go in, all the detective had to do now was actually build up the courage to enter it.

Eventually he crossed the canal by using a road bridge and then walked up the full length of Canal Street, carefully taking in everything around him and then back down the street once more before he had built up enough courage and confidence to enter *'The Last Exit'* bar.

Once inside the glass-fronted façade, Hollister was a little surprised by the bars décor. You walked on bare wooden floorboards, highly polished and echoing your footsteps. The white walls were illuminated by blue lights, casting a warm hue onto the ceiling, which then reflected down onto the floor. To Hollister's right were, what he could only describe as church-like wooden pews with long tables between them, their high backs offering those seated in them a certain amount of

privacy. The bar area was brightly lit and had been decorated with an art deco theme and it was here that the detective found his resting place, sitting on a high stool and ordering a drink of lager as he listened to the non-distinct throbbing of dance music.

He had been sat there for about ten minutes, taking in the growing atmosphere of the bar and all those around him and had virtually finished his first drink in two gulps, partly out of thirst and in an attempt to calm his nerves. His second drink he now sipped more slowly and reflected on him being there. Nobody spoke to him, nobody bothered him and, maybe, nobody even noticed him. When he first passed the three burly doormen, each dressed in identical thigh length black coats, and entered the bar, Hollister felt the dozen or so people inside look over to him. He sensed many pairs of eyes staring at him, an obvious first timer in *'The Last Exit'*, but as he confidently strode up to the bar, they each went back to their conversations and, unless he suddenly grew another head, nobody really cared that he was in *their* bar, all of which helped to steady the nerves of Hollister as he settled down on the stool and ordered his drink.

The detective studied closely the single barman on duty. He was in his mid-twenties, short dark hair and stood about six feet tall. He had a finely trimmed beard that framed his face with a stocky and muscled build, his lower arms decorated with colourful tattoos and he was obviously a fit man that worked out a gym. Dressed in black trousers and a purple shirt, Hollister thought that the barman looked out of place serving drinks. He thought that he would have been more relaxed if he was this side of the bar, being waited on as he enjoyed a few drinks, rather than serving the patrons of *'The Last Exit'*.

Having now had a drink to quell his nerves, Hollister now felt sufficiently relaxed to start asking some questions, "Excuse me," began the detective when the barman had an idle moment, "Can I have a quick word? It'll only take a minute."

The barmen came over to Hollister, all smiles but with a worried look on his face. "Is there something wrong?" he asked.

Hollister returned the smile, "No, there's nothing wrong." A look of relief came over the bartender's face, but as Hollister discretely showed him his warrant card, he looked apprehensive again. "I'm making a few enquiries about somebody and I was wondering if you could help me?"

"I'll see what I can do," was the rather nervous reply.

After looking at the name badge of the barman, "I see your name is Gregory…"

"Oh, please call me Greg," interrupted the bartender.

"Well Greg," Hollister smiled again. "A few weeks ago we found a body, an apparent suicide, but some of us are not that certain and so we're looking into the possibility that it wasn't. From all accounts he was a 'rent boy'…"

"We don't allow their sort in here," protested Greg.

"I wasn't trying to imply that you did," responded the detective. "On the contrary, I can see that this is a decent place."

"You're not gay, are you?" asked the barman.

Somewhat surprised by the question, Hollister shook his head. "No, I'm married."

Greg was beginning to feel a little more relaxed now that he realised Hollister was not trying to chat him up. He offered the detective a warm and genuine smile. "I'll help you any way that I can, officer."

"Mac," interjected Hollister, "Please call me Mac, that's what everybody else calls me. I've got to be honest with you but I'm not here in any official capacity. I'm just doing some personal research. If I showed you a picture of this person, do you think you might recognise him?"

"Maybe," replied Greg, "But then again, I do see a lot of people."

"I understand that." Hollister produced a small photograph of Robinson and presented it to the barman. "Please try though. It's important to us that we try and find out as much as possible about the person."

Greg recognised the face of Robinson immediately. "Yeah, I know him. His name is Martin." The beaming smile on his face quickly disappeared. "I didn't know he was dead though?"

When Hollister heard Robinson called by his alternative name he felt his heart miss a beat and momentarily gasped for breath as he finally got a break. He could not believe that he had struck this lucky at the first bar that he went to. He also noted the smiling expression on Greg's face as he recognised Robinson. "How well did you know him?"

"I didn't actually know him," replied Greg, "But I had seen him about. Nobody could ever forget such a darling like him. He's...was...gorgeous. I knew he was on 'the game'. It was obvious, but I've got a partner and wasn't interested in him. If I was single though, who knows?"

Ignoring the smiling face of the barman, "Where did you usually see him?"

"Mostly on the streets, usually touting for business and usually with the other's hanging around the coach station. I've seen him in a couple

of pubs around there as well. Sometimes I saw him in a couple of clubs, mostly at weekends though. He could usually be found in a club call 'Adonis'. Do you know it?"

"I've heard of it," lied Hollister. "Was he normally on his own or was he usually with somebody?"

"He was never alone. Somebody that gorgeous would never be alone for long out there, trust me. There was always somebody after him. When he went to 'Adonis' he was usually with the owner, a guy called Malka. Because of his club and that he's got loads of money, he always has young lads hanging around him. They're usually blond too. He's got a thing for young blond boys. I'd say that if you wanted to know about any young lad in 'The Village', then he's your man. If he doesn't know them, then nobody does."

"Thanks Greg, you've been a huge help. Before I go and see him, is there anything that you can tell me about him that could help me out, you know, give me an edge?"

Greg thought for a moment, "You can use the fact that he lets young boys into 'Adonis'. The place is usually full of them. All out on the pull and some, I reckon, are barely out of school. It has been rumoured that some of them haven't even left school yet."

"You don't seem to like him?" asked Hollister.

"He's never done me any harm, but his type, the one's that prey on young boys, 'chickens' we call them, give us more respectable gay men a bad name. We all get grouped together and pigeonholed as perverts. Most of us older guys don't go for the young ones. They're usually too much trouble and hard work. If you do fall for one of them, it'll usually mean trouble when you find out their real age or you'll end up in

trouble because of their age. Either way, you can't win and so it's best just to stay away from them in the first place."

By this time Hollister had finished his drink. "You know what Greg, you're all right. Let's have another drink. This time though, have one yourself, I insist."

The young barman looked a little embarrassed by the detectives compliment. "I'm not allowed any alcohol, but I'll have a coke."

Greg fixed each of them a drink and between serving customers he chatted to Hollister. "To be honest with you Greg, I've never been in a gay bar before. When I first walked in, I didn't know what to expect, but this place is okay. I like it here. Do you know that I'd walked up Canal Street twice before I plucked up the courage to come in and..." he paused briefly, hesitating on his words. He was about to tell Greg that he liked him and was glad that they had met, but decided against it. "...I only wish that I was coming here and meeting you under different and happier circumstances."

There was also something that Greg found reassuring about Hollister and it appeared that he had subconsciously tapped into the confused state of mind of the detective. "You can always come back again. Don't worry, I'll look after you," he said with a smile and a wink.

The two men laughed as Hollister responded to the offer, "I think that I can look after myself."

"Don't you believe it. There are some more extreme members of our community that would get really turned on by a real policeman, especially a detective."

Hollister smiled back at Greg as he went off to serve some drinks. By now, Greg had been joined behind the bar by two women and another

man, all identically dressed and Hollister spun around on his stool to face the bar and reflected on what he had been told. The bar was now beginning to fill with a mixture of men and women and Hollister tried to play to himself, trying to figure out who were with friends and who were with lovers. Some were quite blatantly obvious, others not so. Hollister also found that he was totally at ease and very relaxed in the bar, a gay bar and surrounded by homosexuals. He did not feel out of place, in fact he felt the very opposite. He felt like he belonged there and, as he stood up after finishing off the last of his beer, he motioned to Greg to come over to him. When he had again joined the detective, Hollister gave him a smile and a wink, pressed twenty pounds and his calling card into the hesitant hand of the barman, both as a way of saying thank you and also so that he would remember him.

Two mean looking, well-built and burly men, both wearing identical long black overcoats and ear-pieces stood in the brightly lit doorway of the club. It had not been hard for Hollister to find the *'Adonis'* nightclub. In fact the detective had remembered where it was from when he had driven around looking for Spencer and as he approached the steps, one of the doormen barred his path. "This is a member's only club pal."

"Detective Chief Inspector Hollister," he showed the doorman his warrant card, which was scrutinised closely, "I'd like to see Malka."

Not impressed by the warrant card, "What for?" asked the doorman.

"That's for me to know and you to find out. Is he in tonight?" asked Hollister, knowing that he probably was judging by the two-door Bentley car parked just outside the club.

"Wait here." The doorman's attitude was very abrupt. He had been offended by Hollister's rebuke and disappeared inside the doorway to make a telephone call, taking great pleasure in leaving the detective out in the cold. He remained silent after returning to his colleague and Hollister. The two security men had become immovable objects, whilst Hollister paced up and down on the pavement, looking at the various posters advertising future events at the club.

After a few minutes of the tense stand-off, a man came to the door from inside the club and he was flanked by another two gruff looking security guards and despite being a police officer, or because of the fact, Hollister felt a little intimidated. "Can I help you, Chief Inspector?"

Hollister quickly studied the suntanned man before him. He was about six feet tall and around forty years old, average build and had short cropped greying hair with a matching beard. A perfect description, thought Hollister. The man wore an obviously expensive black suit, its cut and style, together with its fit giving away its value, and an open-necked white silk shirt. "Is there somewhere that we speak in private?" asked Hollister.

"Is it official police business?" replied the nightclub's owner.

"No," responded Hollister, "but it could be."

For a slit second, the two men stared deeply into each other's eyes, each trying to psyche out the other. The clubs owner cracked first, "Okay, will you follow me."

The detective did as requested and followed the suited man into the club, with the two minders following them at a close distance. Being fairly early there were only around sixty to seventy people in the club,

mostly men in their mid-twenties and about half of these were dancing to the pulsating beat of dance music. It had been a while since Hollister had been inside a nightclub and he had trouble getting used to the noise and the multi-coloured flashing lights, especially the white strobe lighting, which reflected back into the room from off the mirrored walls.

The group of four men had no difficulty in making their way to the owner's office, which must have been soundproofed because no sooner had the door been shut behind them the pounding bass-line of the music became a dull thudding in the background. Hollister could not help but find himself impressed at the décor of the office, its pale grey walls offering an ideal contrast to oak furniture. The huge 'L' shaped desk stood on the cherry veneered wooden floor, with a black leather chair behind the desk, which the man sat in. Hollister sat in a one of two smaller chairs opposite the desk.

The opening of their conversation was fraught with tension, "What can I do for you Inspector?"

"First of all, Mr…"

"Charnel, Malka Charnel," he replied after Hollister hesitation.

"First of all, Mr Charnel, I'd like to tell you that you don't have to speak to me. I'm not here in any official capacity and anything that we discuss, and I give you my word on this, that it is for our ears only and completely off the record. Anything that you tell me will be treated in the strictest confidence."

Charnel was now intrigued by the detectives visit, but remained very cautious. "Very well Inspector, I'll talk to you but in light of what you've just said but I reserve the right to refuse any questions that I

don't like or, in case you go back on your word that might be used later to incriminate me."

Hollister nodded his head in response, "That's fair enough. I've been told by somebody, whom, I'm not at liberty to tell you, that you might be able to help me with some enquiries regarding this youth."

Hollister placed the photograph of Robinson on the desk before the nightclub owner. He looked at it briefly and shook his head. "Sorry, but I've never seen him before."

"Not only did your facial expression give you away, but somebody has positively linked you and this youth together...in this club. So, let's stop playing games and start being honest."

Not knowing what Hollister knew unsettled Charnel and he replied cautiously, "As you can probably imagine Inspector, I see a lot of young men in here. Surely you don't expect me to remember all of them?"

"But this young man is very unusual. He is very charismatic and everybody else that ever met him has always remembered him. Not only is he extremely good looking, with a fine physique, which I've been told is the kind of young men that you like, not that I am judging you, each to their own. But this particular young man is only sixteen years old and, if he's been in here, he would be two years too young to be in here. He also happens to be a 'rent boy'. Oh and something else, he is dead. Now, look at the picture again and let's try again."

Hearing Hollister say that Robinson was dead clearly unsettled Charnel and he again looked at the picture before him, biding time as he thought fast before he replied to Hollister, his brain in a state of shock. "Yeah, I think I do remember him."

"Funny that. But I thought you might suddenly remember him." Hollister now had the edge over the nightclub owner.

Charnel was not impressed by his sarcasm, "What do you really want, Chief Inspector?" he know addressed Hollister by his correct rank, realising the seriousness and gravity of the situation. "I've got two clubs to run. I'm a very busy man."

"So am I," responded the detective, "and I'm not used to be being jerked around. How well did you know him?"

The nightclub owner thought for a moment, weighed up his options and decided that honesty was probably going to be his best policy. He also knew that if Hollister was acting in any official capacity and had anything on him, then this conversation would be in taking place in a police interview room and not in the comfort of his own office. "I have seen him in here. Not recently though, the last time was around a year ago. I knew he was only young, but I genuinely had no idea he was that young. There was no way that he would've got in here if I knew he was only fifteen. I think his name was Martin. He was the lasted plaything of somebody that I know and Barry brought him in here a couple of times but I made sure that Barry knew that he wasn't welcome in here with him, you know, because of his age."

"Very commendable," replied Hollister, still with a sarcastic edge in his voice. "This Barry, does he have a surname?"

"Fox something I think."

"Could it be 'Foxford' and does he live over in the new apartments over in Salford?"

It was the turn of Charnel to be shocked, "How do you know that?"

"Let's just say a little bird told me. After all, I am a detective. At least you now know that I'm not interested in your club or anything that you might be doing here or whoever comes in here, with the exception of this Barry and this boy. I want you to tell me everything that you know about this Barry Foxford and I do mean everything. After that, you're going to help set up a meeting with him. If you refuse or hold anything back, then I'll give an anonymous tip to Serious Crimes and have them pay you a visit for letting under-aged boys into your club possibly for the purpose of prostitution. And believe me, I will."

"I don't doubt for one minute that you would," replied Charnel.

The two men spent the next fifteen minutes talking, with Charnel telling everything that he knew about the teacher, before finally phoning him up and setting up a meeting between Foxford and Hollister for the following night.

Chapter Ten

As Hollister sat and waited for his 'guests' to arrive he glanced around at his current surroundings as he listened to the modern jazz music that filled the air and created a warm cosy ambiance. The restaurant/bar was only a small place, situated in the cellar of the building that also housed '*The Last Exit*' bar. The restaurant's decor was clean and modern, brightly lit, with small square tables, each of the holding a maximum of four people which added to its intimacy and were on the bare wooden floorboards. What was it about the gay community and wooden floors, mused the detective as he waited? Hollister had always been very choosy about restaurants, highly critical of the food, service and atmosphere whenever he dined out but so far he was very impressed with this recommended venue.

Out of boredom and as the minutes ticked by, Hollister scrutinised his fellow diners. There was a couple of men sat a table, obviously a couple and even though they were trying to be discreet, their body language gave them away to the experienced detective. The majority of the patrons at this early hour were a group of about a dozen business types that appeared to be out celebrating somebody's birthday and getting ever more raucous as they drank more.

Malka Charnel, the owner of the *'Adonis'* nightclub was late. McKenzie Hollister was a man that never liked being kept waiting but on this occasion it gave him the opportunity to go over in his head, once again, the questions that he planned to ask the school teacher, Barratt Foxford. The police officer had already waited fifteen minutes

past their agreed meeting time and was just about to leave when he saw Charnel descending the stairs. Dressed in his usual dark suit and white shirt, followed by a burly bodyguard, which Hollister thought might be over-the-top, the bar owner searched out the detective and crossed the floor to his table.

"You're late," snapped Hollister when Charnel was close enough to hear him.

"And you're very lucky that I'm even here," replied Charnel. There was an underlying current of hostility between the two men, neither of them showing the other any form of friendship. Charnel sat down with Hollister, while his minder took his place at the bar, out of earshot. "It took a great deal of persuasion to get Barry to agree to meet you. I'll be honest with you, he didn't want to come. But I told him that it would be in his interest to meet you somewhere like this rather than you go back to his school and talk to him there, which is what you'd probably have done if he refused to come here."

"It was something that I was prepared to do if he didn't come tonight. It wasn't something that I would've particularly enjoyed doing or that I wanted to do, but I would've done it if he doesn't show tonight," replied the detective, his frosty mood mellowing, but only slightly.

"You must understand that Barry has a great deal to lose, you know from his naming as being gay. Not everybody would be that tolerant of a teacher, especially a PE teacher in a Catholic school, who has a penchant for young boys. How does he know, that if he helps you, that you'll keep your word and not go public or even arrest him?"

"He doesn't. Look, I'm not really interested in what he does or who he does it to. I can't say that I approve or that I'm not a little concerned

about it, especially for the boys at his school, but I'm only interested in one boy and one boy alone. It would serve me no purpose, at the moment at least, other than upsetting this boy's family if I went public, as you so eloquently put it. I can't rule out his arrest in the future if it turns out that he had something to do with this lad's death. He should know this and the fact that if he did have something to hide, that we would catch up with him eventually. However, having already spoken to him, I personally don't think that he had anything to do with this young lad's death and so, he's got nothing to hide."

"So he has your word that you won't use anything against him?" asked Charnel, still wanting confirmation.

Hollister nodded his head. How could he prosecute the teacher for any wrong doings with Robinson when he was wearing the dead boy's clothes and paying for drinks out of money withdrawn from the 'rent boy's' bank accounts, thought Hollister? Even his moral indignation at the prospect of a man having a sexual relationship with a boy, especially a teacher with one of his pupils, was waning. No, he thought to himself, he would not be prosecuting the teacher. In all honesty he wasn't that bothered about him. All he wanted was information about Robinson, possibly some clues as to why Robinson left home and become a prostitute. He also wondered whether Foxford knew where he could find the elusive Spencer.

Charnel nodded his head, this time in the direction of his minder, who then went back up the stairs and seconds later came back down with the Barratt Foxford. The schoolteacher looked haggard and drawn, like he had been awake all night, which he probably had been and he appeared to be a man with the world's problems on his shoulders and nobody to

lessen the load that he carried. He sat at the table, next to Charnel, his fingers constantly twitching, nervously fiddling with the cutlery, a napkin, anything. From his experience Hollister saw this as a sign of nerves, somebody with something to hide.

The suited Charnel whispered something into Foxford's ear, placed a comforting hand on his shoulder, offering some moral support and then left them alone. Hollister ordered some drinks, which were brought over by waiter. When he was far enough away, Hollister began questioning the man.

"I've given my word that anything you disclose to me will remain between just us," the stony faced detective began with enough ice in his voice to freeze the canal outside, "I can't say that I agree with what you do, but I won't do anything about it again I give you my word on this. You will, one day, eventually face your day of reckoning, but I won't be part of it. What I want, and all that I want, is to get to the truth behind the life and subsequent death of Cameron Robinson. Unlike when I spoke to you at the school, this time I want the truth. Piss me about and you'll regret it and believe me, you'll regret it. Do I make myself clear?"

Foxford nodded his head slowly, eventually bowing his head in shame. He did fully understand the gravity of the situation and after talking, at length the previous evening, to Charnel and later doing a great deal of soul searching, he had decided to tell the detective everything that he wanted to know. The schoolteacher knew that if Hollister had intended making a criminal case against him, then this conversation would be taking place in a police station, under caution, and not in a restaurant. What did fascinate Foxford though was why he

was going to such measures to unravel the lifestyle of the dead youth outside of normal policing and investigation? He was, after all, a boy that had turned his back on his life, his family and friends and just disappeared, with nobody hearing from him and forgetting about him until he turned up dead. Foxford was also intrigued as to how much the detective really knew about Robinson.

However, what the teacher did not know was that Hollister did not understand himself why he had become so obsessed by Robinson? Hollister continued his verbal assault on the now intimidated and cowering teacher. "I know that you're gay. I'm not bothered about that. I also know that you like young boys. Again, although I'm alarmed, that doesn't bother me. I'm one of the few people that know that Cameron was also gay. It would not take a genius to come up with a sexual link between the two of you. Now, I recall you saying when we first met, that the two of you developed a close relationship. Just how close was this relationship?"

Gulping down the lager before him, Foxford spoke for the first time, his voice trembling with nerves. "Why don't you just come out and say what you're really thinking and want to ask?"

"Okay, I will. Were you having a relationship, a sexual relation, with Cameron Robinson?"

The following seconds of silence seemed like an eternity, eventually broken by the wavy voice of Foxford. "Yes, I was. But it's not as bad as it sounds."

"I consider it pretty bad when a teacher abuses his position of trust and sexually abuses a child in his care," retorted Hollister, trying to hide his moral indignation of the teacher trying to justify his actions.

"Without wishing to speak ill of the dead or insult his memory, but believe me, Cameron wasn't the naïve and innocent boy that you're painting him out to be. He knew full well what he was doing and the possible implications. But I must stress that I had nothing whatsoever to do with his death. After...you know...he left home and vanished I never saw or heard from him again. You've got to believe me on this. I loved him and I would never have hurt him. I don't mean that I lusted over him, I really did love him."

"I've never thought or said that you did have anything to do with his death. He died alone. Officially, as far as the police are concerned," but not me, thought Hollister, "nobody is being sought regarding his death. I only want to know about him. Now, how did this sexual relationship between the two of you start?"

Another brief and nervous silence followed the question as the teacher wondered whether or not he should answer the question? While he thought, choosing his words carefully, he continued to fiddle with anything at hand and after taking another gulp of the cold beer, "It was one afternoon after school had finished and Cameron had had a solo gymnastics session. It was mid-June, close to the school breaking up for its summer break and Cameron was worried about letting his training lapse during the holidays. I remember that it was really hot in the gym and he had worked up quite a sweat and no sooner were we back in the changing room, he stripped off completely, you know, to cool down.

"He didn't even have any underwear on. He just sat there, completely naked, talking to me without a care in the world that he was naked. He leant back and stretched out and I could see his entire body. I mean I

could see *everything*. From all his gymnastics training he had a terrific body on him. He knew of my nickname, but he certainly wasn't bothered about being naked before me. This was the first time that I had ever seen him completely naked. He just sat there and lightly stroked his body and fanned himself, you know, trying to cool himself down. He knew full well that I was admiring his body, after all Cameron was incredibly good looking and had a superb body on him. Any gay man would've given his right arm to be in my position at that precise moment in time. Cameron kept asking me whether he could do some training during the school holidays and I said that I'd see what I could arrange. He then stood up, stretched again right in front of me and went to the showers. I stood there and watched him walk away, desperately trying to hide my erection.

"I know that I shouldn't have but I secretly spied on him as he stood under the showers. Then I moved to where he would be able to see me. When he saw me he didn't stop showering or tell me to go away, he just smile at me, gave me a mischievous wink and a smile and blew me a kiss. He then turned to face me and slowed his movements down. What had started off as just a shower now took on a certain amount of slow seductive sensuality. It was almost as if he was almost as if he was putting on a show for me, which I now realise that he was. You might find this hard to believe but he was actually trying to seduce me. You also might find this hard to believe but knowing that if anything happened between us was wrong I tried desperately to resist him but my urges and desire for him got the better off me. I succumbed to temptation. I made sure that the changing room door was locked and returned to the showers and stripped off and joined him in the shower.

"I couldn't help myself. I don't know why I did it but I just did it. I've lived with the guilt of doing it every day since, that's the truth. Cameron now knew that the rumours about me were true and that I was gay, but it didn't bother him. As he bathed me, he could also tell just how aroused I was by him and his actions in the shower and that I wanted him. No, that's not true, I needed him. I needed to have him at that precise moment in time more than I've ever desired anybody else in my entire life.

"From the moment that I first spied on him and began secretly watching him in the shower and until I joined him in the shower, I knew that what I was doing was wrong, but I just couldn't help myself. It was like he had cast a spell over me, hypnotised me. He had used his looks, his body and his considerable charm and, without saying a word to me, had seduced me. Honestly, I couldn't help myself. Nobody could have resisted him at that precise moment in time. I was, by now, hard and this seemed to encourage him, you know, egg him on and he started to toss me off. No sooner were we out of the shower then he immediately sank to his knees and started to suck me off. The way that he did it, as if it was the most natural thing in the world for him to do, clearly showed me that this certainly wasn't the first time that he had done anything like this before. When it was all over I was filled with guilt. I still am. I've regretted every minute of it but Cameron knew exactly what he was doing. Believe me, he literally seduced me. Clearly it wasn't his first time and even though I felt guilty about what I'd just done with him, this actually made me feel a little better."

"How old was Cameron when this happened?" asked Hollister.

Foxford hesitated before he answered the detective, this time out of embarrassment. "He was in his second year at St. Anthony's, year eight, which means he was between twelve and thirteen." A brief pause followed as the teacher wondered whether he should actually reveal the boys age. "It was just after Cameron's thirteenth birthday. I know it was wrong and I wish that I could turn back the clock, but I couldn't help myself. He was that beautiful."

Hollister shook his head in disbelief but he also realised that what Foxford had just revealed to him must have been very difficult for him but what worried the detective was that while the teacher was recounting his sexual experience with Robinson he had felt his own penis harden. He too had become aroused by the story. "Did Cameron ever tell you who he'd been with, you know, had sex with before you?"

"Not at first, but he did eventually. You've got to understand that a man/boy relationship is still a great taboo and one based on mutual trust, you don't rush into things. Cameron was definitely not a virgin. He'd had sex before me and I mean full gay sex. I could tell this by the way that he acted in the shower and by what he did afterwards and just by the way that he did things. I can honestly say that I was corrupted by him and not the other way around." Foxford paused briefly, relieved that he was finally able to talk to somebody about his secret nightmares, a chance to clear his conscious and be able to sleep again. "I grew to love him. I'll be honest and admit that at first I lusted over him. He was every gay man's dream, drop dead gorgeous, with a fantastic body and willing to do anything, but the more that I saw him, the more that I wanted him. We began having sex almost daily, after every training session. Even while he was training, I could barely keep

my hands off him, he had such a fantastic body and I couldn't help but keep touching him up. I became obsessed by him. He was all that I ever thought about, morning, noon and night. I couldn't get him out of my mind. When I was with him, I never wanted to leave him or for the two of us ever to be apart but I had to compete with his church and his fucking priest. Whenever he wasn't training, he was at the church. I simply couldn't get him away from the place and I must admit that I got jealous."

"Are you telling me that Cameron was also having a sexual relationship with his priest?" asked Hollister, almost willing the answer to be the one that he wanted.

Foxford nodded his head. "I was so obsessed by him and at first I thought he might be seeing another boy in the school and so, one evening after school, I secretly followed him home. I was very discrete about it. Cameron had no idea that I did it. Parking my car close enough to his house to observe him, but far enough away so that he didn't see me, I watched him go into his house and then up to his bedroom and get changed through his bedroom window. He never closed his curtains and got undressed with the light on and anybody walking past could've seen him. At the time I thought he was doing this to show off his beautiful body. Any way, he came out after a bit and went to his church. After what I later found out was choir practice I watched Cameron and the priest go back to the priest's home. I saw the bedroom light go on and the priest close the curtains. I knew only too well what was happening. I couldn't believe what I was seeing and I was filled with a jealous rage. I could have handled it if he was seeing another boy but not his priest. A priest, a man of the church, a pillar of

society was having sex with my Cameron. You've no idea how much this fucked my head up. I mean him, a priest."

Hollister could hardly believe his ears. Not only were his suspicions about Father Martin being proved correct but Foxford was voicing an unbelievable perverse hypocrisy. He too was a man of trust, if not more so that the priest, but it was all right for him to have sex with a young boy, barely a teenager, but not another man. The detective was not that naïve, he knew that there was a probability that the teacher would tell him things during their conversation that he would find unpalatable, but he found that he was not prepared to hear the truth. He had this ideal image in his mind of the young boy, corrupted into degrading sex with men who should have known better but had not expected to be told that Robinson was in fact the instigator of his own abuse. "Did you ever speak to Cameron about his relationship with father Martin?"

"Eventually yes but I didn't say anything at first. I loved him so much that I just shared him with his priest in bitter silence but each day the jealousy and the anger was building up inside me. The longer that I left it, the more time that passed, the more jealous I became. Then one day, a couple of weeks later and about a month before he vanished, we had an almighty row and I told him that I'd seen him go into his priest's bedroom. He went mad at me. He was really upset that I'd followed him home and that I was checking up on him. I tried to explain to him that I only did it because I was in love with him, but he wasn't interested in hearing my explanations. He was never the same after that argument. He stopped his gymnastics training and tried to avoid me as much as possible. I tried to talk to him but that row killed off our

relationship. We never the same again and we never had sex again after that night."

"How long were you in a relationship with Cameron?" It was only when Hollister had asked the question that he heard his own words in his own ears and realised that his choice of words had actually normalised the sexual relationship between the teacher and one of his pupils. He had used the word 'relationship' as he would have with any other individual being interviewed and this implied that he found the prospect of a man/boy sexual relationship normal.

"A little under a year" was the near whispered and embarrassed reply from Foxford but he soon reverted back to his natural demeanour as he tried to justify his relationship with the schoolboy. "But like I said earlier, I wasn't his first lover. Cameron was a very resourceful lad. If he wanted something, then he would get it. He used anything and everything that he had in order to get something that he wanted. He'd obviously heard the rumours about me and seen the graffiti about me. The stuff you saw wasn't the first comments made about me and he knew that I liked boys. He used my weakness and desire for young boys in order to get what he wanted. He even told me so. He wanted extra training in gymnastics in order to develop and build up a great body and he did this in order to make himself more attractive to the likes of me. He did it, you know, have sex with men to fulfil whatever he wanted. Cameron once told me that he wanted to be either a model or a TV personality and he was prepared to do anything to achieve this dream. As I've said, Cameron was a very clever and resourceful boy. Believe me I know what I did with him was wrong and I now regret every single minute of it. I've had so many sleepless nights you know

after he left home and since his death, but believe me, it wasn't me that took advantage of him, it was Cameron that used and manipulated me."

Hollister still had not got over the shock of Foxford's previous revelation. "I still can't believe that you were able to have a twelve month...relationship, for the lack of a better word, with a thirteen year old pupil at you school and nobody got suspicious? Somebody must've known that something was going on between you two?"

"We were always very careful about being seen together. Apart from when he was training in gymnastics, we were never alone together in public. Neither of us spoke about the other to anybody else. When I wasn't with him, I just hoped that I'd just get a quick glimpse of him, you know, walking around the school. Just seeing him, excited me and I longed to be with him and hold him and kiss him. I now realised that I was obsessed with him. It was, to me, something very special, a secret just between the two of us, our secret. Then the fucking priest came along and ruined everything."

Without revealing so to the teacher Hollister knew exactly what he meant. The detective had become obsessed with Robinson from the moment that he had first seen his naked body on the bed at the bedsit. "Did you see Cameron in the days before he vanished?"

"In what context?" replied the teacher, now feeling more relaxed and at ease talking to Hollister. He had stopping nervously fiddling about with anything close to hand and sipped his second pint of lager, as opposed to taking gulps, as he had with his first glass.

"Did you teach him? Did you talk to him? You know anything like that?"

Foxford shook his head. "No. Around about two weeks before he disappeared, he became very sullen and moody. At first I thought it was just part of his growing up, you know, part of his puberty. He had stopped coming to gymnastics training and when I asked him why, he just shrugged his shoulders and mooched off. I kept an eye on him over the next couple of days, from a distance mind you, and he seemed to be worried about something. He wasn't the Cameron Robinson that I knew and had so recently loved. I wanted to be there for him, to help him, but I couldn't. I knew that there was something wrong with him, but he no longer trusted me enough to confide in me. I've lived with that guilt for over two years now and especially since the school was informed that he was dead. If only I'd put his welfare before my desires, then he might still be at home and alive to this day. That is my personal nightmare. I have to live with this until the day that I die."

Hollister shook his head, "By this time I doubt it would've made any difference. From what I've found out, it seems that he'd already decided to leave home by this time. I honestly don't think that anything that you might have said would've made any difference. I think that he'd been making plans to leave home by this time. He'd planned it and prepared for it. Perhaps this sudden moodiness was his secret sorrow at the thought of leaving his parents."

"But I still have nightmare about it. I still have the guilt."

"And so you should," rebuked Hollister. "What you did was wrong and you know it. If I was you, I'd worry more about your secret feelings and sexual urges towards young boys. It's not natural for a teacher to lust over young boys and if the Education Department ever found out about you, you'll be finished as a teacher."

A look of shame came over the face of the schoolteacher, "Don't you think that I know that? Don't you think that I've tried everything in my power to get rid of these urges? Believe me, I have. It's a cross that I have to carry. I've learnt my lesson though. I've never touched another boy at the school since Cameron."

Secretly Hollister could relate to what Foxford was telling him. Maybe that was why he was not as outraged by what he had just been told and arrested the teacher. He too was having the same thoughts about Robinson and Spencer. Without realising it at the time, reflecting on that day with the benefit of hindsight, Hollister had found himself aroused by the sight of the naked Robinson and marvelled at his strong athletic body and his good looks and for the past few weeks he had not been able to get both him and Spencer out of his mind. He was beginning to have the same feelings and go through the same emotions that Foxford must have had.

The schoolteacher had picked up on this himself. The longer that he spoke to the detective, the more comfortable he felt and he had noticed that Hollister was hanging onto his every word. The teacher could tell that before him was a man that seemed to be enjoying this conversation. It had ceased being an interview, but more like a talk about how to pick up and develop a relationship with a young boy. Foxford could almost sense that the only thing that the detective was actually questioning was his own sexuality, a stage that he himself had reached on several occasions.

He would have been correct. Hollister was indeed now having doubts about his own sexuality and the more that the teacher told him about his way of life, the more that he wanted to hear. He wanted to listen to

every graphic detail about Foxford's relationship with Cameron Robinson, becoming sexually aroused as the schoolteacher recounted their intimate moments, secretly wishing it had been him. "Shortly after Cameron's death and funeral I was contacted by another young lad, a self-confessed 'rent boy'," continued Hollister, deciding that the time was right to go all the way. "He spoke to me about something else, but part of this conversation related around an incident that he had with a man that fits your description. Do you sometimes use 'rent boys'?"

The teachers face suddenly became ashen and he looked a little shocked, but he knew that the detective would have known the answer to the question before he even asked it and so, despite it being an embarrassing admission, he decided to be honest. "I have done at times."

"The one that I'm referring to told me that his name was Spencer and he alleges that you picked him up outside *'Burgerworld'* on Market Street. Do you remember him?"

Foxford nodded his head slowly, "Yeah, sure I do. A runaway, he'd been sleeping rough and I offered him a bath and a bed."

For a price, thought Hollister, but he decided to keep this to himself and not reveal to Foxford his moral indignation at his actions. "Once again, I'm not interested in anything that you and he did but he told me something about Cameron that is a central part of my enquiries and I need to clarify a few points. Have you any idea where I can find him so that I can talk to him again?"

This was only partly the truth. Hollister did want the boy to shed some more light on Robinson and what he did but really the detective

wanted to see him again. He knew that he had been secretly lusting over Spencer since their first meeting.

Once again the teacher seemed genuinely shocked, both by the question and the fact that the two boys knew each other. "Are you telling me that Cameron was on 'the game'?"

"I'm not at liberty to answer that," replied Hollister as he ordered some more drinks with a wave of his hand.

Foxford saw through the smokescreen, "He was, wasn't he? That's why there is a police interest in him and why I'm being interviewed here, in a gay bar and off the record and not in a police station?"

A third pair of drinks was brought over and both men remained silent whilst in the hearing range of the waiter. During this brief interlude Hollister thought carefully about his response to the teacher's question. Once they were alone again he answered the question, "We've got grounds to consider it as a possibility. But that must never be repeated, ever. Do I make myself perfectly clear on that? If I find out you've said anything to anybody about this, I'll jump on you like a ton of brinks."

Foxford was taken aback by the sudden sternness in Hollister's voice. He knew that he would never do or say anything that would tarnish the name and reputation of the boy that he once loved, despite the fact that he now had what seemed like a million questions swimming around in his brain. "Yes, perfectly clear. I give you my word that I'll never repeat it."

"Good, now what about this Spencer?"

Nightfall had descended when Hollister and Foxford eventually left the restaurant by climbing the stairs and exiting through the heavy oak

door and back out onto Canal Street. The sudden blast of fresh came as a welcoming feeling to the two men as they made their way along the street. Despite it being autumn, it was still fairly mild, the once blue sky had been replaced by streaks of silver and crimson as darkness slowly descended on the city and all along Canal Street the masses flocking to 'The Village' sat out at tables or stood around sipping their drinks from plastic glasses, most of whom were openly advertising their sexuality and the area now had a more cosmopolitan feel to it. The two men did not speak to each other on their short journey and instead they listened to the different tunes and rhythms coming from the open doors and windows of the multitude of bars and clubs along their route. At the top of the car-free street, where the seemingly never-ending traffic flowed along Princess Street, they separated, with Hollister telling the teacher that he would be back in touch soon.

The detectives mind was racing, awash with even more questions, but at least he now had the answers to some of his previous questions. He now knew, for definite rather than suspected, that Barratt Foxford, Robinson's former gymnastics coach and the boy's priest were both having sex with him before he disappeared. Having met with Robinson's former teacher Hollister found that he had to fight off his natural desire to go and confront Father Martin immediately but by the time he would have reached the priest it would have been too late to have a meaningful conversation with him and would not have been conducive to his private investigation.

Hollister knew where the priest was and that he probably was not going anywhere soon and so he decided to make the journey first thing in the morning, having had the night to think about the correct way to

approach the priest. Maybe, thought Hollister, that when he approached the priest and revealed everything that he now knew about the boy, that the priest would have the elusive answer to the main question, why had Robinson become a 'rent boy'? This was the one answer that Hollister sought more than any other.

At least he was one step closer to meeting Spencer again, he thought, as he left Foxford and retraced his steps back up Canal Street, marvelling at the openness of everybody and their *laisse faire* attitude towards their sexuality. The schoolteacher had told him that he thinks he can get in touch with Spencer and that he would try to get word to him. What he probably meant was that he knew exactly how to get hold of the young 'rent boy' and would tell the boy to get back in touch with Hollister to prevent the detective from causing any trouble for him. Foxford did explain to him that maybe the youngster might not want to see Hollister again and this might explain why he was being so elusive and hard to find. This thought had already crossed the mind of the detective but he was determined not to relent in his search for the boy.

Hollister had wanted to press the teacher into revealing more about the boy and how he thought he could succeed where he himself had failed, but decided, for now at least, to remain silent. For now at least, happy in the knowledge that he may be one step closer to seeing the boy again, but on reflection, as he took in the pulsating Latino rhythms coming from the bars and clubs, he could hardly contain his excitement at this thought. His heart was already pounding and his mind racing with thoughts of what might come from their meeting, with a hardness forming inside his trousers for the second time that night. But, before

he could think about meeting Spencer he had work to do and set about freeing his mind from fantasies and concentrated on his next move.

Hollister was still a little surprised at how relaxed he felt walking along Canal Street. All around him were people that he once avoided any contact with but now he felt so comfortable being around. He had previously avoided drinking in the known gay bars of Manchester, fearful of the stigma attached to it if he had ever been discovered. Now he felt hypnotically drawn towards them and uncaring about the possible consequences. As he slowly walked past the bar that had been his first encounter of the near legendary 'Village' he had to fight the urge to go in and have another couple of drinks or was it the desire to see Greg the barman again? Instead Hollister had decided that he had drank enough for tonight, anymore and he might have had difficulty in driving home and escaping the eagle-eyes of a traffic officer and he decided to go to a nearby taxi rank and get a lift back to his now adopted home, the former apartment of Cameron Robinson.

As he reached the top of Canal Street and turned onto Minshull Street, an area well known for prostitution, he saw three male youths, each around eighteen to twenty years old coming towards him. Alarm bells immediately rang in the mind of the detective and the thought of getting attacked and robbed came to him. One of Hollister's hands had instinctively gone into his pocket and now clutched his warrant card, ready to flash it to the advancing trio of youths. They were all on in-line roller skates and as they passed him each of them said something. At first the detective did not fully comprehend what it was that they had

said to him but slowly he realised. They had each said the word "business". They were all 'rent boys' touting for business.

Whether it was because he was probing the life and death of a 'rent boy' or it was the beer he had drunk with Foxford or maybe it was even listening to Foxford's account of how Robinson had seduced him at the age of thirteen, possibly a combination of all three, Hollister found himself drawn towards the boys. He watched as they spun around on their wheeled feet and skated back towards him and as the three youths passed the stationary police officer for a second time, they once again offered themselves to Hollister. This time Hollister got a good look at them, singled one of them out and as the youngster realised that Hollister was interested in him, he skated up to Hollister, spinning to a halt.

"Business mate?" the boy asked with a smile.

Hollister took a good look at the teenager. He had bleach-blond hair, which was almost black at the roots and a young, finely sculptured face. His complexion was dark, Mediterranean looking, with eyes that were so dark they could have been black. He was a good looking boy, a little on the small side and rather thin, but he had a warm smile and a certain impish charm. "How much?" asked Hollister.

"Twenty for a blow, fifty for full sex" was the instant reply.

"What's your name?" enquired the detective.

"Call me Johnny," replied the boy.

"How old are you Johnny?"

"Old enough to be legal," he replied cautiously.

"I don't think that you are. The law states that you have to be…"

The youngster cut Hollister short, "Fuck, what are you 'Babylon'? I don't talk, I work. If you're not interested, then I'm off" and he began to skate away.

"Wait, Johnny, I'm just new to this. I've never done this before." The youth gave Hollister another chance and came back, once again a cheeky smile beamed across his face. "How much is it for you to stay all night long?"

"I can't. If I'm not home by morning, me mum'll kill me."

Once again the stark realisation of the world Hollister was moving in to hit him hard. The young boy was prepared to let strangers have sex with him, yet he would not stay out all night because he might upset his mother. Very strange morals, thought Hollister.

"Okay then, we'll start at a hundred if you come back with me and we'll see where we go from there and you might earn a couple of hundred quid. It's up to you."

The youngster was a little wary, but he certainly wanted the money. "I don't know mate. Don't normally go to a punters home."

"You can trust me kid." Hollister tried to reassure him with a smile. "I'll tell you what. I'll even take you home afterwards. Drop you off anywhere you want."

"That's what they all say," was the instant reply.

Hollister tried one more time, by now he wanted this boy and only this one. "I'll tell you what, I'll go and get my car and if you're here when I get back, I guarantee you a hundred for a start. There's more if you want to earn it. It's up to you."

When Hollister returned in his car five minutes later, he found the youth stood barefoot in an office doorway, his roller skates in his hand. He looked a little strange dressed only in a navy blue tracksuit and white socked feet, every inch the young boy that he was. No sooner was Hollister's car stationary, the youth jumped into the passenger seat alongside Hollister, placing his boots on the floor between his legs and wondered what the man would want for one hundred pounds?

They had not travelled very far when Hollister pulled the car over. "I'll have to get some more money."

He left the teenaged boy sitting alone in his car, subconsciously turning off the engine and taking the keys with him. While the boy waited for Hollister to return from the cash-point machine, he had a natural desire to be nosy and looked inside the cars glove box. He was a little surprised when he saw a radio inside. Looking under the driver's seat he saw a small blue light and it was only now that he realised he was with a police officer.

The young boy fought off his natural desire to leap from the car and run off into the warren of streets and the darkness of the night. The fact that he was barefoot and could not have got very far before being caught was another factor that helped him to decide to stay put, the prospect of the money was his main reason. He took a gamble and decided to trust Hollister was not going to take him to a police station. Hollister returned, nodded to the boy, offering him a nervous smile and then they were on their way again.

Hollister took the young boy back to the former apartment of Cameron Robinson. As he let them in, the boy seemed clearly impressed with the décor of the flat and knew that he was going to be

safe with the police officer. No sooner had Hollister put on a light and closed the green curtains, the boy began to undress. Hollister eased himself onto a sofa and watched him. "Stop at your underwear."

Soon the boy was standing almost naked before the detective, his nudity only denied by his white briefs. Fully aroused now Hollister motioned for him to come closer and when he was within reach, he ran his hands all over the soft skin of his muscle-free torso and his hairless legs. Eventually his fingers gripped the fabric of the teenager's underwear and slowly pulled them down. The boy never moved or flinched once as he stepped out of them and stood naked before Hollister, who continued to caress the boy's body with his sweaty hands, leaving no part untouched, until he could stand it no more and led the boy by his hand into the bedroom.

Chapter Eleven

McKenzie Hollister, wracked with guilt as he lay in the bed of the former 'rent boy' Cameron Robinson, the bed that he now considered his own, virtually chain-smoking cigarettes, had crossed over the Rubicon. After spending weeks agonising about his recent fantasies and his desire to have sex with young boy, desperately trying to block them out of his mind, he had actually done it. He had taken a young boy to bed and had sex with him. Not just any youth, but an obviously under-aged 'rent boy' at that. Over the last few weeks, as Hollister grappled with own sexual identity, he had found himself in the position where he wanted to have sex with a young boy. He had paid the more than willing youngster to have sex with him and now this filled the detective with more shame than the actual act.

As a senior police officer, Hollister was meant to protect the likes of the young Johnny, not to exploit them for his own carnal desire and depravity. The contrition he now felt at having the boy perform oral sex on him, before having him commit other sexual acts on him, culminating in Hollister having anal sex with him, lay very heavy on his mind, no matter much the conscience stricken detective tried to justify it.

Johnny, assuming that this was his real name, which Hollister doubted knowing that Robinson and probably Spencer both used aliases, had already been out on the streets of Manchester, touting for business, as he put it, and cruising for men to pay him to have sex with him for money, probably a long time before he had even arrived at the

restaurant for his meeting with Foxford, a meeting that had succeeded in answering many questions but, once again, raised some more. When the teacher told him that it was actually Robinson that had seduced him, rather than the other way around, Hollister had originally doubted it but when he recalled watching the teenager slowly and seductively remove his clothes in the video that he had watched, he thought that he might actually be telling the truth. He could actually envisage Robinson manipulating a situation for his own needs, as had the young 'rent boy' from the previous night. Hollister knew that what he had done was wrong but he had just found himself getting carried away with the situation as no doubt Foxford had with Robinson and the schoolteacher had with Hollister's schooldays friend Ged. Here were three men, covering a timespan of over three decades and each with the same unnatural sexual desires towards teenaged boys, before each of them succumbed to their own lust and temptation, each of them entering into a sexual relationship with less than naïve young boys.

Hollister had, as he tossed and turned, wrestling with his conscious, managed to convince himself by using some form of twisted logic, that unlike Foxford and the other teacher, that he had not taken advantage of the slim bleach-blond young boy but had actually saved him from probably a worse night ahead. If the boy would have allowed somebody to have sex with him for fifty pounds, then he would have had to have had sex with four different men to earn the two hundred pounds that Hollister had given him. So, in the perverse imagination of the detective, it was far better for Johnny to have spent a couple of hours with him, safe in the knowledge that he was not going to hurt the boy, than have him out on the frequently dangerous streets of

Manchester and at the mercy of any pervert that preyed on vulnerable boys like him.

In Hollister's mind, he had actually done the boy a favour. He was already out there working as a prostitute, possibly already having committed sexual acts before meeting him, so if it had not been Hollister then it would have been somebody else. It did not stop him feeling guilty though because he had actually enjoyed himself. As the young boy began to get undress all thoughts that he should not be doing this or even telling the youngster to stop went out of his mind, totally consumed with the moment. As each layer of clothing was slowly removed Hollister found that he was getting more excited, the hairs on the back of his neck standing on end and his breathing becoming more erratic. Once he had started to undress there was no way that he could have stopped the young boy even he had wanted too.

The detective had kept his word and made sure that the youth got home safely. After they had spent nearly three hours together, Hollister had driven the boy home and dropped him off close to the high-rise block of flats where he lived and without drawing any attention to them had bid him farewell. After watching the still barefoot youngster enter the building, Hollister set his car in motion again, with the intention of going back to Robinson's apartment and clean both him and the flat up, getting rid of any evidence of Johnny's visit, but he just did not have the nerve or the resolve to do so. As he drove, he kept seeing flashbacks of his couple of hours of sordid depravity with the young 'rent boy' and could not bring himself to return to the flat in the knowledge with the knowledge of what he had just done there.

The thought that Cameron Robinson himself would have done, no doubt, many of the same things that Johnny had done to and with Hollister, with his own 'clients', entertaining these men in the very same bed that Hollister had just used now filled the detective with moral indignation. There was no way that his conscious, he thought to himself, would allow him to sleep in that bed tonight.

Instead, Hollister still wracked with remorse and guilt, made what was now becoming a rare visit to his own home, his marital home, safe in the knowledge that his wife Kate would not be there. She was still in hospital, recovering from the injuries that he had inflicted on her in a moment of drunken rage. He had literally beaten her to a pulp. She was his loving and caring wife who had checked up him before, so why was this time so different? Was it because he had something to hide, he thought? But, at the time of assaulting his wife, Hollister had not actually done anything and he did not have any reason to hit his wife. Whatever was going on was all inside Hollister's mind, his secret fears and fantasies, his guilty desire of something forbidden.

Now though, he did have a secret, a dark and terrible secret, one that he knew that he could never reveal to anybody but was etched in every furrow of his brow and the shadows cast by the contours of his face. In just a few short weeks the once normal life of Chief Inspector McKenzie Hollister had been turned upside down and he was beginning to think that his wife Kate had been right on the day that he attacked her, maybe he was losing control of his life? Letting himself get carried away by emotions and this, he had found from previous experience, to be a very dangerous road to go down.

Sleep was still eluding him though. After taking a shower and drinking several glasses of whisky, slowly munching through a roast beef sandwich, he eased himself into the second bed of the night. The difference in comfort was immediately obvious to Hollister. His marital bed felt lumpy and uncomfortable when compared to the bed in the apartment of Robinson. As in every other area of his life, the young Robinson had allowed himself, and indeed his clients, the luxury of an expensive bed and mattress, far outstripping the type that the salary of the detective could afford.

It had been shortly before midnight when the tired Hollister had climbed into his bed and for ninety minutes he had tossed and turned in a desperate effort to get some sleep, but it still escaped him. Every time that he closed his eyes he saw the faces of Cameron Robinson, so tranquil and innocent looking in death; the impish smiling and mischievous face of Spencer, the subject of so many recent sordid fantasies; and now Johnny, the young 'rent boy' who had willingly given himself over to the lecherous lust of the detective, only doing so in the knowledge that he was going to well paid for his services, money that had come out of Robinson's bank account that sent the loop of guilt round in full circle. The young 'rent boy' had clearly enjoyed both what he did and what was done to him and at no point did he voice any complaints to Hollister about his treatment. Maybe it was this that now troubled the detective?

What was it about this generation of youngsters that seemed so obsessed with material goods that they were prepared to have sex with men old enough to be their own father's in order to own the latest of

luxuries? No shame, no guilt, just the desire to earn money to buy whatever the latest gadget was?

Hollister looked over to the clock, its red numbers the only light in the darkened bedroom, which reflected his own mood and the clock told him that it was now nearly two in the morning and he finally gave up on the notion of sleep. The detective eased his aching body out of the bed, donned his blue robe and went downstairs for yet another drink in the hope that this would be the one that helped him to blot out the memory of what he had so recently been doing to the teenaged Johnny. This drink led to another and another until he had downed nearly a full bottle of whisky before the combination of tiredness and alcohol finally allowed Hollister the slumber that he hankered, spilling the final drops of whisky onto the carpet as the tumbler slipped from his grasping fingers onto the floor.

It was the sound of a key being inserted into the lock on the front door that eventually disturbed him and woke up McKenzie Hollister. His wife Kate was coming home, her brief stay in hospital was over. It took the detective two attempts to stand up such was the pain in his head, a sharp jolting pain in the centre of his forehead that pierced deep into his brain, as if some unknown assailant was attacking him with a sharp knife. He had to peer through squinted eyes, the bright light of the morning increasing the torment in his head and the dryness in his mouth only added to assault on his senses. Dressed only in his bathrobe, his face haggard and unshaven, McKenzie Hollister looked a pathetic sight.

Barely able to stand on his own, Hollister eventually managed to cross the room, bumping into furniture on his short journey to the hallway. Every step he took sent another piercing stab of pain deep inside his brain and the brightness of the early morning hurt his eyes, adding to his discomfort until he finally faced his wife. "Hello Kate" he began, his voice hoarse and rasping. "I didn't know you were coming home today. You should've called me and I would've come and got you…"

She backed away from the outstretched arms of her husband, her face, once so beautiful and contoured, still bruised and swollen. "Don't you come anywhere near me, you lousy bastard."

Hollister was taken aback by her rage and spluttered out a reply, "Kate, I told you in the hospital how truly sorry I am."

"Did you think that your pathetic attempt of an apology would be enough for me to forgive you for what you did to me? I'm not one of your suspects that won't help you and so you give them a few slaps. I'm your wife. The woman that has always stood by you, the woman who cried herself to sleep worrying about you, dreading the knock on the door telling me that you were dead, only for you to kick the shit out of me and for no reason whatsoever."

"Kate, don't do this to me," pleaded Hollister.

"Don't do this to me," her voice now sarcastically mocking her husband's, "just listen to you. You're pathetic. You're a piece of shit. Now, get out of my way," she demanded.

Hollister refused to move and barred her way to the stairs. "Kate, talk to me, please."

"Talk to you! I'd rather see you rotting in hell than talk to you. I've only come back here because I own it jointly with you. I've not come back to be with you or forgive you or let you get away with what you did to me. I'm only here because I live here, not to be with you. I want you to see me every day so that you'll never forget just exactly what you did to me." A determined look now came over the face of the bitter woman, "Now get out of my fucking way."

The rage was growing deep inside the detective and he struggled with his emotions. "I told you how sorry I was. What I did was wrong, so terribly wrong and I wish that I hadn't touched you, but I did. I can never forgive myself…"

"And I'll never forgive you either or let you forget it," interrupted Kate Hollister as she once again tried to pass her husband and climb the stairs, but he held out and tried to stop her. "Go on, fucking hit me again," she yelled at him. "Prove how much of a man you are and kick the shit out of me again."

Tears welled in the eyes of Hollister as he moved his hand away from his wife, finally allowing her to reach the stairs. "I'm sorry Kate, so very sorry," he whispered as she past him.

His words of apology fell on deaf ears. Whilst she was recovering in hospital she had made up her mind to never forgive her husband's actions and no amount of words or apologising would ever change her mind. She could tell this by his pained expression on his face that he genuinely meant what he said and she did not doubt that he was truly sorry for what he had done to her, but the damage to their relationship was done and could never be repaired, the slamming of the bedroom

door sending echoes through the empty house emphasised the closing of this chapter of both their lives.

A couple hours later, around lunch time, McKenzie Hollister walked into the detectives offices of Heller Street police station. By now he had showered and shaved and looked presentable, a little haggard still, with black bags caused from sleepless nights under his eyes, but presentable. He felt the eyes of every single one of his colleagues burning deep into him as he made his way to his private office and his private inner sanctum. He heard various comments like "Glad you're back" and "How's Kate?" but chose not to verbally respond to them, offering those that spoke to him a cursory nod of his head. Once in his office Hollister eased himself into his chair behind his desk and looked at the messages, hoping to find one from either Spencer of Barratt Foxford, only to find that he was disappointed. Most of them were comments relating to Kate, that he did not want to read or be reminded off, others were now dated information that was now irrelevant. Instead of reading them he just sat in silence and tried to figure out what his wife's next move was going to be?

Was she still going to remain silent about his beating of her or was she going to reveal the terrible truth and end his career? Maybe, he thought to himself, that in time she would mellow and forgive him, but judging by her mood a few hours ago, Hollister doubted it. The thought of her being there, constantly mocking him and reminding of what he had done filled him with anxiety. Even he now doubted that he could live under the same roof as her after what he had done, being subjected to days or weeks of constant ridicule and torment, the fear of losing

control again and attacking her again, this time with possibly unforeseeable consequences.

It was Sergeant Phoebe Boston, Hollister's assistant that became the first officer to directly speak to him. Having knocked on the glass door before entering, she offered him a comforting smile, "Good to see you again Mac. Hope Kate's okay. The boss says for you to go and see him whenever you came in."

Sergeant Boston was referring to Chief Superintendent Mundy, "Cheers Phoebe."

"How's Kate?" she asked.

A lump swelled in his throat as he forced a smile to his face, "She's okay. She came out of hospital earlier, recuperating at home. Better go and see what Mundy wants."

As she watched Hollister leave his office and then the main office, Sergeant Boston could tell that Hollister was a man with his emotions balanced on a knife's edge. Her sixth sense picked up on the fact that all was not well with him. She knew that recently he had been under a great deal of stress and now it was beginning to show. She knew that Hollister's temper had always been kept on a short leash, its fuse ready to ignite at the slightest touch of the litmus paper, having been on the receiving end of his wrath on several occasions, as indeed had many of the detectives working with Hollister. She had learnt, from first-hand experience, the tell-tale signs that he was ready to blow. Sergeant Boston sensed that here was a man waiting to explode.

There was no waiting this time. McKenzie Hollister was allowed straight into the office of Chief Superintendent Mundy by his secretary

with a wave of her hand. Mundy was on the telephone to somebody, looking up when he heard the door being opened by his long-time friend and motioned for him to come in and take a seat. Mundy made his excuses to whoever he was speaking to and hung up. "Mac, how are you feeling and how's Kate? Is she home yet?"

There was genuine warmth and sincerity in the words of Mundy, Hollister could detect it and knew that he was in the company of a true friend. "She came home earlier. She's at home now resting. I thought I'd give her some space and show my face." Hollister wondered whether his friend had seen through his lie.

"It's good to see you Mac," replied Mundy. "Do you want a drink?"

"I'd love a scotch," Hollister answered almost immediately. He had wondered whether he should lay off the alcohol for a while but decided that Kate's attitude warranted another drink.

Mundy made his way to a high cabinet, poured two glasses of whisky and handed one to Hollister, sitting next to his friend, breaking down the barrier of his desk and enabling the two men to talk as friends and not colleagues. "I could not believe it when I got the call that Kate's been attacked, began Mundy, "it's not something that you expect to hear, the wife of one of your most senior detectives being attacked in her own home. If I could find out who it was, I'd...I'd...do them myself. Don't worry Mac, we've dropped everything looking for whoever it was. Haven't got any real leads at the moment, but we'll find the bastard, you can rely on that."

Hollister took a sip of his whisky, the warmth of the liquid burning his throat as he swallowed it. "Kate blames me for it."

Mundy let out a sigh, "That's understandable but ridiculous. She's probably still in shock."

"No Andrew, she means it," continued Hollister, "she says that it was my fault. If I hadn't been so engrossed in my work, if only I'd spent more time with her and less time working or on the piss, then it wouldn't have happened."

Due to their many years of friendship Mundy could detect that Hollister had wanted to go further and say something else and as soon as he had downed the las of his whisky, Mundy refilled his friends glass in the hope that the whisky would loosen up his friend. "Mac, we can both understand how she feels, but she doesn't really blame you. She'll be in shock. We all, at times, get too preoccupied in cases and neglect certain aspects of our lives, but Kate knows all about this. She's always stood by you in the past. She'll get over the shock of what has happened. Let's not forget, she's just been through a terrible experience, in her own home, where she should be safe."

"That's the point Andrew, it was my fault..." Hollister could not finish his sentence as his eyes filled with tears. "...I am at fault and I feel like shit."

Mundy did not reply immediately but thought about what Hollister had just said, watching the tears roll down the cheeks of his friend, something that he had never seen before throughout all their years of friendship until finally he grasped what Hollister was really trying to say. "You did it, didn't you? It was you that beat her up. That's what you're trying to tell me, isn't it? You put your own wife in fucking hospital, didn't you, you bastard?"

"It's not like that...I couldn't help myself...I just lost control." Hollister was now a pathetic sight, weeping and blubbering like a hysterical schoolgirl.

"You did more than lose control..." Mundy could hardly contain his indignation, "...you kicked the fucking shit out of your own wife. You put her in hospital. For fuck's sake, I've pulled coppers of important cases to look for her attacker and it was you all the time." Mundy was by now pacing up and down his office, trying to contain his anger.

Hollister was now beginning to pull himself together, "Andrew, you know me better than most people. I've never laid a finger on her before...but...she's been screwing another guy and I found out."

"Kate wouldn't do that to you." Mundy was not prepared to believe Hollister's lie. "I didn't believe you when you said you thought she was cheating on you and I certainly don't believe you now. Kate has given you her life. She adores you."

Hollister continued with his concocted story, "Andrew, I caught them together...at it...fucking...in my bed. My fucking bed! I just lost it. I did him in. I grabbed him by his throat and kicked his fucking head and all the time she tried to protect him. She didn't give a fuck about me. Then I threw him out on his arse, stark bollock naked. She then started on me! She was saying that she only doing it because I cared more about my job than her and just how shit I was in bed and how I couldn't satisfy her anymore. She began mocking me, taking the piss out of me and that's when I lost it." Hollister paused briefly, sensing whether Mundy had taken the bait. "I only remember hitting her once. After that, I've got no recollection or memory of what happened. I didn't know that I'd hurt her so much until I saw her in the hospital."

Mundy was clearly shell-shocked at this unexpected revelation. "That still doesn't excuse what you did to her for Christ's sake."

"Don't you think that I know that?" At least this statement, probably the only one that he had said to Mundy was true. "My every thought's ever since have been what I did to her. I had a suspicion that she was seeing somebody else, I told you so the other week but I never thought that I'd catch them…at it…in my bed…having sex. I just couldn't help myself. Christ Andrew, what would you do if Melanie was shagging around?"

Hollister had expertly manipulating his friend by turning the tables on the senior officer, by mentioning his own wife's name and putting the emphasis on his own emotions. "Of course I'd be annoyed, but that's not to say that I'd kick the shit of her and put her in hospital." After a brief pause where Mundy took stock of the situation, "I'd better call the troops off and reassign them. What happens next?"

After a brief pause Hollister shrugged his shoulders and finished off his second whisky. "I don't know Andrew. I've got somewhere else to live for now, so fuck her. That little shit, whoever he was, is fucking welcome to her. I don't give a fuck about the dirty fucking whore anymore."

The senior detective had once again fallen for the lies of his friend. Mundy had allowed his judgement to be clouded by their years of friendship and this had left gullible to Hollister's charade. "I don't mind admitting that I'm stunned. No, I'm more than stunned, I'm devastated. I never thought that Kate would ever do something like this. When you first told me of your suspicions I couldn't believe it then and I can't believe it now. But don't worry, your secrets, both of them, are

safe within these walls. Nobody needs to know what has happened and why. It'll remain our secret. You just take care of yourself and take as much time off as you need to sort your head out. I'll take care of HR and watchdogs for you. So don't worry about them."

"Don't worry about me though Andrew, I'll be okay. I'll always bounce back."

Hollister spent the next hour or so at the police station, making the most of what was becoming a rare visit. He went over and over the few known details about Cameron Robinson from his disappearance to his death, searching for that one vital snippet of information that had so far eluded him. Having spent some time at his former apartment, Hollister was now totally convinced that somebody was blackmailing the boy and could well have been involved in his death. His gut instinct told him this and it was the identity of this person that he now sought. The youngster being blackmailed would explain the sudden change in Robinson's mood and behaviour just before he vanished from his home, making him go from a loving and caring son into the sullen and moody teenager that everybody Hollister has spoken to remember about him.

If the detective's suspicions about this mystery person were correct, then maybe Robinson might not be the only boy being forced into committing sexual favours and acts for nothing and if this was the case, nobody could rule out the use of violence to maintain the silence of the young boys. Hollister knew, from experience, that this information was there, hidden somewhere in the statements given by all those that knew him, but where was it? But more to the point, who was it?

It could be Foxford, his gymnastics coach and a man with a self-confessed penchant for young boys. Maybe it was the youngster's priest? A priest that Hollister had discovered that had moved diocese several times throughout his career, spending two or three years in one church before being moved onto another many miles away. Hollister had forgotten that he wanted to talk to the priest again in order to challenge him on his relationship that the detective had been informed included a sexual one. On reflection though, neither man had the need to blackmail Robinson into letting them have sex with him. By all accounts, he had given himself freely to both the men. So, there had to be somebody else, but who?

Whilst at the police station Hollister ran a name check on Barratt Foxford, Father Martin and Malka Charnel through both the police national computer and the Sex Offenders Register but was not surprised that he drew a blank on each of them In fact, very little surprised him about this case these days. The words of Spencer came back to him about all their clients being respectable and legitimate and his fruitless search seemed to prove the boys point.

Hollister also spent some time looking at the endless images of missing boys on the Child Protection Unit's database. He was searching for the elusive Spencer. Sitting alone in a secluded office and searching through the missing persons files of these youngsters Hollister was plunged into a state of deep depression as he realised just how many young boys go missing and are never heard off again. They just seemed to vanish of the face of the earth, never to be seen again and nobody really seemed that bothered about their disappearances. Except for Hollister, but he was only interested in one boy in particular,

Spencer. The detective had drawn a blank searching the police's files for him but he knew that he was out there, living somewhere on the frequently dangerous streets of Manchester, selling his body for the price of something to eat and a bed for the night. It had been Spencer that had first put the notion into his head that Robinson was being blackmailed by somebody and it was now him that he sought more than anybody else.

Not just for the possible identity of Robinson's blackmailer. Hollister also wanted to know who he really was. Having found no record of him being reported as missing on the police's computer databases, Hollister was even more intrigued by the youth. Now, not only did he want to find out who he was, he wanted to know all the details about why he had run away from his home and why he had never been reported as missing? How is it possible in this modern age of mass communication that youngsters can just fade into the twilights of the busy streets of towns and cities up and down the United Kingdom and nobody know that they are there?

Hollister also had an ulterior motive for finding Spencer. The young boy had been forever in his thoughts since that first fateful telephone call and then their subsequent meeting. Hollister knew that he needed to find Spencer for two reasons. The first was to speak to him in detail about Robinson but his main reason was that he *wanted* to find him. When they had met, the youth had spoken so freely and openly about his sexual relationships with men and now that Hollister had himself experienced sex with a young boy, he now knew that he wanted to find Spencer to be able to have sex with him. It was the prospect of this that had kept Hollister awake at nights losing sleep out of repulsion at the

thought of it and the secret desire of wanting to do it. Until he had met the young Johnny, it was the only thoughts in his head throughout the daylight hours.

When he had first embarked on his covert investigation, the thought and very notion of him having sex with a teenaged boy would have repulsed him but the deeper that he delved into the death Robinson, the more that he got sucked into the twilight and illegal world of prostitution and 'rent boys' in particular. He knew that his lust, for that is what Hollister now realises that it was, nothing more, nothing less, for Spencer was wrong, both morally and professionally, but it was all that he thought about. In the now warped and depraved mind of the detective, he thought that if he could not have sex with the person that he ultimately craved, Cameron Robinson, then he was going to have sex with the next best thing, the cheeky and cherubic Spencer. Even while he was having sex with the young 'rent boy' Johnny, it was Spencer that he was thinking about, imagining that it was actually him not Johnny. He had closed his eyes to reality and dreamt of Spencer.

Hollister had almost forgotten about Johnny. He glanced at his watch, it was almost six in the evening and Hollister wondered whether the young boy was out there on the streets, plying himself for those just finishing a day's stressful work and seeking sexual gratification before embarking on their journeys home. As Hollister now knew from personal experience, a great deal of pleasure can be gained in the knowledge that the act itself may still be illegal, but the person performing it was both underage and a boy, creating even greater

excitement. The erection that he got whilst thinking about Johnny and what he had done the previous evening deep inside his trousers decided Hollister's fate and he set out in search of the young boy.

Hollister found him once again on Minshull Street. Johnny skated up to Hollister as soon as he saw him walking along the pavement, greeting the detective with a huge beaming smile on his young face. To look at him, dressed in a pair of navy blue tracksuit bottoms, white T-shirt and a red quilted body-warmer, nobody would have guessed that he had a sordid occupation as a 'rent boy'. He looked just like any typical teenager the world over. However, it was the shameful and debauched side of the youth that drew Hollister, almost magnetically towards the youth.

"Hiya Mac," the youth said excitingly when he was close enough to the detective, taking the initiative himself. "Want some more business?"

"Yeah, if you want" replied Hollister casually but with a smile, trying to hide his excitement at finding the boy so easily.

"Same as last night?" asked the boy, totally at ease and relaxed about what he was offering.

"Yeah, but I've only got a spare hundred and fifty quid tonight."

Hollister walked as the young boy skated next to him, looking like a father and son having had a day's shopping, the obvious reason for their meeting up completely obscured. "No big deal. After what you gave me last night I'd let you do me for free tonight. Like the skates? Got them out of the money you gave me. Eighty quid they were, top of the range. Got the other gear as well, do I look good?" He sounded like

an excited schoolboy having just celebrated his birthday and had bought himself some presents.

Hollister did like the look of the young boy and told him so as they reached his car. Hollister sat behind the wheel while the boy climbed in next to him and unlaced his newly acquired prize possessions, carefully placing them on the floor between his legs. He settled in, fastened his safety belt and made small talk until they reached the flat.

No sooner were they in the lounge, with Hollister settling onto the larger of the two sofas, Johnny began to undress. Now knowing that Hollister liked to watch him strip off, this time he took his time, removing each item slowly and seductively until he was only wearing his underwear briefs. Images of Cameron Robinson doing an almost identical striptease came into the mind of the detective as he sat and admired the near naked youth, with his fat-free and muscled torso, his strong muscular legs and his handsome face. This was a youth that clearly knew that he had excited the man before him, somebody that enjoyed looking at him like this and he exploited it to its fullest. Johnny eventually sank to his knees between the open legs of Hollister, his young fingers unfastening the trousers of the detective, they then gripped the erect penis, immediately taking it into his mouth and sucking it to completion.

An hour later, man and boy lay naked on the bed, with Hollister stroking the boy's soft hair while his head rested on the detective's hairy chest. Hollister had just finished having sex with the youngster and was taking a break before he did so again. He had decided earlier to try and get to his secret lover to reveal a little more about himself. "Can

I ask you something, why do you do this? You know, let men have sex with you?"

The boy seemed a little reluctant at first to answer the question, but eventually opened up to Hollister. "I only have sex with people I like, you know, people like you. I'm not gay or anything. In fact I've got a girlfriend. She doesn't know what I do when I'm not with her, but she likes the way that I spend my money on her."

"How do you explain having so much money to spend?" asked the mystified detective.

"I tell her that I win it gambling or on scratch cards. You can earn some big money on some of them. Also told her I do a part-time job some nights, helping me mates out doing some work, which is not exactly telling any lies."

This brought a wry smile to the face of the boy and the detective. "You're certainly right there but what about having sex with men?"

"I don't," came the adamant reply, "When I have a punter, that's just business, a means of earning some money, nothing more, nothing less. Going with somebody like you, that's different. That's something I like and enjoy. That's sex. When I go with a punter, it's just work, that's all. Queer sex is just something to bring the money in."

"I don't believe that," replied the baffled detective. "You don't just do 'it'."

"You saw where I live last night. Shit, that place is so boring and depressing. Half the kids my age go out robbing things and places just to give them something to do, enjoying give the police a run around if they get caught. The other half, they're probably on 'the game' to pay for their drug habits."

The stark realisation of what the boy was saying was well known to the detective. "You don't do drugs though, do you?"

"Shit no. I smoke a bit of weed now and again with me bird Julie, but that's it, honest."

Hollister moved his hand from the boy's head and placed it comfortingly around his shoulder, drawing the boy closer to him, almost in a fatherly manner. "What made you start doing this in the first place? You know, become a 'rent boy' and sell yourself?"

There followed a brief awkward silence before eventually Johnny sighed and rather reluctantly continued, safe in the knowledge that he was not having to look Hollister in the face and constantly pausing out of embarrassment. "Me brother came home from the pub one night and he was pissed as a fart. He's five years older than me. Our Jimmy had just broke up with his bird and was really pissed off. At the time we shared a bedroom...and...this night...he got in bed with me...and he started to kiss me and touch me up...you know...inside me underpants...must've thought I was his bird or something."

The boy paused and sighed before he continued, "Our Jimmy is bigger than me and he...forced himself on me...and...before I knew it, he was trying to shag me up the arse. I was struggling and told him to get off me and wouldn't let him do anything to me. He hit me a couple of times...you know around the head...I told him I'd do something if he stopped hitting me...he then made me suck his dick."

How old were you when this happened?" asked Hollister, sighing to himself, now regretting asking his young lover as to how and why he started doing what he was doing, but hanging onto his every word.

"I'd only just turned twelve," was the embarrassed and barely whispered reply.

"Did you tell anybody about this? What your brother did to you was wrong and he shouldn't have done it." Hollister regretted his words, realising that no sooner had he said them they made him sound like a police officer.

"I couldn't. I was dead embarrassed about it…and…after all…he was me brother. You don't 'grass' on your own brother, no matter what he does to you."

"I agree, but sexual assault is a very horrible thing…" Hollister cut himself short. He was beginning to sound more and more like a police officer.

"I still couldn't do it though," replied Johnny quietly. "I know that I should've said something and stopped him 'cause he just kept making me do it to him more and more. It got so bad that I dreaded seeing him 'cause I knew that he'd make me suck his dick. It was all the time. First thing in the morning he'd shove his dick in me mouth…he'd make me do it three or four times a day. Then one night he got me pissed and…shagged me up me arse. He'd tried to do it a few times but I wouldn't let him but this night he just got me pissed and shagged me. He raped me. After I felt so cheap…and it hurt me so much. After…I cried me self to sleep, trying to block it out…but the memory and pain of that night was still there."

Hollister felt something damp on his chest and realised that the young boy was weeping silent tears as he continued to recount his nightmare experience. "After that first time…he used to shag me nearly every night. Whenever he wanted to until he got a new bird and he left me

alone for a bit. But soon they split up and he started making me suck his dick and shagging me up the arse again. Except this time he used to batter me as well, blaming me for him and his bird splitting up. He said he couldn't get a hard-on with her except when he was thinking about me. He said it was my fault. Then one day…he was out of work and it was during the school holidays…giro day it was…and me mum was out at work…him and three of his mates watched this porn film…and he was teasing me, telling his mates that I liked to suck dick and take it up the arse and then to prove it, he made me suck his dick in front of them. I wanted to kill the bastard…but by this time him and his mates were all pissed…and they all shagged me up the arse.

"After our Jimmy had finished…they pushed me to the floor and pulled all me clothes off. I was struggling and fighting them all the time…but I couldn't stop them. They were all 'bout the same size as our Jimmy and they took turns in shagging me…all of them…over and over again. While one of them was shagging me, two of the others would hold me down and the other would make me suck his dick. I wanted to bite the fucking things off. After a while…I stopped struggling and just let them do whatever they wanted to me. They were going to do it any way and me struggling and fighting was only hurting me. After that time I decided that if I was going to have to do stuff like that…well…I might as well get paid for it."

"I can do something about your brother and his friends, if you want?" replied Hollister as he absorbed the youngster's horrific account, once again stroking his fine soft hair.

"Yeah, I know you can." The boy was almost telling Hollister that he knew that he was a police officer. "But what'll be the point? Won't

change anything. What happened, happened. Can't take that away. Anyway, our Jimmy's banged up now. He got two years for burglary. Hope someone is raping him like him and his mates raped me."

After a brief pause Hollister planted a reassuring kiss on the boys head. "I suppose you're right. How old were you when we became a 'rent boy'?"

"I was nearly fourteen" the youngster replied.

Hollister was genuinely shocked. "Fourteen! How old are you now?"

"I'm nearly sixteen. I leave school in a couple of months."

"Fucking hell. I don't believe what I'm hearing." The shock was apparent in his voice as he sat up in bed, pushing the boy away from him.

"Come off it. You knew last night that I was young. What's the big deal?"

What the youth said was correct. Hollister had suspected that he was still barely legal and thought that he might still be too young to legally have sex and that he was probably still at school. But this, to Hollister, was the thrill of being with him, adding to his increased state of excitement. Knowing how young he was, the knowledge of his age was the desire, not the actual physical sexual activity. The thought of it made his heart beat faster, his adrenaline pumping through his body, carrying him through the mundane existence of daily life.

For the first time in over a month Hollister was finally beginning to understand some of the emotions that he had been feeling and why he kept thinking about the missing Spencer and now Johnny. He wanted to have sex with Spencer for the same reasons why he had enjoyed having sex with Johnny. It was the thrill of him, a senior police officer, having

sex with an underage boy because it was illegal and morally wrong. Sex with children was still taboo in most societies and it was this that drove some people to actually do it. The thrill of rebelling against the confines of morality, to push the boundaries as far as they could in the need, or desire, for something that they are told that they should not have or even do. Repressing their urges was creating the desire to do it in the first place.

As Hollister started to commit buggery on the young boy for the second time that night, for the first time he not only understood why he wanted to do it. For the first time in two nights, Johnny became a real person and not just a sexual fantasy.

Chapter Twelve

Now armed with the information recently provided to him by Robinson's former gymnastics coach, which had only served to prove that his original suspicions had been correct, McKenzie Hollister felt he was finally ready to confront the boy's former priest about his sexual relationship with Robinson. His own recent journey into the sleazy world of 'rent boys' had opened his eyes, not to mention his mind, to the nether world of homosexuality and the sordid depravity that accompanies sex with teenage prostitutes, literally at times, nothing more than children. Hollister knew that if his dalliances with Johnny were ever discovered and made public, it would totally destroy him personally and ruin his promising career in the police force.

Maybe this was part of the hidden danger, the catalyst that, despite the risks, had spurned him along, that made him want to do it, especially the second time. The knowledge of his secret life and the excitement that it now generated had given Hollister a new sense of belonging. He now identified himself as a 'closet' homosexual. He no longer had any desire to be with a woman or to have sex with one, not even his once devoted wife Kate. The desire to immerse himself into his newly discovered world was all that now carried him from one day to the next. He needed to be part of this 'gay scene', on the inside, not looking at it from an outsiders perspective.

He had found himself to be genuinely upset by the plight of the boy that had introduced him to the dubious pleasures of gay sex. Johnny had been an innocent victim of his own brother's lust and depravity,

substituting his much younger and vulnerable brother for the girlfriend that he could not have and yet Johnny had come out of this terrible experience on top. He had decided that if people wanted him to perform oral sex or have full sex with him, then they were going to have to pay him for it. The boy had manipulated his sexual abuse for his own needs, just as Spencer had done when he allowed Foxford to pick him up on that cold and miserable night, offering him a meal, bath and a bed for the night in exchange for sex. Hollister now began to wonder what kind of world he was living in that created these situations, let alone what kind of generation was being raised in this world, a world in which youngsters could have the initiative to manipulate this terrible experiences for their own benefit.

Spencer, it now turns out, had apparently turned to prostitution out of necessity and need. Johnny had followed the same route for purely financial gains. As to why Robinson had become a 'rent boy' was still a complete mystery to Hollister and he hoped that the boy's former priest might turn out to have the elusive answer.

Once again sitting in the priest's study, the only sound in the room being the loud ticking from a clock which was nestled on a shelf with some books that were almost as archaic as the wooden clock, Hollister rehearsed in his mind the questions that he wanted answering, knowing full well that whether he got them answered or not still depended on the willingness of Father Martin to break the cycle of taboo and be honest to both the detective and to himself. Hollister could, at last, understand the sexual attraction that some men felt towards young boys. Despite it

being wrong, not to mention illegal, Hollister thought it was the most natural thing in the world.

Upon getting to know him better, Hollister had found Johnny to be a desperately sad and lonely young boy. Here was a boy silently crying out for somebody to love him. He had shown Hollister another side to his character, a part of his personality that he usually tries to hide behind his bravado and his streetwise knowledge. He was the complete opposite of Cameron Robinson. Here was a boy that was full of love and happiness, surrounded by those that genuinely loved him or at the very least, cared about him and yet he still ran away from home, turning his back on everybody. In their own way, both boys had touched a raw nerve with Hollister. With Robinson it was because no matter how much you are loved, it sometimes is still not enough. Whereas Johnny had touched him in a gentle, almost childlike way but then again, that was what he was, just a young child.

After about ten minutes of listening to the ticking clock, which seemed to get louder as it echoed around the room and reading the titles of the books on the shelves, Hollister finally heard the door being opened, its ancient hinges groaning out in desperation for some oil, alerting the detective to the priest's presence, as did the creaking floorboards. Turning to face him, Hollister saw that he was dressed in his black cassock and to any other person Father Martin would have looked very intimidating.

"I did not expect to see you again Mr Hollister," Father Martin said immediately. "What is it that you want now?"

Hollister had detected an air of hostility in the voice of the priest and came straight to the point. "You were not exactly honest with me at our first meeting, were you Father?"

The priest's eyebrows furrowed, desperately trying to read the mind of the detective. "Oh, and what exactly do you mean by that comment?"

"I mean about your relationship with Cameron Robinson." It was now the turn of Hollister to watch for any changes in the expression of the priest, searching for any tell-tale sign.

"And I thought that I had answered all your questions with honesty. I've admitted that Cameron and I had a very close and intensely religious relationship. What more is there for me to say?"

Hollister shook his head, unable to accept what he had just heard. "You could start with the fact that you and Cameron were secret lovers…"

Father Martin cut him short, "What a ridiculous thing to say."

Hollister was beginning to lose his patience with the obnoxious and objectionable priest. "I'm saying it because it is true. We both know that so cut the crap and stop hiding behind your robes and start telling me the truth."

Still protesting his innocence, but a little shaken by the bluntness of the detective, "I've never anything so preposterous. I've a good mind to get the Bishop to complain to your superior officer about your harassment of me and these completely unfounded allegations."

"If I were you Father, I'd be more worried about your own Superior Officer," Hollister voice was heavily tainted with sarcasm, which had an icy edge to it. "Father, I would not accuse you of anything of such

magnitude if I could not prove it. Have you ever heard of the name Barratt, or Barry, Foxford?"

"No" came the immediate reply. "Why, should I have?"

Hollister gave a slight smile, "A very sudden and precise answer. Being a priest of over twenty years, you must have met many people in your capacity as their priest and also as a respectable member of the community and yet you know, without any doubt or hesitation that you don't know this man called Barratt Foxford."

Realising that he had been caught out in a trap, Father Martin backtracked and tried to get out of it. "Well…maybe I have. I cannot remember the name of everybody that I meet."

"I would have thought that you would remember this name. He was one of Cameron's teachers. In fact he was more than that. He was not only his form teacher but also his gymnastics coach and so I find it very hard to believe that if you and Cameron had such a close friendship and relationship that he never mentioned his gymnastics coach by name. Barratt Foxford also had a 'special relationship' with Cameron. How do I know this, you might ask? Because he has actually told me so, that's how I know."

Father Martin was now definitely rattled by not only Hollister's insinuations, but his attitude as well. "Cameron might have mentioned him by name…but that was over two years or three years ago. Surely I'm not expected to remember everything that he said to me from all that time ago?"

"Father, let's cut all this crap and bullshit and end this ridiculous charade and let's start again." Hollister was beginning to lose his patience with the priest. "We both know that you and Cameron were

once lovers. This guy, Foxford, told me so. He knows because he once followed Cameron home one night from school and saw him go into your bedroom. Now, obviously I can't prove any of this, Foxford has got too much to lose by going public, but I know that you were abusing him, you know that you were abusing him so do me a huge favour, stop treating me like a fucking idiot."

Father Martin's complexion had turned ashen, his hands were visibly shaking and he sought a chair to sit in, fearing that his legs would give way at any moment. To him, his entire world had just crumbled around him. He gulped for air, almost hyperventilating. "I…I don't know what to say."

"Let me tell you what I either know, or suspect, about you and Cameron and then let's take it from there" began Hollister, gleaming a certain amount of pleasure in watching the priest squirm as his secret life was revealed. "Cameron was a very good looking young boy. He had a great physique, one that he worked on daily because he knew that it was one of his strengths and the weakness of people like you. He was, apparently, a very pleasant and likable young boy, always willing to help others and he had an enormous amount of charm and charisma. He knew only too well that he could manipulate certain situations for his own benefit, as he did when he as good as seduced his gymnastics coach, thus beginning their relationship. Now it appears that at some point you also fell under his hypnotic charm and took advantage of him for your own carnal desires. That I can relate to. Now, in your own words, tell me exactly what happened between you and Cameron Robinson and how it started."

As Hollister spoke, the priest picked up on his hidden meaning. He knew both by instinct and experience that the detective had also sampled the forbidden sexual exploits of a young boy. It had been his comment *'That I can relate to'* that had given Hollister away and now the priest relaxed a little, safe in the knowledge that he was amongst 'one of his own'. Father Martin took a deep breath and then began, "Cameron was by no means the victim. Like you've just said, he knew full well both what he was doing and what he was getting himself into. Maybe, from somebody else's point of view, what we did was wrong, but I refute, in the strongest terms possible any accusations that I either abused the boy or took advantage of him."

"Do you know what Father, I actually believe you," Hollister added in a now warm, almost sympathetic manner. "Now, in your own time and words, tell me how it all began."

The priest spoke very softly, his voice contrite with remorse and regret, "We, that is the church's youth movement, go away camping every year during the school summer holidays. I remember this year because Cameron had just become a teenager, he'd just turned thirteen. One day, I remember it vividly, like it was only yesterday, it was really warm and sunny and the boys, twelve of them there was, spent most of the two weeks only wearing just their shorts, very rarely wearing anything else, like T-shirts throughout the day. One day they all went swimming in the sea. Afterwards, Cameron and this other boy, his name was Robert, went off for a walk along the shoreline. This Robert was a couple of years older than most of the boys and he…sought off…helped us to monitor and supervise the younger boys. To make sure that the boys were safe at all times. They were never allowed off

on their own. An adult always supervised them and so I followed them discretely, from a safe distance, unseen by either of them.

"The two boys went into a secluded cove, safe in the knowledge that they couldn't be seen by anybody else, unaware of my presence behind them. They seemed to know where this place was and I can only assume that this was not the first time they had ventured into it since we had been there. When I went around the rocks and looked into the cove I could hardly believe my eyes. Both boys had taken off their shorts and were naked. Cameron was on his hands and knees whilst Robert was behind him. They were obviously having sex. I was in a state of shock and mortified down to the very core of my heart. Deep in my heart I wanted to cry out and make them stop this dreadful abomination, but I couldn't. My mouth was dry and no words came out. I just stood there, in a state of shock and watched them intensely, feeling myself grow hard as I did. Unknowingly at first I began to rub myself whilst watching them, coupled together, clearly enjoying themselves and loving each other. When Robert had finished having sex with Cameron he lay next to him and performed oral sex on him. I'm almost certain that at one point Cameron saw me watching them. He looked over in my direction and appeared to give one of his sweet angelic smiles of his.

"Later that night, Cameron and I were alone after evening mass and I told him what I had seen him and Robert do and that it was wrong, very wrong, in the eyes of the Lord. At first he seemed a little embarrassed and panicked at the thought that I would reveal what I had seen and that he would have to stop coming to my church. I reassured him that I would not say anything and that it was going to be our secret. I said that

he needed to confess his sins to the Lord and this was when he told me about his sexual relationship with his teacher.

"I closed my eyes and silently prayed for him as he told me all the sordid details of his sexual relationship with his teacher and when I opened my eyes, I was staggered to see him naked before me. Whilst I had been praying for his soul, Cameron had slipped off his T-shirt and shorts and was now naked next to me. Cameron, now knowing that I had seen him and Robert in the cove and did not interrupt them had misinterpreted my actions and thought that I also wanted him. That was how promiscuous the young boy was. I was truly mortified and yet strangely aroused by him. I quickly pulled him to the floor, so nobody could see him and whilst I was telling him to get dressed, he said something like *'let me make you happy'*.

"I wanted so desperately to stop him, believe me, I did. Nobody knows how much I wanted to stop him and thrash the living daylights out of him for tempting me so. But I couldn't. I just couldn't take my eyes of him as he lay there, at my feet, masturbating before my very eyes. That one act of not stopping him has haunted me ever since." The priest paused briefly, made the Sign of the Cross and wiped tears from his eyes. "I have prayed a million prayers for forgiveness since that day, for succumbing to carnal lust and desire, but believe me detective, I simply couldn't help myself. The sight of such a beautiful boy, so handsome and muscular, lying at my feet, naked as the day he was born, masturbating himself was too much temptation for anybody to withstand. It proved to be too much temptation for me, any man. Cameron reached up and began performing oral sex on me…"

Father Martin did not get the opportunity to complete his sentence as Hollister cut him short and interrupted him. "You'll have to pay for your moment of temptation one day, but it's not for me to judge you. I'll leave that for Him." Hollister pointed upwards, towards the heaven's to make his point.

The priest could now detect a certain amount of sympathy in Hollister's voice, where there had previously only been anger and hostility. "Don't you think that I've thought about that ever since? With every passing day I've regretted my moment of weakness and wished that I hadn't succumbed to temptation and handled the entire incident differently and not allowed myself to have been corrupted. For believe me detective, it was I that was corrupted and not, as you think, the other way around."

Hollister did actually believe the priest. He had been recounted an almost identical scenario of boy/man seduction by Foxford. Any doubts that Hollister still had about the innocence of Robinson had now been dispelled. He now knew that Cameron Robinson was by no means the innocent victim of the sexual depravity of older me. "After this first occasion, you know, whilst on holiday, when did you and Cameron begin your relationship?"

Once again, the priest hesitated before he replied to the question, listening to the ticking of the clock. "It was about a week later, after choir practice. All the other choristers had gone home and it was only Cameron and I in the church as we tidied up after practice. This in itself was nothing unusual. Cameron had a genuine interest in the Church and we often talked about various aspects of its doctrine and sometimes I even got the inspiration for my next sermon from talking to him. We

completely lost all sense of timing as we talked, with neither of us mentioning what had happened on the break but, no doubt, we both had thought about it. I know that I did. When I realised how late it was and that his mother was probably worried about him, I went to the office and telephoned his home to let his mother know that he was still at the church and that he wouldn't be long. After we went into the vestment room and he removed his surplice and cassock. To my horror he was naked underneath. How he had somehow managed to remove all his clothes, without me seeing him. It was a complete mystery to me then and a shock and the knowledge that he may have performed the entire practice naked mortified me and yet, it strangely excited me as well. It meant that he had planned what was happening and this became the start of our relationship."

In a strange way the detective admired the boldness and daring of the youngster to do such a thing. "How long did it last?"

"It only lasted a couple of months. It became extremely difficult for me to concentrate on my duties. I also think that some people were beginning to get suspicious about us spending so much time together and so I brought our…relationship…to an end."

Hollister paused for a moment as he digested what the priest had told him and thinking how much it now applied to him. Maybe the priest was trying to warn him about something. "Paedophiles like you…"

"I am not a paedophile," interrupted Father Martin. "I resent even the merest suggestion that I am. Paedophiles are vile and disgusting people."

The priest's outburst took Hollister by surprise. "Anybody that preys on children for sex is a paedophile."

"No they are not, detective and you, of all people, should know that." Hollister twitched nervously in his chair as the priest continued, "Paedophiles prey on innocent children and direct their sordid desires towards defenceless and innocent children. I am not one of *those* people. I love children. I have devoted most of my life to children, taking care of their pastoral and spiritual needs. The ancient Greeks had a name for those like me and, if you feel the need to pigeonhole and categories me, then use it. It was *paiderastes* or pederast. It means *'the lover of boys'*."

Hollister ignorance of such matters had caught up with him. "Are one and the other not the same, just different names or excuses?"

"Absolutely not, detective," Father Martin's voice now had a tone of indignation in it. "A paedophile, as you are aware, is a very dangerous person. To them, their sexual attraction to children lies in their minds. It is this desire that prompts them into abusing children. They usually dream of having sex with a particular child. They have fantasies about this child, frequently acting out these fantasies on animals before they abuse a child. They work their minds up into a frenzy that they end up abusing a child. On many occasions the child that they abuse is not the actual child of their desires. It is just another aspect of their paedophilia. To actually violate the object of their desires would end their desire for their particular child. No child can ever be truly safe around a paedophile.

"However, a pederast loves only one boy, both fatherly and spiritually. In ancient times the word 'pederasty' implied that the man took care of all the boy's needs, with the full consent of his parents, after he had entered puberty and not yet reached manhood. An older

man, a friend of the boy's father and usually a scholar, would...sort off...adopt the boy and make himself responsible for all the boys development, both intellectually and morally. The boy, or 'catamite' as they were known, would then reward his mentor any way that he could and this usually took the form of sexual favours. This would then cement their spiritually love and bond together."

"What a total load of bollocks," protested Hollister.

"Every word is true detective. There are countless examples of this on plates and amphorae in art galleries and museums around the world. Look it up, be the detective and prove me wrong."

Hollister mind was now in turmoil. The priest had expertly managed to turn the psychological tables and gained the upper hand. "Even if it's true, which I doubt, you, as a priest cannot hide behind such ancient ideals and morals. In this day and age, a man cannot have any form of sexual relationship with a young boy..."

"Can't they, Chief inspector?" Father Martin, without knowing about Hollister and the young 'rent boy' had exposed the detective's hypocrisy. "As the Good Lord says, *'He that is without sin among you, let him cast a stone at her'*. You'll find it in the Book of Saint John, chapter eight and verse seven."

Father Martin was now calm and composed and it was the turn of Hollister to nervously wring his hands. "What are you trying to say, Father?"

"Through your words, both spoken and implied, I know that you are not without knowledge of sexual liaison with a young boy. You have as good as told me, Chief Inspector. Don't forget, I have been trained, like you, in searching out the true meaning of the words being spoken, in

order to find and understand their actual meaning. We are not that dissimilar, are we Chief Inspector?"

"I don't think that my sexual preference is an issue..." rebutted Hollister.

"And I don't think that you, of all people, are in a position to judge me."

Verbal hostility had now broken out between the detective and the priest. "I was not trying to judge you Father. All I wanted was an insight into your relationship with Cameron Robinson."

"Well, you now have your 'insight' detective. So, if you excuse me, I have a lot of work to do." Father Martin brought their meeting to an end.

Deeply unsettled by his meeting with the priest, McKenzie Hollister sought solitude and time alone to think before driving back to Manchester and so he spent a while walking around the village that was Father Martin's diocese. Had he been so transparent, he wondered to himself? His words had been chosen with care. He had not, or so he thought, openly shown the priest any emotions and yet he had known, almost instinctively, that he had formed his relationship with Johnny, the young 'rent boy'. If Father Martin had been so easily able to pick up on this, then, wondered Hollister, had anybody else? The thought of this troubled the detective. Just when he thought that he was beginning to think that he had pulled himself back from the abyss, he now found himself once again torn by doubts and guilt.

Having driven back to Manchester, his mind in turmoil, Hollister needed a drink now more than ever. Parking his car in a side street in

the city centre, paranoia descended on the detective and he almost started the engine and drove off but he pulled himself together. As he got out of the car and locked it, he thought that he could feel everybody looking at him, talking about him, knowing just who he was and what he been recently doing with the young 'rent boy'. Making the short journey onto Canal Street, wanting to seek refuge in the one gay bar that he knew, Hollister felt that everybody was staring at him. He felt hundreds of eyes burning into him and he thought that they were all talking about him.

Entering through the glass doors of *'The Last Exit'* Hollister breathed a sigh of relief as he realised just how heavy his heart was beating and how much he was perspiring. He realised that he was having a panic attack. Making his way to the bar, almost pushing past those patrons already in the bar, actually making them look at him, Hollister finally found solace at the bar. He ordered a lager, which he virtually drank in one go and then ordered a second as he finally began to calm down as his paranoia eased and he calmed down.

As the alcohol took effect, Hollister relaxed and began to look around the bar and the people in it. He no longer imagined that they were looking at him or talking about him, the uneasy feeling that some of them might even know that he was a police officer, a though implanted in his brain following his meeting with Father Martin, slowly dissipated and now he realised just how ridiculous the whole thing had been. As Hollister slowly looked around the bar in search of Greg, the barman, he realised that there was no sign of him.

But somebody did lean forward and look him directly in the eyes. Having been previously obscured by the throng of people at the copper-

topped bar, McKenzie Hollister finally looked directly into the eyes of the one person that he had sought more than anybody. He looked straight into the shocked face of Spencer.

Chapter Thirteen

Immediately on making eye contact, both man and boy had different reactions. Hollister felt his heart miss a beat whilst Spencer, on the other hand, spun on his seat and went to leave. Hollister's reactions were faster than the boys. He reached out, pushing aside those that stood at the bar between him and Spencer and grabbed hold of him by his jacket. "Where the hell have you been?" asked the detective abruptly. "I've been searching everywhere for you."

Realising that he had lost his only chance of evasion, Spencer replied to the detective, "I've been around."

"Spencer, what's going on? Who's this?" asked the man that was with the youth, fiercely guarding what he regarded as his property.

The youngster tried to placate the man, "It's okay Chris. He's just some bloke that I met a few weeks ago." Turning to face Hollister, "He'll leave me alone."

The man, who was aged around forty, shorter than Spencer, with dark hair balding at the crown and his pierced ear gave him the appearance of somebody wishing to remember years now long past, was not going to give in easily. "Listen, I don't know who you are or what your connection is with Spencer but…"

"I'm a police officer," Hollister interrupted the man and pushed his warrant card up close to the man's face, so close that he probably could not of read it. Now those that Hollister had imagined were staring at him a few minutes earlier really were looking over towards the

commotion at the bar. "If you don't want to be arrested for being with a minor, then I suggest you fuck off, sharpish."

The man very briefly thought about his situation and decided to take the harshly worded advice of the detective seriously. As he turned to leave, two security men arrived and Hollister showed them his warrant card. Both held their hands up skywards before turning and returning to their previous position at the door. Spencer was livid. "Who the fuck do you think you are and what the fuck do you think you're doing?"

"We need to talk" replied Hollister now calmly.

"I've got fuck all to say to you" snapped back Spencer angrily.

"You've got a great deal to say to me. You can either talk to me now, outside, or I'll take you in and officially question you. The choice is yours and the clock is ticking."

Spencer gave an arrogant laugh. "You won't take me in. You're bluffing."

Hollister stared directly into the eyes of the boy, their noses almost touching, "Fucking try me," his voice full of menace.

Now feeling very intimidated, if not a little scared, Spencer conceded defeat in the battle of wills. "Okay, but not here."

They both walked out of the bar, past the prying eyes and ears that had witnessed their brief diatribe and past the two security guards, who made a mental note of their faces. Hollister made sure that he remained just half a step behind the youth, ready to grab him if he foolishly made a bolt for it in order to avoid the detective's questions. Once out in the fresh air they took a seat on a pair of metal chairs, two out of four that surround a circular table. To make sure that the boy did not attempt to run away, Hollister proceeded to handcuff him to the table. Spencer

tried to object, but the sheer strength of Hollister's grip on his arm made him realise that any resistance was futile and, very reluctantly, he allowed himself to be shackled to the metal table. He then set about trying to hide the handcuffs with his jacket.

They were not the only ones sat out on Canal Street, the cosmopolitan atmosphere of 'The Village' encouraged the patrons of the bars and clubs out onto the street and in full view and to all those out on Canal Street, they looked like a normal couple, sitting by the waist-high wall, sharing a drink, as the canal and life past them by. Nobody gave them a second glance as they talked.

"What do you want?" asked Spencer, his young voice full of anger and bitterness at his treatment by Hollister.

"Where have you been?" demanded the detective. "I've searched 'The Village' from top to bottom, for weeks, looking for you and you've been nowhere to be seen. So, where have you been?"

"I don't have to answer to you," objected the boy.

"Oh yes you do," responded Hollister defiantly. "After all, you're nothing but a kid. You shouldn't even be out here, let alone in a bar, with a client."

"Who said he was a client?"

"I did. Spencer, you're a 'rent boy'. If you're with a bloke in a bar, then he's probably a client. Now if you don't to go straight from here to Hell...my police station, for the last time, where have you been?"

Spencer thought for a few seconds, trying to second guess as to whether Hollister would really take him in for questioning? He decided against pushing his luck too far. "Like I said, I've been around. Canal

Street isn't the only place that I hang around." There was still an icy tone to the teenager's voice.

Hollister persisted, "You're really beginning to piss me off now. For the last time, where the fuck have you been?"

Spencer let out a sigh and bowed his head, finally giving in to the persistent detective, having been wound down by his asking the same question, "Hanging around Ducie Street."

"Where?" asked Hollister with a puzzled look on his face.

"You know the car park on Dale Street near Piccadilly train station, you know near Ducie Street," was Spencer's reluctantly given answer.

Totally confused now, Hollister tried again. "What the fuck are you doing all the way over there?"

Spencer relaxed a little and offered his captor a brief smile, "You've really got no idea have you?" When he saw Hollister shake his head, the youth continued, "That's where we hangout. Everybody knows that. Canal Street and 'The Village' are far too risky for us, so we meet up and hang out there."

"What's over there that 'The Village' doesn't offer you?"

"Privacy," Spencer paused briefly whilst the detective gathered his thoughts. "You just don't get it, do you? Over there..." the youngster points to the canal behind him, "...there is a path that leads to the old canal tow path. If you follow it all the way, going towards Piccadilly station, you get to the arches. It's dark and secretive and there loads of places where you can take a 'John', without getting any grief from anybody. That's where I've been and that's why you couldn't find me. You've been looking in the wrong place."

Hollister found that he was amazed that such a place existed in the centre of Manchester and made a mental note to go there and chick it out for himself, partly out of curiosity and partly to reassure himself that Spencer was telling the truth. Not that the youngster had anything to gain by lying to him, mused Hollister. "I've been trying to find you because we need to talk more about Cameron Robinson or Martin Foxford as you knew him."

Spencer looked away from the detective. Hollister tried to judge whether this was a gesture of embarrassment at having to talk about the dead youth or it had been brought about by his current situation. "I've got nothing to say about him. He's dead. Why can't you just let him rest in peace?"

Ignoring the boy's comment, Hollister pressed his point, "When we met last you told me that you thought Cameron was being blackmailed by somebody into giving him free sex. Having looked into this claim, I now think that you might've been right. Me personally, I'm now convinced that he was being blackmailed and this person might even be responsible for his death and you might know who he is, which then could put you in his sight's."

"I don't know jack-shit." Spencer still maintained both his ignorance and arrogance as he continued to look away from the detective sitting next to him.

Hollister gripped him tightly on his thigh, out of sight from those around them, his strong fingers digging deep into the soft fleshy muscle of the youth, making the youngster wince in pain. "Listen here you little shit," he said through gritted teeth and in a menacing voice, "I've spent weeks trying to find you. I've checked out just about every bar on

Canal Street. I've looked in every darkened street and into every seedy alleyway to see if you were in there with a punter and I've seen some pretty disgusting sights. Now that I've finally found you, I'm not letting you out of my sight until you've told me everything that I want to know. So you'd better fucking wise up young man…fast."

The air of self-confidence had disappeared from Spencer as he realised that the detective meant business. He now felt very intimidated by Hollister and for the first time realised what he could do to him if he really wanted to. Turning to face the detective he looked directly into his cold icy eyes and spoke softly. "What do you want to know?"

"That's better" replied Hollister as he relaxed his grip on the boy's thigh. "Let me go and get us a drink and we'll talk. Give you time to think about what you know and now that you know that I'm not in the mood to be pissed about."

Leaving Spencer safe in the knowledge that he could not run off because he was still shackled to the table, unable to go anywhere even if he wanted to, Hollister went into the bar, passed the glaring eyes of the door security men who he had just shown his warrant card to earlier and he return a few minutes later with a lager for him and a coke for the boy, "Couldn't get you a drink because of your age."

Sitting next to Spencer once again, Hollister pulled his chair up as close as he could to the boy, not wanting anybody to overhear their conversation. "Right, let's start at the beginning. I know your name isn't Spencer. I've checked the police national computer, various registers and the missing persons file at my station and you're not listed on any of them. So what's your name, and I mean your real name and how old are you?"

Spencer took a mouthful of his coke and wondered whether he should tell the detective what he wanted to know, eventually deciding that he will. "Pavel, Pavel Holešovice. I'll be eighteen in a couple of months."

"What do you prefer, Pavel or Spencer?"

"Spencer."

"Where are you from…you know…originally?"

"That don't matter."

Hollister decided not to push this point and offered the boy a smile as he sipped his lager. "Fair enough, for now. Now, I need you to be totally honest with me Spencer. I need you to tell me everything that you know about Cameron, or Martin, no matter how trivial you may think it is. In order for me to understand everything about his death, I need to know everything about his life. After doing some research, without going into too much detail, I now think that somebody was either blackmailing him or using some sort of hold or influence over him and I need to find out who this person is. I'm not interested in anything that you do, that's your business but if we're both right, then there's a very dangerous man out there. He might even be doing the same to another boy and this might even lead to his death. We need to find this man and take him out of circulation before we end up with another dead boy."

"We're definitely talking about the same boy?" asked Spencer.

"Yes, we are" replied Hollister. "His real name was Cameron Robinson, but when he left home, he changed it to Martin Foxford." The detective not letting on that he knew the reason behind the choice of this name.

Spencer nodded his head, almost to the beat of the music that filled Canal Street, noticing that his fear and apprehension had subsided. "I didn't really know him that well."

"I didn't think that you did but you are though, one of the few people that is around the same age as him and knew about his way of life. Just tell me what you know about him. You know, how you first met, any mutual friends or clients you had. Like I've said, I need to know as much as possible about him."

After taking a sip of his coke, wishing it was something stronger and alcoholic, Spencer thought for a moment and then responded. "I first met him about a year ago. I'd been out one night…you know…working and when I'd done this punter I saw Martin…sorry, Cameron, on the street. Where he came from or who he was I didn't know at the time. He was stood near the toilets over at Chorlton Street coach station and was obviously out for business. But the way he acted I could tell that he was a 'green horn'…you know…a new boy on the streets. I noticed him because of his looks. Even I've got to admit that he was really good looking. All our regular punters fell for him straight away and wanted him and he began to take the business from most of us. Then one night, this older and bigger lad, I think his name is Harvey, turned on him and beat him up for taking all our punters away from us. Afterwards, I went over to help him and that's how I got to know him."

"You seemed to know the rules of the streets pretty well, even a year ago," stated Hollister. "How long have you been on the 'game' before this happened?"

"A couple of years," admitted Spencer, the boy's barely audible reply came after a short pause.

"I don't mean to pry, but I'm genuinely interested and fascinated about your lifestyle. Was your first time the night that you told me about, you know, getting picked up outside *'Burgerworld'* on Market Street by this Barry?"

Spencer shook his head. "No. I just took advantage of him."

"How?" replied Hollister with a quizzical look on his face.

"I'd been here on the streets of Manchester for a couple of weeks by that time. Like I said, I'd been sleeping rough on the streets and just needed somewhere to go. When I first ran away from home, I didn't know what to do or where to go and so I just slept rough in..." Spencer hesitated, still not prepared to reveal too many details about his early life or where he came from to Hollister. "...I got to know a couple of lads. Some were okay and about my age now but there were a couple of younger boys, barely in their teens. Most of them were in care homes and used to pull tricks to pay for their drugs and had to be back for ten at night, which left most blokes for us older ones. While these 'chickens' worked early on, we'd hang around waiting for them to go home, doing a bit of robbing here and there and some 'weed' just to pass the time. Nothing big mind you, just some booze and food from a few shops. They weren't all runaways though. Some of them even had homes to go home to, probably nice ones. After they'd made enough for the next day's drugs, they'd fuck off home to their nice warm beds and then we'd be left to fend for ourselves, on our own, living day-to-day on the streets.

"You then ask yourself 'what have you got?' and 'where are you going to spend the night?' The answers were always the same, fuck all. It's a shit life on the streets. You'd give almost anything not to be

scared at nights when you're sleeping rough, alone in an arch or doorway or anywhere where you don't have to sleep with one eye open. In fact, when you're sleeping rough on the streets, you don't actually sleep, you doze. You're far too scared to go to sleep in case somebody robs you of what little you've got or some dickheads on their way home after a night out decides to piss on you because they think it's funny or they just kick the shit out of for fun. You've also got to watch out that the rats don't run all over you or even bite you. That's the reality of having to sleep on the streets and so we do whatever we can just for a bed for the night."

"With you only being so young, did the uniforms never come across you and take you home?" asked the detective solemnly, deeply affected by the youngster's tale of woe.

"Yeah, sometimes and don't take this wrong but there are some really sick bastards in the police force. There are a couple of 'pigs'…sorry, police…out there that once they find out you're a 'rent' they force you to give them a 'blow-job' or they take you somewhere and shag you up the arse in the back of their van. This has happened to me a few times. Other times they just take you home. They don't seem to care that you might actually be running away from something at home in the first place. They just take you home and dump you there. The first time they did this, I got the shit kicked out of me for running away. I was black and blue for days and when I was starting to recover after a couple of days, I got battered again for bringing the police to…our…home. So, when I got better, I ran away again. Then I got picked up again, took back home and got battered again. This time I was so badly hurt that I ended up in hospital but not even they gave a shit. They believed the

bullshit that…about me getting jumped by a gang of lads. No sooner was I out of hospital, I ran away again to get away from…them. That's when I moved to London.

"Down there the police don't give a fuck about you. They know we're there and what we're doing but, as long as we don't cause them any problems, mostly they leave us alone. Sure, we get the odd sicko that'll pick us up for a 'blow-job' or a quick shag, but that's just life. Mostly they just drive past us and laugh at you. Sometimes they think they're being kind to you and throw you some scraps of food but what they're really doing is saying we're nothing better than animals. They probably think what's the point in picking you up? All it does is create a lot of paperwork for them, arrange for Social Services to pick you up and take you back home, only for you to probably run away again. Nobody ever asks what you're running away from because nobody really gives a fuck about you or even cares what happens to you."

"I care Spencer and I'm asking," Hollister said genuinely. "What are you running away from? Maybe I can help you."

After a brief pause Spencer shook his head, "Don't want to tell you yet. It's not important to your case and it's private. Maybe one day though I'll tell you."

"Fair enough," replied Hollister with a disappointed shrug of his shoulders, deciding not to push the youngster too much for now. "You can tell me that when you're ready too. Now, how long did you spend in London?"

"Not long, only a couple of weeks. God, that place is so full of sickos and weirdos. I remember seeing something on telly once about King's Cross and how all the 'rent boys' hang out there and so I made for

there. Not even I could believe how many kids were sleeping rough around the station and in the streets around it. Christ, some were barely in their teens. Not all were 'rent boys' though, some were part of gangs that controlled the begging or were pickpockets, but a lot of them were 'rent boys'. It appeared the younger they were, the more in demand they were and some sick bastard was always there ready to prey on them. I got to know this lad who was only thirteen and having to score punters all day long to pay for his 'crack' habit. Said he'd already been on the streets a couple of years before I met him. He needed a couple of hundred quid a day for his 'crack' and if he was desperate, then he'd virtually give himself away, going with who knows who and just for a couple of quid. He'd do "blow-job's" for a fiver, you know, for the price of a 'rock'. Tell you, London is one fucked up place.

"I soon learnt that if I was gonna survive down there, then I'd have to 'turn tricks' like them. While I was there, I got raped twice, one being a gang-rape. I had me nose broken and generally worked over three or four times by some dirty bastards that'd kick the shit out you after fucking you rather than pay you. To them, I was just a piece of meat, just some young boy to fuck. Couldn't stand it any longer and then I came up to Manchester for some so called northern hospitality."

"And if I remember rightly, after a couple of weeks you met up with Barry and saw him as a ways and means of getting you sorted out."

"Yeah, that's about it," replied Spencer.

"Although I'm genuinely concerned about you and I really do want to help you but I'm not going to pry into your past. You obviously have your reasons for leaving home in the first place and you can tell me about this whenever you want. At the moment though, I'm only

concerned about Cameron Robinson. Going back, what happened after this lad Harvey beat him up?"

"I took him back to my place…you know…to clean him up and get him sorted. He had a bath, then I sorted his cuts and bruises out, cleaned him up and then we went to my bedroom…" The detective's ears pricked up, expecting to hear something exciting, but he was disappointed. "…nothing happened though that night. We just talked, had something to eat and crashed for the night."

"Can you remember what you talked about?" asked Hollister.

Spencer shook his head, "I really can't remember and that's the truth. No shit. He told me that his name was Martin and that he's new to the 'game' and that he wasn't a virgin."

"Did he give you any indication as to why he was turning to prostitution?" asked the detective, relieved that there was no longer any hostility in the voice of the youngster that he had spent weeks looking for. He did find himself once again hanging on to every word that the teenager spoke in sheer fascination, needing to know more about this secretive world he had stumbled upon.

"Not at first though. He did tell me that he'd been shagged by a PE teacher and that he let him do it because he wanted to get a great body and become a model or maybe get a part on TV or in films. That's what he said he wanted to be. If he was still alive, I think he'd be one by now. He knew what he wanted and was prepared to do anything to get it. He knew what he wanted to be and nothing was going to stop him. He knew that if he had to have sex with a bloke to get something that he wanted then he'd do it. He really didn't care what he did."

So that was it. Hollister finally had the answer to the question that he had sought for so long now. Robinson wanted to be a model and a television star. That was it. That was why he concentrated so much on his gymnastics training. He wanted to get a good body and in order to get this physique, if he had to have sex with his gymnastics coach, he simply did not mind. Sex with Barratt Foxford was just a means to an end. In the eyes of Robinson it was just something that he needed to do in order to achieve his ultimate goal in life.

"How about his home life, did he ever talk about his family?"

Once again Spencer shook his head. "He never mentioned them once. But, then again, most 'rents' never do. Half the time it's things at their homes that they are running away from and then they end up on the streets and then on the 'game' to survive."

"Would it surprise you to know that Cameron was different? He came from a really good home with a loving and caring family."

"You know what, it wouldn't" replied Spencer with a shake of his head. "I could tell from the first night that we met that he was different from most of us. Could tell by the way he talked and looked that he had been brought up in an okay place. He just seemed…" Spencer paused briefly and rotated his hands in mid-air, trying to find the correct expression, "…well…normal."

"That," exclaimed the detective "is precisely what's been bugging me all along. Here's a young lad, from a good and loving home, doing well at school and then just giving it all up, leaving home without any apparent reason and becoming a 'rent boy'. It just doesn't make any sense. That's why I've been trying so hard to find you in the hope that you could explain why he did it." Hollister paused briefly before he

continued, "Not only that, I like you. There is something about you that fascinates me about you."

Now the youngster understood why the detective had wanted to meet him again and relaxed a little, allowing himself a brief smile. He had thought that Hollister was only after him in order to exploit him, to exploit him sexually, but having heard what he had just been told he now thought differently and decided to open up. "After that first night, me and Martin we sort off became friends. We looked out for each other. If there was a dodgy punter out there, we'd warn each other about him. Like I said, Martin...sorry Cameron...wanted to be a model and asked me if I knew any bokes that were photographers and did lads like him so he could have a portfolio done? I introduced him to one that I knew called Will and after that, I hardly saw him out on the streets. He seemed to have used me just like he used everybody else."

"Is this photographer still going?"

"Yeah," came the softly spoke reply.

Both had finished their drinks and Hollister left the youth alone for a second time while he went back into the bar and refilled their glasses, joining Spencer a couple of minutes later and letting the boy know that he had put something a little stronger into his coke this time.

Hollister removed the handcuffs from Spencer's wrist and the table and pocketed them. "Don't think we need these anymore," commented Hollister as he did and watched the boy massage his now sore wrist. "Where can I find this Will? He's next on my list."

"He's a little shit" came the unexpected reply, "a proper sicko. I don't know where his studio is, that's assuming that he has one, but he works at a bail hostel for juveniles over in Stockport."

Without even meeting him, Hollister had taken an instant dislike to the man. Like Robinson's priest and gymnastics coach before him, he had apparently exploited Robinson for his own gratification. "Do you know where this bail hostel is?"

"Yeah, it's in Cheadle Heath, a big house, on its own."

"I know it. I'll get the boys to give it a knock…"

Spencer interrupted the detective, "You can't let them know I told you about it. I'll be dead for sure if he ever found out."

On realising just how scared he was, Hollister tried to placate the boy. "Don't worry Spencer. I'll make sure you're not mentioned. I'll find some reason to raid the place and then find something on the Will." This soothed the nerves of Spencer and Hollister continued, "Don't forget there isn't really an investigation into Cameron's death. It was officially closed after the *post mortem* concluded it was suicide. I'm still doing all this on my own."

"You must be pretty certain that there was something more to his death to do all this?"

"I am," replied Hollister. He thought long and hard before he spoke again, "Listen, don't take this the wrong way but it's getting late, not to mention cold. I'm in a difficult position. There is still so much that I need to ask you, but I can't run the risk of being seen with you in 'The Village'. I'd like you to come back to my place…no strings attached…where we can talk in private. I'll even pay you whatever you'd lose out on by not working. You never know, I might even give you a bonus…if you catch my drift."

Even Spencer was beginning to feel the cold and understood the predicament of the detective. He also had his own reputation to think

off. He could not be seen talking to a police officer in the middle of Canal Street but he was still a little uneasy about trusting Hollister, but reluctantly he decided to chance it. "Yeah, okay. I'm not exactly dressed to stay out any way."

As they both emptied their glasses, Hollister noticed that the youth was a little unsteady on his feet and thought that this might be as a result drinking alcohol without eating anything and decided to get some food on their way to Robinson's apartment. "There's something that I need to tell you. Since the last time that we met, I've had some personal problems, which I won't go in to. Anyway, I've moved into Cameron's old flat."

"Do you mean that's where we're going?" asked Spencer. After the detective nodded, the youngster continued, "I'm not sure about this."

"What better place for us to go? Except for us two, nobody even knew that he had the place and it'll be a shame to ruin it by clearing it out. In there, we can talk in complete privacy, safe in the knowledge that nobody will see us talking or overhear anything. We can get something to eat and even have a drink there."

Spencer was still a little hesitant, but what the detective said did make sense, he thought to himself. The need for something to eat and the prospect of getting something to drink, not to mention to possibly get paid by Hollister, were the final factors in making up his mind.

On the way to Robinson's apartment, Hollister stopped off at a bank and withdrew some money, then called into a Chinese take-away shop and finally at a convenience store for some alcohol, where he once again used a cash-point machine to draw some more money out. What he did omit to tell Spencer was that he was using money from

Robinson's bank accounts and not his own to pay for the food and drink. Hollister saw no need to burden the youngster with this information, not wanting him to change his mind and have second thoughts about going back to Robinson's former flat. Having spent weeks looking for him and finally having found Spencer the detective was not going to let him out of his sight until he was satisfied that the boy had told him everything that he knew about Robinson and answered some of the many questions still buzzing around in the mind of the detective. Hollister, if he was honest with himself though, felt like a schoolboy on his first date, with the thought of finally being alone with the person of so many recent fantasies.

"I'm still not sure about this," Spencer commented as he and Hollister entered the former flat of Cameron Robinson for the second time. Despite his reservations, the youth knew that this was probably the best place for them to talk.

"It's perfectly all right," replied Hollister, "I've been using this place as a base for the last couple of weeks."

Hollister led the still wary youth into the lounge while he went into the kitchen and emerged a few minutes later with a plate of food and a drink for the youngster before he disappeared for a second time, emerging this time with some food and a can of lager for himself. He got straight down to business, "Tell me more about this photographer."

"He's a little shit, pure scum, an absolute arsehole," replied Spencer as he wolfed down the food before him. "He'll encourage some young lad at the hostel to either break the conditions of his bail or his curfew or something like that and then he'll take advantage of the situation. He

threatens the boy saying that unless he does what he wants them to do for him he'll put it in his bail report for the courts that they constantly broke the conditions of his bail. Most lads have no option but to go along with him. Those that don't usually end up getting sent to a young offenders unit because of what he's said about them. The one's that do go along with him and these are usually the younger ones that are too scared to say no to him become his models."

"What sort of pictures does he take with them?"

"He doesn't just photograph them, he makes videos as well. Real sick ones," answered Spencer. "He'll have boys going with each other...you know...doing sex things to each other. Some he'll get to have sex together and others he'll get blokes in to shag them while he photographs or films them. It appears the younger the boys, the bigger the market. The more innocent that they look, the more sick and perverted are the things that they have to do."

Hollister could hardly believe his ears. Here was a man in a position of trust, employed by the legal system to look after the very youngsters that he exploited and took advantage off, in order to satisfy his own perverse desires and the needs of others. "I've seen a couple of videos like this, one of them featuring Cameron. Could these have been done by this bloke?"

"Yeah they probably were. There ain't that many sickos out there that have ready access to boys for these kind videos. I saw one once, a real sick one. This young blond lad gets tied to a bed and five blokes go through him and I mean they did the works on him, especially this black bloke. He was massive...if you catch my drift. Not once did the boy struggle or say no. He just did everything that he was told to do. It

wasn't rape or anything like that but there was no way that he could've enjoyed what they did to him. Not even I've done half that shit. This Will guy must've had some real big hold on this kid in order for him to take part in something like that."

"Do you think this blond boy could've been drugged first?" asked Hollister, searching for an excuse to raid the bail hostel.

"He didn't seem to be. He appeared to be awake and actively taking part. Maybe not willingly but he never objected to what they did to him. He did seem a little spaced out though."

Hollister mind was now racing into overdrive. From the description given to him by Spencer and based on his prior knowledge of such things, he was beginning to suspect that some kind off pharmaceutical medication, a 'date rape' drug, had been given to the youngster prior to his terrible ordeal. If this was the case, then it would give the detective grounds for initiating a raid on the bail hostel. "I'll respect you if you don't answer this, but…have you ever made any videos with him?"

Washing down a mouthful of food with a swig of lager, Spencer seemed embarrassed when he replied to the question. "Not with him but yeah, I made one once…a while back. Wasn't for me."

Hollister was both mortified that the youngster sat with him had appeared in a porn movie and fascinated that he had. If he had told the truth that he was nearly seventeen years old and he said that he had made this film some years ago, then he would have been barely a teenager when he did it. "We're going to have to get this scum-bag out of operation and pretty quickly."

"It won't do any good though," Spencer added in a very matter-of-fact way. "He'll quickly be replaced by somebody else."

"What makes you say that?" asked the detective.

"He works within the system and that system always covers up for those that get caught out. It's just the way it is. He's been at it for so long that somebody high up and I don't just mean in the probation service, must know what's going on and be turning a blind eye and some top copper must be covering up for him as well. Might even be you, for all that I know."

Hollister shook his head, "No Spencer, it isn't me. Until you've just told me about it, I had no idea anything like this was going on in Manchester. I understand what you're saying though, somebody has got be looking out for him but it is not me. I'm different though."

Having finished off his plate of food, Hollister washed it down with his lager. He certainly was different and if only Spencer knew the truth about the sleepless nights he had endured looking for him, the nights that he had masturbated whilst thinking about him, secretly wishing that it was Spencer doing it and not him. He now knew that he had wanted to be alone with him from the very first time that he had seen him. He had dreamt and fantasised about being alone with him, in this very scenario, for weeks now and if Spencer had known this, then maybe he might not have been so willing to have been alone with the detective in the first place.

Hollister looked closer at the youth sat across the room from him. His mid-brown hair had grown a little, helping to frame his handsome face. The boys green eyes did not give any indications of any pain or suffering that he might be secretly concealing. He just seemed like a typical teenaged boy. There was nothing overtly special about him and

yet there was something about the youth that attracted the detective to him.

"How different though?" asked Spencer with a mischievous grin, despite having a mouthful of food.

"I'm straight down the line," replied the detective. "I'm either your best friend or your worst enemy. That depends on you though. If I'm your friend, then I'll move heaven and earth for you and help you out any way that I can. If you cross me though, I'll be your biggest nightmare. I'd jump on you like hitting you with a ton of bricks."

"Don't tell me, let me guess. Your birth-sign is cancer?"

A rare smile lit up on Hollister's face, "How do you know that?"

"Let's just say that in my line of work that I'm a good judge of character," replied Spencer with another impish smile.

The bitterness and the antagonism from earlier in the evening had gone from both the detective and the youth as Hollister continued to study the boy before him. He did not look like somebody who was nearly seventeen years old and approaching adulthood, but the young boy that he really was and it was only now that Hollister realised what the fascination was about him. He reminded the detective of his school friend Ged, the boy that he had experimented sexually with until they had been ultimately caught out and humiliated.

For weeks after, once alone in his bedroom and under the cover of darkness, he had allowed his imagination and his hand to run rampant and fulfil the remainder of their interrupted passion and now, many years later, he found himself alone with somebody that not only looked like him, but had helped to open up his long dormant feelings for Ged. He had thought about Spencer on the two occasions that he had been

with Johnny, the 'rent boy' with which he had finally realised his true sexuality, but now, whether it was due to the alcohol, he again longed for Spencer.

Hollister motioned for the teenager to join him on his sofa and was a little surprised when the youngster crossed the room and sat next to him. "Don't tell me you're gay?" asked Spencer.

"Let's just say that I like you. I like you a lot," replied Hollister. "I've been thinking about you for weeks...longing to be with you." There was no hint of embarrassment or shame in the detective's voice as he finally revealed his true feelings to the youngster.

It was the turn of the teenager to appear surprised. "Have you done anything like this before?"

"Only twice," came the reply. "Both times they've been with a 'rent boy' Maybe you know him, Johnny Simons?"

"What...the skater?" the shocked Spencer replied.

"Yeah...that's him. I must admit though that I was thinking about you all the time we...I was with him, secretly wishing it was you and not him."

"Yeah, I bet you did," Spencer said with a wry grin. "I saw him the other day and he said he'd been with a copper. Thought he was pulling me leg. Had no idea that it was you though. Do you know he's younger than me and still at school?"

Hollister was in such a state of shock that he failed to hear the last part of Spencer's sentence. He had not realised that Johnny knew he was a police officer. He certainly had not told him and wondered how he had known, making a mental note to find the boy again and ask him. But for now he had other plans.

Chapter Fourteen

Dawn was just breaking when Hollister woke the following morning. He was momentarily startled to discover that he was not alone, but soon relaxed when he remembered who it was sleeping next to him. At first he thought it was Johnny, the other 'rent boy' that he was having sex with, who was in the bed. He thought that he had kept the boy out all night, worrying his mother so much that she would have called the police and reported him missing. Hollister found himself relieved, not to mention pleased, that it was Spencer who lay next to him.

Slowly and carefully he eased himself out of the bed, taking great pains not to disturb the sleeping youth and he could not but wonder just how long it had been since the youngster was this peaceful? The detective padded over towards the window, with the curtains drawn, preventing the early sun from shining through and studied the sleeping boy. The covers had been pushed back and barely covered him, exposing most of his body to the detective and he again wondered when the youngster had been this at ease as his chest gently rose up and down, his breathing so slight that he could have easily have been mistaken for dead. As he gazed on the boy, the image of Cameron Robinson once again flashed through his mind.

He too had looked so peaceful on that fateful day when Hollister had answered the call to attend the scene of his death. The more that the detective had pried into the youth's brief life, on the surface so happy and full of life and yet now the detective now realised just how desperately sad and unhappy he must have really been. Knowing more

about the boy now than he did on that day the words on the 'suicide' note were now beginning to make a little sense, *'...All my life I have cried out for love, but nobody ever loved me...a nameless person amongst others...maybe in death I might achieve something."*

Achieve what though, wondered the detective? What exactly was he trying to say with these words? For the first time since he began his personal quest, Hollister was beginning to think that maybe Robinson had committed suicide after all. Maybe his original 'gut feeling' and instinct had been wrong all those weeks ago. Recalling the remainder of the 'suicide' note, its contents now etched deeply into his memory, Hollister being unable to forget them, it really did now sound like a cry for help or a plea for somebody to love him.

Two men had claimed that they had loved him. The two men that were the most prominent and life-influencing people and so prominent in his life at the time, Father Martin, his priest and Barratt Foxford, his gymnastics coach, probably did not love him but lusted over him and each had abused their positions of trust and had sex with the boy. Hollister doubted that either man had truly loved Robinson. To them, he was probably just been their latest plaything, quickly being replaced by another boy after he had disappeared and possibly soon forgotten. At least that part of the note now made sense.

As he thought about it, the only real thing that Robinson's death had achieved was to turn his own life upside down. Seeing the youngster lying naked on the bed, almost angelic looking and at peace, had disturbed him so much that not only had it cost him his marriage, but it had brought out into the open his long dormant feelings regarding his own sexuality, ones that even he had, over the passage of time,

forgotten. At first Hollister had found himself questioning his sexual orientation but when he had finally found the courage to have had sex with a young 'rent boy', he had overcome these suppressed feelings and embraced them he realised that he was, and probably had always been, homosexual and his true path in life was revealed to him. He also realised that he could never go back to his previous existence and this meant turning his back on his once loving wife, not that she wanted him now any way.

At first Hollister thought about getting back in bed with the sleeping teenager but instead he chose to face the curtained window, pulling it back just enough to look out onto the park opposite. The detective thought that it offered an incredible sight first thing in the morning. Shafts of golden sunlight breaking through the greyness of the night and highlighting the multitude of hues of the trees and the ground, the grass sparkling as the sunlight reflected of the early morning dew and the only sounds to be heard was the distant singing of the birds, offering Manchester a dawn chorus before the humdrum of daily life shattered the peacefulness of the early morning.

For the first time in weeks Hollister felt completely at ease with his own conscience and the view in front of him added to his feeling of tranquillity. He thought that he could wake up and see such a beautiful sight every morning. What he had done to and with Spencer the previous evening had been morally wrong, possibly teetering on illegal, but they had both wanted it to happen and so, thought Hollister, no harm had been really done. Spencer would probably have spent the night with the mystery man that he had seen him with in the bar and probably may have done everything that he and the youth had done and

so Hollister thought that it might as well have been him and not some complete stranger. They had both enjoyed their hours of passion, their love making at times being very intense and neither of them had regretted it. So, in the mind of the detective, they had done nothing wrong.

Many people though, especially his own colleagues at Heller Street police station and the police force as a whole, would have disagreed with this sentiment had they known about it but Hollister no longer cared about their opinion. He was finally at ease with himself and was no longer being forced to be living a lie. He had paid a heavy price for his newly discovered sexuality though, losing his wife and probably coming perilously close to losing his job in the process. Spending so many weeks away from official police investigations and cases looking for Spencer, running maverick and trying to come up with answers to questions regarding the life and death of Cameron Robinson had taken its toll on him but none of this mattered to McKenzie Hollister as he turned away from the window and once again stared at the sleeping youngster. As long as he had Spencer beside him at night, even if he could never openly admit to anybody, nothing else mattered to him. He was in love with the boy.

There was a spring in the step of McKenzie Hollister as he walked into the detectives offices at Heller Street police station. For the first time in weeks his mind was free of all nagging doubts and worries about his own sexuality, the whereabouts of Spencer and the death of Cameron Robinson. He had made his mind up that he was now going to turn his back on his previous existence and set up home in the former

apartment of Cameron Robinson and, hopefully, begin a new life, this time with Spencer.

When he had set off on his private investigation into the secret life of the schoolboy little did he know that it would lead to the course of events that it had. It was his search for Spencer that had brought him into contact with Johnny, which itself had led to his sexual encounters with the boy and revealed his own hidden and latent homosexuality and now he fully embraced who he was and he did not care who knew about it. Naturally he could not reveal to anybody who he was living with, this would have caused too many questions to be asked and so for now, all he could do was embrace the moment.

Hollister had spent the weekend with Spencer, getting to know him better and having sex with him as often as the youth had allowed him too. His peace of mind and inner happiness made him feel like a teenager himself and all the other detectives working that Monday morning noticed it, especially Phoebe Boston. She alone had been one of Hollister's strongest supporters during his enforced absence and was genuinely pleased to see him sitting behind his desk again. "It's really good to have you back Mac."

"It's good to be back," replied Hollister with a smile. "Tell me Phoebe, what's been going on while I've been away."

"As you know, we've wrapped up the Hulme case and he's currently locked up awaiting his trial. Some of the squad are working on a rape and some others on a couple of drug related armed robberies, you know, just all the usual stuff." Sergeant Boston paused briefly, "How's Kate these days?"

Hollister had known this question was going to be asked by somebody and had prepared for it, "She's fine and making a good recovery. However, because she blames me for putting her life at risk in the first place, we have unfortunately split up."

"Oh Mac, I'm so sorry to hear this," Boston was genuinely upset at Hollister's revelation. "You were such a nice couple."

"Don't worry about it Phoebe, it was really for the best. Over the past few months we'd grown apart and her getting attacked was the final straw for her. It's really for the best in the long run." There was not the slightest hint of any emotion in his voice as Hollister said his much-rehearsed speech and hoped that the shock of hearing that they had separated would have been enough to disguise the fact.

Sergeant Boston did not pick up on it, "You seem to be all right though Mac?"

"Sure, I was upset at the time but these things happen so let's move on. There's no point in dwelling on the past. I'd better go and see the boss and let him know I'm back."

"Mundy isn't here at the moment," answered Boston, "he's been sequestrated by The Met. He's in London working on something."

"Well, what do I do?"" asked Hollister with a smile, holding his hands out.

A knowing smile flashed across the face of the young sergeant, "A package came for you the other day. It looked a bit suspicious and so we got the bomb squad to check it out. Turned out to be okay, it's just a video tape."

"Well, let's go and see what's on it shall we?" replied Hollister.

McKenzie Hollister had no need to watch the tape, he knew exactly what was on it and what his sergeant and assistant did not know was that he had actually sent it to himself. After giving it a great deal of thought, he had decided that the best way to orchestrate a raid on the bail hostel at which the photographer worked was to send in an anonymous tape and note. This way the police would have grounds to raid the building and Hollister would be able to keep his word to Spencer and not involve him. After spending weeks searching for the youngster and now having found him and they had become lovers, he certainly was not going to do anything that might jeopardise their blossoming relationship.

It was not long before Hollister and Detective Sergeant Boston were watching the video. After putting on a pair of surgical gloves, he had removed the tape and the note from within the *'Jiffy'* bag. The note was a collection of words cut from newspapers and magazines saying *'This was filmed at the Dawson Hall by a member of staff called Will.'* It was a chilling note, reminiscent of the classic hostage demand notes and it offered no indications as to what was on the tape. Sergeant Boston was appalled at what she was watching, whereas Hollister found that he was getting sexually aroused by the contents of the tape. He knew only too well what was on the tape.

Hollister had actually sent the tape himself. After viewing all the tapes at Robinson's apartment he had chosen one with great care and one of the mildest, cleaning it off any fingerprints and posted it to Heller Street police station. Even though it was the mildest one, it was still very graphic. As he watched a youth of a similar age to his

teenaged lover being abused by two men the detective could not help but get aroused and hoped the Sergeant Boston did not notice.

Once the short tape had finished, it was time for Hollister to resume his charade, which was now something he was getting used to doing. "We've got to take this scumbag out and quickly," declared Hollister, acting as if he was shocked and appalled by what he had just watched.

Still in a state of shock, Sergeant Boston found it hard to talk, "I can't believe what I've just seen. How can he…anybody…get turned on by that stuff? Christ…he was just a kid."

"We've got to move fast." Hollister was relieved that the detective had taken the bait and felt a little uneasy that he had become excited by the tape and realised that he had to keep his relationship with Spencer a secret. "Let's do a copy and then send the original and the note over to forensics to see if they are any fingerprints on them. I doubt it, but it's worth a try, so let's give it a shot. Who's running the station while Andrew is in London?"

"Chief Superintendent Jacobson" was the reply.

Excellent, thought Hollister. Jacobson, he knew, was a family man and once shown the copy of the tape, Hollister knew that he would be appalled by its contents. "Right, I'll take the copy up to Jacobson and then you take the original and the note over to forensics. Tell the lab to drop everything for this. This is now our number one priority."

"Right Mac, I'm right on it."

The two detectives separated. The ploy had worked.

Within minutes of reading the note and viewing the copy of the tape, Chief Superintendent Jacobson was arranging for both arrest and search

warrants for both the bail hostel and the home of Wilfred Vigrass. It had been easy for the detectives to acquire the surname of the man named in the note, all it had taken was a telephone call to the Probation Service and now, armed with his full name, finding his home address was equally that simple. Jacobson had as a matter of routine ran Vigrass' name through the police's data base and the Sexual offenders Register and, as expected, neither of them revealed anything about Vigrass.

The course of events had unfolded even faster than Hollister had imagined. Once the tape was viewed by Jacobson and the warrants applied for and issued, in a little under three hours Jacobson, Hollister and Sergeant Boston found themselves outside the Dawson Hall bail hostel.

Somebody inside the building must have seen the convoy of vehicles descending onto the carpark and the street outside the bail hostel because the door was opened before they reached it. Hollister was greeted by a man in his forties, his blond hair having turned almost white and wearing a pair of glasses that magnified his blue eyes. "Yes officers, can I help you?"

It was Jacobson, as the ranking officer, wearing his full uniform, who took the lead, "Are you Wilfred Vigrass?"

"Yes" came the rather hesitant and quizzical reply from the man.

"I am Chief Superintendent Jacobson from Heller Street police station," Jacobson's voce was both harsh and uncompromising, "these are my colleagues including Chief Inspector Hollister. Wilfred Vigrass, we have a warrant for your arrest on the suspicion that you are involved

in the production and distribution of child pornography. You do not have to say anything, but it may harm your defence if you do not mention, when questioned, something which you later rely on in court. Anything you do say may be given in evidence. Do you wish to say anything at this moment?"

As he was being cautioned, both Jacobson and Hollister watched the blood drain from the face of Vigrass. He was shocked into turning an ashen complexion and he shook his head. Jacobson continued, "For the record, we will record that the accused did not comment when asked. We also have warrants to search here, your home and any other address associated with you. Do you understand?" Once again Vigrass nodded his head in a state of shock. "We understand that you are a photographer, do you have a studio?"

"Yes," replied Vigrass in a dry rasping voice. "I'll take you there."

"Good. At least you're co-operating," stated Jacobson as Hollister handcuffed the man. "Can we go inside now?"

All the detectives followed Vigrass into the building, whilst the uniformed officers remained on the car park, moving along those curious enough to ask what was going on.

Nightfall was once again descending on Manchester as the frustration grew in the minds of the detectives investigating Wilfred Vigrass. They had searched the bail hostel without finding any evidence of the crimes which he was suspected off. None of the police officers were surprised at this. In fact, they would have been more surprised if they *had* found anything incriminating at the place of work of the probation officer but they had to be extremely thorough in their work and still search the

building, just in case. The names and addresses of every person that was either a current resident or had passed through the hostel in the last five years was taken, with the intention of interviewing those concerned once Vigrass was in police custody.

A search of Vigrass' home, conducted by a second team of officers, had also found no obvious evidence of child pornography, with the possible exception of the scores of tapes and computer discs that were sealed in clear plastic bags, together with the computer of Vigrass, all marked as possible evidence and then carried away to waiting police vehicles, whilst officers searched every nook and cranny of his home, all to no avail and this had been relayed to Jacobson and Hollister.

As the searches proved fruitless, Hollister was beginning to have his doubts as to the wisdom of his move against Vigrass. Maybe he was not involved in the production of the video tapes that he had found in the home of Robinson. After all, he only had the word of his teenaged 'rent boy' lover that Vigrass was actually involved. Perhaps Spencer had given him false information and they were probing into the life of a wronged and innocent man. Hollister had not doubted the sincerity of his teenaged lover as he had revealed to the youth the course of action that he had intended to pursue, questioning the youngster in great detail about his knowledge of Vigrass' activities and gleaming as much information from the boy as possible. But maybe Spencer was wrong? Being a naturally suspicious person, rarely trusting anybody and only ever taking them at face value, Hollister was even beginning to think that Spencer was deliberately leading them all in the wrong direction while he warned the real culprits that the police were on their trail. However, he quickly disregarded this notion.

The preliminary search of Vigrass' photographic studio had also refused to yield any evidence of anything sordid or perverse in the nature of the photographs taken by the man, who had remained dignified throughout his ordeal. Hopes of finding anything incriminating were pinned on the two metal filing cabinets that had been sealed and taken from the studio to be examined in detail back at Heller Street police station, but a random selection of the files contained in the drawers of the cabinets had indicated that they were going to be harmless, nothing than happy smiling families or joyous brides and grooms on their wedding days.

Hollister was getting frustrated, as was everybody else involved in the day's activities and they were all feeling tired and hungry as he, Jacobson and Boston all took a break in a police car. They had all worked throughout the day, with only the barest minimum of breaks and refreshment in their desire to find any possible that would help them rid the streets of Manchester of somebody they viewed as a very dangerous paedophile.

"Maybe we're barking up the wrong tree Mac?" declared Detective Boston.

"No Phoebe," snapped back Hollister, "we're not. This guy's a scumbag. I can feel it."

"But we've not found anything to justify that McKenzie," added Jacobson, "maybe he's not our man after all."

"That bastard's guilty as sin," remonstrated Hollister as he got out of the car, slamming the door shut behind him, making the car shake on its stationary wheels.

"Is he always this agitated?" asked Jacobson.

"Only when things don't go right, sir," replied Boston as she stared out of the window at Hollister and the building in front of them.

Vigrass' studio was a converted flat located over a grocers shop. The owner of the convenience store had been interviewed earlier in the day and had failed to reveal anything of great important about Vigrass or his activities, neither had the proprietor of the newsagents next door. They both had recognised Vigrass from his photograph but could not remember seeing him with any young boys. The flat over the newsagents was boarded up, while the exterior door, or the wooden sheet covering it, showed any signs of it being disturbed for a while. Detective Boston looked at the building and then around the neighbouring streets and had a thought. "Sir," she began hesitantly, "the shop over the newsagents is boarded up. The newsagent said it had been for sale and yet there is no 'For Sale' or 'To Let' sign on it."

"Yes, well," replied Jacobson, a little on the slow side.

"Look around Sir. There are a few houses around here for sale and they all have signs in their gardens but the flat over the newsagents hasn't got anything advertising that it's for sale."

Jacobson was slowly catching up to the woman's thoughts. "Do you think that there might be something up there? You know, accessible through his studio?"

"Maybe Vigrass is using the other flat as well, you know, as an extension to his studio."

"That could certainly be a good point. Good thinking detective," replied Jacobson, as Jacobson and Boston got out of the car. He called over to Hollister, "McKenzie, come here."

Hollister, cigarette still in hand, obeyed his superior officer and walked towards them. "What is it?" he asked frostily.

"Detective Sergeant Boston might have something here. See the flat over the newsagents shop? It's empty and all boarded up. The newsagent told our uniformed that it had been for sale. But there are not any 'For Sale' signs on it. Don't you think that it's a tad odd, especially when there are 'For Sale' signs on the houses nearby?"

Hollister caught on quicker than Jacobson had. "That's it. That's where the bastard's got his stuff. Have we got jurisdiction to go in there?"

"I think so," replied Jacobson. "We've got the right under PACE to search anywhere relating to the addresses on the warrants. So yes, I think we can enter the property if we can prove that the only point of access is via the address on the warrant. Has the address on the warrant got a loft?"

Both Hollister and Sergeant Boston looked at each other and shrugged their shoulders in unison. "I presume so," replied Hollister.

"Right, on my say so, we're going in," declared Jacobson. "But I think Mr Vigrass and his solicitor should be present when we do. You know, just to cover ourselves in the case of any flak," stated the ever cautious Jacobson.

What the Chief Superintendent said had made sense to Hollister. Nobody, especially him, wanted to come up with the evidence that Vigrass was guilty and then have the evidence ruled inadmissible due to a technicality. Hollister knew that the man was guilty but he still needed solid and concrete evidence to prove this, something that would

stand up in court as part of a prosecution case against the photographer and so they all could do nothing except wait for Vigrass to be brought to the address from Heller Street police station.

Detective Sergeant Boston had suggested to the two senior officers that there should also be a representative from the Crown Prosecution Service present when they entered the flat. With his adrenaline pumping through his body, Hollister had failed to realise that with the new address about to be searched not the original one on the warrant, then this was the type of scenario good barrister's could argue and have anything found there ruled inadmissible by a trial judge and so he had contacted the Crown Prosecution Service, whilst Jacobson was arranging for Vigrass to be brought to his studio, and the search team had been joined by a senior lawyer.

Eventually they all saw the dark blue car, with its two-car escort, advancing towards them, their blue lights flashing, making other vehicles move out of their journey. Once stationary, Vigrass emerged from the saloon car, handcuffed to a detective and a suited man, balding, pot-bellied and aged around fifty years old, get out of one of the marked police escort vehicles. He marched straight over towards Jacobson, "Adam, I really must protest…"

Jacobson offered the solicitor an outstretched hand and cut him off in mid-sentence. "Gideon, I'm sorry about this, but we are dealing with something very important. May I introduce you to Detective Chief Inspector McKenzie Hollister and his assistant, Detective Sergeant Boston," hands were shock all around and the arrival of Vigrass completed the circle. "This is Gideon Copner, he is representing Mr Vigrass."

Turning to Vigrass, Jacobson continued, "Mr Vigrass, may I remind you that you are still under caution and may I also remind you that you do not have to say anything…" a nodding Vigrass indicated that he understood what Jacobson was telling him. "We suspect that the property adjoining your photographic studio is being used as an illicit continuation of the property that has been found to be your photographic studio, which we have a warrant to search. Do you have anything to say before I continue?"

Vigrass remained silent and shook his head, his solicitor answering on his behalf. "Let it be recorded that my client did not say anything."

Jacobson continued, having acknowledged the solicitor's comment with a nod, "Upon information received, we applied for a warrant to search the photographic studio of Mr Vigrass where we discovered that he might be using the adjoining property as an extension of his own property. We contacted the Crown Prosecution Service for advice, they've sent a representative to overview the search, and the CPS stated that the warrant to search the property would be valid if we can only gain access to the new property via the address stated on the original warrant. I wanted both you and your solicitor here as well to overview the search, in case of any legal issues or technicalities later on. Mr Vigrass, do you fully understand what is going on?"

Realising that any objections would only delay the inevitable search, which would then be held against him if he was charged, Vigrass nodded his head.

"Once again, let the record show that my client has exercised his right to silence and that he is not objecting to or opposing the search of the

said property," stated the solicitor, who looked as visible shaken as his client.

"I would also like to have it recorded," added Jacobson, "that your client, Mr Wilfred Vigrass, has helped us all day and not once has he impeded or refused to assist us. Right, let's get it on."

With that they all once again entered the photographic studio of Wilfred Vigrass. The lights were on and the detectives did not need the torches that they carried as they made their way up the stairs and into the brightly lit rooms. Once up the stairs, with no chance of escaping, the shackles that bound Vigrass' wrists together were removed and he quickly surveyed the studio for any sign of damage by the police. They all made their way to the landing and congregated under the loft access, while a uniformed officer, under the instruction of Jacobson, climbed up and pushed aside the small square wooden cover, revealing a retractable ladder, which extended as it was lowered.

One-by-one and in single file they all climbed the ladder and disappeared into the apex roof that had been converted into one large room, a red-bricked wall, partially knocked down, marking the divider of the two flats. The uniformed officer first into the cramped space had found a light switch and this had illuminated the 'V' shaped room. Watching carefully where they placed their feet, fully aware that a forensic team might be following in their footsteps, everybody followed the constable as he walked along flooring that ran the length of the two flats. He released another metal ladder which again extended as it was lowered, this time into the supposedly empty flat next to Vigrass' studio. One-by-one, like lemmings jumping off a cliff, they all emerged from the roof space and gathered in the hallway. Yet again

Jacobson asked Vigrass if he objected to them searching the property and once again he shook his head, indicating that he did not.

Jacobson opened the first door at hand. The instinct of Detective Sergeant Boston was proved correct as a switched on light revealed a bedroom. Surrounding the bed were three video cameras, each mounted on metal tripods, with a battery of lights behind the cameras. Hollister recognised the room immediately as the one where Robinson had been filmed with the sex aide before having oral sex with the man. Hollister could feel his heart pounding in his chest as the door to another bedroom was opened revealing another room with cameras and lights, except this one had no bed. In the centre of the room, suspended from the ceiling, was a six-foot cage and on a wall was a huge 'X' shaped cross. Doted around the room was a variety of sex aides, together with spanking paddles and whips, clearly a room used for the making of sadomasochistic videos.

What was once the lounge of the flat was now filled with about fifty video recorders all linked to an editing suite and all along the walls were literally thousands of video tapes and on a desk under what was once a window were three computers that were linked to video recorders and these were recording internet images of child abuse, recording the images directly onto tapes rather than downloading them onto the computers memories and thus eliminating any risk of getting detected. Clearly a very sophisticated set-up which all the senior police officer made no secret of discovering with pats on the back and congratulatory comments, mostly aimed at Detective Boston while Wilfred Vigrass and his lawyer hung their heads in shame.

"Mr Vigrass, do you wish to say anything about what we have discovered?" asked Jacobson. A slow shake of his head indicated that he had no wish to reply, his face now gaunt and beneath his wire-rimmed glasses his eyes had seemed to shrink into the dark bags of his suddenly accumulated stress at the discovery of his secret and as Jacobson continued Vigrass looked a broken man. "McKenzie, will you show to Mr Copner that the only means of access from the street is sealed from the inside and that access can only be gained by the studio owned by Mr Vigrass."

Hollister nodded and led the solicitor down the stairs to confirm that this was correct. Once they were back in the lounge Jacobson, who was now in his element and relishing the glory that was going to be heaped on him, continued to address those in the room, "Officers, you can take Mr Copner and his client back to Heller Street. I want this place sealed up tight. It's too late to search it tonight. We'll do it first thing in the morning. Mr Copner, you can be present if you wish. I want this place treated as a serious crime scene, as if it was a murder scene. I don't want anything touched until it's been photographed. I want forensics in next to dust the place and lift as many fingerprints as possible. Then I want SOCO to be brought in for a minute search, the finest that they have ever done. Everything is to be logged as they remove it. I don't want this case getting away from us on a technicality."

"Should we notify the Vice or the Child Protection Unit," enquired Hollister.

"No" came the emphatic reply from Jacobson. "This is our baby, not theirs. We'll tell them when we're good and ready. They're not getting the credit for this one, I…we are." Jacobson turned and spoke directly

to Hollister and Detective Boston, "Good work you two. We wouldn't have got this if it wasn't for you two."

If only Jacobson really knew how he had come by the information on Vigrass and that it was him that had sent in the original tape and note, thought Hollister. If the pompous Chief Superintendent knew this, and the fact that Hollister's teenaged loved, who could so easily appear in one or more of the tapes on the shelves, had helped to reveal Vigrass, then maybe Jacobson might not have been so smug with himself. On the other hand, despite the hypocrisy of the situation, Hollister could barely disguise his own glee and excitement and could hardly wait to return to his new home and into the loving arms of his paramour and tell him, that with his help, the police have arrested Vigrass and shut down his video operation.

Chapter Fifteen

It took the police two entire days to remove everything from the photographic studio of Wilfred Vigrass. The previously sealed exterior door to the adjoining property had been forced open, allowing the police direct access to the flat and they were able to remove the contents of the rooms with the minimum of knowledge of the local inhabitants and despite the interest and questions by those in neighbouring properties, the police had maintained an air of secrecy about their search. They refused to reveal anything about their exhaustive and round-the-clock activities to the locals for fear of provoking a climate of hysteria regarding Vigrass' secret profession and then being inundated with questions demanding to know whether their children had been involved. The police would not have been able to reveal to the concerned parents whether their children had come under the lecherous grasp of the photographer because they simply did not know themselves whether they had or had not.

Even the most hardened of detectives were shocked by both the sheer volume and the perversity of the material that they had unearthed and each one of them were deeply relieved that the person responsible for it was safely locked behind bars at Heller Street police station. The three detectives which had led the investigation into Vigrass were each going through different emotions. Chief Superintendent Jacobson was basking in his newly achieved glory, relishing in the praise being lavished on him by his own superior officers and, for once, not being the butt of locker-room jokes. Jacobson's career at Heller Street had not

always been as illustrious and he had frequently had to be led by junior officers, as in this particular case, but now, even his harshest of critics were looking at him in a different light.

The feminine instincts of Sergeant Phoebe Boston, so often hidden from view, could not believe the images that she was being forced to watch. Her tough exterior, hardened through her upbringing in Mansewood, a suburb of the Scottish city of Glasgow, had been rocked to its core as she sat through video after video. Access to the room now containing the vast collection of tapes, photographs and computer generated images seized from Vigrass was highly restricted and Detective Boston supervised those under her charge as they spent hour after hour, day after day, watching the sordid material. She found the images truly shocking and deeply disturbing and very hard to believe that anybody could get sexually aroused by the sheer depravity enclosed on the tapes, let alone those sick enough to participate in the making of the films or posing for the photographs, knowing full well that the youngsters involved were probably doing it by coercion and clearly not enjoying what was being done to them.

There seemed to be a core of about dozen youths that kept appearing in the movies, most seemed to be in their late teens whilst there were others that appeared to be younger, although Detective Boston knew from experience that sometimes people looked younger than they actually were, but it was the prospect of these youngsters being abused by men, many of whom were clearly identifiable because they had not disguised their faces and were clearly old enough to be their father's that horrified her. The brazenness of the abusers, so confident that

nothing would come from their depravity that they had not even tried to disguise their faces appalled the young police woman.

Detective Boston, like so many people in modern society, accepted the fact that homosexuality was an everyday part of modern life, but not where children were involved. She knew that most gay people found the thought of children being sexually abused as abhorrent as everybody else and that the number of those involved in such exploitation were minute compared to The sexual grooming and abuse of children had been highlighted by some very high profile cases, many of the involving youngsters in care homes, but the thought that somebody working within the judicial system was preying on these children, forcing them to commit sexual acts in order to prevent them getting sent to these homes mortified her. She had also resigned herself to the fact that what they have stumbled across must surely just be the tip of the iceberg.

This thought had also crossed the mind of McKenzie Hollister. He knew that Vigrass would only have been able to exploit these youngsters with the collusion of others in power. Experience has told him that at some point Vigrass would have overstepped his mark and that at least somebody would have objected to his advances and complained about them and yet the probation officer had been able to continue both in his professional duties and in his hobby. It did not take a genius, thought Hollister, that he was being protected by somebody who may or may not have been employed by the Probation Service and that person could carry enough influence to divert attention away from Vigrass. It had actually been Hollister's young lover that had planted this thought in his head upon returning home the night of the raid on

Vigrass' studio, a night of glee and satisfaction at being able to offer Spencer some protection, knowing that the youngster will never again fall unto the clutches of Vigrass but also using the arrest of Vigrass as a means of proving his love for the boy.

His pleasure and satisfaction had proved to be short lived upon returning to his adoptive home and telling Spencer that not only had Vigrass been arrested, but a search of his photographic studio had produced enough evidence that would surely put him in jail for a very long time. Spencer was pleased in a subdued way and when pressed by the detective he had revealed that he was worried about being recognised on any of the films. Hollister reassured the boy that he would protect him as much as possible and the apprehensions of the teenager subsided a little when Hollister reminded him that he would not even have got to Vigrass if it was not for the teenager and that he had, so far at least, been able to protect him as the informant.

Forty eight hours after his arrest, Wilfred Vigrass was formerly charged with multiple offences of the possession, the taking, making and distribution of indecent images of a children and looked at pending a very long time locked behind the bars of a prison but there was very little evidence, at the moment, that he was actually involved directly in the abuse of these youngsters and could not be charged with any indecency offences. However, Detective Boston was still supervising the viewing of the tapes and the cataloguing of the photographs and every police officer involved knew that at some point in the future the evidence would present itself and Vigrass would be charged accordingly,. But for now they had to be content with what they had

and that he had been reminded in custody. At least Vigrass was off the streets and out of harm's way while Jacobson planned the next phase of his operation that would elevate him above his current rank.

When Jacobson had revealed to Hollister what he intended to do next, Hollister was plunged into a state of panic and inner turmoil. His previous joyous mood had been replaced by apprehension and doubts nagging in his brain. The senior of the two detectives wanted to simultaneously raid every bar and club on around Canal Street and search out anybody under the age of eighteen years. Hollister knew from his own recently acquired knowledge, which he could not share with Jacobson, that most of the licensed premises refused to have anything to do with under-aged patrons.

"But there are children involved," Jacobson was adamant.

"Well…yes, maybe…but only on video and photographs and even these are only a very small number," argued Hollister. "The sheer manpower that is needed to carry out such an operation would be phenomenal and at best, we might only a couple of kids. Even then, we're not certain of getting any. You might as well raid every pub and club in Manchester. You'd probably get better results that way."

"There are risks involved yes, but even if we save one child from an ordeal like those poor defenceless young boys on the videos have suffered, then it's worth the risk. For God's sake McKenzie, what are you thinking off, there are children involved here."

Hollister was getting annoyed at the persistence of Jacobson and was glad that their heated exchange was taking place in Chief Superintendent Mundy's office, which was currently being used by

Jacobson in Mundy's absence and not in the squad room being witnessed by all the other detectives. "Yeah, I know that but don't you think that you're using a sledgehammer to crack a nut?"

"I understand your reservations McKenzie, but we're going to move with this because there are children involved. I know that I won't always be here and that eventually Andrew will return and the last thing that I want to do is rock any boats but trust me, this is the right thing to do considering the circumstances. You have two options, you can either remain here at Heller Street and supervise any arrests or you can join me in the control van, it's your choice which but this is going to happen tonight whether you like it or not."

Hollister had no option but to concede defeat to his superior officer and wondered how he could distance himself from what he thought was a disastrous plan. Hollister also found himself in a difficult predicament. He was known as a patron in four or five bars and had been asking questions about 'rent boys' and him charging in with uniformed officers would not only expose him as a police officer but somebody might recognise him as being seen with Spencer, sitting outside a bar on Canal Street having a lengthy conversation and a few drinks with the young boy.

This was his biggest fear. If anybody at Heller Street found out that he had been frequenting the bars on Canal Street, then their inference could make him a suspect in the ongoing case with Vigrass not to mention the humiliation and ridicule that he would no doubt face. Hollister had known that there was a risk of being discovered in a gay bar ever since he had embarked on his personal investigation into the life and death of Cameron Robinson but now his fears were about to

come to fruition. At least he had the option of remaining in the background and not actually being out there on Canal Street and actually being recognised offered him some consolation. His newly discovered lifestyle was having one positive effect on Hollister, he thought to himself. He had realised that he had a conscious.

It was this new found conscious that led Hollister to walk into *'The Last Exit'* bar three hours before it was due to be raided along with every other bar and club on Canal Street. He had been in this bar a couple of times since first meeting the barman Greg and they had built up a welcoming and friendly relationship. It had been Greg that had put him in touch with the owner of the *'Adonis'* who in turn had put him in contact with Barratt Foxford and Hollister finally getting some definite information on Cameron Robinson's choice of lifestyle. After the help from Greg, Hollister thought that he owed him one.

The face of the barman lit up with a broad smile when he saw Hollister enter the bar and walk towards him. "Hi there Mac," he said when Hollister was close enough, "don't see much of you these days. Been busy have you?"

"Yeah, something like that," replied Hollister. "Listen Greg, I need a word. Is your boss in?"

"No. Not yet. He doesn't normally come in until around midnight. You know, when we start to get busy. Why, what's up?"

"Listen, I owe you a favour. Is there somewhere we can talk, you know, in private?"

Sensing that something was wrong Greg indicated for one of the other bar staff to cover him and motioned for Hollister to follow him

out past the doormen and onto the street. Hollister was a little reluctant to follow him at first but thought that without Greg he would not have got the breaks he had with Robinson and so he though the risk of being seen on Canal Street was worth it. Once out in the fresh air the detective scanned the street for any advanced police 'spotters' and came straight to the point. "Greg, remember when we first met and I told you that I was a copper?"

"Yeah, why, what's wrong?" asked Greg with a worried look on his face.

"Well," began Hollister, "the other day we picked up this scumbag that exploits children. I can't tell you too much about it because it's an ongoing investigation but it's led to this real prick of a Chief Super planning on raiding every bar and club on and around Canal Street at midnight tonight looking for any kids or 'rent boys'. You can't tell anybody about these raids Greg and I do mean anybody. If they get wind that I've been here and warned you, then I'll be in deep shit."

The barman was visibly shocked, "I understand the risk you're taking but like I said, we don't let kids in."

"Well just make sure that the guys on the door do their job tonight and you do keep them out, tonight of all nights and make sure your boss is in here when the plods hit. You're an okay guy Greg and I think you deserved the heads up but for Christ's sake, please don't tell anybody else."

"I won't, promise. Christ, this is going to be some raid."

"Believe me Greg, the wanker that's leading it is going to make sure it is. I've got to get going now, get ready for the shit to hit the fan. You be careful Greg."

The barman responded with a nervous smile, "I will. Thanks for the warning and I'll see you soon."

With that, Hollister returned to Heller Street police station and waited for the midnight raid.

Midnight came and on a synchronised signal given by Jacobson the police descended *en masse* onto Canal Street and the surround streets. The two pedestrian ends of Canal Street were sealed off at Minshull Street and Princess Street, together with all the minor streets that led onto the 'The Village' by dozens of police vehicles as around one hundred police officers sprang from mini-buses parked nearby in the warren of narrow streets and alleyways and ran onto Canal Street sealing off every establishment along the street, all caught on camera by the assembled media, who had been personally invited Jacobson, capturing the ensuing panic and pandemonium.

'The Village' had never seen or known anything like this before, with the gay community previously having a fairly good relationship with the Greater Manchester Police force and this heavy handed approach by Jacobson was only going to alienate the police and the gay community for many years to come. Every type of licensed premises that was either on Canal Street or off it was visited by the police, with uniformed officers preventing anybody leaving the venues until every patron had been spoken too and anybody that looked like they might be under-aged were asked to produce identification, which was then checked and recorded. Those that could not produce any form of identification was taken, in handcuffs, to a waiting van and then into custody and held until somebody could vouch for them.

Not surprisingly, the police came in for a great deal of criticism, not to mention verbal abuse from those whose night out enjoying themselves had suddenly been interrupted. Not even Jacobson's aim of trying to protect juveniles from harm helped to quell the ever-increasing furore. To the gay community the raids were seen as yet another heavy handed attack on their way of life and Hollister had anticipated this reaction and had tried to warn Jacobson, but to no avail. Hollister derived a great deal of smug satisfaction that it was going to be the Chief Superintendent that was going to have to face the mounting criticism the following morning when both the mainstream media got hold of the story, as would the more senior officers of the Greater Manchester Police.

From early indications, Hollister had been proven correct. The raids had been a total disaster. A token number of sixteen and seventeen year old boys had been detained, along with the men that they were with and were taken to Heller Street police station. Only two teenaged prostitutes had been detained and these were also taken to Heller Street. Even Jacobson was disappointed by the results.

"What the fucking hell are you lot doing up there?" The question was almost yelled down the telephone to McKenzie Hollister. He had recognised the voice immediately as that off Andrew Mundy, the Chief Superintendent that Jacobson was covering for.

"I assume you're referring to last night's raids?" asked Hollister back, trying to remain calm, a man never at his best first thing in the morning and especially when he was being shouted at.

"Don't get fucking smart with me Mac," was the riposte from Mundy, "of course I'm referring to that fuck up last night."

Even Hollister, with their years of friendship between them, was glad that he was facing the wrath of Mundy over a telephone and not face-to-face. "I tried telling Jacobson that it was going to be a mistake but you know what he's like? He just wouldn't listen to me or anybody. I wanted no part of it, believe me."

"I don't blame you Mac," said Mundy, somewhat calmer now, "that guy's nothing but a fucking liability. He's a fucking idiot. I've had call after call all fucking night about him and his raid. At first I thought it might be you running rough shot..."

Hollister interrupted Mundy, "Don't blame me for this fuck up. I tried to warn him but he wouldn't listen to me. That fucking idiot is taking the heat for this one, not me. I didn't want anything to do with it. I didn't even go out with him. I stayed here at Heller Street."

"I realise that now and I'm sorry that I yelled at you. What the fuck made him do such a thing? That's what I want to know."

"I'm sorry Andrew, can't tell you the details over the phone but we're involved with a case and Jacobson thought that raiding 'The Village' was a good idea and might help the case."

"And has it?" asked Mundy.

"Personally, I don't think so. All we appear to have done last night was piss off the gay community and disrupt the night out for a lot of innocent people."

"I'm going to have his bollocks on a plate for this. Have you any idea where he is? I've tried Heller Street but nobody has seen him."

"I've no idea where he is. He's probably gone to ground. Heller Street has only got a skeleton staff in. He had just about everybody out on last night's raids," the answer from Hollister was laced with an amount of smug satisfaction.

"Christ, what a fucking mess." Mundy hesitated a moment and then continued, "What can you tell me about Wilfred Vigrass being arrested?"

Hollister was so shocked at hearing this that he almost dropped the telephone. It took him a couple of seconds to compose himself before he replied, "Nothing over an open-line except to say that he's facing some very serious charges."

"I know what he's currently charged with and with what might follow." Mundy paused briefly, "Listen, I'm coming up in a couple of hours to try and calm things down and so you can tell me all about him then. If you come across that bastard Jacobson, tell him that I'm going to fucking kill him." At that, the line went dead.

Hollister was shocked. How had Mundy found out about Vigrass' arrest? It had not yet been made public knowledge and surely nobody at Heller Street police station, knowing the gravity of the case, would have broken ranks and told Mundy about the arrest, jeopardising the ongoing investigation into Vigrass. A hand was placed on the detectives shoulder, making him jump and this was followed by a kiss on his cheek. "What's up? You look like you've seen a ghost," asked Spencer.

Hollister turned to face his young lover who was still in bed with him, "It's my boss down in London. He knows about us lifting Vigrass," replied Hollister.

"How, I thought it was a secret until he appeared in court this morning?"

"I've no idea Spencer. Somebody must've told him."

"Do you think he knows about us?" concern was now showing on the face of the youngster.

Hollister reassured him with a kiss on his cheek, stroking the other with his palm, "Not a chance kid. Nobody knows about us. Even if he did, I wouldn't give a fuck. You're my life. You're all that I care about and I won't let anything happen to you."

The teenagers face lit up with a smile which revealed him for what he was, a young boy. Hollister knew that he was playing with fire in forming a relationship with Spencer, but he really did not care anymore. He found himself finally happy. Spencer was also happy. Finally the boy had found some happiness in his young life. He had found somebody who cared about him and wanted to be with him for himself and not just for sex. This was what he portrayed to Hollister but secretly he was already having doubts.

Having showered and shaved, put some clean clothes on, making himself presentably for the day ahead, McKenzie Hollister decided to pay a visit to Eileen Robinson, Cameron's mother. He knew that there was a very strong possibility that some of the videos seized from Vigrass' studio would contain images of her son and Hollister thought that it was his moral duty to warn the grieving mother that it would only be a matter of time before the police once again began to investigate the life, and death, of her son. He knew that whoever arrived on her doorstep would not understand her unremitting love for

her firstborn and Hollister wanted her to know the details of her son's activities and secret life before they were made public.

Where this new found conscious had come from was a mystery even to Hollister but the teenaged Robinson had affected his life like nobody else has for many years and yet he had never even met the young boy whilst he was alive. He had only spent around five minutes with his body and yet the impact that these minutes have had on the detective were nothing short of colossal, which is why he found himself once again sat in the lounge of the Robinson's family home.

Nothing had changed since his previous visits. Eileen Robinson still wore a black dress as her private mourning and personal suffering continued. The largest framed photograph of Cameron still had black silk sashes on its corners and this time, as he sat there, he felt the eyes of the boy were on him, staring into his soul, judging his current lifestyle and behaviour.

"I'm so glad that I caught you Eileen," began Hollister, "there is something very important that I have to tell you."

"Have you finally come to tell me that my Cameron didn't commit suicide?" asked the defiant mother, unshaken in her belief that her son had not taken his own life.

Her forthright question threw Hollister of balance, "No, unfortunately not. At this precise moment in time, Cameron's death is still viewed as and is being treated as a tragic suicide. In that aspect, nothing has changed. However, certain new developments have come to light regarding another case, which unfortunate I cannot go into because it's currently a live case, but there is a very strong possibility that you Cameron's death may be reinvestigated. At this precise moment in

time, no matter how much that I wish to, I simply can't tell you what this new line of questioning will take."

"Mr Hollister, you're one of the few friends that I've got left, one of the few people that come to see me these days so please, spare me the niceties and tell me what I need to know to protect the memory of my dead son. No matter how painful you think it might be to me, it's nothing compared to the pain that I've felt since losing my darling Cameron. Please tell me," pleaded the grieving mother.

Hollister was visibly shaken to his core by the heart-wrenching plea of mother, still mourning the death of her firstborn child, unable to comprehend why he had done what he had. The detective took a deep breath and wondered what he was about to do was the correct thing but looking directly into the red-rimmed, heavily bagged eyes of the still distraught mother helped him to make up his mind. "What I'm going to tell you must, for now at least, remain confidential between us. If word got out that I'd even told you, I'd be in deep trouble. It could literally end my career."

"You have my word, Mr Hollister. I won't say a word. I just need to know the truth about my Cameron."

Taking another deep breath, or was it a sigh at the sadness of the woman before him who was so obviously struggling to hold in another batch of tears? "When we first found your son and discovered who he was we also found out how he survived for the two years that he was missing. The police, at a higher rank than me although I supported their decision, decided to withhold this information in order to protect you and your family and not to cause you any further suffering than losing

your son. This is going to be painful for you but...do you know what the term 'rent boy' means?"

The mother shook her head, "I've never heard it before."

"I'm so sorry that I have to tell you this but it's a slang term used to describe a teenage male prostitute. Your son was one of...these."

Looking confused, Mrs Robinson was too naïve to understand what she had just been told, "What exactly does one of these 'rent boys' do?"

"He...well...er...he has...sex with people for money," eventually came the embarrassed and barely audible admission from Hollister.

"Oh!" replied Mrs Robinson in an almost matter-of-fact way. "This still doesn't prove that my Cameron took his own life, does it?"

Hollister was visibly shaken by this question, "Well...no...not exactly. However, it could shed some light on why Cameron left home in the first place."

The mother thought for a moment before she continued, "Do you think that my Cameron was hurt by somebody when he was one of these 'rent boys'?"

"I've really no way of knowing Eileen, but there is certainly a possibility that he may have been harmed at times."

"Do you think that he left home to become one of these 'rent boys'?"

"It appears so." Hollister found it very strange the Robinson's mother had so readily accepted his prostitution and possibly his homosexuality, assuming that the naïve woman truly understood the meaning of him being a 'rent boy' and yet she blatantly refused to accept that he had taken his own life.

This disturbed the detective and lay in the back of his mind as he eventually told Cameron's mother everything that he knew about his life after leaving home and his death. He thought that she needed to know that both his former priest and gymnastics coach had both had sexual relationships with her son but decided not to tell her that it appears Cameron had initiated the sexual liaisons himself, sparing the mother of details that would, in all likelihood, cause her even more pain and suffering. Hollister decided against telling her of his own feelings about her son and how his life had been impacted and influenced ever since the day of his death, only mentioning that he wished that he would have been able to get to know him whilst he was alive and just what a loving son he must have been.

With his secret thoughts and desires about Cameron Robinson kept firmly locked inside his brain, he now fully understood why his mother could still not accept that he had taken his own life, despite the fact that Hollister, despite his original thoughts, was now certain that he had.

There was well dressed, tall, blond-haired stranger aged around fifty behind the bar of *'The Last Exit'* who turned to face Hollister as he entered the near deserted bar. Despite the lateness of the hour, past midnight, even the detective could not but help notice that there were only a handful of customers. Two nights ago this place, like all those on Canal Street, would have been crammed full of people, both gay and straight, enjoying a night out. Twenty four hours ago the very same people would have been interrogated by the police and made to feel like second-class citizens in their home town because of the disastrous

raids orchestrated by Chief Superintendent Jacobson, with Hollister still feeling seismic aftershocks and fallout from Jacobson's actions.

He had come directly from Manchester's Piccadilly train station and a brief meeting with Chief Superintendent Mundy, held in a late-night coffee shop, who offered Hollister some advice on how to make this a damage limitation exercise for himself before Mundy returned to London on the next train. Hollister had told Mundy that the raids were a response to the arrest of Vigrass and the discovery of his studio where he made pornographic videos involving some young boys. Upon hearing the details and the facts behind the implementation of the raid on Manchester gay 'Village', even Mundy had to concede that Jacobson had no option to do something, but he still could not concede the later action that he took, raiding every bar and club in 'The Village'. Mundy kept repeating that he wished Hollister had contacted him prior to the raids.

Hollister was himself reluctant to inform Mundy how the operation came to be initiated, in fear of exposing his and Spencer's relationship and that his teenaged lover had been the main informant that led to Vigrass' arrest and the search of his studio, and Mundy himself hesitated short of coming out and asking Hollister directly, but because of the long term closeness of both men they each picked up on the hidden subtext that each of them was withholding something from the other. The short meeting between the two senior detectives had left Hollister both confused and intrigued and in desperate need of a drink, which is what took him to *'The Last Exit'* bar.

As Hollister casually ambled into the bar, he noticed Greg say something to the suited stranger, who then waited for Hollister. "So you're the detective that warned Greg about the raid?" he asked.

Hollister nodded, "I thought I owed it to Greg to give him a heads-up and warn him. He'd helped me out on a case I had been working on and guided me towards a conclusion so I thought that I owed him one."

"I don't mind saying that you've really fucked up 'The Village'. Nobody is out because they don't trust the police not to come back. The police are definitely not welcome, well, in most places."

"I can understand the feeling of 'The Village' but believe me the raids had nothing to do with me. The guy that orchestrated is an absolute arsehole. He's was already a laughing stock, a fucking idiot. Believe me, I tried to tell him that they were a bad idea but he insisted and so he can take the shit and the fallout for them. I wanted nothing to do with them." Hollister could detect the open hostility towards him coming from the man.

"I don't know whether to believe you or not," stated the man.

"Listen…" Hollister paused while the man told him his name.

"Edwards. Stephen Edwards, I own this bar."

"Mr Edwards," began Hollister, "I can fully understand how you must be feeling but remember I didn't have to come here and warn Greg in the first place. I was taking one hell of a risk coming here in the first place. I could've easily been seen and recognised by the advanced spotters that we had out and I would've had some very difficult questions to try and come with answers to. I was dead against the raids, so much so that I didn't even take part in them. I chose to remain at the station."

A realisation came over Edwards and a smile appeared on the face of the bar owner, "I get it. You're a closet gay. That's why you tipped us off, isn't it?"

Hollister actually felt himself blush with what he thought was embarrassment, "Let's just say that I've come to realise that I've got more in common with the gay community than most police officers."

Edwards laughed, "That's the strangest 'coming-out' speech I've ever heard."

The ice and hostility broken, Hollister offered Edwards a smile. "It was the truth when I told you that I wanted no part of the raids. I tried telling the dick that planned them that they were a bad idea but he wouldn't listen to me or anybody else. Like I said, Greg did me a favour a couple of weeks ago and so I thought I owed him one."

"He's a good lad, he's like that. Listen, I'm sorry about my attitude earlier, have a drink on me."

Hollister accepted the apology with a shake of their hands but more importantly, the drink. Over the next hour or so he talked to Edwards and Greg and got to know everything about the raid the previous evening and how it had affected the businesses in 'The Village'. Hollister actually felt embarrassed about being a police officer and ashamed at the actions of the police force as a whole when he heard details of exactly how customers of 'The Last Exit' had been treated and spoken too and he could assume that this story would have been repeated in every other bar raided by the police. The uniformed officers had been deeply offensive about the sexuality of those interviewed, being overly abusive and insulting, with words being used such as 'faggot', 'queer' and 'arse bandits' and Hollister made a mental note of

trying to find out the names of those officers who had raided *'The Last Exit'*. He also advised Edwards to make a formal complaint about their behaviour with the Police and Crime Commission, giving Edwards the name and phone number of its leader.

The three men got to know each other well over a few drinks in the half-empty bar, even Greg was allowed a couple, with Edwards relaxing his previously strictly enforced rule. Despite his initial hostility, Edwards got to like the detective and Hollister in turned opened up to the bar owner. He revealed that he had only just discovered his true sexuality and that he was fairly new to life in 'The Village' and that his experiences were very limited. What Hollister failed to mention that his sexual experience consisted of having sex with two 'rent boys' and he had begun to secretly wonder what it must be like forming a relationship with a more mature person? The evening in 'The Last Exit' culminated with Hollister being invited to a private and exclusive party after the bar finally closed, which he accepted and was more than a little intrigued by the secrecy involved.

The reason for all the secrecy became apparent the moment that the three of them entered the club. Having first passed four very large and menacing doormen, all dressed in black and eyeing the new-comer with suspicion, it was only the presence of Edwards that actually got him inside the venue the trio went down a flight of steep steps and into the dark club. The dank smell of sweaty bodies greeted them immediately. White flashing strobe lights accompanied the very loud thud of drum and bass dance music and it took Hollister a couple of seconds to adjust

to the conditions and when he became accustomed to the noise and lighting he was shocked and instantly aroused by what he saw.

To his left there was a small stage area and this had three completely naked men on it, each of them writhing about and performing various sexual acts on one another. Immediately in front of the stage was the dancefloor, again occupied with men, this time each of the clad in various items of leather clothing and some were dancing while others appeared to be copulating. To his right was a seating area where men were clearly performing oral sex on other men and this area continued towards the bar. Despite being warned that it was not an ordinary 'party', Hollister was shocked at the sight of so many men openly indulging in sexual acts with one another within the club.

The 'party' that Hollister had been taken to was a secret and underground sadomasochistic event. The detective had no idea that anything along these lines even took place in Manchester and wondered what Jacobson would have said and thought if he had stumbled across this event as part of his raids? Even Hollister could hardly believe his eyes at what was going on and felt a little embarrassed by the erection in his pants and hoped that nobody could see it. But then again, everybody that Hollister could see was either engrossed in their own sexual activity or watching others enjoying theirs. Hollister stood sipping a cold beer straight out of the bottle that he had been presented with upon entering the club and watched the events on stage. Both Greg and his boss had left him alone while they went off to find their friends and the detective felt a little uneasy on his own.

He soon felt somebody start to squeeze his backside. At first he was shocked and wanted to turn and confront the owner of the hand,

possible even hit him, but found that he could not move. The mystery hand gripped his buttocks harder and this time Hollister did turn to confront the man, who turned out to be about forty years old, with short ginger hair and a goatee-type beard and moustache, which gave him the appearance of a wizard. He was dressed in black leather trousers and wore a harness of leather straps that criss-crossed his hairy torso. He was fairly good looking, and the two men smiled at each other. Hollister then felt the strangers hand move to his crutch and begin rubbing his hard penis. Panic filled Hollister as the man began to undo his fly's and pulled out his member but still the detective did not move. Nothing like this had ever happened to him before and, despite his surroundings, he was not sure what he should do. Part of him wanted to flee the club in horror but another part of him kept him transfixed to the spot.

"I see you've made a friend," a familiar voice said to Hollister, as he was presented with another drink.

He turned to see Greg and took the beer. The barman was with another man about the same age and build as him, and both men were dressed in black leather shorts and vests. "Great place, isn't it? This is my partner, John. See that nun over there…" Greg pointed out a man dressed as a nun, except they were made out of rubber and not fabric material, "…that's Stephen's partner Martin. Oh, and your friend, that's Scott."

At least Hollister finally knew the name of the man masturbating him, not stopping when Greg and his partner approached him and only stopping after had involuntarily ejaculated onto the dancefloor. As calmly as he had approached Hollister and upon completion, the man

smiled and walked away, no doubt in search of another man. The detective was dumbfounded. He had never experienced anything like this before and, after passing his beer to Greg while he replaced his now limp penis in his trousers, he sought out the toilets.

A red sign indicated that they were around a corner and Hollister headed in that direction, the thud of the music not as loud and the strobe lights having been replaced by a dim red light. The sight that befell him was even more shocking than the activities he had just left behind in the main club. A group of men were surrounding another person, who was laid across a circular table, his knees resting on two barstools and he was being abused by a huge dildo, whilst taking turns in performing oral sex with anybody within his distance. Hollister watched briefly in utter fascination, but his bladder needed relieving and so he cut short his viewing and headed towards the toilets. It was only now that he saw the face of the person lay over the table and upon seeing the face, Hollister felt like he had been hit by a bolt of lightning. It was Spencer, his teenaged lover.

Chapter Sixteen

The short journey back to the former apartment of Cameron Robinson was an arduous one, conducted in total silence, with an air of tension between the two occupants so thick that it could have been cut with a knife. Throughout the twenty minute journey Hollister was trying to find something to say, but he was lost for words.

The shock of seeing Spencer in the club had even surpassed his astonishment at what was going on between the leather clad men, not to mention the complete stranger that had masturbated him so casually and in a matter-of-fact way. Upon realising that it was his young lover that was splayed over the table, Hollister was not only mortified with what was being done to Spencer but the fact that he seemed quite relaxed by it, with no coercion being involved. The repulsed detective physically pushed away the men that stood in front of the prostrate teenager and when they fought back it was only the production of his police warrant card that finally drove them away.

The man holding the dildo, upon seeing the warrant card, dropped the rubber phallus onto the floor and disappeared into the crowd. It was only now that Spencer looked up and stared into the shocked face of Hollister. Gripping the youngster by his hair, Hollister dragged the struggling boy across the room to where he could see a pile of clothes that he assumed were Spencer's and ordered him to get dressed. The teenager had no choice but to comply. By now, two of the doormen had descended on the area looking menacing and ready for trouble, having been alerted by party-goers, but they too backed away on seeing the

detectives warrant card. Once dressed, Hollister gripped the youth by his upper arm tightly and virtually dragged him out of the club and up the street to where Hollister's car was parked.

Finally Spencer's nightmare journey was over and still gripping him tightly by the arm, Hollister used his considerable strength to both pull the youngster up the stairs and into the flat before pushing him into the lounge. Spencer lost his balance and crashed onto the floor, cowering in a corner as Hollister stood over him, intimidating the youngster. "What the fucking hell were you doing there?" yelled the detective.

"I could ask you the fucking same," came the immediate response, regretting his words the moment he had uttered them when he saw the anger in Hollister's eyes, "Who the fuck do you think you are treating me like this? I'm not your property. I can do anything that I want."

"Why you ungrateful little bastard, I've been taking care of you…"

"No you haven't," interrupted Spencer, "you've been paying to fuck me, that's what you've been doing." By now Spencer had scrambled to his feet and faced Hollister, "You've not been taking care of me. It's me that's been taking care of you, showing you what to do because you haven't got a fucking clue."

"I've treated you right. I've looked after you. Bought you things and you fucking do this to me you…you…you ungrateful little bastard," Hollister yelled back, trying to ignore the truthful comments made by the youngster.

"You've been rewarding me and paying me for sex, that's all you've done. You can call it whatever you like but don't fucking kid yourself, that's what you've been doing. It's only what my other 'John's' do. Pay me to fuck me."

Their argument was now in full flow, "What about at that…stuff you were doing in the club, you dirty little bastard?"

"I was getting paid good money for that and you've fucking spoilt it for me. Hello, that's what I do. I'm a fucking 'rent boy'. I get paid to get fucked by blokes like you. If you don't like it, just fuck off and leave me alone."

Hollister was finding it increasingly difficult to contain the rage that was building up inside of him. "What do you mean 'I can fuck off'?"

"I've got as much right to this place as you have. Probably more so, if the truth was known. If it wasn't for me, you wouldn't even know about it. Martin, or Cameron or whatever his fucking name was, was a friend of mine, not yours. You didn't even know him and yet you've moved into his flat like some fucking grave robber…"

"Don't speak about him like that," Hollister said through gritted teeth.

Spencer realised that he had struck a raw nerve and continued to press his point, almost in a mocking way. "You move in here because it suits you. You pimp of Martin's gear and fuck me whilst probably wishing you were fucking him."

Hollister snapped. A slap across the head sent Spencer crashing to the wooden floor. The open-handed blow was followed by a kick into the stomach of the youngster, still cowering on the floor, now gasping for breath. "Shut the fuck up. Shut the fuck up. You know nothing," yelled Hollister.

Spencer, realising that staying on the floor left him vulnerable, managed to quickly scramble to his feet, gasping breath, holding his stomach where Hollister had kicked him. However, he was not giving

up easily, "You're nothing but a bent dirty bastard copper that enjoys fucking little boys."

Hollister, having now completely lost control of himself because of the taunts of the teenager, lashed out again except this time he punched Spencer in the face. "Don't fucking push it, you little shit."

Falling to the floor for a third time, this time tasting blood in his mouth, the enraged teenager leapt back to his feet. "Or what?" he asked, before he continued, "You'll kick the fucking shit out of me like you probably do to those that you arrest? I'm not scared of you. You wouldn't be the first punter to beat me up and you probably won't be the last. I'm out of here."

Like a cat stalking its prey, Hollister pounced on the boy, gripping him by the throat. "You're not going anywhere."

"And whose gonna stop me, you?" gasped the youngster, fighting for breath as he struggled to free himself from Hollister's vice-like grip, "I'm not you fucking prisoner, you can't stop me."

Another punch, this time a full powered one from short range caught the youth full on in his face. Spencer's nose shattered, sending blood gushing out, covering his mouth. "That's right, beat me up. That's all you can do. You think I'm letting you get away with this."

Spencer had somehow manager to prise Hollister's fingers from around his throat and free himself. Just as the detective made another lunge for the teenager, who in turn grabbed the nearest object, which turned out to be an empty beer bottle, smashing it against the wall and thrusting the jagged remnants towards the oncoming police officer, in a desperate attempt to protect himself. "Take another step and I'll fucking do you. I fucking mean it."

Ignoring the shouted threat from the boy, Hollister charged at him, knocking the bottle out from his hand and once again gripped him by the throat. "You're nothing but a cheap little whore," he yelled as he threw the youngster across the room.

After hitting the opposite wall, Spencer fell to the floor and remained motionless. Hollister pounced on him again and kicked him twice in the stomach shouting at him to get up and get out but still the teenager did not move. Hollister kicked him again and it was only now that the detective noticed the pool of blood forming under his head and on the wooden floor. The detective bent down and gripped the boy by his shoulders and shook him and it was only now that he realised that Spencer was no longer breathing. He continued to shake the lifeless body and called out his name. There was still no response from the teenager. The detective placed a hand on the boy's chest, searching for a heartbeat and again he felt nothing. Hollister knelt over his body, placed both hands over the area of his chest and started pushing down rapidly, desperately starting to restart his heart, again to no avail.

Still no response from the teenager and slowly, the stark realisation began to dawn on Hollister and panic set in as realised that Spencer was dead and that he had killed him.

A state of shock came over a numbed McKenzie Hollister as he stared down at the limp and lifeless body of the young boy. Everything had gone so terribly wrong over the past few days for the detective and this had culminated in Hollister being responsible, albeit accidently, for the death of the youngster. It was Spencer's mocking that had pushed him over the edge and made him throw the youngster across the room

and against the wall. Looking at the body as he drank whisky neat from the bottle, barely being able to hold the bottle at his lips due to trembling hands, he wondered what he should do next. Knowing full well what he was and despite everything that he had seen Spencer do, he had genuinely cared about the boy and now seeing his lifeless body filled the detective's heart with enormous remorse and regret, not to mention guilt. The youngster had not deserved to have ended up like this. Hollister rubbed his eyes, wiping away tears, trying to clear his head and think straight.

The blood that flowed from the gash in Spencer's skull was beginning to make a large puddle on the floor and the sight of this spurred the detective into action. He went into the kitchen and returned with a couple of towels and a plastic carrier bag. The detective wrapped the towels around the youngster's head and then placed the shopping bag over the dead boys head, preventing even more blood spilling onto the wooden floor. Returning to the kitchen Hollister sought out something to clean the blood up. It was only now that he realised he had never cleaned anything in the apartment before and it took him a while to find a mop and bucket.

Soon the blood on the lounge floor was cleaned up and Hollister was left with the body of Spencer. The towels and the carrier bag had succeeded in preventing any more blood going onto the floor and Hollister sat on the largest of the sofas, puffing wildly on a cigarette, hoping that the nicotine would succeed in calming him down, where the alcohol had failed. He was now wondering what he should do with Spencer's body? How could he, a Detective Chief Inspector, have got himself into such a situation, that at nearly four in the morning, he had

the body of a teenage 'rent boy' lying lifeless on the floor of his adoptive home, which itself was the former home of another 'rent boy'? He could never have imagined that, when he began his investigation into the life of Cameron Robinson, it would have eventually ended up like this.

Hollister knew what he should do but there was no way that he could do it and remain a police officer. He should have called the police and notified them of Spencer's death and explained that it had been a tragic accident. The simple fact of the matter was that in doing so, he would be placing himself in a terrible position, one that not even he could guarantee that he could get himself off by simply explaining away the facts of the incident. First he would have to explain who Spencer was and how he knew him, before he would have to explain what caused the argument that led to his death, in the apartment of another dead 'rent boy' that Hollister may now be suspected of having something to do with his death. Too many questions with no way that Hollister could answer them without jeopardising himself and his career. Another mouthful of whisky finally wiped this thought from his head. He had to think of something else and quickly.

Maybe he could just leave the teenager where he was, having first removed the bloodstained bag and towels from around his head, and simply let the cleaner find him? This was certainly an option that appealed to him but in doing this it created another problem, Hollister would then have nowhere to live and having wrecked his marriage to Kate, he would not have been able to move back in the matrimonial home, assuming she would even let him. He certainly would not be

able to continue living his new-found lifestyle whilst under the roof of his former wife and so the detective quickly ruled this option out.

Hollister quickly realised that his current circumstances dictated that he had to be completely mercenary. At this precise moment in time, he *needed* the former home of Cameron Robinson. He began to weep tears of genuine remorse for the dead boy that lay only feet away from him as he took another swig of whisky straight from its bottle, his entire body shivering as he swallowed it and placed his head in his hands, unable to comprehend how he had managed to get himself in such an awful mess. The detective thought about going for a walk and let a little fresh air clear his head, which was something that he frequently did whenever he needed peace and quiet to think. He also realised that the whisky was not helping him and replaced the lid, deciding not to drink any more.

After sitting in silence for about five minutes, his head in his hands, tears running freely down his face an idea came to the detective. He had to treat Spencer's death like he would a murder he investigated and devoid himself of all emotions. He had to let his training kick in and clear his mind of any personal feelings that he had felt for Spencer and treat his death as that of a complete stranger.

Spencer was, after all, a prostitute and so would have been expected to be out on the streets, working on the night of his death. Unfortunately, it was not that uncommon for prostitutes to be attacked and even murdered and then just left out on the streets and this was what Hollister had decided to do with his body. Considering the affection that Spencer had shown towards him, whether it was genuine or just purely for financial gain, it would be a very undignified end to

his young life but one that Hollister thought he could easily arrange. The question was could he get away with it? Another question was where he could dispose of the body without being seen?

'The Village' was too well lit and there were always people milling around the warren of streets, either just finishing work or about to start their daily shift and so 'The Village' was quickly ruled out by Hollister as a place to dump the body. Another option was to leave Spencer's body in a park, but the detective also ruled this out in case it was discovered by some children and the last thing that he wished to do was give some children the heartache and the grief, not to mention any future nightmares, that he was now feeling. Then the solution of what to do next suddenly came to him and ironically it had been Spencer that had told him of the location that was going to be final resting place. When the detective had finally met up with the youngster again and before they had become lovers, Spencer had told him about the canal towpath that led from a car park on Dale Street. This, thought Hollister, would be an ideal place to leave a body, safe in the knowledge that it would soon be discovered.

Hollister had soon bundled up the body of the young prostitute, his former lover, somebody that he had become obsessed with finding, only to eventually kill him out of a drunken jealous rage, onto the rear seat of his car. The detective had used the duvet from off of Robinson's bed to wrap around the body and used some tape he found in the bedroom, no doubt used for other purposes, to prevent the duvet from coming open. Fortunately for Hollister he was not that drunk and Spencer, still only being a teenager, did not weigh too much, making

the lifeless body less of a dead-weight. After covering the head with another plastic bag to prevent any seepage of blood, he found it fairly easy to manoeuvre the body, still heavy enough for the detective to become a little breathless as he struggled to carry the body out of the building, down into the street and onto the rear seat of his car, pausing several times to make sure that there was nobody around that could later identify him.

Within ten minutes Hollister drove onto the public car park on Dale Street and parked as close as he could to the canal. Despite the lateness of the night, or was it the earliest part of the morning, there were a couple of cars already parked there but none of them showed any signs of being occupied or about to be driven off. Hollister was a little surprised at how well lit the area was and got out of his car, looking around for anybody. There did not appear to be anybody else in the area and Hollister knew that he had to be quick and setting off, his feet crunching on the gravel, towards the canal. It was now that he saw the archway. This must be where the 'rent boys' go, thought Hollister as he entered the small niche in the brickworks. The dark tunnel bent to the left and led down towards the silently passing canal. The first thing that Hollister noticed was the smell of damp and that of stale urine. It clogged your nostrils and made the uninitiated feel nauseous. The towpath of the canal was only a few feet wide and Hollister had to watch his footing as he made his way along, searching for an appropriate location to place Spencer's body.

An arched area behind some railings, completely devoid of any lighting, seemed to be the best place and once the eyes of the detective had become accustomed to the darkness, he glanced around. It had used

condoms and wrappers, together with clumps of tissues on the ground and was obviously a site for homosexual activity. If a body was discovered here, all the hallmarks would indicate to some form of homosexual activity that had gone terribly wrong and resulting in the death of a 'rent boy'. All very tragic and not a very dignified place to leave the body of somebody that he thought he loved, thought Hollister, but it was certainly a believable scenario and, if he was honest with himself, a practical solution to a very difficult problem and retraced his footsteps to go get the body of Spencer.

After placing the now stiffening body onto the damp and mildewed ground Hollister released it from the duvet. The detective heard a noise and stopped moving and held his breath, relieved to see that it turned out to be a couple of rats running over some discarded foil condom wrappers, but it did act as a reminder that he needed to be quick.

Gently he raised the body up to its standing height and walked until Spencer's body was flush against the slimy brickwork. Hollister had realised that in order for his death in this location to be believable that the youth needed traces of the wall on his clothing to imply that at some point of his *liaison de amour* he had been up against the wall. Next Hollister took hold of the head of the teenager and feeling very reluctant and heavy-hearted at doing it, banged the boy's skull against the brickwork, nearly vomiting at hearing the crunch of bone against the wall. As with his clothing, Hollister realised that he needed to leave residues of the wall on his head and in the gash that had seeped blood but most importantly, Hollister knew that he needed traces of Spencer's blood on the wall. Finally he let Spencer drop to the ground. This was going to be his ultimate resting place and position.

Hollister gathered up the duvet and looked one last time at Spencer. As if had seen a ghost, the image of Cameron Robinson lay on his own deathbed came into the mind of the detective as he looked at Spencer's lifeless body. It seemed fitting to Hollister that the youth which had first awakened all the long dormant homosexual feelings within the detective had been the final thought that he had as he walked away from the body that he was now leaving for somebody else to find.

Hollister had succeeded in getting the body out of the flat and to its final resting place without anybody having seen him and the question that now filled the detectives mind was whether he could actually get away with it?

Hollister had to literally force himself to go into work a few hours after dumping Spencer's body, desperately trying to put the nightmare of the previous few hours behind him, hoping that in reporting for duty it would give him something, anything, to think about other than Spencer and enable him to take his mind off his own self-inflicted nightmare. Everybody in the detective's offices could tell that Hollister, from the moment that he walked through the doors, had not slept and was possibly still the worse for the drink from the night before and so they all decided to give him a wide berth. Only Chief Superintendent Jacobson, possibly unaware of Hollister's reputation for being bad tempered from the lack of sleep or the effects to alcohol, braved the wrath of Hollister.

Jacobson was now realising that his well-intentioned raid on the bars and clubs of Canal Street and 'The Village' as a whole had been a total disaster and found that he needed the help of the next senior officer at

Heller Street police station to help him sort out the public relations mess that was beginning to explode all around him. The local media had picked up on the story and were accusing the police of being both heavy-handed and homophobic, a claim that the Greater Manchester Police were vigorously denying. Everybody realised that it was only going to be a matter of time before the national press picked up on the story and even the police now had to concede that despite all their good intentions, the raids had not been successful and had, in fact, been a total failure.

The Greater Manchester Police had also been forced to reveal the reason behind the operation and very reluctantly disclose details of Vigrass' arrest, something that they had so far managed to prevent. The investigation into Vigrass' sordid and depraved activities were still ongoing and this disclosure might have forewarned other currently unknown guilty parties into disposing of any incriminating evidence if they were to follow the photographer into the police cells. Jacobson had been summoned to the forces headquarters to explain his actions and it was this that he was planning with Hollister when Detective Sergeant Boston interrupted them.

Having acknowledged the presence of Jacobson with a courteous 'Sir', she then addressed Hollister, "Sorry to trouble you Mac, but we've just been informed that a body has been found."

"Where?" asked a troubled and worried Jacobson.

So soon, thought Hollister. He had thought that several hours, possibly days, would pass before the body of Spencer was found, an epoch that would have given him time to think.

"On the towpath of the Rochdale Canal, near to Piccadilly train station," she replied.

"Do we know who it is?" asked Hollister, first letting out a sigh and then plucking up the courage to say what he would have been expected to say, his voice trembling with disguised emotion, already knowing the answer.

"Only that it's a young lad, probably a 'rent boy'," answered Detective Boston.

Jacobson seized upon this point immediately, "Oh and what makes you think that?"

"Well sir, where he's been found is a notorious haunt and hang out for 'rent boys'," she replied, realising what Jacobson was going to say next.

"Sergeant, if you knew that there was another place that these 'rent boy' prostitutes hung out at, don't you think that you should have made me privy to this knowledge before we decided to go onto Canal..."

Hollister leapt to the defence of his assistant and interrupted Jacobson. "Adam, I can read your mind. My detectives in this office are not going to be scapegoats for your momentous fuck up. I tried telling you that raiding Canal Street was a fucking bad idea but you wouldn't listen. So back off my officers and sort your own shit-storm out. I've got a murder scene to attend."

Jacobson sat there, flushed with rage at having been spoken to the way that he had and was unable to say anything as he watched Hollister and Detective Boston walk out of the office. "Thanks Mac."

"That guy's a fucking arsehole Phoebe, he deserved it," replied Hollister. "What else do we know about this body?"

"In there Mac you said it was a murder, we don't know that for sure yet," replied Sergeant Boston.

Realising that he had just slipped up, Hollister had to think fast, hoping to deflect any suspicions of the junior detective. "Well, it's pretty obvious, isn't it? If we've got the body of a possible 'rent boy' in a known haunt, then it's hardly like going to suicide, is it?"

"I suppose you're right." Detective Boston had accepted the given explanation because it made sense and now referring to the sheet of paper that she held, "This kid's apparently got head injuries. Early indications point to something going on wrong whilst with a punter, possibly a fight over payment, who knows."

Hollister nodded, letting out a sigh that he had got away with his slip of the tongue and realising that he had to be much more careful in the future. "Have you got the team on their way?" he asked.

"Yeah Mac, did it before I came to get you. Forensics, SOCO and the doc are all on their way. Uniformed have sealed the area and the press, as far as I know anyway, don't know about it yet." Detective Boston knew that this well practised procedure had been implemented before breaking up the meeting between Hollister and Jacobson.

"It might not be a bad idea to leak the story to the press. After that fucking arsehole fucking over with Canal Street, we certainly could do with something to deflect attention. Might even provide some justification for what that knob-head did," added Hollister.

Secretly though Hollister felt a little sympathy for Jacobson. The man had looked devastated, as if his career was finished, which it might be but he had his own problem to currently deal with.

An ever-increasing state of foreboding descended over Hollister as the vehicle he was travelling in was driven across the centre of Manchester and towards Spencer's body. The closer the car got to Piccadilly train station, the darker the mood of Hollister got. Even Detective Boston had picked up on this sullen aspect of her superior officer's mood but put it down, from experience, to the effects of too much alcohol from the night before.

Detective Boston's dark blue car turned onto Ducie Street and through a police cordon and then onto Dale Street and the car park, so familiar now to Hollister, stopping next to a collection of marked and unmarked police cars and vans and a yellow ambulance. Hollister was reluctant to get out of the stationary vehicle but knew that, as the most senior ranking police officer on site, all his colleagues' eyes would have been on him, watching his every movement, some no doubt hoping that he would dig himself a grave, just as Jacobson had done so, and finally he eased himself from the front passenger seat. Detective Boston had already got out of the car and approached a uniformed Inspector before Hollister joined them.

"According to Inspector Pitt," the detective began updating Hollister immediately, "the body was found earlier this morning by somebody out walking his dog. Not very likely though, but it is certainly possible. Apparently, according to what I know, this place is popular with young boys before they go to school."

She knows more about this kind of lifestyle than I do, thought Hollister, being brought back to the present by a male voice. "My men have taken the man, and his dog, to Shaw Street," added the Inspector, a man in his fifties and used to seeing bodies turn up on the streets of

his division, leaving him devoid of all emotions and it showing in the monotonous tone of his voice. "Yes, he does have dog but we can't rule out the possibility that he was here for something else."

"Have you got an ID on the dead boy yet?" asked Hollister.

The Inspector was slightly taken aback by Hollister's abruptness. "No, not yet," he replied, "the medical examiner has only just arrived and we haven't touched the body yet."

"Down here, is he?" asked Hollister, motioning towards the archway and the constant hum of the portable generators.

"He's had a bad few days," whispered Detective Boston to the Inspector once they were out of hearing range of Hollister. The uniformed officer offered half a smile, but was clearly unimpressed by Hollister's attitude.

"Still no excuse for bad manners," he replied.

Hollister, Sergeant Boston and Inspector Pitt made their way through the arch and down towards the water's edge. The noise of the generators that powered the portable arc lights reverberated through the tunnel and making them appear much louder than they actually were, the lights bathing the entire area in brightness, casting giant shadows from those caught in there beams and illuminating the area that contained the body. The artificial light revealed the true squalor in which the corpse lay to Hollister. All around were used syringes and other drug paraphernalia, used condoms, their wrappers, wads of tissue, empty drinks cans and bottles and the general waste of the city. Hollister felt even more guilty than he originally had at leaving the body of the boy that he had loved in such a location but, as he let out a deep sigh, a lump forming in his throat and desperately fighting back

the tears that involuntarily formed in his eyes. He alone knew that there was nothing else that he could have done.

He looked at the lifeless form that was Spencer. Clearly moved and having to fight back tears, the detective shook his head. A gesture that was read by those around him as remorse for the youngster but was really an indication of the guilt he had at first accidently killing the teenager that he had cared so much for and given away so much for and then leaving his body in such a location, treating his corpse as if it was just another piece of trash left to rot. He was so glad that the deafening sound of the generators masked anything that was said to him as he watched in morbid silence, consumed by his private grief, as the doctor made a brief examination of the body.

A sense of deep foreboding engulfed Hollister as he recalled watching a similar scenario only a few weeks before with the discovery of Cameron Robinson's body. Hollister had dealt with death and grieving before, having lost friends and colleagues over the years, but this time it was different. To stand there, staring at a body of a person that you had killed and that you had placed where it now was, unable to grieve for the loss of somebody that only a few days ago he was sharing intimate moments with, ripped deep into his human psyche. Hollister found that he was overcome with both guilt and self-loathing, grieving privately for the young life that he had snuffed out, albeit accidently, and hating himself for putting him here in such a revolting and degrading place.

Hollister had seen enough. He turned and walked back up the path, pushing past the ever growing mass, comprising mostly of uniformed police officers. Once out onto the Dale Street car park and into the light

of the grey sky, he began gulping at the fresh air and found a concrete boulder to sit on just before his legs gave way and lit up a cigarette, consumed by guilt but unable to confess to his crime. Hollister realised that his life had reached rock-bottom and things could not get any worse for him.

Chapter Seventeen

The following morning Detective Sergeant Boston knocked on the door of Hollister's office and, as she usually did, walked straight in without waiting for a reply. "We've got an ID on the dead kid Mac." What she saw even took her by surprise, "God Mac, you look awful. You okay?"

Hollister did look and feel terrible. Sleep had eluded him for another night and this showed by the dark circles under his eyes. He now spoke in a rasping hoarse voice. "Spare me the bullshit. Who was he?"

Detective Boston had got used to Hollister's grumpiness and simply ignored him, "His name was Jan Rodesh. He was seventeen, going on eighteen. He's from the Holešovice district of Prague, you know, the Czech Republic. Apparently he lived in Bolton with his cousin. He's also an illegal immigrant and he was known to our Vice Squad."

Hollister found that even now, despite everything that had happened to him and his life over the past couple of months, he could still be shocked. He had run a check himself through the police's databases but he had used the alias used by Spencer and not his real name. He had told the detective that his name was Pavel and that his surname was Holešovice, no wonder the detective could not find any trace of the teenager because he simply had not trusted Hollister with his real name. He had been right though about him being from somewhere in Europe by his accent and his dark complexion. "How do you know all this?"

"I took his fingerprints and ran them through the computer and there he was," replied Detective Boston. She sat down in front of Hollister,

"So I then contacted the Czech embassy and they've given me everything that they've found out from the authorities over in the Czech Republic. There's a lot more as well. Even at seventeen, he was well known to the Czech authorities. He was first picked up by them when he was only eleven. He was caught having sex with a German national in a changing room at the *'Podolí'* swimming pool complex in Prague. Apparently it's a well-known hang-out for young 'rent boys'. This German sex tourist had paid him three hundred crowns for sex, which is about seven quid in our money. About six months later he was again picked up by the Czech police. This time it was during a purge on 'rent boys' in Prague and this time he was in an amusement arcade in the main train station in Prague called *'Lazer Game'*. For this he got sent to a sort of care home but not even this stopped him. When he was thirteen he was again arrested for working as a prostitute. This time he was with another German bloke in *'Letna Park'*, which is apparently a notorious gay 'cruising' area. His family also thought that he might have been making gay porn movies because apparently a lot of young Czech 'rent boys' do over there and so they moved to England to get him away from everything there.

"They applied for asylum but it all fell through, don't know all the details yet. I'm waiting on Border Force to get back to me. It appears that the Vice Squad picked him up once about a year or so ago. He claimed that he was lost but they thought he was out soliciting but couldn't prove it. They took him home to his cousin. She lives on Spencer Street, over in the Brieghtmet district of Bolton. His cousin, Anya, she's a known 'hooker' in the Bolton area, works out of Shiffnal

Street. Even she's been lifted a couple of times. She's only two years older than him."

Hollister was, as usual, extremely impressed with what Sergeant Boston had found out but was a little curious as to how he had ended up living with a known prostitute and after asking Sergeant Boston this, she answered his question, "Apparently even his mother was a 'hooker' back in Prague and is now a house-bound alcoholic. The cousin Anya, she's been known to do drugs as well and Jan got arrested after getting caught dealing in drugs to other schoolkids while they were waiting for their asylum claim to go through. He got a caution. The school threw him out and no other school would touch him and so Social Services got involved and placed him in care. He ran away virtually straight away. The police in Bolton found him and took him back to the care home and...guess what? He ran away again, got picked up, got took back and he ran away a third time. This was when his cousin stepped in and vouched for him with Social Services who handed him over to her and he was just left to his own devices. He was barely a teenager, what a shit life."

"So Social Services and the Education Department just wiped their hands with him?" asked Hollister in disbelief.

"It seems that way. It also seems that, despite his denial to Vice that he'd followed his sister onto 'the game' and had become a 'rent boy'. There was evidence that he'd recently had anal sex and there were three different types of semen in his mouth. But I've saved the best for the last..."

"Happy little soul this morning, aren't you?" interrupted Hollister. "Go on then, what is it?"

"He didn't die there. He was killed somewhere else and then dumped there," the female officer replied.

A feeling of panic descended on Hollister, which he desperately tried to hide. "Oh…right. And how can you tell?"

"The *post mortem* revealed that he'd died after a blow to the head but it was done against a clean wall or floor. There was no evidence of mould or slime or anything else that we found on the canal towpath's walls in the wound. It was a clean wound. Whoever had killed him then dumped his body there to make it look like he'd died there. The killer even banged his head against the wall to make it look like that it had happened under the arches on the towpath."

Hollister's mind was racing. He should have realised that the *post mortem* would have revealed this but his thoughts at the time had been clouded by his guilt ridden alcohol consumption. "Have you got any DNA to indicate who he'd been with?"

"Apart from the sperm, it's too early to say yet. Forensics are checking for anything as we speak," she replied.

"Has he been positively identified yet?" asked Hollister.

"No, not yet. Uniformed are picking up Anya as we speak."

"You'd better get over to the morgue and wait for her." Hollister paused briefly, "Good work Phoebe, you'll go far. Andrew's back from London tomorrow and I'll make sure that he knows about the effort you've put in so far."

"Cheers Mac," replied the slightly embarrassed Detective Sergeant, secretly basking in Hollister's praise. However even she was concerned about him. This was the worst that she had ever seen him looking and hoping that the imminent arrival of Chief Superintendent Mundy would

sort him out. There was no way that Mundy would allow him to work looking the way that he did. The two men were old friends and even Detective Boston knew that, during their years together as police officers that they had taken care of each other and looked out for one another.

Around two hours later, Sergeant Boston knocked on Hollister's office door and then entered, this time she was accompanied by a suited and bespectacled man in his fifties. "Mac, this is Douglas Nash. He's head of Manchester Social Services."

"Thanks Phoebe," Hollister replied standing up and offering an outstretched hand. "Mr Nash, come in and take a seat." There was a patronising tone to Hollister's voice that Detective Boston had detected but the man from Social Services had missed.

"Chief Inspector, I really must object..." Nash protested, being interrupted by Hollister.

Hollister got straight to the point. "Does the name Jan Rodesh mean anything to you, Mr Nash?"

"I don't think so. Should it?" replied Nash, uncertain of what Hollister was getting at.

"Seventeen years old and lives in Bolton?" continued Hollister.

"Chief Inspector, I'm a busy man..."

"So am I, Mr Nash, so am I, but I still have to find the time to pick up the pieces of your incompetence."

"Just what are you implying Chief Inspector?" asked Nash, getting more and more impatient with every passing moment.

"Apparently this Jan Rodesh is on your 'At Risk Register'."

"So are literally hundreds of other children. What's so special about this one?" asked Nash.

"Because he's fucking dead, that's what," yelled Hollister, banging a hand on his desk making both Nash and Detective Boston jump. "Yes, he's fucking dead. We found him under the arches on the towpath near Piccadilly station this morning. He was on your 'At Risk Register' and yet he was working as a 'rent boy' and he's been murdered."

Nash was lost for words and felt very intimidated by Hollister and the fact that Sergeant Boston stood over him. "Chief Inspector, I really must object at being treated like this. There is no need to raise your voice. I can fully understand your annoyance and possibly your frustration…"

Hollister's tone now took on a mocking form, "Oh, you can understand my frustration, can you? We've got a young girl having to identify the body of her seventeen year old cousin who is then going to have to tell his mother that he's dead, a young boy that your shitty organisation was supposed to be taking care off. Do you think his mother will be 'frustrated'?"

"Chief Inspector, without access to my department's files I simply cannot comment on any particular individual. We have literally hundreds of young men and girls that we are…"

"Well, Mr Nash," interrupted Hollister, his voice heavily tainted with sarcasm, "may I suggest then that you fuck off back to your office and find out who he was and how you managed to let him work as a 'rent boy' and end up dead. I'm personally going to be all over you and your fucking department over this. The lot of you are unfit to look after animals let alone the lives of human beings. Now get out."

Nash was clearly shaken by both Hollister's words and by the way in which he had just been spoken to and he looked ashen faced as he stood up and was escorted out of the office by Detective Boston and then out of the building. A few minutes later Hollister himself followed him, visibly unsteady on his feet.

A short time later Hollister was once again waiting in the office of Dr McIlvenna, the head teacher of St. Anthony of Padua school, Cameron Robinson's former school. The genial man had offered Hollister the use of his office when the detective had turned up at the school and requested another meeting, this time in private, with Barratt Foxford. Dr McIlvenna went personally to get the teacher, having to once again cover his class for him and Hollister was left alone with his thoughts for a good five minutes. Eventually he was joined by the track-suited Foxford. "Detective Hollister", he began, "I'm a very busy…"

"Sit down and shut up," ordered Hollister. Somewhat shocked, the teacher obeyed the command, realising that this was going to be more than a polite conversation. "I've come to warn you that the police, if they follow normal procedure, are about to reopen and reinvestigate Cameron Robinson."

Foxford felt the life drain out of him as a state of panic came over him. "Why?" he asked in a wavering voice.

"Remember that other 'rent boy' that I asked you about, Spencer? You know, the one that you picked up outside *'Burgerworld'*?" Foxford nodded his head in acknowledgement and Hollister continued. "Well, he's also turned up dead. We found him this morning in the canal tunnels over at Dale Street."

With every word out of Hollister's mouth, Foxford felt his world falling apart. "Was he…you know…murdered?"

"Yeah," replied Hollister. "A blow to the back of his head killed him and then somebody dumped his body there to make it look like he died there."

"You've got to believe me," pleaded the devastated teacher, "I had nothing to do with his death. I've not even seen him since that night. Honest I haven't. In fact, I've been too scared to go out ever since you came to see me."

Hollister tried to reassure the trembling and frightened teacher, "I'm not here to accuse you, far from it. I never thought for one minute that you had anything to do with his death. I've come to warn you that no doubt somebody will come and see you and ask you about Cameron. With two 'rent boys' turning up dead within a month or so, the police are bound to try and see if there's a link between them."

The words of the detective seemed to calm Foxford a little, "Thank you for the advanced warning," he said in barely a whisper.

"But understand one thing though," pressed Hollister, moving closer to Foxford, his voice now low and intimidation, "if you ever tell them that I was asking about Spencer, then I'll fucking kill you. I'll expose you for what you are, a paedophile teacher. There is no way that you can tell anybody that I was asking about him. It'll put me in a very difficult position, with questions that I wouldn't be able to answer without dropping you in it."

"You've got my word on that. I swear that I won't say anything detective," replied Foxford, realising that Hollister was himself in trouble. "Believe me. They won't hear anything from me."

"Just make sure they don't or I'll have your bollocks on a plate."

With that final statement, Hollister left the office and the deeply shocked teacher. Foxford would, having been given the time and the opportunity to compose himself and to be able to come up with an explanation for Hollister's second visit to Dr McIlvenna and also to be convincing enough if the police did indeed visit him again. He was after all a master of deception, being able to hide his secret life and sexual preference from his colleagues. Hollister's secret was safe with him, thought Foxford, but he knew that it might cost dearly at some possible date in the future.

Hollister made his way back to Heller Street police station, feeling slightly more relaxed. He was now confident that Barratt Foxford would not reveal, if questioned, that he had been asking about Spencer and Hollister also knew that he would have to speak to Greg, the barman, and Stephen Edwards, the owner of 'The Last Resort' and use the same kind of threats to ensure their silence. This time, he was going to use the threat of exposing the secret sadomasochistic party that he had been taken too and that he would personally guarantee that it be raided and the party-goers identities be exposed.

They were not idle threat's either. Each of them would be genuine enough. Hollister knew that if he was backed into a corner and if he had too, he would reluctantly expose them all, in order to save his own career and reputation, whatever was left of it any way.

The shock of accidentally killing Spencer/Jan had been enough to snap Hollister out of his fantasy world and back to the reality of life. He thought that he had genuinely cared for him but now realised that all he

had done was to lust over the boy. Spencer had been right, thought Hollister, in what he had said as part of their fatal argument. All he had really wanted the teenager for was sex. Now he was faced with the reality of the situation that Hollister had used the youth to satisfy the crisis in his own sexuality. All he had wanted to do was to experience the thrill of having something that he should not have. Hollister now realised that the repression of his homosexuality had actually created the desire to experiment with it when the opportunity had come along. Now he knew that he had to put all these thoughts back into the internal box from which they had come from, bury them deep into the recesses of his brain once again and get on with his life and this positive thought was in his mind when he walked into the detective's offices at Heller Street police station.

There to greet him was Chief Superintendent Mundy, newly arrived back in Manchester from his secondment down in London. "Andrew, welcome back. I thought you weren't due back for another day or so. What you doing back?"

"My office, now," replied Mundy to Hollister's question, more of an order than a request.

Hollister followed Mundy up to his office, both men maintaining an awkward silence for the duration of their short journey and with Mundy closing the door behind them once they had reached the sanctity of his office. Mundy came straight to the point. "What the fuck is wrong with you? I've just had Douglas Nash from Social Services screaming at me about your attitude and look at you, you're a fucking disgrace. You're a disgrace to the police force."

"I've been under a lot of stress but I'm alright now," responded Hollister, somewhat surprised by his friend's outburst.

"Fuck off McKenzie, you're clearly not all right and even if you were, that doesn't excuse you balling at Nash."

"Andrew, have you met him? He's a pompous prick. He doesn't give a fuck about any kids on their register. As long as he's getting his massive salary, he doesn't give two fucks about them." The usually amiable mood between the two friends was rapidly deteriorating into open hostility.

"That maybe the case," replied Mundy, "but it's not for you to pass judgement. You, of all people, in the state you're in judging somebody else. It doesn't excuse your behaviour. Nothing does. Now, what's this about this kid that you've found on the towpath?"

"He appears to be another 'rent boy'. His name is Jan and he's only seventeen. He was being abused back home in the Czech Republic and so his family brought him here, for a better life and to get him away from his abusers. Things went tits up and he ended up in care. He's on the 'At Risk Register' with Social Services and yet he was able to become a 'rent boy' and now he's dead. That's why I blew it with that prick Nash. Turns out he was killed somewhere else and dumped on the towpath, left to rot while Nash should've been looking after him."

Mundy had calmed down on hearing the details of the discovery of the body and who he was. "That's two dead 'rent boys' within a month or so. Didn't you once say that you suspected Cameron Robinson's death might not be suicide?"

"A while back, yeah, but I think I was probably wrong."

"Well maybe you were right all along. We've now got two dead 'rent boys' and we can't rule out, at the moment, that there might be some connection between them. This coming after the raid on Vigrass and 'The Village' is the last thing that we need. Maybe there's a connection and some sicko is out there killing 'rent boys' to cover his tracks. Are there any similarities between the two boys?"

"I...really...don't know," Hollister was flustered, "It's too early to say."

Mundy thought for a moment and then spoke to Hollister, "Because you led the investigation into Cameron Robinson's death and that at the time you raised doubts that it was suicide, I want you to lead this investigation..."

"No Andrew, I can't. I can't do it," interrupted a stunned Hollister, now pleading with Mundy.

"What do you mean that you can't? You're my best officer..."

"I just can't. I just can't," Hollister looked devastated.

Mundy was astonished by Hollister's response. "McKenzie, what the fuck are you going on about?"

Hollister was adamant with his refusal to investigate the death of Spencer/Jan, much to the chagrin of Mundy. "Please Andrew, not this one. I just can't do it. Give it to somebody else but please don't ask me to investigate this..."

Mundy had never seen his friend this upset about a case in all their years of friendship and he interrupted Hollister in mid-sentence. "For fuck's sake Mac, give me one good reason why not?"

"I can't tell you," replied Hollister.

The Chief Superintendent was beginning to lose his patience, "Will you calm the fuck down and start talking sense."

Hollister's temperament was now bordering on hysterical. "I can't tell you. I just can't tell you."

"For fuck's sake McKenzie," Mundy had finally reached the end of his patience and snapped. "You're going to lead this invest…"

"No, I can't," yelled Hollister back at Mundy, "I've told you that I can't do it."

"You will and that's a fucking order," Mundy shouted his reply.

"No, no, no," Hollister said as he crumpled into a chair before suddenly getting up and storming out of the Mundy's office and past the astonished police officers that had heard the tirade.

Mundy met up with Hollister again on the car park. A light rain had begun to fall from the grey leaden sky, which matched the mood between the two senior detectives. By the time Mundy had caught up with Hollister he had his head buried in his arms on the roof of a police car. Mundy marched up to him, ignoring the rain that dampened his shirt and demanded answers. "What the fuck was all that about?"

"Andrew, be a friend and leave me alone," came the muffled response from Hollister, clearly crying into his arms.

"At this precise moment in time I'm not your friend, I'm your superior officer. After that…that…disgrace in there, you can kiss goodbye to any friendship."

"In that case," replied Hollister as he turned to face Mundy, glaring into his eyes, "just fuck off and leave me alone."

At this point Mundy had had enough. He gripped Hollister by his shoulders and shook him violently, "Pull yourself together for fuck's sake. Pull yourself together. What the fuck's wrong with you?"

Hollister brushed away the hands of Mundy and pushed him away, only another parked police vehicle preventing Mundy from falling onto the car parks gravel. "I killed him," whispered Hollister.

"What did you just say?" asked a disbelieving Mundy, not sure if he had heard correctly.

"I killed him," replied Hollister still in barely a whisper. "That's why I can't investigate the case."

Mundy was completely dumbfounded by Hollister's claim. "Do you realise what you're saying?"

"We were having an affair," began the now weeping Hollister, "we had an argument and I lost my temper and pushed him away. He fell and hit his head. I didn't mean to kill him, honest to God I didn't. I didn't know what to do. I panicked and took him to the Dale street towpath. Oh God, I'm so sorry. I'm so sorry. I didn't mean to kill him. It really was an accident."

Mundy began pacing up and down between the two police vehicles, in a state of shock at Hollister's disclosure, frantically thinking what to do next while Hollister once again leant on the roof of a police car, his head buried in his arms in shame and embarrassment. Finally Mundy stopped pacing, turned to face Hollister and once again took him by his shoulders, this time gently and he spoke softly to Hollister. "Mac, come back up to my office and let's talk about this in private. This really isn't the place. Let's get away from prying eyes and ears."

Hollister wiped away his tears, "What am I going to do?" he asked.

"Let's go upstairs. We'll sort something out." The calming influence of Mundy was enough to placate Hollister and, almost solemnly, the two rain-sodden police officers returned to the building.

Hollister and Mundy were now seated in Mundy's office. Each of them had a large drink in their hands and both were now calm and composed. They had dried themselves off as best that they could, but their damp clothes still clung to their bodies. As he sipped the whisky, Hollister revealed to Mundy how he had been secretly investigating the life and death of Cameron Robinson and how this had brought him into contact with the now deceased Spencer/Jan. He tried to explain how their relationship had begun and then flourished, about his visit to sadomasochistic party and what he saw his young lover doing. Mundy was spared no details as Hollister told him about the argument that followed and resulted in his death and the disposal of his body. Hollister felt relieved that he had finally been able to tell somebody of his secret life and the recent tragic events.

Mundy had sat in complete silence as Hollister narrated his story, barely able to believe what he was hearing, especially from his lifelong friend. When Hollister was finished, Mundy responded in barely a whisper, "I simply can't believe it."

"It's all true, Andrew," replied Hollister. "I wish to God that it wasn't, but it's all true."

"Oh, I believe you. It's just that I'm stunned. I had no idea that you were like that...you know...gay."

"I don't think that I was until I began investigating Cameron's death. Well, I suppose that I must've been...you know...deep down, but I

didn't really know though myself until I started coming into contact with these 'rent boys'."

"I understand what you're trying to say Mac," replied Mundy reassuringly.

"You've no idea what I've gone through," added Hollister, thinking that Mundy was only trying to placate him. "It's why I've been so moody. Why I've been drinking so much and all the stuff with Kate. You can't understand…"

"Oh I can," replied Mundy letting out a deep sigh.

Hollister, despite how troubled his mind currently was, picked up on a certain undercurrent in Mundy's voice, but because of his fragile state of mind, was not quite certain what he friend was trying to say.

It was only now that Mundy opened up, relieved that he was finally able to tell somebody of his darkest secret, one that had been haunting him for the past few years, but which had been rekindled a few months ago with the discovery of Cameron Robinson's body.

"You were wrong about Cameron. He really did commit suicide. I came across him again about eighteen months after he had disappeared from home. He was once my secret lover. That photographer you picked up…you know, Vigrass, he made me a video a while back and I recognised him immediately from when he had disappeared. He was one of those people that you could never forget once you'd met him. I got Vigrass to arrange a meeting and then I told Cameron that unless we became lovers, that I'd have him picked up and returned to his family. He said that he'd do anything not to go home. He was so close to achieving what he'd always wanted to be, a model and he begged me

not to send him home. He used all his considerable charm against me and I just fell for him. Like you, I couldn't help myself.

"I tried to warn you off from investigating him after he turned up dead but obviously I didn't try hard enough. He took his own life though Mac, honestly he did. I had nothing to do with his death. I just covered it all up so I wouldn't be implicated. Like you, I've got too much to lose. After his body was found, I went to his flat over in Whalley Range and took away the medication that I'd got for him and anything else that might incriminate me. Things began to unravel with the arrest of Vigrass. He was under my protection. It was his lawyer that told me about his arrest. We're all part of the same group. There's even a possibility that I knew this Jan."

It was the turn of Hollister to be shocked as he tried to come to term with the disclosure of his friend, something that he never saw coming. "Christ, what a mess. What are we going to do now though?"

"Nothing," was the brunt and brutal reply. "Now that we both know about each other, it's business as usual. This is to remain just between the two of us. If anybody ever finds out, then we're both fucked." Mundy paused and thought for a moment and then continued. "I'll head the investigation into this Jan, not you. You can work alongside me on it though. Point me in the right direction so that I can cover your arse. I'll get it all wrapped up as quickly as I can, without finding out too much. I'll put it down to some mystery punter killing him and then panicking and dumping his body. Which is not that far from the truth really, is it?"

"Can we pull it off?" asked Hollister in disbelief.

"As long as you get yourself sorted out, get off the booze and keep your mouth shut, then yes. After all, it wouldn't be the first time. As regards to what happened earlier, I'll tell the troops that you're upset because you've found out that Kate was cheating on you left you and that you've only just found out."

"And you really think that we'll be able to get away with it?" asked Hollister for a second time.

Mundy nodded his head. "Yes, we can. Unknown to you, we've got some pretty influential 'friends'. You don't need to know who they are, but don't worry about anything. For Christ's sake though, you'd better lay off the booze. That's a sure fire way to slip up. I know that at the moment you're pretty fucked up, I was after Cameron turned up dead. You have to find some other way of living with the stress and the guilt at what you've done. Nothing can change what happened and I believe you that it was an accident. I've checked the details of the *post mortem* and the type of injury corresponds with how you've described what happened but it's going to be hard for you to live with, but you can do it. Just move on to something else. Plough yourself back into your work, anything, as long as it takes your mind off it."

Hollister sat in a stunned silence, trying to digest what his friend had just told him and what he was being asked to go along with. He already knew that he had no option but to go be part of Mundy's plan, he had far too much to lose if he did not, but it still rested heavy on his conscious and he still had his doubts. There were still some unanswered questions that he needed to know about Cameron Robinson and his death. They had haunted him ever since he had first seen the teenager dead in the bedsit. They had caused him many sleepless nights and

plunged him headlong into this current nightmare. Finally he had the courage to speak, "Andrew, can I ask you something?"

"If you must," replied Mundy, his attitude curt and unfriendly.

"I need to know two things about Cameron Robinson. I need to know these answers before I can move on," Hollister paused briefly and then continued, fully aware that he could be opening a can of worms that he did not really want to look into. "I need to know why he left home and why he became a 'rent boy' I need these answers Andrew?"

Mundy sighed heavily. He had no desire to answer Hollister's questions but the prospect of finally being able to relieve the burden and the guilt that he had been carrying ever since Robinson's body had been discovered proved too tempting an opportunity to turn down and so he took a deep breath and replied to Hollister's questions. "He left home simply because there was no way that he could have continued his kind lifestyle whilst still living with his parents. He knew that it would have only been a matter of time before they found out what was doing and then who knows what would have happened next. 'Pud'…that is Cameron was beginning to think that his father was getting suspicious.

"He had this punter, a bloke called Dave, who turns out to be a real sick bastard, well into young boys and all kinds of kinky stuff. He works in a warehouse over in Trafford Park and he used 'Pud' on a regular basis. He was introduced to him by his gym teacher, Foxford. Anyway, this guy Dave who is originally from London and still got friends down there and when 'Pud' told him that he wanted to leave home, he said that he knew somebody who had a couple of flats and then he helped 'Pud' leave home. Naturally there was a price that 'Pud'

had to pay and this Dave and his friend introduced him to somebody else and together they got him doing all kinds of sick stuff but 'Pud' just went along with it all because they said they'd help him to become a model. When they didn't and the London scene got too much, Cameron got this Dave to help him move back to Manchester. Once back here, this Dave got him the flat over in Whalley Range to live in and then the bedsit where he was found dead as an escape place and a mailing address and he turned to prostitution because he needed money.

"He became a 'rent boy' simply to pay the bills. He said that he'd quit once he'd made it as a model or a film star. I met up with him by chance about eight or nine months ago. Like I said earlier, I asked Vigrass to make me a video with a young blond boy in it and when I watched it, I immediately recognised Cameron. I nearly died of shock. I'd led the initial investigation into his disappearance and so I recognised him immediately. I got Vigrass to arrange a meeting between us and over a few weeks we became lovers. It only lasted for a few months though, it was far too risky to continue seeing him and I never saw or heard from him again until he turned up dead. Then I panicked. While we were together, 'Pud' told me that he was always depressed and that everybody in his life just wanted him for sex and so I got another friend of ours, this doctor, to get me some pills for him. These were the ones that he used to take his overdose."

Both Hollister and Mundy were relieved, but for totally different reasons. Mundy at finally having the opportunity to talk to somebody about his relationship with Cameron Robinson and Hollister at finally knowing why the young boy had left home and become a 'rent boy' but there was still one remaining question unanswered. "Andrew, when I

first met this Spencer as I knew him, he said that Cameron was being blackmailed into giving free sex to a...client that recognised him and that he may have been responsible for his death. Were you this client and did you have anything to do with his death?"

"His death was just a tragic suicide. Nothing more, nothing less," Mundy replied, letting out a deep sigh, deeply moved and upset by the inevitable question. He refilled their glasses with whisky and continued, "There was nothing anybody could have done to prevent it. Having made the film with Vigrass, Cameron asked him if he knew anybody that he could help him to get onto television. Vigrass pulled a few strings and got him an audition, but the director only wanted to have sex with him. He didn't even get the part. This plunged Cameron into a state of deep depression and this was when he asked if I could get him any anti-depressants. He was beginning to realise the futility of his hopes and dreams and how everybody just used him for sex.

"But not me, I really did care about him. I might even go as far as saying that I was beginning to fall in love with him which was why I had to end things between us. He was all I lived for but I couldn't risk being seen with him. Do I feel guilty? Yes. Every minute of every day the guilt eats me up. As regards to 'Pud' being blackmailed, once again there is absolutely no truth in it whatsoever. Nobody could've blackmailed him. He simply wouldn't have let them. He would've just moved on somewhere else and started all over again in another city, under a new name. It seems this Jan, the lad that turned your life upside down like 'Pud' did to mine, was lying to you all along.

"The very resourceful Cameron Robinson was the one that blackmailed you. Using you, fucking you, taking you for a ride just so

that he could get what he wanted. Once you'd fallen for him he pulled all the strings all along. If I was honest and had to say something I'd say that the little bastard got what he deserved."

Hollister was devastated. He had lost just about everything that he had ever cared about because he chose to listen to a seventeen year old boy that he later became infatuated over. His life had been turned upside down, forced to face up to long forgotten memories from his past, reliving decades old nightmares and for what? Nothing. He had once pledged Spencer his undying love and now he found himself hating the boy, feeling glad that he was dead, that he had killed him. He felt nothing but contempt for the dead boy.

Printed in Great Britain
by Amazon